AFTER LONG SILENCE

The marvel, the mystery, the exaltation only came when Tasmin left deepsoil. He anticipated the moment with a kind of hunger, never knowing exactly when it would happen, but always sure it would.

He led the group west past the citadel. Behind them lay the food crop fields, the dwellings, the nondenominational chapel. Behind them lay Deepsoil Five: very ordinary, very real, very day to day.

All around them lay dream country.

They moved slowly, scanning the monstrous crystals. South at the limit of vision, a mob of pillars marked the site of the Presences. There, as here, the soil barely covered the crystals. Everything around them vibrated to the whining buzzing cacophony that grew louder as they moved toward the ridge.

The Watchers knew they were there.

I give [Sheri S. Tepper] full marks for a tremendously exciting and inventive novel, with excellent characterizations and a taut plot. Particularly clever is the communications gap between species . . . Absolutely fascinating.
—*Anne McCaffrey*

AFTER LONG SILENCE

Sheri S. Tepper

BANTAM BOOKS
TORONTO • NEW YORK • LONDON • SYDNEY • AUCKLAND

AFTER LONG SILENCE

A Bantam Spectra Book / December 1987

ISBN 0-553-26944-5

Published simultaneously in the United States and Canada

Bantam Books are published by Bantam Books, Inc. Its trade-
mark, consisting of the words ''Bantam Books'' and the por-
trayal of a rooster, is Registered in U.S. Patent and Trademark
Office and in other countries. Marca Registrada. Bantam
Books, Inc., 666 Fifth Avenue, New York, New York 10103.

AFTER LONG SILENCE

When Tasmin reached for the gold leaf, he found the box empty. The glue was already neatly painted onto the ornamented initial letter of the Enigma score, and it would dry into uselessness within minutes. He spent a fleeting moment wanting to curse but satisfied himself by bellowing, "Jamieson!" in a tone that was an unequivocal imprecation.

"Master Ferrence?" The boyish face thrust around the door was wide-eyed in its most "Who, me?" expression, and the dark blond hair fell artfully over a forehead only slightly wrinkled as though to indicate "I'm working very hard, now what does he want?"

Undeceived by all this, Tasmin waved the empty box and snarled, "One minute, Jamieson. Or less."

The acolyte evidently read Tasmin's expression correctly for he moved away in a nicely assessed pretense of panic mixed with alacrity. The gold leaf was kept in a storeroom up one flight, and the boy could conceivably make it within the time limit if he went at a dead run.

He returned panting and, for once, silent. In gratitude, Tasmin postponed the lecture he had been rehearsing. "Get on with what you were doing."

"It wasn't important, Master."

"If what you were doing wasn't important, then you should have checked my supplies. Only pressure of urgent work could have excused your not doing so."

"I guess it was important, after all," Jamieson responded, a quirk at the corner of his mouth the only betrayal of the fact that he had been well and truly caught. He let the door shut quietly behind him and Tasmin smiled ruefully. The boy was not called Reb Jamieson for nothing. He rebelled at every-thing, including the discipline of an acolyte, almost as a matter of conviction. If he weren't almost consistently right about things; if he didn't have a voice like an angel . . .

Tasmin cut off the thought as he placed the felt pad over the gold leaf and rubbed it, setting the gilding onto the glue, then brushed the excess gold into the salvage pot. It was a conceit of his never to do the initial letter on a master copy until the rest of the score and libretto was complete. Now he could touch up the one or two red accents that needed brightening, get himself out of his robes and into civilian clothes, and make a photostat of the score for his own study at home—not at all in accordance with the rules, but generally winked at so long as the score didn't leave his possession. The finished master manuscript would go into a ceremonial filing binder and be delivered to Jaconi. They would talk a few minutes about the Master Librarian's perennial hobby horse, his language theory, and then Tasmin would borrow a quiet-car from the citadel garage and drive through the small settlement of Deepsoil Five, on his way home to Celcy.

Who would, as usual, greet his homecoming with sulks for some little time.

"This whole celibacy thing is just superstition," she pouted, as he had predicted. "Something left over from old religious ideas from Erickson's time. We've all outgrown that. There's no reason you shouldn't be able to come home at night even if you are copying a score."

The phrases were borrowed; the argument wasn't new; neither was his rejoinder. "That may be true. Maybe all the ritual is superstition and nonsense, Celcy love. Maybe it's only tradition, and fairly meaningless at that, but I took an oath to observe every bit of it, and it's honorable to keep oaths."

"Your stupid oath is more important than I am."

Tasmin remembered a line from a pre-dispersion poet about not being able to love half as much if one didn't love honor more, but he didn't quote it. Celcy hated being quoted at. "No, love, not more important than you. I made some oaths about you, too, and I'm just as determined to keep those. Things about loving and cherishing and so forth." He tilted her head back, coaxing a smile, unhappily aware of the implications of what he had just said but trusting her preoccupation with her own feelings to keep her from noticing. Sometimes, as now, he did feel he stayed with her more because of commitment than desire, but whenever the thought came to him he reminded himself of the other Celcy, the Celcy who, when things were secure and right, seemed magically to take this Celcy's place. She didn't always act like this. Certain things just seemed to bring it out.

"I sure don't feel loved," she said sulkily. He sighed, half in relief. She might not take less than a day to forgive him for having been away for the seventeen days it had taken to orchestrate and copy the new Enigma score—or, more accurately, the putative Enigma score since it hadn't been tested on the Enigma yet, and might never be—but she would come around eventually. Nothing he could do would hurry the process. If he ignored her, it would take even longer, so he set himself to be pleasant, reminding himself of her condition, trying to think of small things that might please her.

"What's going on at the center? Something you'd like to see? Any good holos?"

"Nothing good. I went to a new one that Jeanne Gentrack told me about, but it was awful." She shivered. "All about the people on the Jut, starving and trying to get out through the Jammers after their Tripsingers were assassinated by that crazy fanatic."

"You know you hate things like that, Celcy. Why did you go?"

"Oh, it was something to do." She had gone alone, of course. Celcy had no women friends and was too conventional to go with a man, even though Tasmin wouldn't have objected. "I'd heard it was about Tripsingers, and I thought you might like it if I went." She was flirting with him now, cutely petulant, lower lip protruding, wanting to be babied and cosseted, making him be daddy. He would try to kiss her; she would evade him. They would play this game for some time. Tonight she would be "too tired" as a punishment for his neglect, and then about noon tomorrow she might show evidence of that joyously sparkling girl he had fallen in love with, the Celcy he had married.

He put on a sympathetic smile. "It's great that you'd like to know more about my work, love, but maybe seeing a tragic movie about the Jut famine isn't the best way to go about it."

Of course, she wasn't interested in his work, though Tasmin hadn't realized it until a year or two after they were married. Five years ago, when Celcy was eighteen, her friends had been the children of laborers and clerks, and she had thought it was a coup to marry a Tripsinger. She had listened to him then, eyes shining, as he told her about this triumph or that defeat. Now all their friends were citadel people, and Tasmin was merely one of the crowd, nothing special, nothing to brag about, just a man engaged in uninteresting activities that forced him to leave her alone a lot. He could even sympathize with her resentment. Some of his work bored him, too.

"It's not just that she's bored, Tas," his mother had said, fumbling for his hand through the perpetual mists that her blindness made of her world. "Her parents died on a trip. Her uncle took her in, but he had children of his own, and they wouldn't be normal if they hadn't resented her. Then, on their way to Deepsoil Five, there was a disaster, one wagon completely lost, several people badly maimed. Poor little Celcy was only eight or nine and hardly slept for weeks after they got here. She's frightened to death of being abandoned and of the Presences."

He had been dumbfounded. "I never knew that! How did you?"

She had frowned, blind eyes searching for memory. "I think Celcy's uncle told me most of it, Tas. At your wedding."

"I wonder why she never mentioned it to me?" he had mused aloud.

"Because she doesn't want to admit it or remember it," his mother had answered in that slightly sharpened voice reserved for occasions when Tasmin, or his father before him, had been unusually dense. Tasmin remembered his father, Miles Ferrence, as a grim, pious man who said little and expected much, given to unexpected fits of fury toward the world and his family, interspersed with equally unexpected pits of deep depression. Miles had gone into peril and died at the foot of the Black Tower the year after . . . well, the year after Tasmin's older brother had. . . . Never mind. Tasmin had been surprised at how difficult it was to mourn his father, and then had been troubled by his own surprise.

Celcy was still talking about the holodrama, her voice

becoming agitated and querulous. "I couldn't see why they didn't build boats and just float down the shore. Why did they have to get out through the Jammers."

He closed his eyes, shutting out other thoughts and recollections, visualizing the map of the Jut. The far north-west of Jubal, an area called New Pacifica. A peninsula of deepsoil protruding into a shallow bay. At the continental end of this Jut were two great crystal promontories, the Jammers—not merely promontories but Presences. Between them led a steep, narrow pass that connected the Jut to the land mass of New Pacifica and the rest of Jubal, while out in the bay, like the protruding teeth of a mighty carnivore, clustered the smaller—though still very large—offspring of the Jammers, the Jammlings.

"Jammlings," he said. "Scattered all through the water. I don't think there's a space a hundred yards wide between them anywhere. The Juttites would have needed a Tripsinger to get through there just as they did to get between the Jammers."

"Oh. Well, none of the characters said that in the holo. They just kept getting more and more starved until they got desperate." Her face was very pale and there were tiny drops of moisture on her forehead. "Then they tried rushing past the Jam . . . the Jam . . . the Presences, and somebody tried to sing them through and couldn't and everybody got squashed and ripped apart and . . . well, you know. It was bloody and awful." Her voice was a choked gargle.

Well, of course it was, an inner voice said. As you should have known, silly girl. He pulled her to him and quelled the voice sternly, annoyed with himself. Her hysteria was real. She had been genuinely upset by the drama. Sympathy was called for rather than his increasingly habitual impatience. "Hey, forget it. All past history and long gone. Now that you're pregnant, you need more cheerful influences." With a flourish, he produced his surprise. "Here, something I picked up."

"Oh, Tasmin!" She slipped the ribbon to one side and tore at the paper, pulling the stuffed toy from its wrappings and hugging the gray-green plush of the wide-eyed little animal. "It's so cunning. Look at that. A viggy baby. I love it.

Thank you." She stroked the feathery antennae, planting a kiss on the green velour nose.

He suppressed the happy comments he had been about to make. The toy had been intended for the baby, a symbol of expectation. He should have said something to that effect before she opened it. Or perhaps not. She was more pleased with it than a baby would be.

He tried with another gift. "Except for a preceptor trip next month, I've told the Master General I won't be available for any extended duty until after the baby comes. How about that?"

"I wish it was already next month," she went on with her own thoughts, only half hearing him.

"Why? What's next month?"

"Lim Terree is coming to do a concert. Less than three weeks from now. I really want to hear that. . . ."

Lim Terree.

He heard the name, then chose not to hear it. Not to have heard it.

Instead, he found himself examining Celcy's smooth lineless face, staring at her full lips, her wide bright eyes, totally unchanged by their five years of marriage. She was so tiny, he chanted to himself in his private ritual, so tiny, like a doll. Her skin was as smooth as satin. When they made love, he could cup each of her buttocks in one of his hands, a silken mound. When they made love his world came apart in wonderful fire. She was his own sweet girl.

Lim Terree.

She was pregnant now. An accident. The doctor had told them she couldn't possibly get pregnant unless she took the hormones he gave her, but she wouldn't take the drug. Could not, she said. It made her sick. Impossible that she could be pregnant, and yet she was. "Sometimes we're wrong," the doctor had said. "Sometimes these things happen." A miracle.

Tasmin was amazed at his own joy, astonished at his salesmanship in convincing her it would be fun to have a child of their own. Too soon for a test yet, but he hoped for a son. Celcy wouldn't mind his caring for a boy, but she would probably hate sharing him with a little girl. "Fear sharing him," he told himself, remembering his mother's words. "Not hate, fear."

He coughed, almost choking. He couldn't just go on staring at his wife and ignoring what she had said. He had to respond. "When did you hear he was coming?"

"There are big posters down at the Center. *'Lim Terree. Jubal's entertainment idol. Straight from his triumphant tour of the Deepsoil Coast.'* I got his most recent cube and it's wonderful. I don't know why you couldn't do concert versions, Tasmin. Your voice is every bit as good as his. He started as a Tripsinger, too, you know."

He let the implications of this pass. It wasn't the first time she had implied that his profession was not very important, something that anyone could do if they were foolish enough to want to. *Mere* Tripsinger was in her tone if not in her words, betraying an ignorance shared by a significant part of the lay population on Jubal. She was wrong about Lim, though. He hadn't been a Tripsinger, mere or otherwise.

Lim Terree.

"I know him," he said, his voice sounding tight and unnatural. "He's my brother."

"Oh, don't make jokes," she said, the petulant expression back on her face. For a moment she had forgotten her recent neglect. "That's a weird thing to say, Tasmin."

"I said he is my brother. He is. My older brother. His real name is Lim Ferrence. He left Deepsoil Five about fifteen years ago."

"That's just when I got here! He was a Tripsinger *here?*"

Not really, he wanted to say. "You were only a schoolchild when he left. And yes, he did some trips out of here."

"Did he really do the Enigma? Everyone says he did the Enigma." She was suddenly eager, glowing.

It was hard to keep the resentment out of his voice. "Celcy, I don't know who 'everyone' is. Of course Lim didn't sing the Enigma. No one has ever got by the Enigma alive."

She cocked her head, considering this. "Oh, people don't always tell the truth about things. Tripsingers are jealous of each other. Maybe he went with just a small group and got through, but it was never recorded or anything."

He made a chopping, thrusting-away gesture that she hated, not realizing he had done it until he saw her face. "Lim Terree did not do the Enigma trip. So far as I remember he led two caravans east through the Minor Mysteries, one out to Half Moon and back, and one through the Creeping Desert to Splash One on the Deepsoil Coast and that was it. He didn't come back from that one."

"Four trips?" She gave him a skeptical look, making a mocking mouth. "Four trips? Come on, Tasmin. Sibling rivalry, I'll bet. You're jealous of him!" Then she hastily tried to undo some of the anger he realized he had let show in his face. "Not that I can blame you. He's so good looking. I'll bet the girls mobbed him."

Not really, he wanted to say again. They—most of them, at least the ones his own age—knew him for what he was, a man who . . . better not think about that. He wasn't even sure that it was true anymore. Dad had screamed and hammered his fist, calling Lim filthy, depraved. Was that it? Depraved? Something like that, but that was after Lim had gone. Tasmin had only been sixteen, seventeen when Lim left. Lim had been five years older. Memory didn't always cleave to the truth, particularly after someone had gone. Perhaps none of what he thought he remembered had really happened.

"I don't remember," he equivocated. "I was just a kid, just getting out of basic school. But if you want to go to his concert, love, I'll bet he has some tickets he'd make available—for his family." Which seemed to do the trick for she stopped sulking and talked with him, and when night came, she said she was too tired but didn't insist upon it after he kissed her.

Still, their lovemaking was anything but satisfying. She seemed to be thinking about something else, as though there were something she wanted to tell him or talk to him about but couldn't. It was the way she behaved when she'd spent money they didn't have, or was about to, or when she flirted herself into a corner she needed his help to get out of. He knew why she did those things, testing him, making him prove that he loved her. If he asked what was bothering her before she was ready to tell him, it would only lead to accusations that he didn't trust her. One of these days, they'd have to take time to work it out. One of these days he would get professional help for her instead of endlessly playing daddy for her in the vain hope she'd grow up. He had made himself this promise before. Somehow there never seemed to be time to keep it—time, or the energy to get through the inevitable resentment. Looking at her sleeping face, he knew that Celcy would regard it as a betrayal.

Sighing, unable to sleep, he took his let-down, half hostile feelings onto the roof. It was his place for exorcising demons.

Virtually every house in Deepsoil Five had a deck or small tower from which people could watch approaching caravans or spy on the Presences through telescopes. He had given Celcy a fine scope three years ago for her birthday, but she had never used it. She didn't like looking at the Presences, something he should have realized before he picked out the gift. Back then he was still thinking that what interested him would interest her.

"A very masculine failing." His mother had laughed softly at his rueful confession. "Your father was the same way." And then, almost wistfully, she added, "Give her something to make her feel treasured. Give her jewelry next time, Tas."

He had given her jewelry since, but he'd kept the scope. Now he swung it toward the south. A scant twenty miles away the monstrous hulk of the Enigma quivered darkly against the Old Moon, a great, split pillar guarding the wall between the interior and the southern coast. Was the new score really a password past the Presence? Or would it be just one more failed attempt, ending in blood and death? The Enigma offered no comment, simply went on quivering, visibly occulting the stars at its edge in a constant shimmer of motion.

He turned to the west in a wide arc, ticking off the Presences along the horizon. Enigma, Sky Hammer, Amber Axe, Deadly Dozen, Cloud Gatherer, Black Tower, the Far Watchlings, then the western escarpment of crowded and mostly unnamed Presences. A little south of west were the Twin Watchers. The Watcher score was one of the first Passwords he had ever learned—a fairly simple piece of singing, with phonemes that were easy to get one's tongue around. "Arndaff duh-roomavah," he chanted softly, "sindir dassalam awoh," wondering as he occasionally did if there was really any meaning in the sounds. Official doctrine taught there was not, that the sounds, when properly sung and backed up with appropriate orchestration, merely damped the vibration in the crystalline Presences, thus allowing caravans to get through without being crushed. Or dismembered. Or blown away by scattering shards of crystal.

Although ever since Erickson there had been people who believed implicitly in the language theory. Even now there were a few outspoken holdouts like Chad Jaconi, the Master Librarian, who believed that the sounds of the librettos were really words, and said so. Jaconi had spent the last forty years making a dictionary of tripsong phonemes, buying new translators from out-system, trying to establish that the Password scores were, indeed, a language. Every time old Jaconi thought he'd proved something, however, someone came along with a new libretto that contradicted it. There were still Explorer-singers out there with recorders and synthesizers and computers, crouched just outside the range of various Presences, trying endless combinations to see what seemed to work, coming up with new stuff even after all these years. Tasmin had actually heard the original cube made a hundred years ago by Ben Erickson, the first Explorer to get past the Far Watchlings to inland Deepsoil, an amazing and utterly mysterious, if not mystical, achievement. How could anyone possibly have arrived at the particular combination of phonemes and orchestral effect by trial and error! It seemed impossible.

"It had to be clairvoyance," Tasmin mused, not for the first time. "A crystal ball and a fine voice."

Erickson had sung his way past the Presences for almost fifty years before becoming one more singer to fall to the Enigma. During those years he had made an immortal name for himself and founded both the Order of Tripsingers and the Order of Explorers. Not bad accomplishments for one man. Tasmin would have been content to do one-quarter as well.

"Tassy?" A sad little whisper from the stairway. "I woke up and you weren't there."

"Just getting a little air, love." He went to her at the top of the stairs and gathered her into his arms. She nestled there, reaching up to stroke his face, whispering secret words into his ears, making his heart thunder and his arms tighten around her as though he would never let her go. As he picked her up to carry her downstairs, she turned to look out at the line of Presences, jagged against the stars.

"You were looking at those things. I hate them, Tasmin. I do."

It was the first time she had ever said she hated the Presences, and his sudden burst of compassionate understanding amazed him. They made love again, tenderly, and afterward he cuddled her until she went back to sleep, still murmuring about the concert.

"He really is your brother? He'll really give us tickets?"

"I'm sure he will."

In the morning, Tasmin wondered whether Lim might indeed make some seats available as Tasmin had promised. To be on the safe side, he bought a pair, finding himself both astonished and angry at a price so high as to be almost indecent.

The streets of Splash One were swarming with lunch-seekers and construction workers, military types, and bands of belligerent Crystallites, to say nothing of the chains of bewildered pilgrims, each intent on his or her own needs, and none of them making way for anyone else. Gretl Mechas fought her way grimly through the crowds, wondering what in the name of good sense had made her decide to come down to Splash One and make the payment on her loan in person. She could have sent a credit chit down from the priory in Northwest City by messenger, by comfax, by passenger bus—why had she decided to do it herself?

"Fear," a remembered voice intoned in answer. "Debt is a terrible thing, Gretl. Never get into debt." It was her father's voice, preserved in memory for Gretl's lifetime.

"Easy for you to say," she snarled. Easy for anyone to say. Hard to accomplish, however, when your only sister sent an emergency message from Heron's World telling you that she'd lost an arm in an accident and couldn't pay for her own regeneration. In advance, of course. No one did regeneration anymore unless they were paid in advance. And equally, of course, if you needed regeneration, no one would lend you any money either, except on extortionate terms that sometimes led to involuntary servitude. The stupid little twit hadn't thought she'd need regeneration insurance. Naturally not, when she had Gretl to call on.

"Shit," she said feelingly, finding her way through the

bruising crowds to the door of the BDL building, ignoring the looks that followed her. People had been looking at Gretl since she was five, men particularly. Perhaps it was her skin, like dark, tawny ivory. Perhaps it was her hair, a mahogany wealth that seemed to have a life of its own. Perhaps it was figure, or face, or merely some expression of lively unquenchable interest in those wide, dark eyes. But men always looked. Gretl didn't look back, however. Her heart was with a certain man back on Heron's World, where she'd be, too, as soon as this contract was over.

"What was that name again," the credit office clerk asked, mystified. "Here, let me see your code book."

Gretl handed it over. One got used to this on Jubal. It cost so much to bring in manufactured materials that everything on Jubal was used past the point of no return. Nothing ever worked quite right. . . .

"It's been paid," the clerk said with a look of knowing complicity.

"Paid?" she blurted in astonishment, only half hearing the clerk. "What do you mean, paid?"

"Your loan has been paid in full," the clerk said, glancing suspiciously from under her eyelashes. "You didn't know?"

"I sure as hell didn't. Who paid it?"

The clerk fumbled with the keys, frowning, then shaking her head.

"Well?"

"Justin," the clerk whispered.

"Who?"

"Oh, come on, lady." The whisper was angry.

"I asked who that was. For God's sake, girl, tell me. I've only been on this planet for a few months, and I haven't any idea. . . ."

The clerk nodded, a tiny nod, upward and to the right. Gretl looked up. Nothing there but the glass-enclosed offices of the Brou Distribution Ltd., or BDL, hierarchy. In one of them, a curtain quivered. "Him," whispered the clerk, suddenly quite pale. "Harward Justin."

"The Planetary Manager?" Gretl fell silent, full of a sick uneasiness. She had met him. When she was here to arrange the loan, and only for a moment in passing. He had stopped at the desk where she was waiting, introduced himself, asked her to have lunch with him. She had refused.

A man with no neck, she recalled. Greasy rolls of fat from his jaw to his shoulders. Eyes that looked like half frozen slush peering at her between puffy lids. A drooping, sensual mouth. Wet, she remembered. He had licked his lips continually.

Abruptly she asked, "Do you have an envelope?"

The clerk gave her a curious glance as she passed one over. Gretl inserted the payment she had been about to make, scribbled a few words on the outside, then handed it to the clerk.

"I am not interested in other people paying my debts," she said. "I'll repay my loan on the terms I specified. See that Mr. Justin gets this."

She turned and strode away, the inner queasiness giving way to amazement and then anger. Wait until Don Furz heard about this! Unbelievable! The gall of the man!

She had almost reached the door when the hand fell on her shoulder.

He was a tall man, an expressionless man, an uninterested man. He did not look at her as other men usually looked at her. It was almost as though he did not see her as a person at all. He said very little, but he did not release her as he said it.

"My name is Spider Geroan. I work for Harward Justin, and he'd like to see you. Now."

_____ **2**

During Tasmin's orchestral effects class, it turned out that the air pump had been rigged to make farting noises, always good for a laugh. Practice for the neophytes shuddered to a halt while Tasmin dismantled the instrument.

"That particular sound is used, so far as I'm aware, only in the run through the Blind Gut," he remarked to the class. "The only instructive thing about this incident is that there are sounds that work better when produced instrumentally rather than by synthesizer, which is why we have drums, bells, pumps, and other paraphernalia. . . ."

"You're running perilously close to expulsion, Jamieson," he growled when the class was over. "That equipment is your responsibility."

"Some of the pre-trippers are kind of uptight," the boy remarked, not at all disturbed at the threat. "I thought a laugh might help."

There was something in that, enough that Tasmin wasn't inclined to press the matter. As was often true, Jamieson had broken the rules to good effect. This close to robing and first trip, many of the neophytes did get nervous and found it hard to concentrate. "Sabotaging equipment just isn't a good idea," Tasmin admonished in a fairly mild tone. "Some idiot kid fooled around with a Jammer drum once, seeing if he could sound like some 'Soilcoast singer, and it got put into a trip wagon just as it was. Do you need me to tell you what happened?"

"No, sir." Slightly flushed, but so far as Tasmin was able to discern, unrepentant, Jamieson agreed. "I remember."

"Well, double check that air pump. Be damn sure it does what it's supposed to do before you leave it."

Jamieson moved to change the subject. "Are we taking any of the first trippers out, Master?"

"On first New Moon, yes. There are only three I'm a neutral preceptor for, three I haven't had in my own classes—let's see, James, Refnic, and that Clarin girl with the astonishing voice. . . ."

"Renna. Renna Clarin." Jamieson cocked his head, considering.

"Right. Anything I should know?"

"James will fade, definitely if there's a clinch, and probably anyhow. He spends half his life wetting his pants and the other half drying himself off and asking if anybody noticed. Refnic's reliable. The tougher things are, the more he settles. I don't know that much about Renna Clarin except she looks funny bald. She transferred in."

Tasmin ignored the impudence, as Jamieson had known he would. "Evidently female neophytes don't have their heads shaved at Northwest, and it came as a shock to her when she got shaved down here. She had excellent personal references. Her records from Deepsoil Seven choir school were good."

Jamieson shrugged eloquently, a balletic gesture starting at his shoulders and ending at his fingertips, which twitched a little, showing their contempt for good records. Excellent choir school recommendations might mean little except that a candidate had an acceptable voice or got along well with the Choir Master. Jamieson himself had had terrible choir school grades and had set a new school record for demerits, a fact that Jamieson knew Tasmin was well aware of. Again he changed the subject. "What's the route?"

"Oh, I think we'll do my usual first trip loop. Past the Watchers on the easy side, down through the False Eagers, along Riddance Ridge to the Startles. Then down the deepsoil pass to Harmony, stay overnight there, give them a good scary look at the Tower while you and I sing them past, then back through the Far Watchlings."

"If it was me," Jamieson said, greatly daring, "I'd use James on the Startles. He likes that score and he can't do much wrong there."

"Rig him to pass, that it? Then what happens the first time some caravan depends on him?"

"Oh, I just thought a little more experience maybe . . ." Jamieson's voice trailed off, embarrassed. He obviously hadn't thought at all. Now he flushed and ducked his head in a hinted apology, a courtesy he accorded Tasmin but very few others.

"Think about it," Tasmin recommended, testing the final adjustment of the air pump. He sat back then, musing. "Jamieson."

"Sir?"

"You're of an age to pay attention to the 'Soilcoast singers. What do you know about Lim Terree?"

"Oh, hey, apogee. Way up in the ranking. Best-seller cubes, last three out. The girls are brou-dizzy over him."

"What's his music like?"

Jamieson gave this some thought. "Kind of hard to describe. There's a lot of Tripsinger stuff in it, but he takes way off from that. Of course, all the 'Soilcoast singers bill their stuff as being real Passwords, but you couldn't get anywhere with it. I don't think you could, anyhow."

"What do you mean?" Tasmin was really curious. He had so deeply resented Lim's misuses of Password material that he had not kept up with the 'Soilcoast singer cult, although he knew it was extensive and bled money at every pore. "What do you mean, you couldn't get anywhere with it?"

Jamieson pursed his lips, gestured toward a chair, and Tasmin nodded permission to sit. "You know the score for the Watchers? Minor key intro, two horns, and a tuned drum. Diddle, diddle, diddle in the strings in that rhythmic pattern, then the solo voice comes in with the PJ, ah the Petition and Justification, right? Kind of a simple melody line there, pretty straightforward, not like those key and tempo shifts in the Jammer sequences? Well, Lim Terree does a kind of takeoff on that. He uses the melody of the P, ah the Petition and Justification, but he kind of—oh, embroiders it. Trills and little quavers and runs and grace notes. Where you sing 'Arndaff duh-roomavah,' it comes out 'Arn-daffa-daffa-daffa-duh-uh-uh-uh-duhroo-duhrooma-vah-ah-ah.' " It was a marvelous, tumbling cataract of sound.

Jamieson had a good voice. Tasmin tried briefly and without success to convince himself he was listening to an obscenity. The phrase had been hypnotic.

"And it goes on like that?"

"The phrase 'sindir dassalam awoh' takes about three minutes with all the cadenzas and rhythmic repetitions and stuff. If you tried that out on the Watchers . . . well, I just don't think it would get you very far. They'd blow and you'd be gone."

"I see what you mean. What's the attraction then?"

"Well, it's great music. Really. Lots of noise and what they do on stage is pretty erotic. He wears something that looks sort of like a Tripsinger robe, only fancier, open down the front practically to his downspout." Jamieson leapt up, gestured as though unzipping himself from a spraddled stance, at once potent and aggressive, making Tasmin see what he was talking about. "The orchestral stuff is wild, too. Loads of percussion and heavy power assists." He collapsed into the chair again, legs over the arm.

"Which couldn't be used on a real trip."

"Not unless you had a trip wagon the size of a coastal broubarge to hold the power source."

"So, how's he going to do a concert here? He'd never get that power by the Presences. And even if the Presences would let it past, which they won't, the widest trail on Riddance Ridge barely passes a standard brou wagon."

"Most of it'll probably be holo. He'll be live against his own recorded setup with maybe one or two live backup musicians along."

"Why would he bother? If things are so great in the Deepsoil Coast, why come inland?"

The acolyte shrugged, a minimal shoulder twitch. "I can't figure it. Too much exposure, maybe? I read the fanstats sometimes. There's a lot of competition among what they call the Big Six. Terree's oh, about number three, down from one or two a year ago. This new kid Chantry is a favorite with the Governor's crowd, and he's gone up like a balloon. Maybe Terree figures he'll be more of a novelty after he comes back from an inland trip."

"Tripsinger Lim Terree," Tasmin quoted from an imaginary poster. "Back from a six-month tour of duty leading desperate caravans in the interior. . . ."

Jamieson grinned. "Something like that, yeah. Why all the interest, Master Ferrence?"

"Oh," Tasmin fell silent. "I knew him once, years ago. He came from around here."

"No joke! Really? Well, I guess it'll be old friends at the bar then."

"Not really. I didn't know him that well."

"I wonder why he didn't let me know he was coming?" Tasmin's mother stared toward him in wonder, though for years Thalia Ferrence had seen nothing but blurred outlines through those wide eyes. "It seems odd he wouldn't let me know." Her voice was aching and lost, with an agonizing resurgence of familiar pain, made strange only by renewed intensity.

He probably didn't know you were still alive, Tasmin thought, not saying it. "Lim was probably too embarrassed, Mother. Or, maybe he didn't know Dad was gone and thought he might not be welcome."

"His father would have forgiven him. Miles knew it was nothing that serious." She shook her head, smiling. She seemed determined to reform Miles Ferrence in memory, determined to create a loving and forgiving father where Tasmin could remember only hostility and harsh judgment.

Not only her eyes that can't see, Tasmin reflected. Her heart can't see either. Maybe that's part of being a wife and mother, having a blind heart. If she's blind to Lim's faults, well, she's blind to mine as well. He tried to feel generous about her warmth to Lim but couldn't. Something about it sickened him. Sibling rivalry? That would be Celcy's easy answer to everything. No, it was the senseless expenditure of emotion on someone unworthy of it that offended him.

Or jealousy. It could be that. He could be jealous of Lim. It would be nice to have only oneself to worry about instead of juggling three or four sets of responsibilities. Celcy. Work. His mother, whose blindness could be helped at one of the 'Soilcoast medical centers if he could only get her there and pay the bills. Since Miles Ferrence had died, BDL provided no more medical care for her.

Not that she ever reproached him. "Your wife has to come first, Tas. Just come see me when you can. I love it when you do."

Now she leaned forward to take his hand and stroke it. "Are you going out on a trip soon?"

"First New Moon, Mom. First trip for some recently robed singers. Be gone two days is all. I don't like to leave Celcy alone very long, not in her condition."

"She's not still pregnant, is she?"

"Why—" He had started to say "of course, she is" and found the words sticking in his throat. "Why did you think she wasn't?"

"Oh, I don't know." That perceptive stare again, as though the mind saw what the eyes could not. "It just seemed sort of unlikely. Tell her she's welcome to stay with me while you're away."

He patted his mother's hand, knowing that she knew he would tell Celcy and Celcy wouldn't care. Sibling rivalry wasn't the only kind of rivalry she knew about.

On the first of New Moon he led a small caravan out of

the ceremonial gate of the citadel, itchily anticipating the transition from reality to marvel. Deepsoil Five was reality. Celcy, who had been entirely marvelous at one time, was mostly reality these days. Work was entirely reality. Though the citadel tried to evoke a sense of exhalation and mystery, its ornamented ritualism had become increasingly matter-of-fact over the years. Chad Jaconi called the constant ceremonies "painfully baroque" compared to the sense of the marvelous that had permeated Tripsinging when he was young. Maybe it was something you could feel only when you were young. Tasmin didn't feel it at all when he was in the citadel.

The marvel, the mystery—and almost always the exaltation—came when he left deepsoil. He anticipated the moment with a kind of hunger, never knowing exactly when it would happen, always sure it would.

He led the group through the sparsely populated area to the west of the citadel, past heavily planted fields of euphoric brou, Jubal's only export crop. Behind them lay the citadel, the food crop fields, the dwellings, the nondenominational chapel, the service and entertainment center. Behind them lay Deepsoil Five: very ordinary, very real, very day-to-day. . . .

And all around them lay dream country.

They stopped at the edge of a brou field to put soft shoes on the mules while Tasmin picked pods for each of them, a privilege that Brou Distribution Ltd. granted only to "licensed Tripsingers going into peril." The pomposity of the phrase never failed to amuse Tasmin. Any kid who was fast on his feet could pick brou under the noses of the field guards, and often did. In the last analysis, however, no matter how pompous the organization was, they all worked for BDL; BDL who maintained the citadels and paid for the caravans and the Tripsingers to get them through, and for the Explorers to find the way, and for the farmers to grow the food they all ate, and all the infrastructure that kept the whole thing moving. Tripsingers, Explorers, mule breeders, service center employees, hundreds of thousands of them, all working, in the end, for BDL.

"May we achieve passage and safe return," Tasmin intoned, cleaving to the ritual, distributing the pods.

"Amen." A stuttered chorus from the first-timers amid a

crisp shattering of dry pods. They chewed and became decidedly cheerful. Tasmin smiled, a little cynically. The brou-dizzy would have worn off by the time they came near a Presence.

Soon the planted fields gave way to uncultivated plains, sloping gently upward toward the massif that formed a sheer-sided wall between the deepsoil pocket of Five and all the shallow soiled areas beyond. The stubby, imported trees gave way to taller growths, mythically slender and feathery, less like trees than like the plumes of some enormous bird. They smelled faintly spicy and resinous, the smell of Jubal itself. Among the grasses, smaller shrubs arrayed themselves like peacock's tails, great fans of multicolored, downy leaves, turning slowly to face the sun. Out in the prairie, singly or in groups, stood small Watchlets no taller than a man. They glowed like stained glass, squeaking and muttering as the wagon passed. Tasmin noted one or two that were growing closer to the road than was safe. He had not brought demolition equipment along on this trip, and in any case he preferred to pass the word and leave it to the experts. He made quick notes, sighting on the horizon.

The balloon-tired wagon was quiet. The mules wore flexible cushioned shoes. There were no rattling chains or squeaking leathers. More than one party had met doom because of noisy equipment—or so it was assumed. They rode silently, Jamieson on the seat of the wagon, Tasmin and the students on their soft-shod animals. Part of the sense of mystery came from this apprehensive quiet. Part came from the odors that always seemed to heighten Tasmin's perception of the world around him. Part came from the intrinsic unlikelihood of what they would attempt to do.

That unlikelihood became evident when they wound their way to the top of the mighty north-south rampart and looked down at what waited there. At Tasmin's gesture, they gathered closely together, the mules crowded side to side.

"What you see before you, people," Tasmin whispered, "is the so-called easy side of the Watchers." He didn't belabor the point. They needed only a good look at what loomed on either side of their path.

Before them the road dropped abruptly downward to curve to the left around the South Watcher. A few dozen

South Watchlings stood at the edge of the road, tapering monoliths of translucent green and blue with fracture lines splitting the interiors into a maze of refracted light, the smallest among them five times Tasmin's height. Behind the Watchlings began the base of the South Watcher itself, a looming tower of emerald and sapphire, spilling foliage from myriad ledges, crowned with flights of gyre-birds that rose in a whirling, smokelike cloud around the crest, five hundred feet above.

On the north side of the road a crowd of smaller North Watchlings shone in hues of amethyst and smoke, and the great bulk of the North Watcher hung above them, a cliff formed of moonstone and ashy quartz, though chemists and geologists argued that the structure of the Watcher was not precisely either of these. In his mind, Tasmin said "emerald" and "moonstone" and "sapphire." Let the chemists argue what they really were; to him whether they were Presences hundreds of feet tall, or 'lings a tenth that size, or 'lets, smaller than a man, they were all sheer beauty.

Between the Watchers, scattered among the Watchlings, was the wreckage of many wagons and a boneyard of human and animal skeletons, long since picked clean. Behind the Watchers to both north and south extended the endless line of named and unnamed Presences that made up the western rampart of Deepsoil Five, cutting it off from the rest of the continent except through this and several similar passes for which proven Passwords existed.

Jamieson feigned boredom by sprawling on the trip wagon seat, although he himself had only been out twice before. Refnic, James, and Clarin perched on their mules like new hats at spring festival, so recently accoutered by the citadel Tripmaster as to seem almost artificial, like decorated manikins. "Put your hoods back," Tasmin advised them quietly. "Push up your sleeves and fasten them with the bands. That's what the bands are for, and it gets your hands out in the open where you need them. I know the sleeves are stiff, but they'll soften up in time." Tasmin's own robes were silky from repeated washings and mendings. The embroidered cuffs fell in gentle folds from the bands, and the hood had long ago lost its stiff lining. "Put the reins in the saddle hook to free your hands. That's it."

With heads and arms protruding from the Tripsingers' robes, the students looked more human and more vulnerable, their skulls looking almost fragile through the short hair that had been allowed to grow in anticipation of their robing but was still only an inch or so long. They could not take their eyes from the Watchers, a normal reaction. Even experienced caravaners sometimes sat for an hour or more simply looking at a Presence as though unable to believe what they saw. Most passengers traveled inside screened wagons, often dosed with tranquilizers to avoid hysteria and the resultant fatal noise. These students were looking on the Presences at close range for the first time. Their heads moved slowly, scanning the monstrous crystals, from those before them to all the others dwindling toward the horizon. South, at the limit of vision, a mob of pillars dwarfed by distance marked the site of the Far Watchlings with the monstrous Black Tower hulked behind them, the route by which they would return. They knew that there, as here, the soil barely covered the crystals. Everything around them vibrated to the eager whining, buzzing, squeaking cacophony that had been becoming louder since they moved toward the ridge.

The Watchers knew they were there.

"Presumably you've decided how you want to assign this?" Tasmin usually let his first trippers decide who sang what, so long as everyone took equal responsibility. "All right, move it along. Perform or retreat, one or the other. The Presences are getting irritated." Tasmin controlled his impatience. They could have moved a little faster, but at least they weren't paralyzed. He had escorted more than one group that went into a total funk at the first sight of a Presence, and at least one during which a neophyte, paralyzed with fear, had flung himself at a Presence.

"Clarin will sing it, sir, if you don't mind. James and I will do the orchestral effects." Refnic was a little pale but composed. Clarin seemed almost hypnotized, her dark brows drawn together in a concentrated frown, deep hollows in her cheeks as she sucked them in, moistening her tongue.

"Get on with it then."

The mules hitched to the trip wagon were trained to pull at a steady pace, no matter what was going on. Refnic climbed into the wagon and settled at the console while James crouched over the drums. Clarin urged her animal forward, reins clipped to the saddle hook, arms out.

"Tanta tara." The first horn sounds from the wagon, synthesized but not recorded. Somehow the Presences always knew the difference. Recorded Passwords caused almost instant retaliation. The drum entered, a slow beat, emphatic yet respectful. Duma duma duma. Then the strings.

"Arndaff duh-roomavah," Clarin sang in her astonishingly deep voice, bright and true as a bell. "Arndaff, duh-roomavah." With the first notes, her face had relaxed and was now given over to the music in blind concentration.

The squeaking buzz beneath their feet dwindled gradually to silence. The mules moved forward, slowly, easily on their quiet shoes, the muffled sound of their feet almost inaudible.

Flawlessly, the string sounds built to a crescendo. The drum again, horns, now a bell, softly, and Clarin's voice again. "Sindir, sindir, sindir dassalam awoh."

The mules kept up their steady pace, Clarin riding with Tasmin close behind, then the wagon on its soft-tired wheels, and the two riderless animals following. The synthesizer made only those sounds it was required to make. Muffled wheels and hooves were acceptable to the Presences, though any engine sound, no matter how quiet, was not. No mechanical land or aircraft of any kind could move about on Jubal except over deepsoil where the crystalline Presences were cushioned by fifty meters or more of soft earth from the noise going on above them. Since such pockets of soil were usually separated from other similar areas by mighty cliffs of ranked Presences, there was no effective mechanical transportation on the planet except along coastal areas and over the seas.

"Dassalom awoh," Clarin sang as they moved around the curve to the left. "Bondars delumin sindarlo." Few women could manage the vocals for the Passwords needed around Deepsoil Five, though Tasmin had heard there were a lot of female Tripsingers in the Northwest. He gave her a smile of encouragement and gestured her to continue, even though they were in safe territory. If there had been a caravan with them, the Tripsingers and trip wagon would have pulled aside at this point and gone on with the Petition and Justification variations until every vehicle had passed. Tasmin felt she might as well get the practice.

Clarin began the first variation. If anything at all had been learned about the Presences, it was that they became bored rather easily. The same phrases repeated more than a few times were likely to bring a violent reaction.

At the end of the second variation, Tasmin signaled for the concluding statement, the Expression of Gratitude. Clarin sang it. Then there was silence. They pulled away from the Watchers, no one speaking.

A thunderous crack split the silence behind them, a shattering crash echoed from the far cliffs in retreating volleys of echoes. Tasmin swung around in his saddle, horrified, thinking perhaps the wagon had not come clear, but it was a good ten meters beyond the place where the smoking fragments of crystal lay scattered. Behind them, one of the Watchlings had violently shed its top in their general direction.

"Joke," muttered Jamieson. "Ha, ha."

Clarin was white-faced and shivering. "Why?" she begged, eyes frightened. "Why? I didn't miss a note!"

"Shhh." Tasmin, overwhelmed with wonder, could not speak for a moment. He took her arm to feel her shaking under his hand, every muscle rigid. He drew her against him, pulled the others close with his eyes and beckoning hands, whispered to her, and in doing so spoke to them all. "Clarin, I've never heard the Watcher score sung better. It wasn't you. What you have to remember is that the Presences— they, well, they're unpredictable. They do strange things." He stroked the back of the girl's head, like a baby's with the short hair.

"Joke," murmured Jamieson again. "It was laughing at us."

"Jamieson, we can do without that anthropomorphic motif!" Tasmin grated, keeping his voice level and quiet with difficulty. He didn't want to talk, didn't want to have to talk, wanted only to feel the adrenaline pulsing through him at the shuddering marvel of the Presences. With an effort, he focused on the frightened first trippers. "These are crystals, very complicated crystals. Certain sound combinations cause them to damp their own signals and stop their own electrical activity. It's complex, it's badly understood, but it isn't supernatural."

"I wasn't thinking supernatural," Jamieson objected, the everlasting rebel. "Laughter isn't supernatural!"

"It is if a crystal mountain does it," Tasmin said with finality, aware of the dichotomy between what he said and what he felt. What he said was doctrine, yes, but was it truth? He didn't know and he doubted if any of those promulgating the position knew for sure. Still, one didn't keep a well-paid position in the academic hierarchy by allowing unacceptable notions to be bandied about in front of first-timers, or by speculating openly about them oneself, particularly when the BDL manual laid out the official position in plain language. It was in BDL's interest that the Presences be considered merely . . . mineral. What was in BDL's interest was in Tasmin's interest. He contented himself with a fierce look in Jamieson's direction that was countered with one of bland incomprehension. The trouble was that he and Jamieson understood one another far too well.

He gave Clarin a shake and a pat, then watched with approval as she sat up on the mule and wiped her face. She was very pale but composed. Her hair made a dark shadow on her skull, and the skin over her high, beautifully modeled cheekbones was softly flushed. She had made a quick recovery.

"Ooh, that makes me seethe," she grated. "I'd like to . . ."

"To demolish a few Presences, right? I know the feeling. Look at them, though, Clarin! Look down there!"

He pointed down the long slope in front of them where the False Eagers stood. She followed his gaze. Light scintillated from the Eagers in ringed rainbows, corruscating and glittering, a rhapsodic symphony of color, the flocks of gyrebirds twisting around them, a swirling garment of changeable smoke.

"Would you want to destroy that?" he asked.

"No," she said at last. "I really wouldn't."

"To say nothing of PEC orders to the contrary," Jamieson remarked drily. "The Planetary Exploitation Council strictures do prohibit demolition of anything except deepsoil encroachment."

"Little ones," she sighed. " 'Lets or 'lings. Nothing like that."

"Nothing like that," Tasmin agreed. "Now, I'd like you to pay some attention to the aspect of the Watchers from this direction." He dropped into his dry, lecture-time voice, trying to turn their attention to something besides the possibility of totally arbitrary annihilation. "The score is different coming from the west, of course, and it's an uphill climb, which means a longer reach, musically. It's called the 'trouble side,' though the westside score is actually simpler, both vocally and in orchestral effects. I'd suggest we get a move on. We have the False Eagers, the Startles, and Riddance Ridge to pass yet today before we go down the deepsoil pass to Harmony."

The first-timers took turns on the winding road beside the Eagers, a repetitive canon on one simple theme. James started well enough, but he got worse as the trip progressed. Refnic sang them through the Startles with practiced ease. As Jamieson had predicted, James froze in mid PJ on Riddance Ridge during an a capella series of phrases without any orchestral effects to cover the quiet. There was a moment of hideous silence. The ground began to tremble beneath them, but just as Tasmin opened his mouth to pick up the vocal Jamieson began singing, missing hardly a syllable, his voice soaring effortlessly. The ground beneath them quieted. When they had come across, Tasmin stopped them and passed his field glasses around, pointing out the wreckage of wagons that lay in a weathered tumble at the foot of the ridge.

It was hard to make a point in a whisper, but Tasmin could not let it wait. "James, that's the result of too little knowledge, too many assumptions, bad preparations, or Tripsingers who freeze. There's nothing wrong with being a good backup man. The orchestral effects are just as important as the vocals. If you can't depend on yourself for the vocals, for Erickson's sake, don't risk your life and those of other people." James was white with shame and frustration. He had been badly frightened by the explosion at the foot of the Watchers, but so had they all. Jamieson's face was bland. He was too bright even to hint at I-told-you-so.

After the trip, Harmony was blessedly dull, a small deepsoil pocket, entirely agricultural. Still, the food and beds were good, and Tasmin took half an hour to pay a condolence call on his mother's sister Betuny, a woman not close enough to ever have been called "aunt." Her husband had died only recently, and Tasmin brought a letter from his mother. After this duty call, he returned to the Trip House to find Renna Clarin on the porch waiting for him. She had wrapped a bright scarf around her head and wore a matching robe, vividly striped. For the first time he noticed how lovely she was, a thought that caught him with its oddness. He was not accustomed to thinking of the neophytes as lovely.

"I wanted to thank you, sir."

"For what, Clarin? You did a good job out there."

"For . . . for not jumping all over me when I got scared."

She was standing slightly above him on the porch, a tall girl with a calm and perceptive manner. Without the Tripsinger's robe she looked thinner, more graceful, and he remembered the feel of her body against his when he had hugged her. One always hugged students at times of peril, but he realized with a flush that she was the first female student he had ever precepted. "So you were scared?" he asked softly. "Really scared?"

"Really scared." She laughed a little, embarrassed at the admission.

"So was I. I often am. After a while you . . . you look forward to it. When you're really scared, the whole world seems to . . . brighten."

She considered this, doubtfully. "That's hard to imagine."

"Trust me. It happens. Either it happens, or you get into some other line of work."

She flushed, thanked him again, and went down the hall to her room. In his own room, Tasmin lay awake, conscious of the towering escarpments all around the town, gathered Presences so quiet that one could hear choruses of viggies singing off in the hills. Echoes of that surge of emotion hitting him that morning were with him still, a welling apprehension, half pleasurable, half terrifying. It had seldom come so strongly. It had seldom lasted so long. He lay there, his body tasting it, listening to the viggies singing until almost midnight.

He had his first-trippers up and traveling as soon as there was enough light. They stared at the Black Tower long enough to be impressed with the sheer impossibility of the thing while Tasmin, Jamieson close behind him, read silently from the prayers for the dead. The remains of Miles Ferrence lay somewhere in that welter of crystal trash at the bottom of the tower. After Miles Ferrence had died, Tasmin had gone

back to the original explorer's notes and done a new Black
Tower score, dedicated to the memory of his father. He had
really done it to please his mother, and so far no one using it
had died. Today he got them through by singing it himself,
with Jamieson doing backup.

After the Black Tower, the Far Watchlings seemed minor league stuff, good practice, but with nothing very interesting about them. James asked to be excused. The sense of
awe and mystery that Tasmin had been reveling in departed
as they came through the last of the Watchlings and saw
Deepsoil Five awaiting them at the bottom of the long slope.
Back to reality again. Tasmin heaved a deep breath. He
would be home in time for supper.

"How did your boysies do?" Celcy said, patting his face
and reaching up to be kissed. "Were they in frightfully good
voice?"

"All but one, yes." He didn't really want to talk about
James. Or, for some reason, Clarin.

"Oh, poor poopsie, did he get popped off?"

"Celcy, that's not funny. And it's in damn poor taste."
He snapped at her, regretting it instantly.

Her good spirits were undampened, however. "I'm sorry,
Tasmin. Really. I just wasn't thinking. Of course, he didn't
get popped off with you there. That's what you're there for,
isn't it? To keep the boysies safe and sound."

"Among other things."

"I missed you. I missed you a lot." She opened his robe
and came inside it, against him, pummeling his ribs with her
fists. "Did you hear me, did you?"

"I heard you." He laughed, suddenly joyous. "I heard
you, Celcy."

"So. Do something about it."

His weariness left him. The aftertrip letdown was postponed. She was as giddy and playful as a happy child, eager
to please him, and the evening passed in a tangle of lovemaking and feasting.

"I have been cooking dinner all day," she announced at
one point, pouring him a third glass of wine. "All day long,
without sur-cease!"

He rubbed his stomach ruefully. If he hadn't married

Celcy for quite other reasons, he might have married her for her cooking. "You're very good to me."

"That's because," she said, running her hands under his shirt. "Because."

There was an interlude.

And then, sleepily, "Tassy, sweetie, *he* called."

"Who?" He could not for the moment imagine whom she might be talking about, and then it came to him with a blow of almost physical force. "Lim? He's here?" He had to be on Deepsoil Five or he couldn't have called.

"He's up at the power station. They're camping there for a day or two to get some equipment fixed, he said. Then they'll come on into town. He talked to me for the longest time, and he's the sweetest man! Tassie, you never told me how wonderful he really is. He wanted to know all about you and me and how we met and everything."

There was a cold, hard lump at the base of Tasmin's throat. He tried to swallow it away, but it wouldn't go.

"What else did he want?"

"To give us tickets to the show, of course. To have dinner with us after."

"Did he ask about Mother?" It was the wrong thing to have asked. Her mood changed abruptly.

"Yes. He asked if she and your father were still living at the same place, and I told him your father died, but she was still there. It's funny he wouldn't know that, Tassy, about your father. I imagine he'll call her, too."

Tasmin doubted it very much. When Lim had left Deepsoil Five, he had gone without a word. It wasn't until almost four years later that they had found out he was alive and well on the Deepsoil Coast, doing nightclub concerts of trip songs, moving young women to passionate abandon, making money with both hands. After Tasmin's father died, his mother could have used some of that money, but Lim had never offered, not even after Tasmin wrote. . . .

Funny. In the letter, he had told Lim that Mother was in need, but he had not said his father was dead. He had supposed Lim knew. And yet, how would he have known?

"What else did you tell him?"

"Oh, just that we wanted tickets. I said lots and lots, so we could bring all our friends. . . ."

Your friends, he thought. Your boyfriends and their wives. Celcy had lots of boyfriends, most of them married. Just friends, nothing to get jealous or upset over. Just boyfriends. No girlfriends, though. All women were rivals, no matter how young or old. Poor Celcy. Dear Celcy.

"You said dinner?"

"After the show, he said. He wants to talk to you."

Jaconi caught him at lunch, very full of his newest theory. "I'm convinced I've found a repetitive sequence, Tas! A similarity that crops up in over ten percent of all successful Petitions and Justifications."

"Don't be pedantic, Jacky. Call them PJs like everyone else does."

The older man flushed, ran his fingers through his gray beard as though he were combing mice out of it. "Habit. Trying to stay dignified in front of the students. Hell, you were my student."

"I remember. And you were a good teacher, too. You should have stayed with it instead of taking the library job."

"Well, it gives me time to—you know. I know you call it my hobbyhorse, Tas, but it isn't just that. Really. Some days I think I'm that close." He held up a pinched thumb and finger, almost meeting. "That close. I know we're actually talking to the things! It almost seems I can understand what the words are. . . ."

"Until someone comes along with a new PJ?"

"No, that's been the trouble up until now. I've been assuming all the . . . PJs should have a common element, right? But what if Erickson was right? What if it is really language." Jaconi's voice dropped to a conspiratorial whisper, and he looked around to be sure no one was listening. "I mean, we don't always say the same things under similar circumstances. Suppose I step on your toe. I could say, 'Gee, I'm sorry,' or 'Excuse me,' or 'That was clumsy of me,' or 'Oh, shit,' or any one of a dozen other things, all equally appropriate."

"That's true." Tasmin was interested, despite himself.

"Always before, I was looking for identical elements. All those translators I bought, I was always looking for words or phrases or effects that were the same and had the same effect. But if we don't always say the same thing to convey the same emotion, then maybe the Presences don't either and what I should be looking for is clusters. Right?"

"It sounds logical."

"Well, so that's what I'm looking for now. I may even have found some. There are similar elements in about ten percent of all PJs."

"What do you mean, similar?"

"Tone progressions of vowel sounds, mostly. With similar orchestrals. Horns and drums. There's percussion in ninety-five percent of the clusters and horns in over eighty percent, and the other twenty have organ effects that are rather like horn sounds."

Jaconi's description had set of a chain of recollection in Tasmin's mind, and he reached for it, rubbing his forehead. "Jacky, I brought you the new Enigma score a week or so ago."

"You poor guy. I looked it over after you left it and it was a bitch."

"Well, yeah, it was complex, but not that bad, really. The Explorer's notes were excellent; I've never seen better. It did have a long sequence at the first of the PJs, though, lots of vowel progressions in thirds and fifths and percussion and horns."

"Who came up with it?"

"Some explorer who normally works way up in the northwest. Don Furz? Does it ring a bell?"

"Furz's Rogue Tower Variations. Furz's Creeping Desert Suite. Furz's Canon for Fanglings." He pronounced it "Farzh."

"Oh, *Farzh*. I should have realized."

"When's it scheduled for trial?"

"It isn't. The Master General wanted it on file, that's all."

"No volunteers?"

"That's a bad joke, Jacky. We've been trying the Enigma for about a hundred years and what's the score by now? Enigma, about eighty. Tripsingers, zero. We won't have a volunteer unless we have someone set on suicide."

Celcy had spent the week prior to the concert creating a new dress. Deepsoil Five was hardly a hotbed of fashion,

and she often made her own clothing, copying things she saw
in holos from the Coast where the influences of the star ships
coming and going from Splash One and Two kept the style
changing. Her current effort was brilliant orange, shockingly
eye-catching with her black hair and brown skin, particularly
inasmuch as it left bits of that skin bare in unlikely places.

"You're beautiful," Tasmin told her, knowing it was not
entirely for him that she'd created the outfit. She took his
admiration for her physical self for granted.

"I am, aren't I?" She twirled before the mirror, trying
various bits of jewelry, settling at last on the firestone ear-
rings he had given her for their fifth anniversary after saving
for two years to do so. He still felt a little guilty every time he
saw her wear them. The money would have helped a lot on
what he was saving for his mother's medical treatment, but
Celcy had really wanted them, and when she got things she
wanted, she was as ecstatic as a birthday child. He loved her
like that, loved the way she looked in the gems. They, too,
glittered with hot orange flares.

He stood behind her, assessing them as a couple, he tall,
narrow faced and towhaired, like a pale candle, she tiny and
glowing like a dark torch. Even in the crowded concert hall
after the lights went down, she seemed to burn with an
internal light.

He had told himself he would detest the music, and he
tried to hate it, particularly inasmuch as he recognized the
Password bits, the words and phrases that had cost lives to
get at, here displayed purely for effect, used to evoke thrills.
Here, in a Tripsinger citadel town, Lim had sense enough
not to bill anything as a tripsong, not to dress as a tripsinger,
and to stay away from the very familiar stuff that anyone
might be expected to know. Except for those very sensible
precautions, he used what he liked, interspersing real Password stuff with lyrics in plain language. Even though Tasmin
knew too much of the material, he still felt a pulse and thrill
building within him, a heightening of awareness, an internal
excitement that had little or nothing to do with the plagia-
rized material. The music was simply good. He hated to
admit it, but it was.

Beside him, Celcy flushed and glittered as though she
had been drinking or making love. When the concert was

over, her eyes were wide and drugged looking. "Let's hurry," she said. "I want to meet him."

Lim had made reservations at the nicest of the local restaurants. None of them could be called luxurious by Deepsoil Coast standards, but the attention they received from other diners made Celcy preen and glow. Lim greeted them as though he had never been away, as though he had seen them yesterday, as though he knew them well, a kind of easy bonhomie that grated on Tasmin even as he admired it. Lim had always made it look so easy. Everything he did, badly or well, he had done easily and with flair. Tasmin found a possible explanation in widely dilated eyes, a hectic flush. Lim was obviously on something, obviously keyed up. Perhaps one had to be to do the kind of concert they had just heard. Tasmin looked down at his own hands as they ordered, surprised to find them trembling. He clenched them, forced his body into a semblance of relaxation, and concentrated on being sociable. Celcy would not soon forgive him if he were stiff and unpleasant.

"Place hasn't changed," Lim was saying. "Same old center. I thought they'd have built a new auditorium by now."

Tasmin made obvious small talk. "Well, it's the same old problem, Lim. Caravans have a tough enough time bringing essential supplies. It would be hard to get the BDL Administration interested in rebuilding a perfectly adequate structure, even though I'll admit it does lack a certain ambience."

"You can say that again, brother. The acoustics in that place are dreadful. I'd forgotten."

"I just can't believe you're from Deepsoil Five," Celcy bubbled. "You don't look all that much like Tasmin, either. Are you really full brothers? Same parents for both of you?"

There was a fleeting expression of pain behind Lim's eyes, gone in the instant. "Ah, well," Lim laughed. "I got all the looks and Tasmin got all the good sense." His admiring and rather too searching glance made this a compliment to her, which she was quick to appreciate.

"Oh, no." Celcy sparkled at him. "It takes good sense to be as successful as you've been, Lim."

"And you must think Tasmin's pretty good looking, or you wouldn't have married him."

They were posing for one another, advance and retreat,

like a dance. Celcy was always like this with new men. Not exactly flirtatious, Tasmin sometimes told himself, at least not meaning it that way. She always told him when men made advances, not denying she liked it a little, but not too much, sometimes claiming to resent it even after Tasmin had seen her egging some poor soul on. Well, Lim wouldn't be around that long, and it would give her something to remember, something to talk about endlessly. "He really liked me, didn't he, Tas. He thought I looked beautiful. . . ."

"Speaking of success," Tasmin said mildly, raising a glass to attract Lim's attention. "Now that you're very much a success, could you offer some help for Mother, Lim? She's not destitute, but I'd like to send her to the coast. The doctors say her vision can be greatly improved there, but it costs more than I can provide alone. And now with Celcy pregnant. . . ."

She glared at him, and he caught his breath.

"Sorry, love. Lim is family, after all."

"I just don't want our private business discussed in public, Tas. If you don't mind."

"Sorry." Her anger was unreasonable but explainable. As ambivalent as she felt about having a baby, of course, she would be equally ambivalent about being pregnant or having Lim know she was. Tasmin decided to ignore it. "About Mother, Lim? You are going to see her while you're here, aren't you?"

Lim was evasive, his eyes darting away and then back. "I'd really like to, Tas. Maybe tomorrow. And I'd like to help, too. Perhaps by the end of the season I'll be able to do something. Everyone thinks this kind of work mints gold, but it's highly competitive and most of what I make goes into equipment. If you'll help me out with a little request I have, though, things should break loose for me and I'll be able to put a good-size chunk away for her." He was intent again, leaning forward, one hand extended in an attitude Tasmin recognized all too well. The extended wrist was wrapped in a platinum chronocomp set with seven firestones. Not the yellow orange ones, which were all Tasmin had been able to afford for Celcy, but purple blue gems, which totaled in value about five times Tasmin's annual salary.

Tasmin felt the familiar wave of fury pour over him. Let it go, he told himself. For God's sake, let it go.

"What request?" Celcy, all sparkle-eyed, nudging Tasmin with one little elbow, eager. "What request, Lim? What can we do for you?"

"I understand there's a new Don Furz Enigma score."

"That's right," Tasmin said, warily.

"And I understand you have access to it."

"I made the master copy. So?"

His face was concentrated, his eyes tight on Tasmin's own. "I need an edge, Tas. Something dramatic. Something to make the Coast fans sit up and scream for more. Everyone knows the Enigma is a killer, and everyone knows Don Furz has come up with some surprising Passwords. I want to build my new show around the Enigma score."

Tasmin could not answer for a long moment, was simply unable to frame a reply.

"Oh, that's exciting! Isn't that exciting, Tas? A new Lim Terree show built about something from Deepsoil Five. I love it!" Celcy sipped at her wine, happier than Tasmin had seen her in weeks.

And he didn't want to spoil that mood for her. For a very long time he said nothing, trying to find a way around it, unable to do so. "I'm afraid it's out of the question," Tasmin said at last, surprised to find his voice pleasantly calm, though his hands were gripped tightly together to control their quivering. "You were at the citadel for a time, Lim. You know that untested manuscripts are not released. It's forbidden to circulate them."

"Oh, hell, man, I won't use it as is. It would bore the coasties to shreds. I just need it . . . need enough of it for authenticity."

"If it isn't going to be really authentic, you don't need it at all. Make up something."

"I can't do that and use Furz's name. The legal reps are firm about that. I've got to have something in there he came up with." Lim looked down. Tasmin, in surprise, saw a tremor in his arms, his hands. Nerves? "That's just the lead in, though. There's something else." Lim gulped wine and cast that sideways look again, as though he were afraid someone was listening.

"I've met someone, Tas. Someone who's put me on to something that could get us into the history books right up there next to Erickson. No joke, Tas. You and Cels can be part of something absolutely world shattering. Something to set Jubal on its ear. . . ."

"Oh, don't be stiff about it, Tas." Celcy was pleading now, making a playful face at him. "He's family and it's all really exciting! Let him have it."

"Celcy." He shook his head helplessly, praying she would understand. "I'm a Tripsinger. I'm licensed under a code of ethics. Even if we ignored the risk to my job, our livelihood, I swore to uphold those ethics. They won't permit me to do what Lim wants, I'm sorry."

"Hell, I was a Tripsinger, too, brother," Lim said in a harsh, demanding tone. "Don't you owe me a little professional courtesy? Not even to make a bundle for old Mom, huh?" Said with that easy smile, with a little sneer, a well-remembered sneer.

The dam broke.

"What you spent for that unit you've got on your wrist would get Mom's eyes fixed and set her up for life," Tasmin said flatly. "Don't feed me that shit about putting it all into equipment because I know it's a lie. You were never a Tripsinger. You broke every rule, every oath you took. You set up that ass Ran Connel to help you fake your way through the first trip, then after you were licensed you led four trips, and your backup had to bail you out on all of them. You got through school by stealing. You stole tests. You stole answers. You stole other people's homework including mine. Whenever anyone had anything you wanted, you took it. And when you couldn't make it here, you stole money from Dad's friends and then ran for the Coast. The reason I have to support Mom as well as my own family is that Dad spent almost everything he had paying off the money you took. You never figured the rules applied to you, big brother, and you always got by on a charming smile and that damned marvelous voice!"

Celcy was staring at him, her face white with shock. Lim was pale, mouth pinched.

Tasmin threw down his napkin. "I'm sorry. I'm not hungry. Celcy, would you mind if we left now?"

She gulped, turning a stricken face on Lim, "Yes, I would mind. I'm starved. I'm going to have dinner with Lim because he invited us, and if you're too rude to let childish bygones be bygones. . . ." Her voice changed, becoming angry. "I'm certainly not going to go along with you. Go on home. Go to your mother's. Maybe she'll sympathize with you, but I certainly don't."

He couldn't remember leaving the restaurant. He couldn't remember anything that happened until he found himself in a cubicle at the citadel dormitory, sitting on the edge of the bed, shivering as though he would never stop. It had all boiled up, out of nothing, out of everything. All the suppressed, buried stuff of fifteen years, twenty years. . . .

Over twenty years. When he was seven and Lim was twelve, Dad had given Tasmin a viggy for his birthday. They were rare in captivity, and Tasmin had been speechless with joy. That night, Lim had taken it out of the cage and out into the road where it had been killed, said Lim, by a passing quiet-car. When Tasmin was eight, he had won a school medal for music. Lim had borrowed it and lost it. When he was sixteen, Tasmin had been desperately, hopelessly in love with Chani Vincent. Lim, six years older than she, had seduced her, got her pregnant, then left on the trip to the Deepsoil Coast from which he had never returned. The Vincents moved to Harmony, and from there God knows where, and Dad had been advised by several of his friends that Lim had stolen money—quite a lot of it. With Dad it had been a matter of honor.

Honor. Twenty years.

"Oh, Lord, why didn't I just say I'd think about it, then tell him I couldn't get access to the damn thing." He didn't realize he had said it aloud until a voice murmured from the door.

"Master?" It was Jamieson, an expression on his face that Tasmin could not quite read. Surprise, certainly. And concern? "Can I help you, sir?"

"No," he barked. "Yes. Ask the dispensary if they'd part with some kind of sleeping pill, would you. I'm having a—a family problem."

When he woke before dawn, it was with a fuzzy head, a cottony mouth, and a feeling of inadequacy that he had

thought he had left behind him long ago. He had ruined
Celcy's big evening. She wouldn't soon let him forget it,
either. It was probably going to be one of those emotional
crises that required months to heal, and with her pregnant,
the whole thing had been unforgivable. The longer he stayed
away, the worse it would be.

"You childish bastard," he chided himself in the mirror.
"Clod!" The white-haired, straight-nosed face stared back at
him, its wide, narrow mouth an expressionless slit. It might
be more to the point to be angry at Celcy, he thought
broodingly, but what good would it do? Being angry with
Celcy had few satisfactions to it. "Idiot," he accused himself.
"You can sing your way past practically any Presence in this
world, but you can't get through one touchy social situation!"
His eyes were so black they looked bruised.

He borrowed a quiet-car from the citadel lot and drove
home slowly, not relishing the thought of arrival. When he
got there, he found the door locked. Few people in Deepsoil
Five locked their doors, but Celcy always did. He had to find
the spare key buried under one of the imported shrubs,
running a thorn into his finger in the process.

She wasn't at home. He looked in their bedroom, in the
study, in the kitchen. It was only when he went to the
bathroom to bandage the thorn-stuck finger that he saw the
note, taped to the mirror.

"Tasmin, you were just so rude I can't believe it to your
very own brother, I gave him the score he wanted, because I
knew you'd be ashamed of yourself when you had some sleep
and he really needs it. He really does, Tas. It was wrong
what you said about his not being a Tripsinger, because what
he found out will make us famous and we're going to the
Enigma so he can be sure. You'll be proud of us. It would be
better with you, Lim says, but we'll have to do it just ourselves.

"You were mean to spoil our party, after I decided to go
ahead and have the baby just because you want it even
though I don't, and I'm really mad at you."

So, that's what she hadn't been telling him. That's what
she had been hiding from him. A desire to end the preg-
nancy, not go through with it. The letters of the note were
slanted erratically, as though blown by varying winds. "Drunk,"
he thought in a wave of frozen anger and pity. "She and Lim

stayed at the restaurant, commiserating, and they got drunk."
There were drops of water gleaming on the basin. They
couldn't have left long ago.

He went to his desk to shuffle through the documents he
had brought home for study. The Enigma score was missing.

Surely Lim wouldn't. Surely. No amount of liquor or
brou would make him do any such thing. He wasn't suicidal.
He couldn't have forgotten his own abysmal record as a
Tripsinger; he wouldn't try the Enigma. He was too pleased
with himself. Surely. Surely.

Tasmin ran from the house. It was possible to drive to
within about three miles of the Enigma, but deepsoil ended
suddenly at that point. From there on, travelers went at their
peril. With cold efficiency he checked the gauges. The bat-
teries would carry him that far and back. There were standard field glasses in the storage compartment.

He was through the foodcrop fields in a matter of minutes and into the endless rows of carefully tended brou. Ten
miles, fifteen. BDL land. Miles of it. BDL, who controlled
everything, who would not like this unauthorized approach to
the Enigma.

Who would have his hide if he wrecked their car, he
reminded himself, focusing sharply on a five-foot Enigmalet
that had appeared from nowhere, almost at the side of the
road, miles out of its range. Sometimes the damned things
seemed to grow up overnight! As 'lets they were easy to
dispose of, and someone should have disposed of this one.
When they got to 'ling size, it was a very different and
difficult thing.

He could see the Enigma peaks clearly. The great Presence was bifurcated almost to its base, rearing above the
plain like a bloody two-tined fork. Five miles more. At the
end of it he found his own car parked against the barricade.
He could feel the ground tremble as he set his feet on it, and
he hastily removed his shoes and took the glasses from the
compartment. How high would Lim have dared go? How high
would Celcy go with him, and how high would he dare go
after them?

The world shivered under his feet, twitching like the
hide of a mule under a biting fly. It wanted him off. It wanted
him away. Moreover, it wanted those others off as well. He

bit his lip and kept on. It was three miles to the summit from
where one could actually see the faces of the Enigma itself,
shattered plane of glowing scarlet, fading into a wall that
extended east and west as far as had ever been traveled, a
mighty faceted twin mountain that stood in an endless forest
of Enigmalings, looming over the plains along the empty
southern coast.

He climbed and stopped, scarcely breathing, climbed
again. To his left, a pillar of bloody crystal squeaked to itself,
whined, then shivered into fragments. He cried out as one
chunk buried itself in a bank a foot from his head. One of the
smaller fragments must have hit him. He wiped blood from
his eyes. Other pillars took up the whine. He controlled his
trembling and went on. Surely Celcy wouldn't go on. As
frightened of the Presences as she was? She wouldn't go on.
Unless she had no choice. Lim had always taken what he
wanted. Perhaps now he was simply taking Celcy, because he
wanted her.

He reached the top of a high, east-west ridge from which
he could peer through a gap in the next rise. A narrow face of
scarlet crystal shone to the left of the gap and another to the
right, the twin peaks of the Enigma. From somewhere ahead,
he heard a voice. . . .

Lim. Singing. He had a portable synthesizer with him, a
very good one. All around Tasmin, the shivering ceased and
quiet fell. Desperately, he climbed on, scrambling up the
slope, finding the faint path almost by instinct. Something
traveled here to keep his trail clear. Not people, but something.

The voice was rising, more and more surely. Silence
from the ground. Absolute quiet. Tasmin tried to control his
breathing; every panting breath seemed a threat.

Then he was at the top.

The path wound down to a small clearing between the
two faces of the Enigma. Celcy sat on a stone in the middle of
it, pale but composed, her hands clasped tightly in front of
her as though to keep them from shaking, her face knitted in
concentration. Lim stood at one edge, his hands darting over
the synthesizer propped before him, his head up, singing. On
the music rack of the synthesizer, the Enigma score fluttered
in a light wind.

Tasmin put his head in his hands. He didn't dare interrupt. He didn't dare go on down the path. He didn't dare to call or wave. He could only poise himself here, waiting. Silently, he sang with Lim. The Petition and Justification. God, the man was talented. It should take at least three people to get those effects, and he was doing it alone, sight reading. Even if he had spent several hours reviewing the score before coming out here, it was still an almost miraculous performance. He had to be taking something that quickened his reaction time and heightened his perceptions. There was no way a man could do what he was doing otherwise. . . .

"Go on down," he urged them silently. "For God's sake, go on down. Get down to the flatland. Get out of range."

Celcy's eyes were huge, fastened upon Lim as though she were in a concert hall. Through the glasses he could see the eggshell oval of her face, as still as though enchanted or hypnotized. She did not look like herself, particularly around the eyes. Perhaps Lim had given her some of the drug he'd been taking? Go on down the trail, Celcy. While he's singing, go on down. Or come back up to me.

But Lim wouldn't have told her to go on. He wouldn't have thought how he was to go on singing and carrying the synthesizer and reading the music all at once. Perhaps she could carry the music for him. Lim began the First Variation.

"Move," he begged them, biting his lower lip until the blood ran onto his chin. "Oh, for God's sake, Lim, move one way or the other." Lim's back was to him; Celcy's hands were unclenched now, lying loosely in her lap. Her face was relaxing. She was breathing deeply. He could see the soft rise and fall of her breast.

Second Variation. Lim's voice soared. And the Enigma responded! Unable to help himself, Tasmin's eyes left the tiny human figures and soared with that voice, up the sides of the Enigma, his glance leaping from prominence to prominence, shivering with the glory that was there. He had not seen a Presence react in this way before. Light shattered at him from fractures within the crystal, seeming to run within the mighty monolith like rivers of fire, quivering. Leaping.

A tiny sound brought his eyes down. Celcy had gasped, peering up at the tower above them, gasped and risen. Tasmin barely heard the sound of that brief inhalation, but Lim reacted to it immediately. He turned, too quickly for a normal reaction, his eyes leaving the music. Tasmin saw Lim's face as he beamed at Celcy, his eyes like lanterns. Oh, yes, he was on something, something that disturbed his sense of reality, too. Reacting to Celcy's action, Lim abandoned the Furz score and began to improvise.

Tasmin screamed, "Don't. *Lim!*"

The world came apart in shattering fragments, broke itself to pieces and shook itself, rattling its parts like dice in a cup. Tasmin clung to the heaving soil and stopped knowing. The sound was enormous, too huge to hear, too monstrous to believe or comprehend. The motion of the crystals beneath him and around him was too complex for understanding. He simply clung, like a tick, waiting for the endless time to pass.

When he came to himself again, the world was quiet. Below him, the small clearing was gone. Nothing of it remained. Blindly, uncaring for his own safety, he stumbled down to the place he thought it had been. Nothing. A tumble of fragments, gently glowing in the noon sun. Silence. Far off the sound of viggies singing. At his feet a glowing fragment, an earring, gold and amber.

"To remember her by," he howled silently. "Joke."

He wanted to scream aloud but did not. The world remained quiet. There was blood in his eyes again; he saw the world through a scarlet haze. Under his feet was only a tiny tremor, as though whatever lived there wished him to know it was still alive.

"I'm going," he moaned. "I'm going." So a flea might depart a giant dog. So vermin might be encouraged to leave a mighty palace. "I'm going."

As he turned, he stumbled over something and picked it up without thinking. Lim's synthesizer. Miraculously unbroken. Tasmin clutched it under one arm as he staggered over the ridge and down the endless slopes to the place he had left the car. Not a single pillar whined or shattered. "Joke," he repeated to himself. "Joke."

Then he was in the car, bent over to protect the core of himself from further pain, gasping for air that would not, did not come.

3

He heard his mother's voice as though through water, a bubbling liquidity that gradually became the sound of his own blood in his ears.

"That acolyte of yours? Jamieson? He was worried about you, so he called me, and we went to your house and found the note she left you, Tas." His mother's hand was dry and frail, yet somehow comforting in this chill, efficient hospital where doctors moved among acolytes of their own. "He got a search party out after you right away. They found you in the car, out near the Enigma. You'd been knocked in the head pretty badly. You've got some pins and things in your skull." She had always talked to him this way, telling him the worst in a calm, unfrightened voice. "You'll be all right, the doctors say."

"Celcy?" he'd asked, already knowing the answer.

"Son, the search party didn't go up on the Enigma. You wouldn't expect that, would you? They'll get close shots from the next satellite pass, that's the best they can do." She was crying, her blind eyes oozing silent tears.

"They won't find anything."

"I don't suppose they will. She did go there with Lim, didn't she?"

He nodded, awash in the wave of pain that tiny motion brought.

"I can't understand it. It isn't anything I would have thought either of them would do! Celcy? The way she felt about the Presences? And Lim! He wasn't brave, you know, Tas. He always ran away rather than fight. You know, when he was a little fellow, he was so sweet. Gentle natured, and handsome! Everyone thought he was the nicest boy. You adored him. The two of you were inseparable. It was when he got to be about twelve, about the time he entered choir school, he just turned rotten somehow. I've never known why. Something happened to him, or maybe it was just in him, waiting to happen."

"You were right about Celcy's not wanting to have a baby," he murmured, newly sickened as he remembered. It wasn't only Celcy who had died. "I thought she'd become excited about it, but she really didn't want it."

"Oh, well, love, I knew that," she said sympathetically. "You knew it, too. A girl like that doesn't really want babies. She was only a little baby herself. All pretty and full of herself; full of terrible fears and horrors, too. Afraid you'd leave her as her parents did. Hanging on to you. Not willing to share you with anything or anybody. Not willing to share you with a child. She needed you all for herself. When I read her note, I wondered if she would have been able to go through with it after all. I'm sorry, Tas, but it's true."

It rang true. Everything she said was true, which simply made Celcy's scribbled confession more valiant. "She was going to have the baby because I wanted it. She did things for me that no one . . . no one ever knew about." He breathed, letting the pain wash over and away. "When she wasn't afraid—she wasn't at all like the Celcy you always saw. I wanted her not to have to be so . . . so clinging. But I loved her. I got impatient sometimes, but so much of it was my fault. I never took the time with her I should have, the time to make her change. I just loved her!"

It came out as a strangled plea for understanding, and his mother answered it in the only way she could to let him know she knew exactly what he meant, her voice filled with such an access of pain that his own agony was silenced before it.

"I know, Tasmin. I loved Lim, too."

Under the circumstances, the Master General was inclined to waive discipline.

"I don't want any more unauthorized removal of manuscripts, Tasmin. I know it's often done, but the rule against it stands. The fault wasn't proximately yours, but the responsibility was. You have been punished by the tragedy already. Anything further would be gratuitously cruel."

Tasmin was silent for an appropriate time. He was not yet at the point where he could feel anything. He was sure a time would come that would demonstrate the truth of what the Master General had said about responsibility.

"Master."

"Yes, Tasmin."

"I was actually on the Enigma when it blew."

"So I've been told. You have the devil's own luck, Tasmin."

"Yes, sir. The fact is, sir, my bro . . . Lim Terree was singing the Furz score. He had a portable synthesizer, I'd swear it was an Explorer model, and he was good, sir. He really was good. I haven't heard any better. . . ."

"If you're trying to justify. . . ."

"No, sir, you misunderstand. The score was *effective*. It wasn't until he forgot himself and started improvising that the Enigma blew."

"Effective!"

"Yes, sir. There wasn't a quiver. He got through the first variation and well into the second before he deviated from the score. If they'd been able to go on down the far side, they'd have been well away." He choked, remembering Celcy's face as she had looked joyously at the singer. "Well away, sir. Well away."

There was a long silence. "I'm fascinated, Tasmin. And quite frankly, I'm surprised and puzzled. I remember Lim when he was here. I wouldn't have said this was in character at all. Your wife was a very attractive girl. Could she have—oh, egged him on, so to speak?"

Tasmin shook his head, "No, sir. She was terrified of the Presences. She wouldn't even look at them through a 'scope."

"How do you explain it?"

"I can't, sir. I really can't."

"But the score was effective, a real Password."

"Yes, sir. I think so, sir."

"Well. Thank you for bringing this to my attention, Tasmin. I'm sincerely sorry for your loss."

"Thank you, sir."

And then home again. Sick leave. Dizziness and nausea and a constant gray feeling. Jamieson dropping in each evening to fill him in on what was going on. A Jamieson oddly tentative and uncharacteristically kind.

"James dropped out of Tripsinging. He's going to specialize in orchestrals."

"Good."

"Refnic's moving to the Jut. They've still got a shortage of Tripsingers there, even after—what is it now, six years? I guess most singers are still afraid of the Crystallite fanatics. Anyhow, Refnic's going."

"Good for him."

"Clarin's staying in Deepsoil Five. When I finish my acolyte's year, I thought you might like to have her. She'd like to work with you. You know, Master Ferrence, there's a lot to her."

It was as though Jamieson was offering him something he could not quite see. Tasmin tried to respond but couldn't. Jamieson left it at that.

The synthesizer lay on the table in his study where the medical team had dropped it off. There were prints of the satellite pictures, too. The Master General had known he would want to see them even though they showed nothing at all except tumbled crystal.

The synthesizer was the best one Tasmin had ever seen, if not an Explorer model, something close. It had some kind of transposition circuits in it that Tasmin wasn't familiar with. He fooled with it for over an hour before he was able to get it into play, and then what emerged was a mishmash that must have accumulated over weeks or months. Lim's voice. Rehearsals. Lim's voice again, cursing at a technician. "Damn you, I've told you twenty times I want. . . ." Then again, "Get it right this time or get off the job. . . ."

Fragments of music. Real Tripsinging, as pure as air. Lim's improvisations. The Enigma score. Celcy's voice. ". . . Tasmin will be so proud! Everyone will know who we are, won't they? You, and Tasmin, and even me."

Then back to the recording session, Lim's voice again. "You'd think after all this time they could say something meaningful . . . that was petulant of you . . . pisses me off when they don't know who I am. . . ."

And finally great swaths of music, a full concert of it, uninterrupted hours of Lim's music, indomitable and triumphant.

When it was over, Tasmin sat in the silence of the house for most of the night, staring at nothing.

"It wasn't you, Tassy. It wasn't your fault." Tasmin's mother wept, agonized by his guilt.

"In a way it was. If the Enigma score hadn't been at the house, she couldn't have given it to him. If he hadn't had it, he couldn't have gone there." He reached for her hand, taking it in his, wishing she could see him.

"Tassy, it was he who asked for it, and she who gave it. All you did was . . ." His mother stared in his direction, intimidated by his silence.

"All I did was break a rule. Me. The one who was always telling her how important the oaths were. The one who always talked about honor."

"What you did was make a mistake. Not a dishonorable one. You only wanted the score to study. It was just a mistake, not a matter of honor. . . ."

"Mother, it feels like a matter of honor to me. I can't explain it. I know I'm not guilty of having any evil intent. I know I'm not guilty of anything perverse or dreadful, but I can't just let it rest. If I'd obeyed the rules, there wouldn't have been a mistake. Celcy would be alive. And Lim."

"All right," she spat at him, her decade's old resignation giving way at last to something alive and angry. "So you did something wrong. God forbid you should ever do anything wrong. Everyone else, but not you. You're so much above mistakes. So damn good. And now you're going to punish me because you made a mistake." She began to weep, tears running down her face in runnels from those wide, blind eyes. "You're all I have left!"

"The money I got for the house will take care of you," he said at last, unable to meet her pain with anything but this chilly comfort. "I bought a BDL annuity, and I've written to Betuny in Harmony. She sent word by the last cavavan through. She's coming from Harmony. One of the laymen from the Citadel will look after you until she gets here."

"We never really got along."

"You will now. She's your sister, and she's very grateful to have a place since her husband died."

"She thinks I'm crazy." It was half a laugh.

"Let her think what she likes. And I won't be gone forever."

"I wish I understood why you have to go at all."

He wanted to tell her, but it would only have confused her as much as it confused him, so he said none of the things he had been thinking for days. Instead he murmured, "I have to know why, Mother. I can't go back to my own life until I know why. Right now all I can think of is questions with no answers. Please—if you won't give me your blessing, at least tell me it's all right." He did not want to weep. He had already wept enough.

"It's all right," she said, drying her eyes on her sleeve. "It's all right, Tasmin. If you feel you have to, I guess you have to. I just wish you'd forgive yourself and let it go. We can all blame ourselves because people die. I blamed myself over your father. And over Lim."

"I know you did. This is just something I have to do."

"All right." She twisted the handkerchief in her hands, wringing it, reaching up to run it under her eyes. "Just be sure you take warm clothes with you. And plenty of food. . . ." She laughed at herself. "I sounded so . . . motherlike. We never outgrow it. We just go on fretting."

"I will, Mother. I'll take everything I need."

He went out to the quiet-car and sat in it, too weary to move for the moment, thinking aloud all the things he had wanted to say but had not.

"I've always been your good boy, Mother. Yours and Dad's. I never asked questions. I always did what I was told. If I broke any rules, they were always little rules, for what I thought were good reasons. I loved someone, even though I knew she loved me in a different way. I wanted a child, and she wanted to be my child. Still, I really loved her, and sometimes—oh, sometimes all that love came back to me a hundredfold. And I thought if I went on being good, life would be like that always. Something bright and singing, something terrible and wonderful would come to me. Like my viggy Dad gave me when I was seven. Like the medal I won. Like Celcy the way she was sometimes. Something joyful.

"And instead there's this thing caught in my throat that won't go down. Two people dead, and I don't know why. One I loved, one I hated, or maybe loved, I don't know which. Maybe the other way around. All the things I thought I wanted . . . I don't know about them anymore. . . . I thought Celcy was everything to me, and yet I didn't ever take the time to get things growing between us. I thought I loved her, yet right there at the end, I was thinking about the Enigma! Why? Why was I thinking about the music instead of about her?

"What did Lim know or think that was so important to him? What was he trying to prove? What made her go with him? *Why did she die!*"

"Celcy," he cried aloud, as though she would answer him, forgive him. "Why, Celcy?"

The Enigma listened, then it didn't. Jamieson called what the Watchling did during our last trip a joke. He was it was laughing at us. Maybe it was. Lim said he knew something, something to knock Jubal on its ear. . . .

He started the car. There was a mount waiting for him at the citadel. The things he was taking with him were already there, packed by the Tripmaster's own hands into two mule panniers and slung on Tasmin's saddle. All the supplies a Tripsinger needed to travel alone, a rare thing in itself and one for which the Master General had been evasive about granting permission.

On the seat beside him was another bag that Tasmin had packed for himself. His favorite holo of Celcy was there, and the note she had written him, and the earring that was all the Enigma had left him of her.

The toy viggy baby was there, too. He didn't know why he was taking it, except that it couldn't go with the house and he couldn't bear to throw it away.

He laid his hand on the bag. Through the heavy fabric, Lim's recording synthesizer made a hard, edgy lump. One puzzle was inside that lump, preserved. His brother's music. Unexpected and glorious, not what he had thought it would be, not a music the Lim he thought he knew could ever have created.

The other puzzle was inside himself, in a place he couldn't reach, something he had to touch, could not rest until he touched . . .

Why had she gone there? Despite her terror? What possible reason could there be?

Whose fault was it? Why had she and the baby died at all?

_____ 4

The Ron River stretched its placid length along a gentle deepsoil valley sloping down to Deepsoil Five from the north. In the valley, deepsoil was no more than a mile wide at any point, less than that in most places. There were isolated farmsteads along the Ron, small crofts tenanted by eremitic types, many of them engaged in crop research for BDL. Most were doing research on brou, but some were engaged in improving the ubiquitous and invaluable settler's brush, a native plant that had been repeatedly tinkered with by the bioengineers, a plant on which both mule and human depended during long journeys and which, it was said, the viggies and other local fauna ate as well.

Tasmin was greeted variously as he went, sometimes with friendliness and other times with surliness. He returned each greeting with a raised hand and distant smile. He did not want to stop and talk. There was nothing to talk about. Certainly not about the weather or the scenery. The weather was what it always was on this part of Jubal, sunny, virtually rainless.

As for the scenery, there was little enough of it. Wind sang in the power lines stretching from the reservoir down to Deepsoil Five; the distant hydroelectric plant squatted at the top of the visible slope like a dropped brick; the fields were neatly furrowed; each dwelling was impeccably maintained.

Like a set of blocks, Tasmin thought. All lines crossed at right angles. Even the Ron had had its major meanders straightened, its banks sanitized. Few crystals. No singing. No peacock tailed trees turning toward the sun. No trees of any kind.

A demolition crew was working at one point on the road, lowering a heavy mesh cone over an intruding 'ling. A noise box directed a loud burst of low frequency sound at the shrouded crystal, and the pillar exploded into a thousand fragments within the mesh cone. Tasmin spent a few idle minutes watching the crew gather up the knife-edged pieces and truck them a few thousand yards to a vacant spot of prairie, well away from the road. In time, every shard would seed another 'let and a new forest of crystals would grow. From the color of the one destroyed, Tasmin thought it might be a Watchling, probably from the North Watcher. That particular ashy shade was rare elsewhere. How it had come here was anyone's guess. A piece picked up on a wheel or popped into a wagon, perhaps. A shiny gem thrust into a pocket and then carelessly thrown away. Then the dews of night had dissolved minute quantities of mineral in the soil, and the crystal had grown, but how it had reached 'ling size without demolition was someone's culpable oversight. The thing had been twelve feet tall!

By evening, he had passed the hydroelectric plant and the dam, circled the shining lake, and reached the top of the long ridge that backed the reservoir. Here the flora was more typical of Jubal, the fanshaped trees relaxing into their nighttime fountain shapes as the sun dropped. His lungs filled with the faintly spicy aroma he loved.

He had almost decided to place his camp in a small clearing among a grove of the plumy Jubal trees when he heard a voice behind him.

"Master Ferrence? Camp is set up over here, sir."

"Jamieson? What the dissonant hell are you doing here?" He turned to see the boy standing beside an arched tent, which was so well hidden among the trees that he had missed it on his walk through the grove.

"Acolyte's oath, Master."

"Don't be ridiculous! Acolyte's oath only applies in the citadel."

"Not according to Master General, Master Ferrence. He

says I owe you most of a year yet, and where you go, I go. So says Master General with some vehemence." The boy was downcast over something, not his usual ebullient self.

"How did you know which way I was going?"

"You and the Tripmaster discussed it. He told Master General and Master General told me. I left a few hours before you planned to."

"I don't suppose it would do any good to ask you to go back and say you couldn't find me."

"Master General would just send me looking. He said so already." The boy turned away, gesturing toward the pile of wood laid by and the cookpot hung ready. "We've got some fresh meat."

Tasmin followed him in a mood of some bewilderment. It had certainly not been his intention to travel in company, and had he chosen company, he would not have chosen Jamieson. Would he? "Master General didn't say anything to me."

"He didn't want to argue with you. He told us to make ourselves useful and not intrude on your privacy."

"Us?"

"Me and Clarin, sir."

"Clarin!"

"Yes, sir?" The girl came out of the tent, touched her breast in a gesture of respect, and stood silently waiting.

"You don't have acolyte's oath as a reason," he snarled, deeply dismayed. Clarin!

"Master General said I might have oath, sir. If your journey takes you past Jamieson's year, sir, then you would be starting on mine."

"I didn't even say I'd take you as acolyte!"

"Well, but you didn't say you wouldn't, sir, so Master General. . . ."

Tasmin shook his head and said nothing more. He was too weary and too shocked to deal with the subject. The pins in his skull had set up a tuneless throbbing at the first sight of Jamieson, and he wondered viciously if the Master General would have been so generous with acolytes if he knew the effect they had on Tasmin's injured head. He had been peaceful, settling into the wonder of Jubal, letting it carry him. Now . . . Damn!

He sat down beside the laid fire and watched while Jamieson and Clarin moved around the camp, making it comfortable. His acolyte seemed subdued, and Tasmin could appreciate why. An almost solitary trip into the wilds of Jubal would hardly appeal to Jamieson's gregarious nature. Though it wasn't mere social contact Jamieson craved. The boy would rather chase girls than eat, but he'd rather sing than chase girls, and he liked an audience when he did it. The thought of Jamieson's discomfort and unhappiness damped his own annoyance with a modicum of sympathy. Obviously, this hadn't been the boy's idea.

Clarin led Tasmin's mule off toward the patch of settler's brush just beyond the trees. The mule would eat it now; they might be eating it later—the roots and stalks would sustain life for human travelers, though no method of preparation did much to improve the taste. Clarin returned, leaving the mule munching contentedly.

"Why in God's name . . ." he muttered.

Clarin threw a questioning glance in Jamieson's direction. The boy avoided meeting her glance. "I believe the Master General didn't think you should be alone, sir." She was respectful but firm.

"What did he think I was going to do? Throw myself at the foot of a Presence, like some hysterical neophyte or crazy Crystallite, and yodel for the end?"

Jamieson still refused to look at her. Something going on there, but Tasmin was too weary to dig it out.

"I don't know, sir. I think he just thought you needed company."

Tasmin snorted. He didn't want company. He wanted to sink himself in Jubal. Breathe it. Taste it. Lie wallowing in it, like a bantigon in a mudhole. Wanted to be alone.

Which wasn't healthy. Even in his current frame of mind, he knew that. Well, did he need company? Certainly it would be easier traveling with three. There were routes that were passable to a single singer, particularly a good singer—and Tasmin was good, his peers and his own sense of value both told him that. However, two or three singers could do better, move faster.

"Did the Tripmaster enlighten either of you as to where I was going to end up on this trip?" he asked resignedly.

"No, sir." Jamieson was heating something over the fire, still subdued.

"The Deepsoil Coast." Where Lim Terree had lived. Where he had talked to people, left clues to himself. Lim's territory.

"What!" Jamieson turned, almost upsetting the pot, not seeing Clarin glaring at him as she set it upright once more and took his place tending it. "No joke? Apogee! I've always wanted to go there!" His face was suddenly alive with anticipation.

"We're a long way from there. Weeks."

"Yes, sir. I know."

"What route?" asked Clarin, stirring the pot without looking at it, the light reflecting on her hair. It had grown into tiny ringlets, Tasmin noted, and she looked more feminine than he had remembered. In her quiet way, she seemed to be as excited as Jamieson.

"The only way I could get the Master General to agree to my going at all was to offer to do some mapping on the way. We've got some old scores he wants me to verify. Little stuff, mostly. Challenger Canyon. The Wicked Witch of the West. The Mad Gap."

Jamieson put on his weighing look. "Mapping is Explorer business. Besides, nobody travels that way."

"Which is why he can't get an Explorer to do it. They have more important things to do. For some reason, Master General wants the scores verified. Nobody's been that way for ten or twenty years. Nobody's used the Mad Gap password for about fifty. I had quite a hunt to find a copy of the score, as a matter of fact. We have no idea whether the Passwords will still work." It sounded weak, even to Tasmin, and yet Master General had been adamant about it. Something going on there? Tasmin would have bet his dinner that the hierarchy of the Order was up to something.

Jamieson was unaccountably subdued again. "It sounds like it will take forever," he said with self-conscious drama.

"Not forever. A few weeks, which is what I said to start with. Good practice for you two."

"I suppose." The boy growled something to himself, and Clarin muttered a reply.

"You don't sound overjoyed."

Jamieson grunted, "Right at the moment—I'm sorry. I shouldn't mention personal things."

"Mention away." Tasmin stretched out on his bedroll, feeling through his pack for the flask of broundy he usually carried.

"Right at the moment I'm mainly concerned that Wendra Gentrack will still be single when I get back to Deepsoil Five. She was madder than anybody I've ever seen when I told her . . . told her I had to go."

"Ah," Tasmin murmured. Wendra Gentrack was a very social young lady. Daughter of Celcy's friend Jeannie and of Hom Gentrack, one of BDL's Agricultural Section Managers. "You have an understanding?"

"I have had what I regarded as an understanding, yes. She seems to have whatever seems to be most fun for her on any given day."

"I told Jamieson he was brou-dizzy," the girl said from her place beside the fire. "Wendra is virtually brain dead."

Jamieson poked the fire viciously, pulled the kettle off and set out three bowls. "Are you ready to eat now?" he asked Clarin in a poisonous tone. "Would that activity possibly occupy your mouth with something besides giving me advice I didn't ask for?"

Oh, marvelous, Tasmin thought. All I need. A juvenile feud. Without thinking, he said, "There are relationships that strike others as being inappropriate, Clarin, which are, in fact, very rewarding to those involved."

She flushed, and he realized with sudden shock what he had just said. He felt his face flame, but kept his eyes locked on hers. "We're evidently going to be traveling together. There is only one way I can see that this will work. From this moment you both have equal acolyte status. I expect citadel courtesy between the two of you as well as toward me. Right?"

They nodded. He thought Clarin had an expression of relief, although perhaps it was more one of quiet amusement. Amusement? At what?

Doggedly, he went on. "And, Jamieson, I do understand how you feel about leaving 'Five just now. Believe me, I do. I would send you back if there were any way to do it." And I will keep trying to think of a way, he told himself grimly.

"Now, what have you fixed for our supper?"

They sprawled near the fire with their bowls, a savory dish of fresh vegetables and grain served with scraps of broiled meat. A little wind came down the slope behind them, bringing the scent of Jubal and the sound of viggies singing. "I had a viggy once," mused Tasmin. "For a few hours."

"No joke? I didn't know anyone could catch them."

"No, they can be caught. They just die in captivity, is all. But this was a young one that was found with broken legs along the caravan route. Somebody splinted the legs and kept the viggy and it lived. Later they sold him to my father."

"Did it sing?" Clarin asked, her voice hushed.

"Not while I had it. It might have. It . . . got away."

There was a long silence, interrupted only by the sound of chewing, the clatter of spoon on bowl.

"Master?"

"Clarin."

"You know I transferred in from Northwest."

"Yes. I never knew why."

"Oh." She seemed to be searching for a reply that would be appropriately impersonal. "My voice was too low for a lot of the scores up there. Nine out of ten of them are soprano scores, and I'm no soprano. The Masters thought I'd have a better chance of being steadily employed down around Five or even Northeast, over toward Eleven. It wasn't until I got to Five that I ever heard much about the Crystallites. And then you mentioned Crystallites a little while ago. Are they really set on killing off all Tripsingers, or is that just a horror story?"

"Well, there was that one notorious assassination on the Jut about six years ago," Tasmin replied. "I'm sure you've heard of that, even though you'd have been very young at the time. It was no campfire tale. All twelve Tripsingers at the local chapter house were killed by a band of Crystallite fanatics. The Jut has no food source of its own. The Jut Tripsingers made regular trips to bring in supplies by caravan, but there had been bad weather and food was already short. They were killed just as they were about to leave on a provisions run. There were about one hundred people there, and when they tried to get out between the Jammers, they all died but two.

We have their accounts of what happened, and some accounts found on the Jut, written by people who died. . . ."

"And the Crystallites?"

"They got away, clean away. As far as I know, no one has ever found out how. They had to have had help, that's certain. Help from outside, somewhere. Anyhow, that was really the first occasion when anyone heard much about Crystallites."

"I don't understand them!"

"They seem to have picked up Erickson's beliefs and carried them to a ridiculous extreme," Tasmin said. "Erickson believed the Presences are sentient, and by that he meant conscious, capable of understanding. He believed when we do a PJ we actually use meaningful words, even though we don't know what the meaning is. He started the Tripsingers as a quasi-religious order—the Worshipful Order of Tripsingers—and we've still got a lot of the old religious vocabulary and trappings left.

"The Crystallites picked up the belief in the sentience of Presences and built on it. In their religious scheme, the Presences are not merely sentient but godlike. The Crystallites believe either that Tripsinging is diabolical or that all Tripsingers are heretics, I'm not sure which. Quite frankly, their theology doesn't seem to be very consistent or well thought out. Sometimes I think two or three people just invented it without bothering to do a first draft. At any rate, they seem to consider it blasphemous for people to speak to the Presences at all. Not up close, at any rate. If we do so, we're tempting the gods who may, if they grow sufficiently agitated, destroy everything." Tasmin smiled at her. Stated thus baldly, it sounded silly. At the foot of the Black Tower, staring up, it often seemed quite reasonable.

"What do the Crystallites want us to do?"

Jamieson answered in a sarcastic, singsong voice. "They want us to stay on the coast, build cathedrals, burn incense, sing prayers all day, and bring in pilgrims from the known universe. Pilgrims who slap down consumer chits with both hands just to look at a Presence through a scope and even more to get within a few miles of one. That's about it."

"Stated with Jamieson's usual contempt for complexity," Tasmin chided, "but essentially true. They have quite a commercial empire built around pilgrimage. And, sad to say, the emergence of the Crystallites seems to have been what caused BDL to revise its own position on the Presences."

Clarin thought about this. "Oh, of course! If people really thought the Presences were sentient, and if the Planetary Exploitation Council thought so, too, then BDL probably couldn't have had exploitation rights to Jubal anymore. BDL might be deported, and it wouldn't like that one little bit. But . . . if BDL defines the Presences as nonsentient . . ."

"Not *if*," said Jamieson. "*Since*. BDL's been defining the Presences as nonsentient for fifty years. Even though we all know they are. . . ."

"Jamieson!"

The boy threw up his hands, saying in an argumentative tone, "Well, we do, Master Ferrence. I don't know a single 'Singer who believes they're nonsentient. No matter what he may say on the outside, inside he knows."

"He or she," said Clarin in a patient tone. "There are women singers, too, you know." It was obviously not the first time she had reminded Jamieson of this.

Tasmin sighed. Did he really want to spend effort cleaving to the BDL line on this trip? Did he want this continuing tug of war with Jamieson? Jamieson, who was, Tasmin reminded himself, one of the most talented singers it had ever been Tasmin's duty to try and whip into some kind of acceptable shape. Reb Jamieson? The everlasting mutineer? Who sang as he sang at least partly because he believed the Presences heard and understood what he sang? And Clarin. Clarin the what? He looked at her, but her face was turned down and he saw only the unlined curve of her forehead and the busy working of her hands on her bootlaces.

He chose peace. "All right, Jamieson, say what you like on this trip. Say it to me. Say it to Clarin; she seems to have good sense. Say that the BDL has been trying to redefine the Presences as nonsentient for the last fifty years so BDL won't be threatened with expulsion. Say that most of us, Tripsingers and Explorers, don't really believe that. Say it here by the campfire. But don't, for God's sake, say it out loud in the citadel when we get back, or in any other citadel we may stop at. I won't flame in on you if you'll be halfway discreet." He astonished himself with an enormous yawn.

The boy nodded, his face bright red in the fire glow. "Even though we all know they're sentient, it's different from being sure. I mean if anybody could prove it, the Planetary Exploitation Council might make BDL pack up and get out, so BDL won't let that happen."

"BDL means you and me, too," sighed Tasmin. "If we're being honest, none of us wants it to happen. So, be halfway discreet."

"It's a kind of hypocrisy, isn't it?" Clarin asked softly.

Jamieson shook his head at her warningly.

"It's interesting," mused Clarin. "I hadn't paid much attention to all of this Crystallite business. We were very isolated up Northwest, and it's closer there to the 'Soilcoast than it is to the interior. There are a number of Crystallite temples on the 'Coast, though. I do know that."

"Lots of temples," Tasmin agreed drowsily. "And lots of pilgrims coming in. Business versus business. Brou Distribution Limited against the Crystallites."

"Us in the middle," said Jamieson, nodding.

"Sleep," Tasmin suggested again, rising and moving toward the tent. Inside the cloverleaf tent the packs were distributed, each in a separate little wing, privacy curtains half lowered. Tasmin's bedroll was stretched out for him, the cover turned down. Clarin's touch. Clarin? A complex person, he thought. It took a good deal of courage to come halfway across Jubal, come as a stranger to a new citadel in an area where women were not as well accepted as Tripsingers as they were in the Northeast. Well. He would undoubtedly get to know Clarin rather well.

Sighing, he lowered himself onto his bedroll and dropped the curtain, thinking about the whole BDL-Crystallite fracas. "Us in the middle," he said, intoning Jamieson's sentiment as though it were some kind of bedtime prayer rather than the invocation of a troublesome truth.

5

The Explorers Chapter House at the Priory in Splash One made up in class for what it lacked in homey comforts. Or so Donatella Furz had always thought. Built in the first enthusiastic flush of planetary exploitation—back in the time before BDL realized how limited access to Jubal was actually going to be—it was a symphony of rare woods inlaid with Jubal coral, squat pillars of vitrified earth, and enormous beveled glass windows looking out onto the sea and the city. Donatella's room had three such, a protruding roomlet facing in three directions, furnished with an elegantly laid table and two comfortable chairs. Eating breakfast in this extravagant bay window was an experience in both seeing and being seen. Half of Splash One seemed to be aware that it had a more or less famous personage among its more ordinary citizens, and a good number of them seemed to know where she was staying. Five or six young gawkers were gathered on the opposite sidewalk when she wakened that morning. They had gathered in front of a dilapidated structure, which seemed to be half saloon and half something else, both halves in danger of imminent collapse. "Looky, looky, Don Furz, the Explorer knight," their gestures said, though they didn't shout at her, which she appreciated. When she sat down to breakfast, the same ones or substitute ones were still there, pointing and nudging one another.

Among whom, she warned herself silently, might be one with a laser pistol or an old-fashioned garotte or just a plain steel knife. The last one had had such a knife. Donatella still had it in her Explorer's case, wrapped in a bloody shirt, and she had a half-healed slash in her left arm to remind her of the cost of naive enthusiasm.

She finished her brou-pod tea, set the cup down with a

little click of finality, and wiped her lips. Rise, she instructed herself. Rise to the occasion. Smile at the people. Wave. Go back in the room where they can't see you. Do not, repeat, do not shut the curtains. Only someone with something to hide would shut the curtains.

Why in heaven's name had she decided to stay at the Chapter House? She hadn't remembered it being this public, this exposed. And why in heaven's name had they built the stupid Priory right in the middle of town? She asked the services man this question when he came for her dishes.

"I think the town grew up around it, Ma'am. Some of the nearby buildings have gone up during the past year. Sixty or seventy years ago, as I understand it, the Priory was quite secluded." He busied himself with the table and with a quick inspection of the room. As he left, he paused by the door to say, "I am, by the way, instructed to ask if you have any special wishes during your visit? Special food or drink, entertainment?"

She knew the man's job description included entertainment of several very specific sorts, but despite his obvious charm and intelligence, he didn't appeal to her except as a source of information. If she needed to avail herself of a service employee sexually, she'd stick to Zimmy.

"How about a concert?" she asked, apparently with her usual dangerously naive enthusiasm channeled this time. Used for advantage. "Chantry or Pit Paragon—one of those." She gave him an eager, expectant look.

"It's not considered . . ." He frowned, his darkly handsome face expressing disapproval neatly mixed with a proper degree of subservience, torso ever so slightly bent toward her, respect and good advice, impeccably offered. Oh, he was slick, this one.

"Oh, hell, man, I know what it's considered. Slumming, right? Undignified? Why would an Explorer knight want to listen to some revisionary rip-off of the sacred calling?"

He grinned, and she suddenly liked him better.

"Tell you what, what's your name?"

"Blanchet, Ma'am."

"All right, Blanchet, we won't scandalize the natives by appearing in public as ourselves. You shop for me today. Buy me a wig. Let's see. Something red, I think." She turned to catch a glimpse of herself in the mirror, smoothing the wide, short bell of golden hair with one hand. Dark blue eyes. Straight nose, a little too long she had always felt. All that climbing about had kept her figure slim, what there was of it. She could get away with a red wig. "Are they still wearing masks at public events down here? Well, buy me a small one that'll hide my eyes and nose. And a dress. I need a bright blue dress."

The man was openly laughing now. "Size, Ma'am?"

"One of those wraparound things with the straps that go all which a ways. They only come one size, you know what I mean? Stretch to fit? In some cases, stretch to rip?"

He nodded. "Is that all, Ma'am?"

"Concert tickets. Any one of the top six will do fine, and you might keep your mouth shut about it, if you're allowed to do that. No point in distressing your Prior or mine . . . or the Explorer King."

"I can be discreet."

"You'll find me most generous if you are."

He bowed himself out with the breakfast dishes, almost certainly going to report directly to someone from the Exploration Department. Probably the local Prior, who would want to know what the visiting knight was up to. So, let him report: The Explorer knight had a taste for night life; the Explorer knight wanted a new dress; the Explorer knight didn't want to be recognized. Everything on the list slightly against the conventions and everything perfectly harmless. The conventions would have had her making a ceremonial procession of herself, dressed in tall boots and worn Explorer leathers, avoiding questionable entertainment and signing autographs with a slightly distant smile. Theoretically, they should suspect her more if she were more compliant. Surely someone on the edge of treason wouldn't be dressing up for a 'Soilcoast singer concert.

She gritted her teeth in concentration. Since someone had tried to kill her, she had to assume that everything she did was watched, every word she said was overheard. Making contact was up to her trusted friend. All she had to do was get herself out in public where it could be done without being noticed. The Chapter House would be watched for the agreed-upon signal—a red wig and a blue dress. Pray God her trusted friend had managed everything according to plan.

And pray God the arrangement had been made with Lim Terree.

When evening came, she decided she rather liked the effect of the red wig, an almost devil-may-care gaiety, in no sense diminished by the impish half mask with the feathery eyebrows. And the blue dress, which clung satisfactorily, was a success also, drawing attention away from her face. Blanchet would accompany her, of course. Explorer knights, male or female, always had at least one escort when in the larger 'Soilcoast cities, if for no other reason than to keep the celebrity seekers in order. If she and Blanchet were lucky, they would be taken for just another couple out on the town; tourists from Serendipity or even from out-system, perhaps; or minor BDL officials in from a deepsoil pocket, a dirt town. They would have dinner, see the sights, attend the concert, and return to the Chapter House. Where she either would or would not invite Blanchet to share her bed for the night. He was an attractive enough man. But he wasn't Link. He wasn't even Zimmy.

She poured herself a drink and sat down on the couch that fronted the extravagant windows, far enough back in the room that she could not be seen. There were at least ten gawkers outside her window now, all staring upward as though hypnotized. In a few minutes she would go and lean out of the window, wave to them, call out "Hi, how are you? Great night, isn't it?" Watching for any move in her direction, any weapon. Anything that might betray another assassin.

Though there might not be another one. Not yet. Whoever had sent the first assassin could not know that the would-be killer was dead. For all the sender knew, the assassin might be alive and well and ready to try again. She could say that phrase to herself calmly, "try again," say it almost without fear. It was only when she took the thought further, "try again to kill Don Furz," that her stomach clenched into a knot and bile burned in her throat. "Try again to kill Don Furz because Don Furz knows something she is not supposed to know."

Not that she'd been trying to find out any such thing! She had been sitting in the large underground library of the Chapter House, three floors below where she was sitting right now, poring through some old papers for references to the Mad Gap. Her Prior thought there might be some early Explorer comments that would suggest a useful method of approach. The Gap was currently impassable. BDL wanted it passable. Thus, Donatella Furz, who thought she remembered reading something about it years ago, was immured in dusty papers and unintelligible correspondence, bored to tears, yawning over the ancient stacks, and longing for dinner. She was skimming the letters between a virtually unremembered third decade Explorer and his Prior when she came upon a page in a completely different handwriting. The half-stretched yawn died on her face and she stared at it in disbelief. She did not need to see the signature to know whose it was. Erickson! She had seen faxes of that handwriting a thousand times. She had seen the handwriting itself a hundred times in the Erickson Library at Northwest City, a library that was supposed to contain every extant scrap of original Erickson material.

But here it was, a letter in the master's own hand! It had obviously been misfiled and had lain unread for the last seventy years. Misfiled by whom? Reading the entire letter made it very clear. Misfiled by Erickson himself.

It was a letter to the future, couched in such subtle and evasive terms that only an Explorer—and one of a particular turn of mind at that—would find it intelligible. It hinted at possibilities that Donatella Furz found stunning in their implications. "I have further outlined this matter," the letter concluded. "Reference my papers on the Shivering Desert, filed with the Chapter House in the Priory of Northwest."

Northwest was her home House. When she had fruitlessly completed the Mad Gap research, too excited to concentrate on it any longer, she returned to Northwest City and found the papers Erickson had referred to. They took some finding because they weren't included in the Erickson material at all. They were buried in the middle of an endless compilation of permutations used in the Shivering Desert, an area that had been totally passworded for eighty years and was, therefore, uninteresting.

"Buried in boredom," she told herself. "He picked two places no one would look for decades, and he buried them there." The pertinent notes were on two pages of perma-paper. Donatella folded them and hid them in the lining of her jacket, then spent hours poring over them in the privacy of her room.

She had taken the papers with a sense of saving them, though protocol would have required her to report them to the Prior at once. Later she examined her motives, finding much there that disturbed her, but coming at last to the conclusion that she thought the papers were safer with her than they would have been with the Department of Exploration.

Even then she had had sense enough to leave other, harmless papers out in her room to explain her study, in case anyone was watching, or wondering.

Erickson had not expected his eventual reader to believe him without proof. At the conclusion he said in effect, "If you want to test this theory, do thus and thus at some unpassworded Presence. If you do it right, you'll see what I mean."

Don had chosen to try it on the Enigma. Everyone and his favorite mule had tried the Enigma, and permission to approach it was almost impossible to obtain. It had taken six months before she had the opportunity to get to the Enigma from the southern coast. She did what Erickson suggested—and more!

When she returned, it was with the recording cubes and notes for the Enigma Score, and she was dizzy with what she knew, bubbling with it. Erickson had only known half of it. If he had had a synthesizer like the current ones. . . . She had hugged the knowledge to herself, glorying in it. Only Donatella Furz knew the whole truth, the truth about Jubal. No one else knew. No one!

Only some time later did she realize that in seventy years there might have been others who knew or suspected, but if they had, they had been ruthlessly suppressed—only after someone had tried to kill her.

On her return, she had arranged for the Enigma notes to be sent to a Tripsinger citadel for transcribing and orchestration—"Send it to that man in Deepsoil Five," she had suggested. "Tasmin Ferrence. The one who did that great score on the Black Tower." Then she had reported a possible breakthrough to the Prior of her Chapter House and had done it with due modesty in language full of "perhaps" and "this suggests." She had made all the proper moves in the proper order; none of them should have aroused suspicion. If only she could have kept it at that! But no matter what motions she went through, what modest little remarks she made when congratulated, she could not hide her elation. Inside herself, she was bubbling with what she knew, what she thought, what she wanted to prove, what she had proved. She had not been so foolish as to blurt it out to anyone—it was obviously information that some people would want to suppress—but neither had she been sensible enough to keep her obvious euphoria hidden.

Who might have observed that euphoria?

Explorers Martin and Ralth, while they were out at dinner one night. "Touch me, boys, because the day will come when you'll tell people, 'I knew her before she was famous.'"

"What are you up to now, Don?" asked Martin, sounding bored. "Another new variation for the Creeping Desert? Don't we have enough Creeping Desert variations already?"

"Bigger than that," she had replied with a laugh. "Much bigger."

"You've got a Gemmed Rampart score that really works," suggested Ralth. "Or a foolproof way to get through the Crazies."

"Why not?" She had giggled.

"Which?"

"Why not both. Why not everything?"

They had laughed incredulously. They had ordered more wine. There had been laughter and arguments among the three Explorers and congratulations on the Enigma score.

Well, what else had she said that night? Nothing. Nothing at all. One bragging phrase. "Why not everything?" Had there been enough in that conversation to give someone the idea that Donatella Furz knew something they would rather she didn't know? Not really. It could all be put down to her euphoria. Even an untested score for a Presence as famous as the Enigma lent a certain cachet to her name. She hadn't really said anything at all!

Who else had she talked to? Zimmy. A services employee. A Northwest Chapter House man. Not unlike this

Chapter House man, Blanchet, except that Zimmy belonged to Don. He was only hers, he kept saying, and had been only hers for some years now, eager to please her, intelligent in meeting her needs for comfort and affection. Zimmy. She thought of him with both fondness and pleasure. What had she said to Zimmy? Nothing much. "Oh, Zimmy, if you knew what I know." Something like that. He hadn't even paid much attention.

And who else? The woman in Northwest City who usually cut her hair.

Don's head had been bent forward while the woman depilated the back of her neck, quite high, so that the bottom of the wide bell of her hair would come just to the bottom of her ears. "How can you do it?" the woman had chattered. "All alone, out among the Presences. I would pee my pants, truly, lady knight, I would."

"It isn't as dangerous as people have thought it was."

"No, it is more. I know it must be. To hear the Great Ones speak, to attempt to pacify them. Oh, a terror, lady knight, truly, a terror."

The woman's use of the words "Great Ones" should have stopped Donatella in her tracks. Those were the words used by Crystallites to refer to the Presences, but Don simply hadn't noticed. "It won't be long before we'll all be able to walk among the Presences much more safely. Not long at all." Don had raised her head, seeing herself and the woman in the mirror.

"Oh, you think some great discovery? Some marvel?" The woman peered at her in the mirror, her black eyes gleaming with something acquisitive and desperate.

And at that point Don had realized what she was saying and had drawn up sharply. "No, no discovery, no marvel, Sophron. Simply the slow accumulation of knowledge. . . ."

Who else had she talked to?

Chase Random Hall, the Explorer King. Could anything she had said to him in the dining room of the Chapter House, during the informal time of day when everyone was on a first-name basis, could anything there have been interpreted as something threatening?

"Randy, you ever think the day may come we'll all be out of work?"

"Mind your manners, silly girl. Don't be obscene."

"No, I mean wouldn't it be terrific if we found The Password?" "The Password" was the apotheosis on Jubal and had been for a hundred years. It was like "The Millennium" or "The Second Coming," a terrible end said to be devoutly desired by some, the single score that would open every pass and permit free travel everywhere.

"I think it's a disgusting thought, one I would appreciate not having raised again in my hearing." Randy had been effete in his youth and was effete still, but there was no arguing with his successes. Now he smoothed his elegantly trimmed moustaches and smiled at her in his best monster-eating-up-a-little-girl smile: glittering eyes in a brown, brown face with his terribly white teeth, teeth that made one weak even while they made one shiver, anticipating voracious kisses. They were inevitable, those teeth, like death. "Do you like living dangerously, stupid child?"

"Is it that dangerous to speculate about The Password?" She had said it lightly. Surely she had said it lightly!

"A little idle speculation here in the Chapter House, over drinks, perhaps not. Anything more than that, decidedly. As a moment's thought—if you are capable of such—should have informed you. Think, silly girl. If you had The Password, there are at least twenty people I could name who would kill you to keep it quiet."

She knew her face had changed then. Changed with horror, in memory. People who would kill! She remembered her friend Gretl Mechas. Or rather, Gretl's body as it had been when Donatella identified it. Remembering this, she turned away. She had had enough of this conversation.

But then he had asked, "Would you like to go to bed with me, Donatella?"

"I am the King Explorer's to command," she had said, stiffly, taking refuge in a ritual answer. This was a new gambit.

"Not at all eager, are you?"

"I . . . I have other affections, Randy."

"Don't we all know it. Your affections are the talk of the House and most unworthy of you. Speaking of danger then, stupid child, what's the news about the Mad Gap?" And they had talked shop as she detailed her attempts to find a Password through the Gap before moving on to other things. Why had he mentioned going to bed together? Everyone knew Randy preferred men, though he would possess a woman if he thought it useful. Had he thought she might be useful? But not quite useful enough? Had he slipped when he spoke of people killing other people? Was he interested in her reaction? Or was it merely a very effective way to change the subject?

It had been an odd, a very odd conversation. With her well-schooled memory for exact words and phrases, exact tones and progressions of tones, she could play it over in her head, again and again, but it made no more sense now than it had then.

Her ruminations were interrupted by tapping at the door. Blanchet came in, dressed to the toenails in a one-piece glitter-suit with a plumed hat and multiple chains of Jubal coral around his neck. She made an appreciative sound. "Don't you look marvelous."

"My poor best will be hardly good enough, Ma'am." He gave her an admiring look. "The outfit becomes you."

"So long as I don't become the outfit." She laughed. "Having got into it, there may be some difficulty getting out. The outfit and I may be inextricable. You'd better not call me 'Don' this evening. That might give our truancy away. Call me Tella. My brother always called me that."

"Very well, Tella. My name is Fyne Iron Blanchet, and my close friends call me Fibe. Or Fibey."

"Fyne Iron?"

"Family names both. I don't think my mother ever thought what it would sound like."

"Well, it sounds very . . . metallurgical."

"So I've always felt." He offered her his arm and they went down the lift to ground level where a city car awaited them. The gawkers were still staring up at her window. None of them seemed to notice her. "Shall I drive?"

"Please. You know Splash One far better than I. It keeps growing! Every time I've been here before I've gotten myself hopelessly lost."

He suited himself to her mood, not talking merely to make conversation but concentrating on his driving. Splash One had grown explosively in recent months, so much so that concentration was a necessity. She stared out at a city raw and gawky in its burgeoning adolescence.

Half the streets were torn up, more were barricaded, though no one paid any attention to the barricades. Stiff, square-cornered new buildings of reinforced brick thrust up beside curvilinear older ones of rammed earth, the hard burnt brown making harsh edges against soft gray. The older buildings were covered with signs offering bargains in entertainment, in used equipment, in new and used clothing, new and used furniture, apartments, rooms. Most of the staff at the military base just outside of the city had dependents housed here in Splash One, and domiciliary space was at a premium.

The newer buildings were labeled with small directories at the entrances; government offices, BDL division offices, purchasing agents, suppliers' representatives, research labs. Every sidewalk was jammed with people; every window had one or two persons leaning out of it, waving, talking to those in the street. Some of those in the streets were engaged in trade of an unmistakable kind, and Don stared.

"Prostitutes?" she asked, breaking her preoccupied silence. There had never been prostitutes on Jubal. At least, none that were visible.

Blanchet nodded. "Recent imports. They say that somebody high up got paid off." He didn't need to specify which somebody. The word among BDL employees was that the Governor had both hands out for himself, which was unnerving. PEC appointed governors were supposed to be unimpeachable, and it made one wonder how high the rot had spread.

At the end of a short side street a building loomed, gleaming like gold and culminating in a high, ornately curved dome. Crowds of people passed in and out through the monstrous doors.

"What in Jubal is that?" she asked, turning to peer over her shoulder.

"Crystallite Temple."

"It's *huge!*"

"It's huge and there are about four more like it up and down the 'Soilcoast. You don't have one in Northwest City yet?"

"No. And I don't look forward to having one. Where do they get the money?"

"Pilgrims. Contributions. If you haven't seen some of the evangelical cubes the Crystallite hierarchy sends out, you've missed something. Very slick, Tella. The money pours in as though it were piped. The people at the top aren't like the ones you see running around on the streets. The assassins, fanatics, and insurgents are a scruffy lot, but those in charge of the temples are something else again. Very smooth. You ought to see them." His mouth compressed into a grim line.

"Well, let's. We're not in any hurry, are we?"

He gave her a surprised look, but obediently brought the car to a halt and walked with her back toward the Temple yard. The paved area was scattered with small groups of pilgrims, each wearing a knot of orange ribbon to identify his status, each group led by a soberly robed guide. Blanchet inconspicuously attached himself and Donatella to the rear of one straggling group as they followed the orange ribboned ones into the enormous structure.

Donatella only with difficulty kept herself from exclaiming. Around them were towering pillars, vaulted ceilings high above, dazzling fountains of light and smoke. "Where do they get all this!" she demanded in a whisper. "How could they get this kind of equipment when we're still short of medical supplies and simple things like computers or lift machinery?"

Blanchet kissed his palm in a derisory gesture and she subsided. Obviously someone had been paid off. And why did it surprise her? She turned as Blanchet nudged her, pointing unobtrusively at three figures that had just come onto an elevated platform at the top of a broad flight of stairs. Two men, one woman. The men could have been brothers, both with extravagant manes of white hair, both tall and well built, robed in glittering, vertically striped garments and wearing high domed crowns. The combination made them appear to be about twelve feet tall. The woman, on the other hand, glittered in quite another way. Her breasts were exposed under sparkling necklaces of gems, and her draped skirt seemed to be woven of gold thread, the extensive train slithering behind her like the body of a heavy snake. She, too, was crowned and plumed.

"Chantiforth Bins and Myrony Clospocket," Blanchet whispered. "Half brothers, I understand, with a long, slippery history. Now Supreme Pontiff and High Priest. And the High Priestess, Aphrodite Sells. The three of them are the real power behind all the Crystallites on Jubal."

"Are they the power behind the assassinations, too? And the terrorism?"

"They claim not. Though they say they 'understand' the frustration that leads their followers to commit such acts."

On the high platform the glittering woman called out a short phrase, which brought the congregation to immediate silence. She had a voice like a knife, as cutting as a shard of crystal.

Don watched for a short time as the three sparkling figures began a ritual that was obviously familiar to most of those in the audience who were cheerfully bellowing the responses. "I've seen enough," she murmured. "Let's get out of here."

They returned to the car, unspeaking, and continued the interrupted trip, passing the farmer's market, a bustling enclave of trucks, mule wagons, booths stacked high with produce, milling vendors, customers, and sightseers, all in one swirling, noisy throng. Across from the market were the fish stalls, a long line of booths fronting the enclosed ponds of the local fish farms, smelling richly of the sea. Beyond the ponds stood the tilting masts of the merchant fleet. Don remarked at the number of ships. "There are more private boats than BDL has!"

Blanchet nodded solemnly. "BDL isn't the sole power in Splash One and Two anymore. At least that's the inside word. More than half the traffic last year was noncommercial. Military, a lot of it. Plus all the pilgrims the Crystallites bring in. And they've added some staff to the Governor's office."

Don started to say, "That's silly, he doesn't do anything," then thought better of it. Her friend Link had been attached to the Governor's office. She contented herself by asking, "Why?"

"Because of the Jut Massacre."

"That was six years ago!"

"Well, you know how long it takes the Planetary Exploitation Council to move."

"I wasn't aware that the PEC moved at all. I thought

they merely existed, like the Core Stars." It was safe to say that, she thought. Lots of people said things like that.

"The story is that the Jut Massacre moved them. Somebody up there had a son or grandson among the slain, and it made them take the Crystallites seriously. You know they're reopening the question of native sentience."

It was safer for her to say nothing at all. "Look at that building," she marveled. "It's all of six stories tall. It's a fortress!" The huge gray structure looked like a monolith, almost windowless, surrounded by high, crenelated walls.

"You've seen it before, but probably not from this angle. It used to have an open square in front of it, right at the eastern edge of town. It's the BDL Headquarters. Behind it is the Tripsingers' citadel, and the Governor's official residence is adjacent, there." He indicated a palacial, terraced edifice set among gardens. "The reason they've added to the Governor's staff is to take care of this upcoming PEC inquiry. And they've beefed up the military in case of further threats from the Crystallite rank and file, though what earthly use we have for this many troopers is anybody's guess. In the process they've made Jubal the garrison planet for the entire system. Everyone assumes someone bribed someone, because the base on Serendipity has been closed and transferred here. And the military have brought their spouses and kids and intimate friends. All of whom need housing and services and food. The town is a mess."

"It certainly is," she agreed.

"Splash Two isn't any better, from what I hear. Nor are any of the smaller cities. Population of the 'Soilcoast cities is supposed to be in excess of two million. Since we haven't the resources to build up, we're spreading out. I'm told at this rate of growth, deepsoil space will run out in a few years. The farmers are already screaming at the cost of land, and we need all the farmlands to feed the people. The whole thing doesn't make sense."

"Amazing," she murmured, shaking her head. "Simply amazing. I think of Northwest City as fairly urban until I come down here. We're really cushioned from all this growth up there, and I can't say I'm not glad. What's that ruckus down there?"

"Hmm. There's a Crystallite street demonstration going

on. Well, you've seen the temple. Might as well see the other side of it. Hear the singing?"

She heard the tuneless wailing, not something that either an Explorer or Tripsinger would have considered singing. "What are they up to?"

"I'll drive slowly enough that you can see, but put your mask in your lap and don't stare at them. These are the shock troops, and they aren't averse to civil disorder. They throw things at people who look like they might be enjoying themselves. As far as they're concerned, anyone enjoying himself on Jubal is bound to be a heretic!" The car moved smoothly down the avenue, and Don watched the mob from the corners of her eyes.

Half a dozen cadaverous figures clad only in loin cloths and sandals were haranguing a scanty and fluid crowd of sightseers. Don caught the words, "blasphemous impertinence" and "the day of punishment is coming," and "we cannot be moved!" As the car came even with the crowd, one of the chanting figures lit a torch, held it high for a moment, then threw it down. Behind the crowd, flames lept up in a blue hot cone.

People screamed and fled, and Don stared in disbelief at the cross-legged figure burning on the sidewalk, its wide white eyes shining in ultimate agony through the flames. "My God," she said, retching. "My God. They're burning a person!"

"An immolation?" Blanchet asked, mouth drawn into a rictus of distaste and horror. He speeded the car to move them away. "Sorry. It's been a moon or more since they did one of those here in the city. Are the soldiers on top of it?"

She looked back. Uniformed figures were moving purposefully through the crowd, one with a fire extinguisher.

"Soldiers are there. Why do they burn themselves?"

"To show the authorities they aren't afraid of death, or pain, or torture, or imprisonment. To show they can't be controlled by police methods. We've got a small scale holy war on our hands. It's just that no one in government seems to realize it yet. People are taking bets on whether the Governor has been paid not to act. And these public immolations are bad enough. The secret, ritual killings are worse. . . ."

"Ritual killings?" she faltered, afraid of what he was going to say to her.

"Killings by torture. Women carved up . . ."

"Blanchet, don't. Please don't. One of them was a friend of mind. Gretl Mechas. She was cut to ribbons. They said it took hours for her to die. I had to identify her body and I couldn't identify anything except her clothes. Oh, Lord, no one in Northwest called it a ritual killing."

"Maybe it wasn't. Sorry, Tella. Your friend wasn't the only one. There have been others. Always women or young boys."

The horrible sight of the immolation, the hideous memory of her friend, as well as Blanchet's comments on the current political scene had ruined Don's desire for dinner or entertainment. Oh, Gretl! Lovely, warm, friendly Gretl. Why! And she couldn't take time to grieve over Gretl tonight. She had to remind herself that there were other, urgent reasons for her to be abroad in the city.

"Where are we going for dinner?" she asked, keeping her voice flatly matter of fact and not caring what the answer might be.

"The Magic Viggy," he told her, shaking his head. "I'd planned it as an appropriate place to take someone with red hair and a very blue dress. I'm afraid it will seem rather trivial, now."

It did seem trivial. They ate imported food at extortionate prices. They drank, albeit abstemiously. Blanchet would have been quite happy to fill her glass more often, but Don let it sit three-quarters full during most of dinner. She didn't need to be more depressed, which the wine would eventually do. They chatted. Though Blanchet was a well-informed and interesting companion, she had trouble later recalling what they had discussed. Magicians and clowns moved about, playing tricks, distributing favors. A neighboring table was occupied by a noisy crowd of elderly sightseers. There was a lot of clutter. When they were ready to leave, Don missed her bag and found it on the floor, half buried under a bouquet of flowers that a magician had pulled from her hair.

"Like a circus," she said. "Like a carnival."

"The most popular place in town," he agreed. "Now, I have tickets to Chantry."

"Not Lim Terree?" she asked, cocking her head. "I really liked him last time I was here."

"Oh, hadn't you heard?" he asked. "It was on the news here a few days ago. Lim Terree is dead."

She made an appropriate expression of dismay without letting the shock show on her face. She felt herself go pale and cold, but the flickering lights in the restaurant hid that. By the time they reached the street, she was in command of herself once more, able to sit through Chantry's concert and pretend to enjoy it. When it was over, she asked to return to the Chapter House, and once there, claimed weariness and was left alone, though Blanchet expressed regret for that decision as she smiled herself away from him. How desirable to be alone! Except, she reminded herself, for whatever listening and watching devices were undoubtedly placed here and there in her rooms.

She rummaged in her bag, as though for her handkerchief, her fingers encountering something that crackled crisply. She palmed it in the handkerchief, wiped her nose, then thrust the note under her pillow as she turned down the bed. Nightly ritual, she told herself. The whole bedtime score with all variations. Shower. Teeth brushed. Hair brushed. Nightgown. Emergency kit on the bedside table. No Explorer would ever go to sleep without the emergency kit within reach. Then, pick up the new exploration digest, delivered to her door in her absence, and read the professional news for a while. A new theory of variation. Which wasn't new. Yawn. Let the eyes fall closed. Rouse a little. Put out the lights.

She let a little time go by, then silently brought the emergency kit under the covers and turned on its narrow beamed light. The note she had put in her purse before leaving, informing her friend that someone had tried to kill her, was gone. In its place were two others. The letters were minuscule, hard to read.

"Terree informed and supplied as per our plans. He is obtaining Enigma score in Five. Took him some time to set up tour. Should return at end of Old Moon."

This was dated weeks previously and was on a tiny sheet of paper, no larger than one-quarter the palm of her hand. Folded inside it was another sheet, even smaller, dated a few days prior.

"Word received two days ago, Lim Terree dead on Enigma. Trying to find out what happened. Make contact."

Both were signed with a twisted line that returned upon itself to make three links of a chain. She put out the light, replaced the kit on the bedside table, then methodically tore the two notes into tiny pieces and ate them.

In the office of the Prior, Fyne Blanchet finished his report with a yawning comment. "I don't know what all the fuss is about. She's all right. I talked about the things you wanted me to, but she didn't say anything much. There's no evidence of her knowing anything I don't. She didn't gripe about corruption or say she was going to murder the governor or anything, just a few snide remarks, the same as anyone."

"She didn't ask you to stay."

"A lot of them don't. Hell, she's got it on with that guy at the Northwest Chapter. Five years? What's his name, Zimble? So, she's monogamous. Lots of women are. Besides, she was really upset over that burning. She saw the whole thing. She didn't eat much, and she was pale all through the concert."

The Prior grunted, thought. After a time, he said, "She has some people she usually sees here in Splash One."

"So?"

"So, she would normally want to visit them."

"And?"

"If she doesn't visit them or any one of them, it might mean something."

Blanchet yawned. He felt the Prior was clutching at straws. Donatella Furz was nothing to worry about. And what was the Prior so worried about? Blanchet, who kept his curiosity strictly in check when it was profitable to do so, told himself he really didn't know. Or care.

"Fibey," she said the next morning over her breakfast fish, "I've got three old friends here in town. I'd like to see them while I'm here. Could you arrange that for me?"

"Certainly, Ma'am. Any particular order? Lunch dates? Dinner dates?"

"No. Nothing in particular. Whatever's convenient for them. There's an old family friend, actually sort of a cousin of my mother's. Name's Cyndal Prince, and last time I was here she lived over in that development south of town, along the bay. Then there's Link Emert. He's still with BDL, but he's recently been attached to the Governor's office. Liaison of some kind. And then there's my niece, Fabian Furz."

"Your brother's daughter?"

"One and only. Bart died about five years ago, one of those wasting diseases no one in the interior knows anything about, and by the time he got to the 'Soilcoast, it was too late to do anything. You'd think by now they'd have improved the medical system in the Deepsoil towns, wouldn't you?"

"I think it's a materiel question, Ma'am."

"Oh, I know, I know. No way to ship the big diagnostic machines in. No way to take in the life support systems. Shit. They take in anything else that suits them, in itty bitty pieces, if necessary, with a whole troop of mechanics to put it together again. Oh, well, no reason to fuss about it now. Bart's long gone, and my bitching won't bring him back. Anyhow, if you could get hold of those people and set up dates for me, this afternoon or tomorrow morning, I'd appreciate it. I'll call you just before noon, if that's convenient."

"You have other plans for this morning?"

"I, Blanchet, am going to have my annual medical checkup. That's why I'm here. Orders from up top."

There was no shortage of diagnostic machines at the Splash One medical center. No shortage of technicians either, Don thought, as she was prodded, poked, bled, and otherwise sampled for the tenth time in as many minutes. "This is the last one," the anonymous white-coated person said with at least a semblance of sympathy. "You can get dressed now."

The physician, who appeared harried and abstracted, leafed through the chart twice before looking up at Don with a furrowed brow. "You didn't have that wound on your arm last time. No record of it in your history. Well, there wouldn't be. It's obviously fresh."

"Yes, it's a recent injury."

"When? How?"

"Oh, about ten days ago. A fall. A 'ling blew its top when I was on a narrow trail, and I fell against a sharp edge. I reported it to the Prior when I got back to the Chapter House. It should be in the record update."

"Oh, I see it. Yes. Well, just checking. Healing clean, is it?"

"Seems to be healing well, yes."

"Do you want the scar removed?"

"Perhaps later. It still takes two or three weeks of regeneration treatment to take scars off, doesn't it."

"With the small machines, which is all we have available, yes. About that."

"Well, I don't have time right now. I've got several explorations to do for BDL before Old Moon's out. I've got some leave coming up next Dead Moon, though. Maybe I'll do it then."

"Suit yourself. If you want it done in Northwest City, don't go to the BDL medical center there. Word to the wise, right? Go to this woman. You'll have to pay for it, but you'll be better satisfied." The physician handed over a note with a name on it.

Don made an appreciative noise, both for the information and because she had been afraid there would be close questioning about the injury. Not that it wasn't very much like a dozen crystal cuts she'd had over the years. It could have been a crystal cut.

But it wasn't.

Shortly after she had returned to Northwest from the Enigma, she had calmed down and begun to realize how dangerous her position might be. This realization was followed by a period of indecision during which she had found an excuse to make a quick trip to Splash One, ostensibly only to attend a government house reception. During the reception, she had managed to get lost on the way to the women's convenience long enough to hold a lengthy whispered conversation in a dark and supposedly vacant office, guaranteed by her friend to be free of ears or eyes.

"I don't suppose it would do any good to suggest you just forget the whole thing?" her friend had murmured.

"I've explained why that won't work," she had said. "This information has to get out. It has to be made public." They both knew it. Don's friend had worked for an intelligence agency at one time and was well aware that this was the kind of information that had to be publicized. As public information, it was a danger to no one. As a secret, it was a death trap. And the consequences to the planet if the information was kept quiet were too terrible for either of them to contemplate.

"BDL isn't going to like it."

"That's why I can't do it," Don had whispered. "They pretty well control me. I know damned well my Priory reports where I go, what I do. Not just me. All Explorers. No. It's got to be someone else who does it. Someone BDL doesn't control."

Together they had crafted a hasty plan, every step of which made the danger more and more clear. When they parted, it was as co-conspirators. Wheels were in motion, very secret wheels. Donatella returned to Northwest with a sense of mixed relief and apprehension, taking refuge in routine duties, everyday activities. Behind her in Splash One, her friend would move things along.

There had been one loose end. She had had to fill out a "lost or stolen equipment" report to cover the synthesizer that she had taken to Splash One and returned without. But after that, nothing had happened. For weeks, nothing at all.

Until ten days ago when she had been sent out on a routine two-day trip to explore a pocket of deepsoil behind an offshoot ridge of the Redfang Range. It had seemed an odd assignment, even at the time. The offshoot, Little Redfang, was only half a day's travel from Northwest. The Passwords to a good part of the range were Donatella's own work, and most of them had been part of the repertory for almost a decade. All that was wanted this time was some minor variation that would get wagons through the Fanglings in a slightly different direction from that taken formerly—a route that Don could see no sensible justification for—and virtually any apprentice Explorer could have done the job.

Still, an assignment approved by one's Prior was an assignment not to be argued with. She remembered being preoccupied with her personal problem, worrying at it relentlessly as she rode. The plan was dependent on so many variables, so many little things she couldn't control. She was having second thoughts, trying to decide if she should make another trip to Splash One or whether it was too late at this point to do anything but ride it out. Indecision was not an ordinary thing with Donatella; it irritated her. Explorers couldn't be indecisive. Those that were didn't last long. The morning's trip made the matter no clearer, moreover, and by noon she reached the peril-point and had to force herself to set the subject aside. She told herself she would think about it again that night, over her campfire.

It took most of the afternoon working with synthesizer and computer, trying permutations of a few phrases that seemed likely, to come up with a new score on the music box that quieted things down very nicely. It was a fairly simple variation of a score she knew well, one she felt competent to use in singing herself through the range—just as a test, and certainly not something that was required of an Explorer—and it was early evening when she started.

The way she chose was a narrow ledge along a towering face and above a sheer drop into a gorge of living crystal. The gorge gleamed with amber and hot orange lights through its generally winey mass. All the Redfang Range was bloody, as evil looking in its way as the Enigma, though a whole lot simpler to get through. Her narrow ledge wouldn't do as a trip-trail, but it would serve to get her into the deepsoil pocket, after which she would find some way out that wagons could travel. As she sang her way along the ledge, she told herself that hell must look much like the gorge below her. The lower the sun dropped, the more it looked as though it were on fire.

She didn't hurry during the transit. Afterward she realized it was entirely likely that someone had followed her from the peril-point. Certainly that someone knew something about Tripsinging, for the attack came at precisely that moment when she moved out of peril. A black clad, black masked form, barely visible in the dusk, came from slightly to one side and behind her.

If it hadn't been that she turned just at that moment in response to some tiny sound; it if hadn't been that the sun glinted on the knife blade as she turned, she would not have seen her attacker at all.

As it was, she dropped without thought, rolled, pulled up her legs to protect her belly and her arm to protect her throat, felt a moment's searing pain along the arm, kicked up and out with both legs, and saw the figure soar over her into the air above the gorge. She had reacted without thought, reacted as she had been taught, as she had practiced a thousand times in the self-defense courses that, since the Jut Massacre, all Explorers had had to take over and over again.

The weapon clattered onto the ledge, but the attacker fell endlessly, without a sound.

For a short time after that, Don was so busy applying emergency care to her gashed arm that she had no time to wonder about the attacker. When the bleeding was stanched, she huddled over a tiny fire, terrified that the assassin might not have been alone. Then, when no further assault came, she began to wonder why she had been attacked at all.

At first light she had attempted to climb to the place the body lay, so far below as to be virtually invisible. If she could find out who, she might find out the reason.

After an hour or two, she gave up. Someone might get into the gorge with a parachute or a balloon. They would not get out again.

Since then it had remained a mystery. Someone had tried to kill her. She didn't know who, and she wasn't sure why. Not a torture killing like Gretl's; nothing weird about it; just a straightforward attempt at murder!

A Crystallite assassin? That's why Explorers studied self-defense, after all, because of the threat posed by fanatics. It could have been. In which case, the intended victim might not have been Don Furz particularly, but simply any Explorer. However, Crystallite assassins were said to scream religious slogans during attacks. Certainly they had done so during the Jut Massacre and in several other assassinations since. This person, male or female, had been silent.

Was it someone who knew what Don had found out? One of those twenty the Explorer King had mentioned? Then how had he or she found out? What did they know?

Was it someone from BDL?

What would her trusted friend think about it? She had been unable to pass the word along until yesterday.

Now she realized the doctor was looking at her oddly, obviously wondering at her long preoccupation. "I was just trying to figure out some way to have the scar removed now," she said to explain her abstraction. "But it can't be done. There just isn't time. Other than the scar, how am I?"

"You're thirty-three years old, in perfect health, in beautiful shape, with no evidence of any disease whatsoever. You've got the muscles of a stevedore and the reaction time of a prime jetball ace. What else can I tell you? Here's a copy of the report. The duplicate will be placed in your record." He cocked his head and looked at her quizzically.

Don grinned. No matter how often she told herself it was foolish, she always approached the annual medical exam with the suspicion it would find her in some lingering illness. Each time, the report relieved her anxiety, and she took the copy now with a sense of reprieve.

She called Fyne Blanchet from a booth in the lobby of the medical building.

"I made a lunch date for you with your elderly relative," he said. "She's a little hard of hearing, so I hope she got it straight."

"When and where, Blanchet?"

"Thirteen hundred at the Fish House on Bayside Street. She told me, among many other things, that she doesn't eat red meat."

"Who can afford red meat? I can't." Pasture land was strictly limited on Jubal, and red meat was the epitome of luxury. Fowl was more usual. Fish, more common yet.

"I'm waiting for a call back from your niece, and Link Emert would love to have cocktails with you after work. He says seventeen hundred at the 'Ling Lounge, just down the block from his office."

"Fine. I'll check back with you after lunch."

Lunch at the Fish House was as predictable as any meal with Cyndal. Close inspection of the menu to determine whether there was anything on it she could not eat. Each such item read aloud. Querulous inquiry into the morals of anyone who would eat said item. Further finicky attention given to ordering copiously from among items that she could eat. And, finally, greedy consumption of said items, right down to the polish on the plate, while discoursing upon the flavor of every mouthful.

If anyone had an ear trained on Cyndal, Don hoped they enjoyed the experience.

"Very nice, Donatella. Very generous of you. What do you hear from your dear mother?"

"Just the usual, Cousin Cyndal. She's still greatly involved with the local gardening group there in Deepsoil Twelve. She asked to be remembered to you."

"Such a lovely woman, your mother."

Donatella, who had quite another view of her parent, smiled and said nothing. When she left the restaurant, the waiter came running after her with her bag, which she, as usual, had forgotten.

"Blanchet? Did you get hold of Fabian?"

"Dinner tonight or breakfast tomorrow, whichever you prefer."

"Oh, make it dinner tonight. Then I'll have the morning to sleep in and luxuriate before starting back to Northwest. Tell her—tell her to pick a place and I'll meet her there at twenty hundred. I'm going to do some shopping before I meet Link Emert. Thanks, Blanchet."

When she arrived at the 'Ling Lounge, she found Link already ensconced behind a table, his mobile chair hidden by it. Link usually arrived early in order to make his disability less apparent.

"Donatella!" He half rose, pushing up with his arms to give the appearance of someone with legs that worked, then seated himself again to reach out for her hand. She did not lean down to kiss him. He had been very explicit about the pain that caused him, so she didn't do it. Also, her hair was flattened and drawn back severely and she was wearing a not very becoming suit that made her legs and torso shapeless.

"I don't want to want you anymore," he had said to her once, the words hissing out between clenched teeth. "Don't you understand, Don! It hurts to want you. I hurts to want anything!"

So, she looked as unwantable as possible, within the bounds of what might be acceptable in a place with the effrontery to call itself the 'Ling Lounge. Predictably, it was decorated with phoney 'lings, plastic crystals that reached from floor to ceiling. Variations on Tripsinger themes pounded from speakers. "Interesting place," she said, gesturing with disdain. "How long has this been here?"

"Oh, less than a year. It's an appalling tourist trap, plain and simple, but the drinks are good."

"Tourists! Lord. That's a word I'd read about but never thought to hear in Jubal, Link. Tourists!"

"More of them all the time, Don. There's even some guy down in Bay City who advertises interior trips for tourists, with Tripsingers and the whole score."

"He's out of his mind!"

"No. He takes them out by the Deadheads, sings them through with some mish mash, then gives them a look at the Crazies, 'accidentally' blows up a Crazeling or two, and brings the tourists back all agog. They think they've been in peril."

"And he makes it with both hands."

"So I hear. What are you drinking, Donatella, my love? It's been almost year since I've seen you, you know that?" He said "my love" casually, as though it didn't matter, but her heart turned over at the words, as it always had. He was thinner. His eyes were sunken. That once glowing face looked pallid. Even his lips were colorless. She shook herself and smiled, pretending not to see.

They ordered drinks. They talked. Little things. Inconsequentialities. Recent explorations. Link's work as Explorer liaison to the Governor's office. The recent announcement that the CHASE Commission was coming to Jubal.

"What the hell is the CHASE Commission?" she asked.

"The Planetary Exploitation Council has set up a new commission to decide once and for all whether there is sentient native life on Jubal."

"Oh, I did know about it. I just didn't remember the name. The services man talked about it last night. And somebody mentioned it at that reception I came down for, last time I was here in town." Donatella's real reason for coming to Splash One had occupied her mind to such an extent that she had been barely able to focus on social rituals. "As I recall on that occasion I forgot who the Governor's wife was and introduced her to someone as Gereny Vox."

"Donatella!" He sounded genuinely shocked. By no stretch of resemblance could the well-known mule breeder be compared in either face or figure to Honeypeach Thonks. Gereny was a completely genuine, if rough-edged, person of considerable charm. Lady Honeypeach was a self-created and ominous device.

"It was just a slip of the tongue. I knew right away I'd got it wrong, and I apologized all over the place. She was very sweet about it, in a poisonous way." Don laughed unconvincingly. It had been a horrible gaffe, one she'd heard about later from the Explorer King and one that, in its way, had perhaps helped to obscure what else she might have been doing in Splash One. "Well, how are they going to go about deciding the sentience question?"

"They're going to hold hearings in a few weeks, just as they did fifty years ago, what else?"

"Remind me what CHASE stands for."

"The Commission on Humans and Alien Sentience: Exploitation."

"Are they going to try to prove human sentience first?" She choked with laughter. "I've had some question about that recently. I have a few nominees for no sentience at all, starting with the Governor."

"Hush, child. You make treasonous utterance. The Governor's stepson is chairman of the commission. Ymries Fedder. He named the commission, I understand."

"Oh, yes. Honeypeach's son." It seemed appropriate to say nothing more, and she contented herself with quirking one eyebrow at Link. He quirked back and she sighed. As always, they understood each other precisely. As always, she ached to hold him. As always, she mourned for him, longed for him. And as always, she kept a cheerful face and let none of it show. He had been in that chair for five years, ever since the trip on which an unexplored Presence blew with Link directly in the way. He should have died, would have died except for Don. Afterward he had accused her of sentencing him to life imprisonment, and she had offered to help him out of it. No Explorer could do less, no lover more. The offer still stood. He had not taken her up on it yet. Thank God.

And as always when she saw him, her mind went frantic, trying to think of a way for a rather minor employee of the Department of Exploration to lay hands on something like a hundred thousand chits. Which is roughly what it would cost to get Link to Serendipity and pay for regeneration of his legs. Half that amount would import a set of bio-prostheses, which would at least let him walk!

No sense thinking about it. She'd thought about it before. Ten years' salary. Damn BDL and their priorities! Brou first, everything else second. And the Explorer Kings, who should be fighting for medical care as part of the contract, seemed content to piddle around with the amenities package. She kept her face calm, crying inside.

Two hours went by and she looked at the comp on her wrist. "Got to run, Link. In one hour I've got a date with my niece, remember her? Fabian? With the Planetary Welfare Office."

"I saw Fabian just last week. She came into the Governor's office for something or other . . . what was it? Oh, I remember. She's working on a settlement plan for the fringe people who get left behind when various military personnel are transferred out-system."

"Fringe people?"

"Ah . . . what shall we say. Unofficial dependents. Uncontracted spouses. The troopers bring them in. Then when they ship out, they decide for one reason or another to go unencumbered."

"Unofficial divorce."

"In a manner of speaking. Kids, too, of course."

"Bastards," she said, with feeling. "Link. Thanks for the drinks." She took his hand in her own, casually, squeezed it, only for a moment, smiled and rose.

"Donatella!" He called her back. "You forgot your bag."

She returned to the Chapter House to shower and change her clothes, entering by the back door and slipping up the stairs when no one was watching, not furtively, simply as though in a hurry. She had no particular wish to explain her unattractive garb to anyone, least of all Blanchet. By the time he arrived with the drink she ordered, she was showered and dressed for dinner, albeit less spectacularly than on the previous night.

"Did you have good visits with your friends?"

"Cousin Cyndal is not really a friend," she confessed with every semblance of candor. "Cousin Cyndal is a pain in the downspout. However, if I don't see her when I'm here, my mother doesn't let me forget it. Seeing Link Emert is also a pain, of a different kind. I keep remembering him the way he was before the accident."

"Ah." Blanchet was sympathetic. "Well, you'll enjoy the evening more, perhaps."

"Oh, Lord," she replied, "I hope so. It's always good to see Fabian. She's fun."

And Fabian was. She told stories of the "fringe people" that made Don alternately laugh and cry; made outrageous conversation with the waiters who delivered their crisp cooked vegetables, wonderfully flavored with strips of broiled fish and fowl; and ended the evening in reminiscences and general conversation. As they left the restaurant, Don said, "Damn, I forgot my bag again," and Fabian laughed. "You always have, every time I've ever been with you, so I picked it up for you. Here."

And back to her room again, duty done. Same procedure with the purse as last night. It was the first chance she had had.

The note was in the bag. Under the bedcovers she read the tiny letters.

"Note received. Terree's brother, Tasmin Ferrence, said to be on way to 'Soilcoast. Has music box. I will contact. Careful."

And the curvy line that made the signature. Chain, or CHAIN, if one wanted to be accurate. The investigative and enforcement arm of the PEC, that was CHAIN. Donatella spent a futile moment wishing that CHAIN was indeed present on Jubal, in force, rather than merely represented by one fairly powerless former employee.

Back to the note. Careful. What did that mean? Careful. Of course she was careful.

Still, the single word appended to the note made her uneasy. Instead of falling immediately asleep as she usually did—as all Explorers did if they wished to be properly concentrated on each day's task—she squirmed restlessly in the noisy dark, staring at the lights from the saloon-cum-amusement park across the street. Refracted through the beveled glass of her windows, the lights made red-purple lines across her bed. There were the sounds of a crowd outside, little muffled by the closed windows. The bustle of people moving along the avenue, shouts of revelry and of annoyance, replies, laughing or threatening or haranguing. Like those fanatics. She remembered the burning Crystallite, eyeballs crisping through a curtain of fire, and set the thought aside with a shudder. Think of something else. Think of Link. Link with his face so carefully controlled. No accusations. Not for years. And yet she would be lying to herself if she thought he had adapted.

Of course he hadn't. He was still the same Link, trapped, trapped forever, and she as trapped without him.

If only. If only she had a hundred thousand chits. If only she could get a hundred thousand chits. He deserved it. BDL owed it to him.

She could not rest. She was not even sleepy. If she had been even drowsy, she might not have heard the sound, so tiny a noise, a click where a click didn't belong.

At the window in the bathroom. Opening on an airshaft, as she recalled. Three stories up.

She did not wait for the click to be repeated. Explorers did not wait. Those who waited, died. Instead, she rolled out of the bed, heaping the covers into a vaguely body-shaped roll behind her, and stood behind the open bathroom door. She had no weapon. A mental inventory of the room yielded nothing of use. The bathroom now, yes. There were useful things there. Spray flasks of various things: dry-wash, antiperspirant, depilatory. She visualized where she had left them, the dry-wash on the edge of the bath, set aside, not useful here in Splash One where there was plenty of water. The antiperspirant was in the cabinet. The depilatory was on the back of the convenience, where she had sat to do her legs and the back of her neck. An almost full bottle.

The click was repeated, this time with a solidly chunking sound as though something had given way. The latch on the bathroom window, no doubt. She began to breathe quietly, deeply. Whoever was breaking in would listen for that. Deeply. Regularly. Breathe.

The figure came through the bathroom door so silently that she almost missed it. Only the movement across the bars of light betrayed it. On feet as silent, she slipped around the door and into the bathroom, feeling for the flask, the barest touch, not wanting to make a sound. She picked it up carefully, her face turned toward the room, trying to see in the intermittent flares of livid light.

The figure was at the bed. It leaned forward, reaching. No knife this time. Something else. A growl, almost like an animal as it realized she wasn't there. It turned toward the switch, and suddenly the room was flooded with light. The hooded figure spun around, saw her, lunged toward her, and she sprayed the depilatory full in its eyes, falling sideways as she did so.

It made no sound except a gagging spit. It kept coming, blindly, reaching for the place she had moved toward. Bigger than she. Stronger, too, most likely. It was like a deadly game of feely-find. The creature couldn't see, but it could hear her. She went across the bed in a wild scramble, then out the door into the hall, leaving it open. The stairwell was directly ahead of her. She breathed, "No, no, don't," just loudly enough to be heard, then stepped sideways and knelt by the wall. As the maddened figure rushed toward her voice, she stuck out her foot, and the careening shape plunged over it, headfirst down the stairs. Don darted back into her room and shut the door.

The crashing sound brought colleagues and visitors out into the hall. Don joined them, sleepily tying the belt of her robe. "What was that noise? Did you hear it? What happened?" Voices from below were raised in incredulous excitement.

A man. Must have fallen down the stairs. No, a man's body. He's dead.

What was he doing in the Chapter House? Did anyone know him?

Why was he dressed that way?

A thief? Who would rob a Chapter House? Explorers didn't carry valuables.

The excited interchange bubbled on while Don half hung across the bannister, staring at the black lump on the floor below. Someone had removed the mask, and a blankly anonymous face stared up at her with dead and ruined eyes. Someone who had known where she was. Someone who had known she was alone. How fortuitous for someone that the intruder had broken his neck. Now no one could ask him who had sent him.

6

Three mule riders approaching Splash One early one morning from the direction of the Mad Gap would have been enough to attract the attention of the locals. Three mule riders followed by a small swarm of Crystallites, all of whom were hooting, cursing, and throwing mud, was enough not only to attract attention but to bring the nearest military detachment into overwhelming action. The Crystallites were promptly face down in the mud they had been using as ammunition, their hands and feet locked behind them, and tranquilizer guns were being applied unstintingly to various exposed portions of their anatomies.

"Sorry about that," the Captain in command of the group said to Tasmin, offering him a clean towel from the riot wagon. "They're getting worse all the time. If the Governor doesn't act soon, our commanding officer, Colonel Lang, probably will. Hope it won't be too late."

"How late would it have to be to be too late?" asked Clarin in a bitter voice, trying to get the mud out of her curly hair with scant success. "That last mud ball had a rock in it." A red lump the size of a hen's egg was rising on her forehead, and she looked as disheveled as she did angry. "Our Master, here, preferred we not use our whips on them."

"I saw your troop coming," Tasmin said to the officer in a mild voice. "I thought we could outrun them until you arrived."

Jamieson was regarding the prone figures vindictively, running his quirt through his hands. Tripsinger mules were so well trained it would be unthinkable to use quirts on them; the device was merely costume. Despite this, Jamieson's intent could be read in his face.

"They'd love it if you took the whip to 'em," the Captain said, gesturing his permission. "Do, if it'll make you feel better. They consider that quite a mark of holiness, being beaten on. That's why we use the trank-guns. They hate that. Keep 'em tranked up for ten days or so, force feed 'em, then turn 'em loose fatter than they were. They just hate it." He spat reflectively, as Jamieson unobtrusively put the quirt out of sight. The officer held out his hand. "Name's Jines Verbold."

Tasmin took the proferred hand. "It's good to meet you, Captain Verbold. I'm Tripsinger Tasmin Ferrence. These are my two acolytes, Reb Jamieson and Renna Clarin."

The Captain nodded to each of them. "Did I misread something, Master Ferrence, or did you three just come down the hills from the Mad Gap?"

"We did. Is there something wrong with that?"

"I didn't know anybody could get through the Gap."

Tasmin expressed amazement. "I used an old, old Password, Captain. I suppose it could have been lost, though that's hard to believe. It's been in my library since my father's time, maybe even his father's. I think it's an original Erickson. It never occurred to me it wasn't generally known."

"Well, that'll be news to please some people I know of. They've had people trying the Gap, trottin' up there and then trottin' down again, for about the last year."

"It's those crazy key shifts in the PJ," said Clarin thoughtfully as she rummaged in one pocket. Something moved beneath her fingers, and she scratched it affectionately. "And those high trumpet sounds. They aren't anything you'd think of, normally."

"And how Erickson thought of them, God knows," laughed Tasmin. He felt a rush of sudden elation. Despite the mud-flinging fanatics, the incident was an omen, a favorable omen. Things were going to go right in Splash One. He was going to find out everything he needed to know. The weight of mystery would be lifted. There would be no more questions. He turned to the acolytes, wondering if they felt as euphoric as he did to be at the end of the journey.

Jamieson evidently felt something. The boy's face shone with interest as he looked down onto the city. During their travels, he seemed to have become less preoccupied with the girl he had left behind and increasingly interested in where they were going and what they were doing. Or perhaps it was the girl who was with them, although Tasmin had not seen him make any obvious move in her direction. Still . . . pro-pinquity. An excellent remedy for absent friends, propinquity—although it would be hard to know whether Jamieson had been encouraged or not, Clarin being so self-contained. She was an inveterate pettifier—Tasmin would have bet she had a crystal mouse in her pocket right now, one she'd caught stealing food from the camp. She was friendly and always thoughtful, but cool. Tasmin had come to appreciate her during this trip. He approved of her restrained manner, her calm and undemanding demeanor, though he did so without ever considering what that approval implied.

"I said," the officer repeated, breaking in on Tasmin's thoughts, "I said, where are you staying?"

"The citadel," he replied, almost without thinking. Where else would a Tripsinger stay but there, among his own kind? "If they have room for us."

"Do you know your way there?"

"Not really. I've been in Splash One before, but it was years ago, when I did a lot of trips to the Coast." This city looked nothing like the smallish town he remembered. This city swarmed, bubbled, erupted with ebbs and flows of citizenry, trembled with noise. "Thank God for one hundred meters of Deepsoil," he murmured only half-aloud, inter-cepting Clarin's empathetic glance.

"It's amazing, isn't it?" she agreed. "I saw it two years ago on my way down from Northwest to Deepsoil Five. I think it's doubled in size since then."

"Well, it's enough changed that I'm going to send a man with you as a guide," the Captain told them. "There are Crystallites in the city, too, and they consider anyone in Tripsinger robes as targets of opportunity. I'm in charge of a stockade of troublemakers, a whole disciplinary barracks full, and I swear they're less trouble than these damn fanatics. I suggest you leave the mules in the citadel stables after this and wear civilian clothes in town. It's not foolproof protec-tion, since they may recognize your faces, but it'll help."

"What are we allowed to do," Jamieson asked, "to pro-tect ourselves?"

"Anything you bloody well can," Verbold replied. "Up to and including killin' a few of 'em. Like I said, once the

Governor gets off his rounded end, we'll have a clearance order on 'em and that'll put an end to it."

"Clearance order?" Clarin asked.

"For the maintenance of public safety, yes, Ma'am. The relocation camp's already built, down the Coast about ten miles. Power shielded and pretty much escape proof. Put 'em in there and let 'em have at each other if they have to have at somebody. Everyone knows it has to be done. What's keeping his excellency is beyond us—all of us. Somethin' devious no doubt." He pulled a face, begging their complicity. It had not been a politically astute thing to say.

"Any rumors about the delay?" Jamieson demanded.

"Oh, there's always rumors," the Captain said, turning away brusquely. He had said too much. Besides, they knew what the rumors were: The Governor was being given a share of the pilgrimage money; he was being paid off by the fanatics.

Tasmin shook his head at Jamieson, and he subsided. Tasmin did not want to discuss planetary politics or the Planetary Exploitation Council here on the public way, surrounded by soldiers who might repeat anything that was said, in or out of context, accurately or not. What the Captain chose to say was the Captain's own business, but Tasmin had a lifelong habit of caution. He leaned from the saddle to take the officer's hand once more. "Thank you, Captain. I'll tell the Master General of the citadel how helpful you've been." The Master General of the Splash One Citadel was also the Grand Master of the Tripsinger Order, Thyle Vowe. Favorable mention to Vowe was not an inconsiderable favor, and the Captain grinned as he stepped back and saluted them on their way.

They reached the citadel without further incident, were welcomed, then lauded when it became known that Tasmin had come down from the Mad Gap with a long lost Password. There was good-natured teasing of the citadel librarian, some not so good-natured responses from that official, followed by room assignments for the travelers, provision for cleaning the clothes they had with them, and obtaining more anonymous garments to be worn in town. Grand Master Thyle Vowe, it seemed, was at the Northwest Citadel and would not return for some days. Tasmin wrote a note, including some laudatory words about Captain Verbold—including his probable political sympathies—and left it for him. It was late afternoon before all the details were taken care of and Tasmin could get away.

The two acolytes were lounging in the courtyard, obviously waiting for him, Clarin, predictably, with a gray-furred crystal mouse—so called because its normal habitat was among the crystal presences—running back and forth on her shoulder.

"Private business," Tasmin said, trying to be more annoyed than he actually was. Now that the time had come, he was having a fit of nerves, and the false hostility in his voice grated even upon his own ears.

"No, sir," said Clarin, apparently unmoved as she pocketed the mouse. "You've told us all about it, and we need to go with you. We can help you find Lim Terree's manager or agent or whatever he is." She was saying no more than the truth. In the long evenings over the campfire, they had learned more about one another than any of them would have shared in the stratified society of the citadel. They were almost family—with the responsibility that entailed.

Tasmin, suddenly aware of that responsibility, found that it made him irritable. "I can do that alone." Could he? Did he want to?

"You might be set upon, Master. We've inquired. It's best for Tripsingers to go in company, so the Master General of this citadel has ordered." Jamieson was factual, a little brusque, avoiding Tasmin's eyes. With sudden insight, Tasmin realized the boy was not speaking out of mere duty and would be wounded if he were rebuffed.

He took refuge in brusqueness of his own. "I hope you two haven't been chirping."

"Master Ferrence!" The boy was hurt at being accused of being loose mouthed.

Jamieson's pain shamed Tasmin for his lack of courtesy, and he gritted his teeth. "Did you get a car?"

"Yes, sir. That greenish one over there."

"Looks well used, doesn't it?" The vehicle appeared to have been used to haul hay, or perhaps farm animals; it sagged; the bubble top was scratched into gray opacity.

"Well, there were only two to choose from, and the other one was pink." Jamieson gave him a sidelong glance, assaying a smile of complicity, still with that expression of strain.

Tasmin flushed. Did he have the right to reject friendship when it was offered? Was he so determined upon his hurt he would hurt others to maintain the appearance of grief? He reached out to lay his hand on Jamieson's shoulder, including Clarin in his glance. "If you're so damned set on being helpful. . . ." Tasmin had already made a few calls from his room, locating one of the backup men Lim had had with him in Deepsoil Five and obtaining from him the name of Lim's agent. "We're looking for a man named Larry Porsent, and we're supposed to find him in the Bedlowe Building, Eleventh Street and Jubilation Boulevard." Under his hand, Jamieson relaxed.

The streets were scarred with new and half-healed trenches; the building they sought was under construction with the first two floors occupied even while all the turmoil of fabrication went on above. They dodged hod carriers and bricklayers and representatives of half a dozen other construction specialties as they climbed the stairs to the second floor.

"When do you suppose they'll start putting lifts in these buildings," Jamieson complained. "I've done nothing in this city yet but climb stairs. They've got Clarin and me in dormitories five flights up."

"They'll put in lifts when lift mechanisms are defined as essential," Tasmin said indifferently. He had been given a pleasant suite on the second floor of the citadel, overlooking a walled garden. "Or when there gets to be enough demand to fabricate them locally. Right now, it takes tenth place behind a lot of other needed supplies like medical equipment and farm machinery and computers. There's the office."

The name was painted in lopsided letters on a raw, new door. Inside they found the tenant crouched on the floor, trying to assemble a desk. He was a short, plump man with a polished pink face that gleamed with sweat and annoyance as he tried to fit a part into a slot that obviously would not hold it. "Larry Porsent," he introduced himself, clambering to his feet with some difficulty. "What can I do for you."

"I'm Tasmin Ferrence."

"Yes." There was no indication the man recognized the name.

"I'm Lim Terree's brother."

The man scowled. "I'll be damned. Really? I didn't know he had a brother. Didn't know he had any kin at all. Except his wife, of course, and the kid."

"Wife!"

"Well, sure. You mean you didn't know? Well, of course you didn't know or you wouldn't be surprised, right. I'm kind of slow on the launch today. Not my day. Not my season, if you want the truth. Perigee time. Lim's death just about finished me off."

"He was a major client?"

"He was damn near my only client. He wanted all my time, and I gave it to him. Would've worked out fine, too, if he hadn't gone crazy. I mean, since you're his brother and kin and all—these your kids? Nice lookin' kids. Why in the name of good sense would a man take every credit he's saved up in ten years and spend everything he's got settin' up a tour of the dirt towns! You can't make that pay. Everybody knows you can't make it pay. I told him. I told his wife, Vivian, and she told him." He ran both hands through his thinning hair, then thrust them out as though to beg understanding. "Why would a man do that?"

"You mean, the tour to Deepsoil Five wasn't a financial success?"

"Hell, man, no tour to the dirt towns is a financial success! They're always a dead loss. Only time we do 'em, ever, is if BDL banks 'em for us. I mean, any of us, any agent, any performer. BDL pays it out every now and then, just for the goodwill, but there's no audience there. How much can you make, stacked up against what it costs to get there?"

Jamieson asked, "You're telling us that Lim Terree used his own money to pay for the trip?"

"Everything he had. Down to the house and his kid's savings fund. And since you're his brother, I can show you a few bills that didn't get paid if you're interested in clearing his good name."

Tasmin shook his head, dizzied by this spate of unexpected information. "Lim had a very expensive comp on his wrist when I saw him last."

"He did, indeed. And I wish I had it now. That was a gift, that was. Guess who from? Honeypeach herself. The

Governor's lady." He spat the word. "Poor old Lim couldn't
sell it or he was dead. He couldn't lose it or he was dead. All
he could do was wear it and try to stay out of her bed. People
that upset Honeypeach end up buried. She's a crystal-rat,
that one. Teeth like a Jammling, and she wanted to eat him."

"Terree's wife," Clarin said, sympathetically aware of
Tasmin's confusion. "Where would we find her?"

"You'll find her at home, such as it is, over the fish
market, down at the south end. Or you'll find her in the
market, guttin' and scalin'. She and the kid have to eat, and
Lim sure left her without the wherewithal. She left a registered job with the Exploration records office to have Lim's
kid, and they sure won't take her back. . . ."

"I may have some other questions," Tasmin said, shaking
his head. "Right now I'm too confused by all this to know.
We can find you here daytimes?"

"If I can make it through the next few days, you can. I've
got a few comers lined up. One of 'em's bound to break orbit.
None of 'em are Lim Terree, though, I'll tell you that. He
was a genius. A damned genius. He could do more with a
music box than any other three people. If you find out what
made him crazy, I wish you'd let me know." He dropped to
his knees and began working on the assembly once more,
oblivious to their departure.

In the car there was a careful silence. Tasmin was trying
to fit what he had just learned into the structure he had
postulated, and it did not fit. A pennyless Lim Terree. A man
who had told the truth when he said he hadn't the funds to
help Tasmin with their mother's needs. Why?

"Do you know where the fish market is, Reb?"

The boy flushed with pleasure. Tasmin seldom addressed
him by his sobriquet. "Clarin and I studied the city map for a
while. I think I can find it."

He did find it, after several false turns, although finding
a place to put the car was another thing. The market was long
and narrow, extending across the length of the fish farms and
the fleet moorings. The wares on display included both native
and farmed out-system fish, finned and shelled and naked
skinned. Though Jubal had a paucity of land life—a few
small animals like viggies, a few birdlike and insectlike
creatures—its shallow oceans burgeoned with species, and

the rainbow harvest made up most of the protein needs of the human inhabitants. They struggled through the crowd toward the south end of the market, asking as they went for Vivian Terree.

Tasmin knew her as soon as he saw her. She was so like old pictures of his mother that she could have been related by blood. That same triangular face, the same deeply curved and oddly shaped mouth in which the lower lip appeared to be only half as long as the upper one, giving her a curiously exotic appearance. That same long, silvery hair—though Vivian wore it braided and pinned to keep it out of her way. Lim must have been attracted by that unbelievable resemblance.

"Vivian?" Tasmin asked.

She pushed a wisp of hair from her forehead with one wrist, keeping the bloody fingers extended. Her other hand held a curved knife. "Yes?"

"I'd like to talk with you, if you have a minute."

"I don't have a minute. I don't have any time at all. They don't like us having conversations while we're supposed to be working." Her face and voice were so full of worry and pain there was no room for curiosity.

"I can wait until after work. My name's Tasmin Ferrence. I'm Lim's brother."

She stared at him, her eyes gradually filling with tears. The knife hand trembled, as though it wanted to make some other and more forceful gesture. "Damn you," she said in a grating whisper. "Damn you to hell."

In his shock, Tasmin could not move. Clarin stepped between them as though she had rehearsed the movement. "Don't say that, Vivian. I don't know why you would say that. Tasmin was only a boy when his brother left home, and he doesn't know any reason for you to say anything like that. See. Look at his face. He doesn't know. Whatever it is, he doesn't know."

The woman was crying, her shoulders heaving. Tasmin straightened, looked around to meet the eyes of an officious and beefy personage stalking in his direction. He moved to meet this threat. "Are you the supervisor here?"

The man began to bluster. Tasmin drew himself up. "I am Tripsinger Tasmin Ferrence. I am on official business for the citadel. I need to talk to this woman, Vivian Terree, and I intend to do so. You can either cooperate or I can report your lack of cooperation to the citadel. The choice is entirely up to you."

The bluster changed to a whine, the whine to a slobber. Tasmin left him in midcringe. "Clarin, find out where we can talk."

Vivian led them out of the market and around to the rear where a flight of rickety stairs took them to the second floor. The tiny apartment was as splintery and dilapidated as the stairs, with narrow windows that did nothing to ventilate the scantily furnished two rooms or ameliorate the overwhelming stench of fish.

The baby was playing quietly in a crib. A boy child, about two or a little older. He turned to look at them curiously as they entered, holding up his arms to his mother. "D'ink."

"Lim's son?"

"Lim's. Of course." She filled a cup and held it to the baby's lips. "Little Miles."

The name came as a shock. Named after their father? Lim's and Tasmin's father?

"Lim didn't live here?" Tasmin fumbled.

"*We* didn't live here. We had a house, a nice house, on the rocks over the bay. There was a little beach for Miles to play on. Lim borrowed against it."

Miles? "You lost it?"

"I guess I never really had it." She turned on him, glaring. "We would have had it if he hadn't done that crazy thing. He borrowed against the house. Against everything we had. A hundred-day note. Due and payable at the Old Moon. He was dead by then." She leaned over the child, weeping.

Tasmin looked at Clarin, pleadingly.

"Let me take the baby out on the stairs," she said to Vivian. "You and Tasmin need to talk." She went out with Jamieson, and he could hear them playing a rhyme game on the landing while the sea birds shrieked overhead.

"Vivian. I don't . . . I don't know why Lim did that. His agent told me about it. I don't understand it."

"He had to get to you."

"To me? I hadn't even seen him in fifteen years! I wrote to him and he didn't even answer!"

"You wrote to ask him for money. Why should he send money to you!"

Tasmin bit back the obvious answer, controlled himself.

"Vivian, I don't know why. Mother was in need; I thought Lim was making it with both hands."

"Let your damned father take care of her!"

"He died. Years ago. Not long after Lim left." After Lim had left, Miles Ferrence had almost seemed to court disaster.

She was shaking. "Dead?" She got up, moved into the next room. Tasmin could hear water running. In a moment she returned. Her hands and face were wet. She had washed off the fish blood. "Dead?" she asked again.

"Why does it matter?"

"I suppose it doesn't, now. Everything he went through. Trying to prove himself to that rotten old man!"

"You didn't even know him!"

"I know about him." She began to weep again. "He was . . . he was terrible. Oh, God, he hurt Lim so."

"Well, Lim hurt him."

"Later. Later Lim hurt him. Later Lim tried to. To get even a little. Because it didn't seem to matter. Poor Lim."

"I don't understand."

"How old are you?" she asked suddenly, eyes flashing.

"Thirty-two."

She counted, shaking her head. "Lim was thirty-seven, almost thirty-eight. He was only twelve when it happened. So, you were only seven. Maybe you didn't know. I guess you didn't." She bent forward, weeping again.

"Vivian, please. Talk to me. I don't know what happened. I don't know what you're saying. Yes, my father was a very unpleasant person sometimes. Yes, I think he was harder on Lim than he was on me because Lim was older."

"Hard! I could forgive it if he'd just been hard."

"I don't know what you're talking about. I'd like to understand, but I don't. I just don't."

"You really don't know?"

"I really don't know."

She got up, wiping her eyes, and wandered around the room, picking things up, putting them down again. She went to the door and looked out at the child, sitting on Jamieson's lap being patty-caked by Clarin. The mouse was on her shoulder once more, and the baby couldn't decide what to look at, Clarin's hands or the little animal.

"When Lim was twelve," Vivian said, "he went to choir school."

Tasmin nodded. All Tripsingers and would-be Tripsingers went to choir school.

"There was this man, the assistant choir master. Lim told me his name was Jobson. Martin Jobson."

"The name doesn't mean anything to me, Vivian."

"He was probably long gone by the time you . . . Well, he was one of those men—what do you call it?" She paused, her face very pale. "A man who screws little boys?"

Tasmin ran his tongue around a suddenly dry mouth. "You mean a pedophile?"

"He did it to Lim."

"Oh, Lord. How awful . . . "

"He could have gotten over that I think. He really could. He said he could have gotten over that, and I believe him. But Lim went home and told his father, your father."

Tasmin shut his eyes, visualizing that confrontation. She did not need to go on. He knew what she would say.

"Your father told him it must have been his fault, Lim's. Your father said he must have asked for it. Invited it. Seduced the man, somehow. Your father told him he was ruined. Debauched. That's the word Lim always said, debauched. He told Lim he was filthy. Perverted. That he couldn't love him anymore."

"No," Tasmin murmured, knowing it was true. "Oh, no."

"Your father had this viggy he was going to give Lim, and he gave it to you instead. Because you were a good boy. Pure, he said."

"My viggy . . . "

"Lim let it loose. If he couldn't have it, he wouldn't let you have it either. He went crazy, he said. He heard the viggy singing to him, words he could understand, like a dream. He had delusions. After that . . . after that it didn't matter what he did. He was already ruined. That's what he thought. . . . "

"So when he ran away. . . . "

"He was just getting even. A little."

"Ah." It was a grunt. As though he had been kicked in the stomach. He got up and went to the door, moved outside it onto the narrow porch, and bent over the railing. The blue-purple of the bay stretched away to the headlands on either side, and beyond the bay, the ocean. At the limit of his vision he could see the towering buoys of the Splash site. Star ships came down there. Ships whose thunder was cushioned from the planet by an enormous depth of ocean. Things came and went, but the foundations of the world remained unshaken.

Unlike men whose foundations trembled when new things came upon them. Unlike brothers, when they learned the loved and despised was not despised at all and had not been loved enough.

"God," he said. It was a prayer.

"Master?" Jamieson stood beside him, his hand out, his face intent with concern.

"I'm all right." He moved back into the shabby room. "Vivian. I'll help. I'll help you all I can. You and the baby."

"How?"

"I don't know. Not just yet. But I will help. Would you go to Deepsoil Five? My mother would make you very welcome there . . . no! Don't look like that. She didn't know. I swear to you, she did not know. My father . . . he was a cruel man in many ways, Vivian, but neither she nor I knew anything about what you've told me. Lim never told us." He put his arms around her.

"He still loved his father," she said, weeping. "And he was ashamed."

Clarin came in with containers of hot tea, obtained from a vendor down in the bustle. Jamieson went out and returned with crisply fried chunks of fish, the chortling baby high on his shoulders, exclaiming, "Fiss, 'ot fiss." Both the acolytes inspected Tasmin as though for signs of illness or damage, and he made an attempt at a smile to reassure them. They were not reassured.

They sat without speaking for a time. Eventually, Vivian said something about the baby, her face softening as she said it.

Tasmin asked, "Do you know what Lim was doing, Vivian? Why he did it?"

"He had to get to you," she replied. "That's all I really

know. He needed something by Don Furz, and you had it.
And he told me if he could get that, we'd be wealthy. His
family would be proud of him, and we'd be wealthy."

"Nothing else? Only that?"

"That's all. It was a secret, he said. A terrible secret."

She knew nothing more. They left her there, promising
to return. Tasmin gave her what money he had with him,
enough to last a few days. "Don't go back to the market," he
told her. "You don't need to do that."

On the way to the car he fished in his pocket, bringing
Celcy's earclip out at last. He stood by the car, staring at it
for a long moment. All he had left of her. All.

"Jamieson."

"Sir?"

"You're a clever fellow, Reb. Somewhere in all this mess
there will be someone who buys gems. I paid four hundred
for a pair of these. Firestones are more valuable here than
they are in the interior. You ought to be able to get at least a
hundred for this one clip, just on the value of the stones. That's
enough to buy passage for a woman and a child, isn't it?"

It was Clarin who replied. "Yes, Sir. More than enough."
There was an ache in her voice, but Tasmin did not notice it.
She was fighting herself not to put her arms around him, but
he did not notice that either. His face was so tired and bleak,
she would have done anything at all to comfort him. The best
she could do was do nothing.

"Can you do that, too?" Tasmin asked. "Get passage.
Earliest possible trip with someone reliable. On the Southern
Route, I think. It's longer, but there hasn't been a fatality on
that route for quite a while."

"Yes, Sir." Jamieson and Clarin shared what Tasmin had
come to identify as "a look."

"I'm all right. You heard the whole thing from the stairs,
I know. It's . . . well, it's a shock to find someone you've—"

"Hated?" Clarin tilted her head to one side, examining
him through compassionate eyes.

"I guess. It's a shock to find someone you've hated didn't
deserve it. It turns the blame inward."

"No more your fault than his," said Clarin, blinking
rapidly. "Excuse me, Sir, but your father must have been a
bastard."

"He was." Tasmin sighed. "In many ways he was, Clarin, he was."

"And then what?" asked Jamieson. "Shall we go back on the same trip?"

"Go back?" he shook his head, for a moment wondering what the boy was talking about. "To Deepsoil Five? Of course not, Jamieson. The mystery is still there, isn't it? I still don't know what Lim was doing. I still don't know why Celcy died!"

"Where next, Sir?"

"To Don Furz. That's the only clue we have left."

Donatella Furz returned to the Chapter House at Northwest late in the afternoon of the agreed-upon day, having come up the coast in a small BDL transport ship and inland from there in a provisions truck. Zimmy would be expecting her, undoubtedly with something special set up by way of dinner and amusement. She needed him, needed to talk to him. Events of the past three days had been as confusing as they were frightening. She kept thinking of Gretl, even though what was happening to her was nothing like what had happened to Gretl except in its atmosphere of obdurate menace. At the moment of peril she had had no time to be frightened. Only afterward, considering it, thinking how close to death she had come both times, did the cold sweat come on her and her stomach knot.

Now she had to confide in someone. Someone close. Who else could it be but Zimmy? She found herself rehearsing the conversation she would have with him, his exclamations of concern. He already knew about Gretl—everyone at the Priory knew about Gretl—he'd understand her fear. Even thinking of telling him made her feel better, as though the very fact she could share her troubles and dangers somehow lessened them. If she could trust anyone, she could trust him. Even though she hadn't told him anything yet, she would now. She had to be able to talk to someone!

Zimmy, however, was not waiting for her.

She didn't want to make an undignified spectacle of herself over the man—he was a services employee, after all, and the Explorer King had said enough on that score already—so she showered and changed and went down to the common room for a drink and the odd bit of chitchat. Chase Random Hall was in his usual place, a high backed chair with the unmistakable air of a throne. She nodded in his direction and received a nod in return.

"All well, Don?" he called, bringing every eye in the room to rest on her.

Damn the man. "All well, Randy," she returned with a brilliant smile. "The doctor says I'll live." She circulated, exchanging the gossip of Splash One for the gossip of Northwest. The evening meal was announced, and still no Zimmy. Now she began to worry, just a little. Had he forgotten the date of her return? He would be full of apologies and consternation if that was the case, busy taking little digs at himself. Or had something happened to him? She turned away from the thought. It was enough that people were trying to kill her; surely there was no reason for anyone to try to kill Zimmy. Of course, there were always accidents.

"I don't see Zimble around," she said to her dinner mate.

"Zimmy? Oh, he went out. Let's see, I saw him go out the little gate about midafternoon. Shopping, he said, and then an amateur show with friends."

"Ah." She kept her voice carefully casual. "After what I saw in Splash One, I grow concerned about any absent face." The conversation switched to Gretl Mechas, and she quickly changed the subject. They talked of Crystallites, suspected and proven, and she remained puzzled. He must have forgotten. Though Zimmy usually didn't forget. Not anything. He was the kind of man who remembered every word of conversations held years before; the kind of man who sent greetings on obscure anniversaries; the kind of man who kept gift shops in business. He had a little notebook full of people's birthdays. This minor talent, or vice, would have made him merely a sycophantic niggler were it not for his humor and charm. No, she could not imagine Zimmy forgetting.

She was in the lounge at a corner table, half hidden by her table mates, when he returned. She saw him in the hallway, checking the message board. Ralth was halfway through a complicated story that she chose not to interrupt, so she did not call out or make any gesture, but merely noticed Zimmy from under her lowered lids. Zimmy turned, his mobile face twisted into a laughing response to someone's remark.

And saw her.

Don let her lids drop closed, frightened at what she had surprised in his face. Shock. Shock and astonishment. He had not expected to see her here. He had not expected to see her anywhere. She gasped and put a hand to her throat, not looking up. Something hard pressed up. She gulped.

"Don? What's the matter?" Ralth was looking at her with concern.

"I swallowed the wrong way. Got so intrigued by your story, I forgot to breathe." She laughed and looked up. There he was. Zimmy. Now he was beaming at her. Waving. If she hadn't seen him for that split second, she would have believed in his apparent pleasure at the sight of her. She waved back, as though she hadn't a care in the world.

Inside, a part of her screamed.

If he had not expected to see her at all, then he had expected her not to be here. Not to be anywhere. To be dead.

Zimmy. So. Well and yes, Donatella. He is a Chapter House man. A hired man. Here for your comfort. Did you think love would change all that? Did you think he loved you just because he said so? A hired man is a hired man, that is, a man who works for money, loves for money.

Who had paid him?

Ralth's story concluded to general and amused disbelief. She excused herself and went to greet Zimmy, hiding her inner turmoil, pretending. "Zimmy! Lord, it's good to be back. Splash One is a madhouse." Her throat was tight, but her voice sounded normal.

"You look all pale around the eyes, lovely. Why don't you go up and get into something more comfortable and I'll give you a nice backrub." He gave her a sly, sideways glance, code for something erotic. No, oh, no.

"Come on up," she said. "Just for a few minutes, though. I'm dead to the world. Couldn't sleep down there in Splash One. Too noisy." She was going on past him, walking up the stairs, still talking. "Zimmy, do you know what I saw?" She described the Crystallite immolation, shuddering dramatically. Once in the room, she sat on a chair and took her shoes off, motioning him to the other chair.

"Don't you want a nice backrub? You'd sleep better."

"Zimmy, old friend, I will tell you the exact truth. There was a man at the Splash One Chapter House you wouldn't believe." She described Blanchet, focusing on certain attributes of his that were only conjectural, hinted at surfeit of all things sexual, and concluded, "So I really just want to fall into bed. Alone."

His chin was actually quivering. Tears were hanging in the corners of his eyes. God, the man should be awarded a prize for drama. Donatella made herself lean forward, made herself pat him on the knee. "Oh, Zimmy. Come on now. It didn't mean anything. It wasn't like us. But I am tired. Run on, now. Don't let Randy see you being all upset or he'll give you a public lecture." She yawned, opened the door for him despite his pretty protestations, and locked it when he was out of earshot.

God. He was good. She had almost believed him. If it hadn't been for that one, split second. . . .

She would bet anything she owned that if he was not directly responsible for the attempts on her life, he was deeply involved.

Who did he work for? In this house, he worked for the manager of services. The manager of services worked for the Prior. The Prior worked for the head of the BDL Department of Exploration—what was that man's name, a new man. Bard Jimbit. Bard Jimbit worked for Harward Justin, Planetary Manager. All of them worked for BDL.

Or perhaps he worked for the Explorer King, unofficially, for Randy's position was one of honor, not actual authority. He had risen to that position, one of three or four current Explorers in various parts of Jubal to do so, through election by his peers. The Kings were elected to represent the Explorers in dealings with BDL, to conduct contract negotiations and resolve disputes. Kings were supposed to be nonpolitical, though everyone knew that a very political favor-trading process led to election. It was part of the whole ritual nonsense the order had been saddled with by Erickson. Theoretically, Don owed fealty to the King, fealty being anything from giving up her seat at dinner to going to bed with him if he demanded it. Chase Random Hall was too clever to cause ill feeling by demanding anything. He got what he wanted without demanding. Did he also want her dead?

Who did want her dead? How had Lim Terree actually died? In an accident? Or had he fallen to some black-hooded figure coming out of the night? She got up and checked the lock on the door, then wandered around the room, casually examining the walls and ceiling. Listening devices? Were there listening devices in the walls? Were there eyes? Had someone watched her in this room as she pored over Erickson's notes? Were those notes safe where she had hidden them in the closet, in the lining of her boots? It was an odd, unsettling feeling to search for spies here in Northwest. She had expected there to be eyes and ears in Splash One; she had not really thought there would be any here.

And why not?

Because this was home.

Who, here at home, had paid Zimmy?

Who, here at home, wanted her dead?

It was almost dawn before she fell asleep.

In the luxurious Executive Suite of the BDL building in Splash One, Chase Random Hall was the dinner guest of Harward Justin, Planetary Manager for BDL. They were not known to be friends, but Justin sometimes commented that he found the Explorer King a witty and amusing companion, whose views on the needs and desires of the Explorers were valuable to management.

At least, such was the overt reason Justin gave for their occasional get-togethers. The covert basis for their real relationship was one of mutual self-interest. Just now they were discussing the upcoming contract negotiations for the Explorers Guild.

"We'll start meeting next week on the new contract," Randy said, sniffing at his broundy glass. "I suppose you want me to go through the motions."

"I've heard the usual nonsense that the Explorers will demand increased medical care," Justin said in his heavy, humorless voice. Justin was a bulky, powerful-looking man of sinister calm. He never allowed himself to do anything that threatened that appearance in public, although his private pleasures were less restrained. His pleasures were indulged in by himself, but his angers were attended to by others, usually by his agent, Spider Geroan. "Very expensive medical care."

The Explorer King sought consultation from the bottom of his glass. "They're getting serious about it, Justin."

"Who is?"

"A good many of them. Our little friend Don Furz, for one. Her lover's still in that chair, you know. Five years now."

"She's only one person."

"There are others."

"Not many. Reprogram them onto the amenities issue again. It's a hell of a lot cheaper to pay for a few additional services employees than it is to ship people to Serendipity and pay for regeneration. Tell them about the progress we've already made. There's minor regeneration already available here on Jubal."

"We have machines only for things like eyes, fingers, wiping off scars. Doesn't mean much if you're missing a leg or an arm."

Justin scowled. "The Explorer contract is not going to make a damned bit of difference, Hall! Go through the motions." The threat in his voice was patent. "Tout them onto amenities and don't worry about it."

"So it won't make any difference," the King said. "Which means. . . ."

"Which means you should ask very few questions, Hall, and engage in no speculation at all."

Justin's voice was oily with malice, but the King chose not to hear it. "The Governor is leaving it perilously late."

"Moving against the Crystallites, you mean?" Justin made a cynical smirk. The Governor was doing what Justin had told him to do. "He may want a major incident."

"He'll get it. It's inevitable."

"He may feel that he must have something irrefutable, unarguable. A notorious assassination, perhaps. Something to justify the forceful use of troops." Justin tilted the glass and drank the last drop of broundy, then touched the button that would summon one of the mute and deaf waiters who served the Executive Suite.

"Presumably the CHASE group can't start hearings until the Crystallites have been moved into the relocation camp?"

"They'll be moved in time, just before CHASE is ready to meet. The Governor's stepson, Ymries Fedder, will be chairman." Justin was not quite happy about this, but there had been some necessary favor trading in the ivory halls of PEC. Governor Wuyllum Thonks had friends there, though Justin could not imagine why.

The King mused, "I presume the findings are already determined. The commission will find there is no reason to believe any sentience exists in the Presences. . . ."

"After which event," Justin said with a chilly and ruthless smile, "I think we would find we have more economical access to the interior than we've had heretofore."

There was an appreciative silence. "The Tripsingers are going to be very upset," said the King. "To say nothing of the Explorers."

"Do you really care?" Justin asked carelessly.

"Each time I check the balance in my account on Serendipity, I care less." He made circles on the table with his glass. Hall felt broundy was an overrated drink. The effect was pleasant, but the taste left much to be desired. He preferred fruit-based liquors, imported ones. "The account comes to a very nice sum. For which I should continue to give my best efforts. And that brings me back to Donatella Furz."

"You've brought her up before. What are you suggesting, Randy? That she has uncovered some cache of secrets? That she has discovered The Password? That she has arrived at some fundamental truth that has eluded the rest of us?" Justin shook his head and leaned back in his chair, accepting a full glass from a blank-faced servitor.

"Oh, unload it, Justin. You understand well enough what I'm worried about. If she has learned something basic to do with language, with sentience, we're slashed off. You, me, all of BDL."

Harward lifted a nostril. Foolish man to think his little worries had not been anticipated by those both more intelligent and more powerful than he. Foolish little man. Still, he

made his voice sympathetic as he said, "Has she said anything to indicate that is true?"

The King thought for a time, then shook his head reluctantly. "No. I have a man very close to her, and he says she's
got something, but she's been chary. He has no proof of what
it is, not yet."

"Well then?" Harward allowed himself a tiny sneer.

"She was wounded a few trips ago. A bad slash on her
arm."

"Not an unheard-of occurrence for an Explorer. Broken
crystals are like knives, I understand."

"I'd wager it was a knife. Somebody tried to get rid of
her."

"Ah. And this makes you suspicious?"

"Wouldn't it you?"

"It would make me ask you, Randy, why you take such
an interest?"

Randy snarled. "The Enigma has been tried and tried
again. She didn't just go out there and solve it all by herself
with her little music box."

"Erickson did."

"Not the Enigma!"

"I mean that Erickson solved various passwords all by
himself with his little music box. Why are you so determined
that Furz did not?"

"I know her. I know how her mind works. She isn't
capable of that. She's bright, but she's not Erickson."

Which was pure jealousy talking, Justin thought. Chase
Random Hall was one of the most politically astute Explorers
on Jubal, but he was not one of the most talented. "Well, as
far as that goes, the score may not work. I understand it isn't
even scheduled for testing. It may be a complete boggle."

The King shook his head, a hungry snarl at the corner of
his mouth, elegantly shaped brows curving upward in an
expression of disagreement. "It's no boggle. The Prior over at
our Chapter House had a communique from the Master
General of the citadel in Deepsoil Five. The thing works."

"So?"

"Just now would be a bad time for Donatella to come up
with something linguistic, wouldn't it?"

"A very bad time. If it got out. On the other hand, Hall,

it would also be a bad time for anything awkward to happen to her. It's important that the CHASE report not be subject to question later on. Don Furz is very high on the list of witnesses to be called. A questionable accident might arouse a good deal of suspicion, and we don't want that."

"I just thought . . ."

"Don't. Don't think, Randy." Justin wanted no underling working at cross purposes. He would make his own final arrangement regarding Donatella Furz. One that would forward his plans. The Explorer knight was very well known. Her assassination would indeed be notorious. He regarded Hall with a sneer. "You dislike her, don't you?"

"Donatella?" Randy laughed, a brittle cackle with no mirth in it. "How can you say such a thing? She's a charming woman. Very lovely. Bright. Dedicated."

"You dislike her, don't you?" the Planetary Manager said again, still amused.

"My dear Justin," Hall sneered. "However did you guess?"

Harward Justin showed his teeth, an expression that the Explorer King knew far too well. When he spoke again, it was with ominous softness. "Don't let your dislike override your good sense, Hall. I've explained that I don't want anything awkward happening to her just now. Spider Geroan still works for me. You wouldn't want to forget that."

The Explorer King smiled. It took every ounce of self-control he had to create that smile. He had met Spider Geroan only once, had seen Spider Geroan's handiwork only once. He never, never wanted to see either again.

_____ 7

His excellency Governor Wuyllum Thonks was at ease with his wife and child in the little retiring room of Government House, having dined well and drunk better yet.

"Wully," Lady Honeypeach Thonks addressed him, tapping the table with her jeweled nail protectors while perusing a printed list, "do I have to invite that awful Vox woman to the soiree? She smells like horses."

"It wouldn't be politic to leave her out," said a quiet voice from across the room where Maybelle Thonks looked up from her book to continue the admonition. "Not if you're inviting all the rest of the BDL higher echelon."

"The rest of them don't smell. And it's really none of your business, Mayzy. You usually don't even show up."

"I wish you wouldn't call me Mayzy, Peachy. I really hate it." Maybelle frowned and returned to the printed page. Twitting Honeypeach, her so-called stepmother, was a dangerous occupation, and Maybelle kept resolving not to do it. Still, she did it. It was like a scab she had to pick at. Damn the woman!

Her stepmother raised one foot and did not answer. The foot was being groomed by a kneeling servitor, and its condition seemed to be of paramount interest. "I don't like that color polish, girl. Try the pinky one." She bent forward to stroke the outer edge of a big toe. "Still a tiny bit of callus there. Rub it a bit more." She returned to the list. "I've invited Colonel Roffles Lang for you, Mayzy."

"He's at least fifty. Why not one of the younger officers, if it's for me?" Actually, Maybelle had already made arrangements for an escort, although it would be extremely dangerous to say so.

"I have to invite him anyhow."

And you want the younger ones for yourself, Maybelle thought, returning to her book. Some people said that Maybelle's father, the Governor, was an expert in masterly inaction, which was code for being well paid to do nothing. Certainly in the case of his wife his inaction was legendary. Maybelle wondered if it were masterly. Perhaps he enjoyed watching Honeypeach lying in wait for her quarry? Or did he enjoy it when she finally caught them? Was he there, watching, at the kill? Maybelle shuddered and tried to bury herself in *The History of the Jubal System*, Chapter Two, "Serendipity and Jubal, the Sister Planets."

"Would you like me to invite some of the Explorer knights, Wully?"

"That pretty one from Northwest," he grunted. "You know."

"Donatella Furz?" Honeypeach smiled sweetly, again examining her foot and giving approval of the color varnish being applied to her nails. "Anybody but, love. She killed my sweet Limmie, that one did."

"Oh, honestly." Maybelle put down the book and rose to the bait. "She did not. Lim Terree died on the Enigma, singing a new score that Don came up with, that's all. He wasn't a Tripsinger, for God's sake. He should never have tried it. He was drugged up and he got himself killed. Don had nothing to do with it. I know her, and she's great."

"Where did you get all that?" her father asked, something threatening in his unexpected attention, as though some mighty and slumbrous reptile had come angrily awake. "All that about Terree? That was private information from the Grand Master's office to mine. I didn't release that information."

"Well, your whole staff was talking about it," Maybelle replied, refusing to be cowed. "They were naturally interested. All of them know that Lim Terree was one of Honey's proteges."

Which is, she concluded to herself, a euphemism to end all euphemisms. Though, come to think of it, Terree had seemed to keep his distance. Unlike some others. Chantry, for example. Chantry was going to be eaten alive. There would be nothing left of him but his teeth. Men that strolled into Honeypeach's lair came out as carrion.

The Lady Honeypeach noted the word *protege* and made a mental tally in her get-even book. Maybelle had quite a number of such tallies after her name. But then, so did others. Donatella Furz among them. "I won't ask Furz," she told Wuyllum. "I don't like her. She killed my Limmie and she was rude to me at the PEC reception. But I will ask those new people. The ones who had the Mad Gap password."

"If you mean the Tripsinger and acolytes from Deepsoil Five, you're too late," murmured Maybelle. "They're leaving for Northwest today."

Honeypeach made a face. From the Governor's palace,

she often used the scope to look right into the courtyard of
the citadel. The blond Tripsinger had looked a lot like her
poor Limmie. All that mass of silvery hair, that narrow,
esthetic looking face, and those long, straight legs. Very
edible. Very, very edible.

_____ 8

Tasmin and the acolytes decided to transport their mules to
Northwest. Riding the animals was not sensible. It would
take six to ten days for the journey, during which Don Furz
could be sent almost anywhere. A truck towing a mule trailer
could make it in one or two, depending on the ferry schedule.

"We can borrow mules at Northwest Citadel," Tasmin
reminded them for the third time. "We don't have to take
our own."

"I like Jessica," said Clarin. "I like her a lot, and I'd just
as soon not leave her here if you don't mind."

He didn't argue. The trust between Tripsinger and mount
had to be absolute. Gentle, unflappable, sensible—Tripsinger
mules were all of these, as well as being sterile, which PEC
rules demanded. The mares and jacks were kept at widely
separated sites on the 'Soilcoast and breeding was by artificial
insemination. Similar precautions were used in breeding foreign fish and fowl. Until there was a final declaration on the
question of sentience, no imported creatures were allowed to
breed freely on planets under PEC control.

Except people of course. The assumption had been that
if it was necessary to evacuate the planet, every human would
be deported. Most livestock, fowls, and fish would be slaughtered before the humans left. The mules would not be—it
was generally accepted that the Tripsingers simply wouldn't
stand for that—but in one generation they would be dead.
The imported trees and shrubs were sterile. The vegetable

crops would be killed except for settler's brush, which was a native species with only slight improvements. If the new commission they had been hearing about was to declare there was native sentience on Jubal and rule for disinvolvement, Jubal could be left as it had been before humans came.

Except that BDL wouldn't let that happen.

"Take Jessica," Tasmin said. "Take your own mule, Clarin. I confess to a fondness for Blondine, as well."

"Not mine," growled Jamieson, fondling his animal's ears. "This old long-ear hasn't got a drop of sense." The mule turned and gave him a severe and searching look, which the boy repaid with a palm full of chopped fruit. "I'll see what I can round up in the way of transportation."

"Clarin and I will get the equipment packed," Tasmin said. They had already made arrangements for Vivian to travel to Deepsoil Five in a wagon train leaving almost at once. Tasmin had sent a message ahead to his mother, though he knew it might not reach her before Vivian did. Messages were sent by heliographic relay between widely separated parts of the planet, but the signal posts were only sporadically manned. Satellite relay worked if the transmitter was directly above the target receiver, but except on the coast or over water, both transmitters and receivers often burned out mysteriously. The Presences simply did not tolerate electromagnetic activity within a considerable distance, as a number of pilots had learned to their fatal dismay in the early years.

Clarin assisted Tasmin in repacking their equipment, checking each item as they went. "You didn't leave this box like this, did you?" she asked, pointing to Lim's synthesizer, standing open on the table.

"Servants," he mouthed softly. "They poke into everything. The story is that BDL pays for all kinds of information. Probably nine out of ten servants in the citadel are selling bits and pieces to BDL informers for drinking money."

She flushed. "Someone told me that before. I'd forgotten. It seems so silly. We all work for the same people."

"Not really," he said, still softly. "If you ask me whom I work for, I'll tell you I work for the Master General of my citadel, and ultimately for the Grand Master of the Order. Explorers work for their priories. I know BDL pays for all of it ultimately, but I don't think of myself as working for BDL. Maybe that's self-serving. There's a lot about BDL I just can't stomach."

She seemed thoughtful, and he waited for the question he knew was coming, wondering what it would be this time. She had displayed a sustained though delicately phrased curiosity about Tasmin's life, but they had pretty well covered his history by now.

"Why do they call him Reb?" she asked.

"Who?" He was surprised into blankness.

"Jamieson. Why do they call him Reb?"

"Because he is one. He was a rebel in choir school. He's been a rebel in the citadel. He's been in trouble more than he's been out of it." Tasmin smiled at a few private memories.

She sat on the bed and fumbled in her pocket, taking out her green-gray crystal mouse, which sniffed at her fingers with a long, expressive nose as it inflated its song-sack to give a muffled chirp. "You know Jamieson wasn't sent after you by the Master General."

"He wasn't?"

"He demanded to come. Because he thought you needed him."

Tasmin was dumbfounded. "What was all that about the girl he left behind?"

"So much smoke. We rehearsed it. So you wouldn't think it was his idea. He thought you'd send us back if it was his idea."

Tasmin dropped to a chair, astonished. "How did you get dragged in?"

"That was the Master General. He said if Jamieson was right, if you needed someone, you needed someone besides Jamieson because a steady diet of Jamieson was too much for anyone." Her mouth quirked as she petted the mouse, curled now in one palm, cleaning itself.

Tasmin stared at her. That kid. That boy. That . . . his eyes filled.

Seeing this she turned, going back to the former subject. "Why did they let him stay in the Order if he was so much trouble?"

"Because more often than not he's been right. And because he's a fine musician, of course." And because he loves Jubal, Tasmin thought. Maybe as much as I do.

"Is he right about . . . about the Presences?" This was obviously the question she had really wanted to ask in the first place.

"What do you think?"

"It isn't what I think. I *feel* he's right. I guess inside somewhere, I *know* he's right. But if he's right, that makes everything else. . . ."

"Hypocritical?" he suggested. "You used that word before, I think." He sat down, looking at her closely. Her eyes were tight on his. The matter was important to her. He decided to give it his full attention.

"Well, I suppose it is hypocritical. I guess we—we Tripsingers—we go along with what BDL demands because it makes it possible for us to go on doing what we love to do. On the surface, in public, we pretend the Presences aren't sentient because that statement allows us to move around on Jubal. Underneath, we believe they are sentient, and that belief is what makes moving around on Jubal worthwhile! We assent to hypocrisy, because it doesn't seem to make that much difference. I guess it's because we don't see anything consequential happening just because we give lip service to nonsentience. It doesn't change anything. We still go through the motions Erickson laid down for us, the quasi-religious, very respectful stuff he ordained, so while we say they're not sentient, we act as though they are sentient. We have to. Otherwise we might lose Jubal, and Jubal's in our blood."

She sat down opposite him, her face eager. "I've felt that, you know. What is it like, for you?"

He lowered himself onto the bed, dangling a sock from one hand, thinking. What was it like for him?

"It's like going into paradise," he said. "We say going into peril, but I've always thought paradise must be very perilous. Anything beautiful, anything that takes hold of your heart and shakes it—that's perilous.

"The peril takes hold of you even before you leave, sometimes. You see the ceremonial gate opening. Everything inside you gets very still. You start to ride, the fields flowing by, slowly changing to Jubal lands. You smell the Jubal trees, and as you go up the trail, they turn, almost as though they're following you, watching you. The ground begins to shiver, only a little, then more. Something is speaking in the ground, something enormous. . . ."

"I know," she whispered. "You go on and the words being spoken in the ground get bigger and bigger until they fill your head. Until you see the Presence before you, glittering. Light comes out of it like daggers, like swords. They pierce you, and you begin to sing. . . . It's like bleeding music instead of blood."

He nodded. She knew. Oh, yes. She knew.

"And if you do it right, quiet comes," he concluded for her. "Something listens."

There was an aching understanding between them, a sympathy that was almost agony. He flushed and dropped his eyes, awash with an emotion he would not allow himself to feel. When she had spoken, he had felt her in his arms, as she had been there on the trail below the Watchers, trembling in his arms. He gritted his teeth, pushing the feeling away. It made him feel disloyal to the memory of Celcy each time he had one of these fleeting feelings.

After a time she pocketed the mouse and said, "Logically, if something listens, something should reply."

He shook his head, smiling ruefully. "That's what Chad Jaconi says. He's spent forty years trying to make sense out of Password scores. I don't know how many so-called universal translator setups he's bought from out-system."

"Did he ever get anything?"

"Nothing sensible."

"What about the other side of the conversation? The Presence side?"

"Gibberish. For decades, people have recorded the sounds the Presences make. They've tried every known translator device. All they get is some kind of noise, Chad says. White noise or brown noise or something. Squeaks, howls, snores, gurgles. Nothing useful. Nothing with meaning."

"What about the viggies? They sing. Maybe they're sentient."

"A lot of people tried to establish that. There were a number of viggies captured in the early years, well treated so far as anyone could tell, and they almost all died—overnight sometimes. A very rare few were said to have lived in captivity. The one I had, the one Lim let loose, was supposed to say a few words, "pretty viggy" and "viggy wants a cooky," but there's no record of any of the things the PEC looks for in determining sentience. No toolmaking. No proof of language. No burial of the dead. And, of course, there's simply no way to go among them and study them as our naturalists would like to do. They're nocturnal, elusive, die when captured, and they don't talk. So much for viggy sentience. . . ."

There was a tap at the door and Jamieson thrust his head in. "I've found an empty brou truck that's leaving for Northwest in half an hour."

"Right," Tasmin agreed, rising. "Let this stuff go, Clarin. I'll finish packing here. You two get your own gear."

There was a brief delay while the truck was fitted with a proper hitch to pull the trailer Tasmin had borrowed from the mule farm. Since there was only space in the truck turret for two passengers, Jamieson chose to ride with the mules. They set out early in the afternoon.

First came the city outskirts, mud houses, mud stores, untidy gardens, these separated from similar stretches by great swatches of hard surfaced road, with more of it building. "Military construction," bellowed the driver over the noise of their travel. "Somebody decided they needed better roads to move the military around. That's why bricks are so short. They've got all the solar furnaces out here surfacin' road."

They passed several of the furnaces, huge mirrors hung on complicated frameworks that both tracked the sun and focused the resultant beam. Behind the furnaces, road surface smoked hotly, fading from red to black.

Once past the construction, though the road was narrow and bumpy, they made better time. They were traveling through fields of grain and narrower strips lined with root crops. Occasionally they could see pens of fowl or small meat animals, chigs or bantigons, omnivores native to Serendipity. Tasmin's mouth watered. He had an insatiable hunger for grilled bantigon. Fried bantigon. Bantigon pie. On this meat-poor planet, Tasmin was an unregenerate carnivore. Clarin, watching him salivate, gave him a sympathetic look. She, too, enjoyed fresh meat.

They reached a wide, shallow river and were ferried

across. They passed a small town on their right, then more
fields and farms, and another small town on their left. They
were bending away from the sea, toward the uplands. Ahead
of them were the only deepsoil hills yet discovered on Jubal,
great sandy dunes pushed up by the sea winds and over-
grown with settler's brush and feathery trees. They wound
among the hills, startling tiny native animals who fled across
the road, once surprising a group of viggies who fled whooping
as the truck came near, turning their heads backward to peer
behind them with enormous pupilless eyes, ears wagging and
feathery antennae pointing at the truck. At the top of the hill,
the largest viggy inflated his song-sack and boomed reproach-
fully at them before the group fled out of sight.

"I had no idea they came this near cultivated lands,"
Tasmin said as he stared at the retreating gray-green forms.
In all his trips he had actually seen viggies only five or six
times, though he had heard them almost nightly all his life.

"See 'em all the time along the coast," said the driver.
"Six, eight at a time. Had engine trouble along here once.
Had to stop and spend the night on the road. Heard 'em
singing real close by. Must've gone on all night. Lots of other
critters around here, too. Ones you don't see very often."

When they came out of the hills, the sun was behind
them, falling slowly into the sea. "We'll spend the night in
Barrville," the driver advised. "There's a BDL agri-station
there. Imagine they'll put you up."

Sandy Chivvle, the local manager, did indeed put them
up, glad of the company and eager to show someone what
was being done with the ubiquitous brou. She insisted that
seeds from this batch be tested against seeds from that batch,
and by the time supper was put before them, none of them
cared if they ate or not. The night passed in a cheerful haze.

Laden with reports to be delivered to Jem Middleton,
head of the BDL Agricultural Division, they left early in the
morning, somewhat headachey and lower in spirits. The driver
dosed them with hot tea from a thermos flask, and they
rumbled along endless fields of brou, the pale green-gray of
newly planted fields alternating with the dark gray-green of
mature crops, passing lines of loaded trucks headed the other
way. They came into Northwest City a little after noon.

They unloaded the mules and then inquired at the neighboring BDL center for Jem Middleton. They found him in the bowels of the building in a remote room in which there was a welter game in progress. At least there were cards and stacks of consumer chits on the table, though the open document cases on the side table argued that something else might have been going on. To Tasmin's surprise, perhaps to his dismay, one of those present was the Grand Master of the Tripsinger Order, Thyle Vowe.

"Tasmin Ferrence! As I live and sing, if it isn't the wonder of Deepsoil Five! And your acolytes, too. Well, this is a surprise. I heard you were coming to Splash One, but I didn't think we'd see you up here. Heard about that Mad Gap thing. Makes me feel like an absolute fool. Should have checked the old files on it someplace besides Splash One, but I never thought of it. Let's see, you'd be Jamieson, wouldn't you? Heard a lot about you." And the white-haired Master knuckled Jamieson sharply on the upper arm, grinning at him expansively. "And you'd be Clarin, the little gal with the astonishin' bass voice, right? Heard about you, too. Word is that Tasmin Ferrence always gets the mean ones—bright but mean."

Clarin submitted to the Grand Master's fatherly caress with what Tasmin regarded as commendable patience. It was almost as though she knew him, or knew of him.

"Tasmin, come meet some people! You know Gereny Vox, don't you? Best mule breeder we've ever had and I've lived through six of 'em." The plain faced, gray-haired woman reached a hand across the table, nodding as Tasmin took it and murmured greetings. The Grand Master went on. "This here's Jem Middleton. Jem's the head of the Agri Division for BDL, heck of a nice guy, good welter player, too. You want to watch him if you ever get into a game, boy. And this other fella is Rheme Gentry. Rheme's new on the Governor's staff from off-world and still sufferin' from Jubal shock. Good lookin' fella, isn't he? Lord, if I'd had teeth and hair like that, I'd of cut me a swath through the ladies. Not Rheme. Very serious fella, Rheme."

The lean and darkly handsome man he referred to shook his head in dismay at this introduction, acknowledging Tasmin's greetings with a rueful nod.

"Now, want to sit in on the game? What about somethin' to eat? What can I get you to drink?"

Tasmin could not keep himself from grinning. The Grand Master had that effect on people. "Thank you, no, Sir. I'm only here to deliver some papers to Jem Middleton from his manager out at Barrville."

"Damn that girl," Middleton growled, drawing great furry brows together in a solid line across his massive and furrowed forehead. "Always gettin' her damn reports in on time. Now I'll have to get to work."

"But since you're here in Northwest, Sir," Tasmin said to the Grand Master, "perhaps you could arrange an introduction for me. To an Explorer knight named Don Furz."

There was a silence in the room, only a brief one, not one of those appalling silences that sometimes occurred during social gatherings following some gaffe, but enough of a pause that Tasmin wondered whether he had put a foot wrong. His prearranged excuse could do no harm. "I wanted to express my admiration for the workmanlike way the Enigma notes were prepared. I had the honor of doing the master copy of the score. . . ."

The silence broke. Thyle Vowe was all affability once more. "Ever met Don Furz?"

"No, sir. I haven't had that pleasure."

"Well, why don't we find out where you can maybe find Don Furz. Gereny, would you mind?"

The roughly clad, gray-haired woman gave him a quizzical look and went to the wallcom. After a few muttered phrases, she returned, a puzzled, half angry expression on her face.

"Don's been sent on a short trip up to the Redfang Range and is expected to return tonight. Something about an alternate route?" She exchanged a quick look with both Vowe and Middleton.

Thyle Vowe seemed very thoughtful at this, turning to rummage among the papers on the nearby table. "Tell you what, Tasmin. The Redfang's only a few hours from here. Why don't you and your young friends ride up that way and meet Don? I'll give you a map so you won't go astray." He rummaged a moment more, than handed Tasmin a small chart, pointing at it with a plump, impeccably manicured finger. "Take the road back of the citadel, ride straight east for about half a mile, then take this turning north. Stay on that road, and it'll deliver you right at the foot of the Redfang canyon by the time it gets dark, if you don't run into Don on the road. Better get a quick start." He was moving them toward the door.

Jem Middleton interrupted. "Just a minute, Ferrence. I wouldn't want you to run into any trouble up that way you couldn't handle. Rarest thing on Jubal, next to red meat, is crystal bears, but darned if I didn't get word there's been a crystal bear sighted up toward Redfang. You'd better take a stun rifle along, just in case." And he was on his feet, pulling a rifle out of a tall cupboard and thrusting it into Tasmin's hands. "You can return it whenever you get back." Then they were in the corridor once more with the door shut firmly behind them.

"What does he think he's playing at?" Jamieson demanded, outraged. "Crystal bears! Nobody's seen a crystal bear for fifty years."

"Shhhh," Clarin demanded. "Something's going on here, Reb. Keep your mouth shut and your eyes open. Do you trust the Grand Master, Master Ferrence?"

Tasmin gave her a grateful look of concurrence. Something was indeed going on here. "Trusting the Grand Master would be my inclination," Tasmin replied, a little tentatively. The four people in the room behind them might have been playing welter, but those open, paper-stuffed cases argued they had been doing something else. As did the fact that some of the face-down hands had had four cards while others had had six. As for the rifle, Tasmin had only fired a stun rifle during the annual proficiency shoots. Rifles were not even routinely supplied to caravans any longer, though they had been standard issue some twenty years ago. The story about crystal bears was nonsense. No one had seen a crystal bear for decades. There was some question as to whether anyone had ever seen a crystal bear or whether they were entirely mythical, and everyone in that room knew it. Unless—one were to substitute *Crystallite* for crystal bear. In which case they had been telling him something without telling him anything. . . .

"Yes," he said in a grim decision. "I trust him."

"Well, then let's trust him. Let's do what he suggested." Clarin looked at the rifle with dismay. "We don't want to walk around carrying that."

"Put it under your robe, Clarin. Yours is stiffer than mine. You can wait at the gate while Jamieson and I bring the mules." Tasmin shook his head at himself as he hurried away across the compound, turning back to see Clarin lounging casually against one wall, the rifle tucked behind her.

The mules were eager to travel after their half day in the trailer. When they had ridden far enough from the city that the rifle would not occasion comment, Tasmin fastened it to the rings of his saddle, trying twice before he got it right. Lord, no one except the military used rifles anymore.

"Crystal bears," mumbled Jamieson, still seething. "Who does he think you are, Master? Everts of the Dawn Patrol?" This was a favorite holodrama of Jubal's children. "When was the last time anyone saw a crystal bear?"

"There's some doubt anyone ever did, actually," said Tasmin drily. "Fairy tale stuff. Early explorers claimed to find a lot of things back in crystal country. Crystal bears were just one of the menagerie. Some of the earliest explorers said viggies could talk and mice could sing."

"Well, they can," Clarin objected, patting her pocket. A muffled chirp followed the pat. "At least sort of. Why would Jem Middleton have had a rifle right there in his office?" Clarin asked.

"Exactly," Tasmin replied. "Why?"

They rode through ascending lands, scattered fields of human crops giving way to Jubal country, the ramparts of the Redfang rising before them as the sun sank behind their left shoulders and the road grew narrower and dimmer. After the last of the farms they passed no one.

"No Don Furz," said Jamieson, giving voice to the obvious.

"Do you get the idea that maybe the Grand Master and the others were afraid of that?" Clarin asked.

"The road tops a ridge just ahead," Tasmin answered, his voice carefully unemotional. "We'll probably get a look down into Redfang canyon from there."

From the ridge top, the road dropped into a basin surrounded on three sides by mixed stony outcroppings and the 'lings and 'lets of the Redfang, then curved to the right around a flat-topped pillar of stone.

There was someone on the pillar!

A gray clad figure scurried back and forth, toppling stones down the precipitous sides. Even from this distance they could hear the grunts of effort, the shattering rattle of stone on stone.

At the foot of the pillar, half a dozen shadowy figures were attempting to scale the rocky walls. The intent of the attackers was clear, and there was desperation in the movement atop the rock. As they watched, one of the plummeting stones tore a climber loose and carried him onto the shattered stones at the foot of the almost vertical face. Other climbers redoubled their efforts to reach the embattled one.

Without a moment's hesitation, Jamieson yodeled "brother, brother, brother," the recognition called gathering strength from the echoes that cascaded in its wake, shattering the silence of the canyon, demanding that any Explorers or Tripsingers within hearing identify themselves. An answering cry came from the pillar top, telling them which side they were on.

Tasmin slid off his mule, dragging the rifle from its scabbard and throwing himself down behind a convenient looking rock. His best rifle scores had always been from the prone position, and he settled into the earth with a wriggle, flicking on the power switch and putting his eyes to the goggle scope all in one motion, tracking the lighted dot across the face of the butte. When it slid across one of the climbing figures he squeezed once, twice, then began tracking once more. One pull would drop a man. Two would keep him dropped for a while. He tracked and pulled again.

Jamieson and Clarin were clattering down the trail toward the pillar at a reckless gallop, the unshod hooves of the mules creating a cataract of echoes, a continuous thunder. The "brother, brother, brother," yodel, leaping the octaves to stir a threatening vibration from the surrounding 'lings, added to the cumulative rumble of avalanching sound that gave the effect of a mounted troop. At the base of the pillar the attackers broke and ran.

Tasmin tracked a fleeing shape, pulled, tracked another, and pulled again before the remaining attackers were lost

behind a forest of crystal pillars. Crystallites? They were very
quiet for Crystallites. By the time Jamieson and Clarin reached
the pillar, all the attackers had disappeared. Tasmin stood up,
brushing gravel from his chest and belly, and restored the
rifle to its scabbard, noting with angry but somehow detached
astonishment that the intensity dial was set to "kill." He
hadn't set it there. He hadn't touched it. Regulation setting
was "stun." Always.

At the foot of the slope, three people moved among the
fallen. Clarin, Jamieson, and the shadow figure from the top
of the bluff who had come down to join the acolytes. Tasmin
mounted and rode to join them. As Tasmin drew nearer, he
saw it was a woman who was turning one of the fallen bodies
face down with a gesture of anger or dismay. She came
toward him, golden hair fluttering in the light breeze, dark
blue eyes fixed angrily on his own.

"I wish to hell you hadn't felt you had to kill them all!"
she announced.

Then, with surprise, "You're Tasmin Ferrence, aren't
you? Your acolyte said 'Ferrence,' but I didn't make the
connection." And then, surprisingly. "I hope to hell you've
got my music box."

Tasmin was gaping at her when Jamieson said "Master,"
in the tone of an adult interrupting the play of children. He
was peering over their heads in the direction the fleeing
attackers had gone. "I hate to bring it up, but the noise back
in those 'lings indicates they haven't gone away. There were
at least ten of them, Sir, and with due respect, you only
dropped four."

"You think they're coming back?"

"I don't think all that hollering presages imminent
departure."

"The Explorer expresses her thanks, Tripsinger," the
woman said. "My mule's over behind that rock, and the best
place for us is back in the range, quickly." She ran toward the
mule, and they followed her, hearing the noise building
behind them as they went. "Those bastards caught up with
me right after I came out of the range," she shouted over the
noise. "There were only four of them at first, but then they
seemed to drop out of the rocks like gyre-birds off a 'ling. I
only had time to get up on that pillar. Two minutes later,

they'd have had me. Or, if you'd been two minutes later, they'd have had me anyhow!"

Only when they were halfway to the range did Tasmin notice the typical Explorer outfitting of both beast and rider and realize who she was. "You're Don Furz?" he exclaimed.

She gave him a quick look. "Who did you think?"

"I didn't know Don Furz was a woman."

"It won't be anything long if we don't get back into the range. Your mules aren't soft-shod. We'll stop just inside." She kicked her animal into a run, and they trailed after her, entering the range between two bloody towers that hummed and whispered ominously. "Pay no attention to them," Don shouted. "They won't blow if we hurry!" She galloped on, making a quick turn to the right, then to the left, pulling up in a shower of gravel.

"Get your mules shod, quick," she said, pulling the cover from her Explorer's box and unfolding the panels around her waist and across her thighs. "We're going down that canyon to the left. The Password is new. I just came up with it this afternoon."

"Then they can't follow us," Jamieson said with satisfaction as he stretched soft shoes over mule hooves.

"They may try," Clarin contradicted. "They weren't making any noise before, but they're certainly making it now." A cacophony of shouts, chants, and religious slogans echoed in the canyon behind them.

"There weren't any witnesses before," Don said. "Now there's the possibility we may get away and talk about this. They want us to believe they're Crystallites."

"You don't think they really are?"

"Those bodies weren't dressed like Crystallites, and they weren't half starved like the Crystallites I've seen," Don commented impatiently. "Finished? Good, come along behind and I'll get us through."

She rode toward a branching canyon, stroking the music box as she went. Her voice was good, not up to Tripsingers' standards, of course, but then it didn't need to be. Explorers rarely sang their way past the Presences, and in any case it didn't take a great deal to get a single person and mule through most places. Tasmin noted with amusement that Clarin was taking notes on her own machine as she rode. He watched her expression, fascinated. The music was there, on her face. Her eyes moved, opened, shut, swung one way and then another as though she saw the notes. Her mouth pursed, opened, widened, pursed once more as it tasted the music. Her hand snapped up and to one side, then back again, all unconsciously. It was like watching someone struggling— perhaps struggling to give birth? Or to conquer something, possess something. Or to be possessed by something! That was probably closer, and Tasmin wondered what his own face looked like when he sang.

Well, if Don Furz didn't sing them out, Clarin could. And Jamieson could, of course, without notes, having heard it only once, though his face showed none of what went on inside.

The score was effective enough, a little thin in places. There were several small tremors, nothing serious. Tasmin saw Clarin rescoring on her box, making lightning decisions as to what effects were needed to flesh out the notes and make them hold for Tripsinging purposes. She was faster at orchestration than Jamieson was. Not that they would ever need such a score. This canyon looked very much like a dead-end to nowhere.

Above them loomed the bloody pillars of the range, almost black in the dusk, with the jagged tooth of Redfang itself behind them. These were not Fanglings they went among. They were far too large for that, and Tasmin wondered briefly if they had been individually named and whether the same basic Password worked for them all.

The sounds of pursuit faded behind them. They came out of peril, down from the crystal pass to find a pocket of deepsoil, a hundred square yards of Jubal trees and shrubs gathered around a tiny spring, which filled a rock cup with reflected starlight.

They dismounted wearily, making no effort to set up camp. "How safe are we here?" Tasmin asked.

Don wiped her forehead with an already dirty sleeve. "Well, if they can get a singer or two to help them, they might come in after us after a few hours' work. More likely, they'll use the standard route and come in east of us, then work this way. If they have access to a set of satellite charts of this area, it won't take them long to figure it out." She stared back the way they had come, her back and shoulders rigid.

"We shouldn't stay here then."

"Just long enough to rest the animals and get some food for ourselves." She was still standing, still rigidly staring.

Tasmin put his hand on her arm. She turned slowly, glaring at him with angry, despairing eyes.

"This is the third time they've tried," she said. "The third time. They almost killed me twice before." She shook his hand away. "That is my synthesizer you've got. Lim gave it to you, didn't he? You're his brother. I didn't know that. . . ." Her voice was ragged, jerky with half suppressed emotion.

"Hush," Tasmin said firmly. "Get hold of yourself, Explorer. Clarin's already brewing tea. I suggest we sit down quietly, have a cup together while you explain what all this is about."

She shook her head, an unconscious gesture of negation.

"We did save your life," drawled Jamieson, looking up from his position by the fire where he was blowing strips of dried settler's brush into reluctant flame, his face speckled with soot. "I know you don't trust anyone. Probably don't know who's coming at you next, but we are the good guys, really."

Don laughed, a slightly hysterical laugh. "I keep escaping by the narrowest margins. As though I had a slightly incompetent guardian angel. Why in heaven's name did you show up when you did?"

"I believe someone thought you might be in trouble," Tasmin told her, digging in his pocket for the message the Grand Master had sent and explaining briefly how they had happened to seek her out near Redfang. "They gave us the rifle just before we left."

"On a very transparent pretext," Jamieson commented.

"And it was set on kill," Tasmin concluded. "It was irresponsible of me not to have checked it before firing, but. . . ."

"But we were in a bit of a hurry," Jamieson concluded, irrepressibly.

"Jamieson!" Clarin said patiently. "Slash it off."

"You don't really act like assassins." Donatella sighed as she opened the message. "But then, Zimmy didn't either."

She sank to the ground near the fire. "I don't know what this means."

"What does it say?"

She spread the small sheet of paper on a rock by the fire and read its contents aloud.

"*The Grand Master is aware*. What does that mean?"

"He's certainly being careful, isn't he?" said Tasmin. "I think he's telling us he knows something, but he's not putting anything on paper that would prove anything against him. Let's get back to you, Explorer Furz. You've been attacked, but you've escaped. You're still alive. On the other hand, my brother is dead. My wife is dead. . . ."

"Your wife! What did she have to do with—"

"Leave that aside for the moment. Evidently the reason they're dead has something to do with you. That's why I'm here. The acolytes are here because one of them is presumptuous and the other got dragged in by the ears." Jamieson flushed, and Tasmin went on. "I suggest that now's a very good time to find out where we all stand."

"I don't know where to start," she said hopelessly.

"At the beginning," suggested Clarin. "Where did it all start?"

"In the library of the Priory at Splash One," Don said quietly. "When I found a letter Erickson had written. . . ."

Half an hour later, she fell silent, the others still staring at her. There were things missing from her story. She knew it and they knew it. Still, they had the general outline.

"Let me see if I understand this," Clarin said. "You found documents of Erickson's that indicated a method of proving that the Presences are sentient."

Don nodded.

"You took some steps, as yet unspecified, to verify this information. As a consequence of this verification, you came up with the notes for the Enigma score."

Don nodded again, slowly.

"And at that point, you decided you had to tell someone what you knew."

"No," Don sighed. "At that point I just bubbled around like boiling sugar for a time, while everyone patted me on the head. Then I got some sense and I decided to keep my mouth shut."

"You didn't say that!" Jamieson complained, while Tasmin gave him a sidelong look.

"It was a fleeting decision," she explained. "Figure it out for yourself, acolyte. If I come up with proof of sentience, somebody will have to do something about it. The Planetary Exploitation Council has to take some action, don't they? I think everyone assumes that once sentience is established, on any planet, not just Jubal, humans have to get out."

"Not everywhere. Not always," Tasmin said.

"No, not everywhere, not always, but those are the rare exceptions. So, why should I want to tip the tripwagon? I earn my living here, just the way you do. My friends are here. My livelihood is here. Besides—it's Jubal! It's home! I don't want to leave here. So after I came down out of the clouds, the first thing I decided to do was keep my stupid mouth shut. Of course, that was after I went giggling around for several days like a damned fool. Anybody who looked at me probably knew I'd found something." She sighed again, rubbing grubby hands up the sides of her face, leaving long smears of soil.

Clarin passed cups of steaming tea and commented, "Presumably you decided differently after a while."

"After I'd had a chance to think, yes. We all know the CHASE Commission is due to meet here very soon. And everyone knows it's rigged. Lord, the chairman of the commission is the Governor's own stepson, and everyone knows that BDL owns the Governor. So, it's pretty sure the results of the commission hearings are prearranged. And we all know what BDL wants those to be. Nonsentient. So then I got to thinking about what will happen after the CHASE Commission reports."

"And," Jamieson said impatiently.

"And what will happen is that BDL won't go on paying Explorers and Tripsingers when they don't have to."

Jamieson gave her a puzzled look. "I don't understand."

Tasmin nodded. What she said reinforced some suspicions of his own. "If the CHASE Commission reports nonsentience, the PEC strictures will be removed. They're the usual strictures imposed by the PEC on any planet where indigenous sentience is a question."

"Nondestruction of habitat," quoted Clarin. "Something like that."

"Exactly like that," Tasmin nodded.

Jamieson still looked puzzled.

"If the strictures are removed," Clarin explained to him, "then BDL can destroy whatever they like."

Jamieson's mouth fell open. "They wouldn't! The Presences are absolutely unique!"

"It's never stopped humans before," Tasmin said, thinking of the histories he had read in the citadel. Rivers turned into sewers. Mountains leveled into rubble. All for the profit of the great agglomerates. "Not where profit is concerned. Think how profits could be increased if BDL didn't have to use Explorers or Tripsingers or wagon trains. Think how much brou could be moved if they could fly the cargo in and out."

"It stinks," said Clarin with feeling.

"It stinks," agreed Donatella. "But it's obvious once you start thinking about it. So, quite selfishly I'd decided to keep my mouth shut, but then I realized it wouldn't make any difference. Most likely I was going to be out of work and off-planet no matter what happened, and so was everyone else I knew. At that point, I decided to do what I should have decided in the first place. For Jubal's sake, not mine."

"To get the word out," Clarin continued. "However, you suspected that if you simply spoke out, you would probably be silenced."

"I think it was a reasonable assumption," Don said, gesturing back the way they had come. "You saw them."

Clarin leaned back on one arm and continued her recapitulation. "At this point the story gets a little confusing for me. You contacted a friend, whom you do not identify to us. . . ."

"For that friend's own protection," Don assented, half angrily. "You say you're the good guys, but how the hell do I know."

"All right. I'll pay chits for that. So, you contact this friend, and you and the friend work up this plan. You decide to get one of the Top Six 'Soilcoast Singers to get the word out for you. You're going to feed this singer certain information, which will then be used as the basis for a show."

"Part of the information was in the Enigma score, and I was the only one who had it at that point. We tried to figure out a way the singer could get the score without tracing it back to me. Then my friend told me Lim Terree could get the score from his brother in Deepsoil Five, Tripsinger Tasmin Ferrence, because I'd already sent it to you for scoring. . . ." Her voice trailed away. "I hadn't known you were his brother. Getting it from you seemed less culpable. I didn't think anyone would be surprised if he got it from someone in his own family. It wouldn't seem like . . ."

"Like a conspiracy," Tasmin finished for her. "It wouldn't make BDL suspicious."

She nodded gratefully. "I thought not. Our plan was that by the time anyone at BDL smartened to what was going on, everyone on Jubal would be talking about the show. Oh, people would doubt that what was in the show was real information, but it would still be widespread by then. Too widespread to stop. And the talk alone would make the PEC pay attention, whether they believed it or not. Then, too, there'd be holo cubes made and distributed. It wouldn't be controllable. Too many people would know."

Clarin asked, "It wasn't part of your plan that Lim Terree would go up on the Enigma?"

"Lord, no! He wasn't a Tripsinger. It wasn't even a proven score yet. He was just supposed to get the score from his brother in a way that would seem natural and unthreatening and then bring it back to Splash One."

"And it wasn't your intention that he should pauperize himself getting to Deepsoil Five? He did, you know. His wife and child are destitute." Clarin sipped at the last of her tea, watching Don's face.

"I didn't know." Don leaned forward, burying her head in her hands. "Nothing went right, did it? I had no idea he'd done that. My friend arranged the whole thing. I should never have. . . ."

"Never mind, Don," Tasmin said gently. "It wasn't your fault. Not any more than it was mine or my father's or Lim's own. He was trying desperately to prove himself. He put everything he had into this—more than he had. Your friend's only mistake was to count too heavily on someone whose own demons were riding him. There's more than enough guilt to go around, but you don't deserve much of it."

"Meantime," Clarin said, going on with her precis,

"two attempts were made on your life. One here in the Redfang Range, one sometime later in the Chapter House at Splash One. But you say you do not know who is attempting to kill you."

"It's true. I don't. I've been over and over everything I said to anyone from the beginning. As I said, I did bubble around a little bit, right at the first, but I never actually said anything. Maybe someone could suspect that I know something I shouldn't, but no one can know, not for sure."

"For some people, suspicion is enough," Tasmin commented. "More than enough. Crystallites, for example. Though I should think they would welcome proof of sentience." He waited for a comment from Don but heard none. "Surely you must suspect someone."

"Someone with BDL, obviously," she said uncomfortably. "We all know how unscrupulous they are. He is."

"He being?"

"Justin. The more profit out of Jubal, the more goes in his own pockets. At least, so I've heard."

"In his pockets, and the Governor's. Some say it even goes to the PEC."

"I don't like to believe that," Don said wearily. "The point is, what am I going to do now?" She stood up and walked around the little fire, swinging her arms, rotating her head, working the kinks out. "I don't know where to go, what to do. All I can think of is to use the com network to send information to everyone I can think of and hope it gets generally disseminated before they catch up to me."

"I doubt they're going to let us out of here long enough for you to do that," Clarin remarked. "We're bottled up."

"Oh, we can get out," Don said. "I know this Range well. Even if they come in after us, there are all kinds of little side canyons and slots you can't even see from the satellite charts. But if we get out, what?"

"I'm still trying to figure out what's going to happen," Jamieson said in a puzzled voice. "There are some pieces that don't seem to fit."

"What do you mean?"

"Well, we met an officer when we were coming into Splash One, and he told us all the Crystallites would be rounded up pretty soon for the sake of public order. They make a lot of noise, the Crystallites, but there aren't all that many of them. Then when we were coming up to Northwest, the driver talked about the military and the roads. They've closed the base on Serendipity and moved the sector garrison here. The Deepsoil Coast is already overcrowded. Jubal can hardly feed its population now, while Serendipity has surpluses all over the place. It doesn't make any economic sense at all. And what I'm wondering is, what are they going to use all those troopers for?"

"It's almost as though they expected general disorder, isn't it?" asked Tasmin in a deceptively mild voice. He had been staring out over the ranges while suspicions gradually solidified within him.

"What kind of general disorder? Who are those troopers going to be used against?"

"Well, considering that BDL will probably start destroying Presences shortly after the CHASE Commission delivers its report, I would judge the troops are to be used against us," Tasmin said.

"Us!"

"Tripsingers. Explorers. All the dependents and ancillary services. All those who earn their living from us, the storekeepers, farmers, and mule breeders. Thousands of us, Reb. If we see the destruction of a few Presences, most of us will forget lipservice to BDL. We might get violent."

"Damn it, we *would* get violent," the boy asserted.

"I think BDL knows that. If I were Harward Justin, I'd be planning to destroy a lot of Presences within minutes of the CHASE report. Before there could be any general uprising. Then I'd use the troops to keep order."

"So what do we do?" Don asked again. "Sit here and die? Try to get out? To do what?"

"Figure something out," said Clarin definitely. "We'll figure something out, Don. But it would help a great deal if you would start by trusting us more than you have."

Donatella shook her head as though she did not understand.

"Oh, come on, Don. You've talked around and around it, for hours. You've told us you found this proof. You've told us you checked the proof. You've told us you have real, factual information. You've told us everything—except what the process was and what the information is. I don't see how we can help you if we don't know."

The Explorer knight rose, stalked away from the fire and stood at some distance from it, her back to them, as rigid as when they had first arrived at the quiet pocket. The fire threw flickering lights along her back, glimmering in her pale hair. "If anyone finds out, they'll kill me," she said.

"They're trying to kill you anyhow. We didn't bring the threat with us. It's already here. I don't think they'll try any harder if they know what the real information is."

Don returned to the fire, rather wild-eyed, like some feral, dirty-faced creature bent over a primordial altar, her face haggard in the leaping light. "You won't believe it," she said at last. "I didn't."

"Try us," suggested Jamieson.

"I talked to the Enigma," she said. "And it talked back."

Dead, disbelieving silence.

"You're joking!" Jamieson said, choking.

"I told you you wouldn't believe me."

"Talked? In words?"

"In words. Real words. And the Enigma talked back. In words."

Silence again. Silence that stretched into moments, each staring at the other, uncertain, unable to believe. . . .

At last Tasmin's voice. "That was a *translator* in the box!"

"A new one," she answered softly. "Very powerful. My friend got it for me. I took the label off."

"I thought it was a transposition program."

"No reason you should have known it was a translator. But the translation is there, in the box. An actual conversation between a person and a Presence. A conversation that makes a kind of sense, too, which is remarkable considering that it's a first of its kind. That's what we were giving Lim Terree. That's why he went to such lengths to get the score from you, Ferrence. He knew what we had."

"God!" Shocked silence once more.

"So, you see," she said, "we have to do something. And all I can think of is what I said before. Spread the word as widely as possible, assuming we could even get access to the com-net, and then hide out until the fallout is over."

"That wouldn't work," said Jamieson.

"I don't understand."

"It doesn't matter that you know the Presences are sentient. You have no witness. The information you've got could have been faked. So long as the CHASE Commission is rigged to give a report of nonsentience, BDL can depend on the military to enforce that ruling, no matter what the truth is. The troopers don't care. Even if you told people and some of them believed you, it wouldn't do any good. BDL would stifle them."

"Maybe not," said Clarin.

Jamieson gave her a challenging look.

"No, really Reb. You haven't taken it all in yet. Listen to what the woman said! She talked to the Enigma. It talked back. If we can actually understand the words of the Presences, there are some very great voices here on Jubal that simply can't be stifled!"

9

Bird-cloud, Silver-seam, Sun-bright, Star of the Mountain, Blue Glory Child of the Twelfth Generation, listening in the quiet of the evening. . . .

To: Bondri Gesel the Wide-eared, Messenger of the Presences.

Bondri singing, along with his troupe in four part harmony, to the outer Silver-seam, the skin, as it were, of the great Presence: "Peace, calm of wind, flow of water, gentleness of tree-frond turning, joy of sunlight, contentment of moonlight and star."

Which did not serve. Silver-seam, Bird-cloud, Star of the Mountain, and so forth returned the song in a series of aching anharmonics: "Discontinuity. Distant: shore thundering. Close, whispering of change. Proliferation of Loudsingers.

Disturbance of one's edges and bits. Fingers itch. Noises in air and earth. Discomfort in the roots. Confusion. Query to Bondri: establish causation?

Bondri the Wide-eared, who had traveled fifty days with his troupe to carry a message to the inner Silver-seam, now paused, his song-sack in limp folds, shaken to the center of his being.

Prime Priest Favel, bent and trembling on his poor old legs, whispered, "Has this ever happened before?"

Bondri flapped his ears in negation, signaling quiet to the troupe. "No Great One has ever asked such questions before. No Great One has really seemed aware of us before, aged one. What shall I sing?"

"Equivocate," suggested the Prime Priest. "Say nothing much at some length. Tell Silver-seam you will seek reasons."

Bondri sang in canon form, which allowed the troupe to follow his lead. After going on at some length, Bondri concluded: "Causation currently unknown. Who knows what passes among the Loudsingers? Who can smell the sunlight? Who can taste the wind? Thy messengers will ascertain."

He had uttered no word of the inner message he had come so far to deliver, even though it was a brief one: "Red Bird to the top of Silver Mountain." Most of the inner messages the viggies carried were no more lengthy than this particular one, which had come from the Great Blue Tooth, Horizon Loomer, Mighty Hand, the Presence humankind called the East Jammer. Prime Priest Favel, who had learned human speech in captivity among the Loudsingers in his youth, was fond of naming the Great Ones with human titles, using human words that he said were thought-provoking in their very imprecision. There had seemed to be no point in attempting to deliver the message that East Jammer had sent. Inner Silver-seam would not even have heard it so long as its skin was quivering like this or while this strange questioning was happening—though the latter seemed stilled, at least for the moment.

"Should I try to quiet it for the message?" Bondri hummed to the priest.

He received a gesture in reply, why not.

Bondri swelled his throat into a great, ruby balloon and sang again to the skin, sang of calm, signaling the troupe to begin an antiphon on the theme of evening, one composed by

Bondri's own ancestor in a season of incessant and troubling storm. It was one of the most efficacious of the surface songs. The troupe composed itself for best projection and howled harmoniously, throats swelled into sonorous rotundity, putting all their energy into it at length and to little effect. The very air quivered with annoyance. Bird-cloud, Silver-seam, Sun-bright, Star of the Mountain, and all—known among humankind as the North Watcher—was not tranquil and would not become so.

"Cacophony, dissonance, melodic lines falling apart," whispered a part leader to Bondri. "Great Bird-cloud is annoyed with his messengers." High Priest Favel stood to one side, bent and waiting, making no comment, though Bondri threw him a nervous glance.

There was no help for it. Bondri stood forward and chirped a staccato phrase. "Tumble down threatens hereabout, dangerous for viggy-folk, go and stay away, away a time, quick, quick." He turned to the old priest. "Your perceptiveness must come quickly."

This was the sense of Bondri's message, though these were not the words. The words had other meanings—leader to troupe, experienced singer to novices in the presence of a Prime Priest of the people—and there were implications of the time of day and the season, modifications of language required by the site in which the words were spoken. When one of the Companions of the Gods quoted another, there was no need for the hearer to ask when or to whom the words were spoken or in what weather or circumstance. The words themselves said it all. The word *taroo*—go—was sung in the early morning. It became *tarou* at midmorning and *tarouu* at noon. It was *itaroo* sung in sunlight and *etaroo* sung in light mist. *Atarouualayum* conveyed the going of a mated pair, sans giligee, at midmorning in driving rain, somewhat north of the Shadowed Cliffs . . . in spring.

So now, Bondri's words conveyed a chill autumn evening in the vicinity of the North Watcher during which a familial troupe of viggies—males, females, giligees, and young, all, except the very newest trade daughters, sharing the same thought patterns—had approached the Great One to deliver a message but could not get past the skin to deliver it and were putting themselves in peril if they didn't move. Bondri felt compelled to reissue the warning to which Prime Priest Favel had not yet harkened.

"Your (autumn chilled but most valued) perceptiveness? The (mighty but not quite trustworthy) Presence in whose (arbitrary and sometimes simply vengeful) decisions we trust grows (dangerously and maliciously) agitated. Best (imperative) we depart."

The priest flicked his elbows in agreement, and Bondri made the wing sign in turn to the pouchmate pathfinders of the troupe, who slithered off at once down an almost invisible track along the side of the North Watcher. This was a proven track on which movement was possible without alerting the Great One. The crystalline structure beneath it had no fractures, no vacancies, no dislocations, no planar defects or interstitials—none of those deviations from uniform crystalline structure that in the Presences served the function served by neurons and neuro-transmitters in fleshly creatures. Not that the viggies, or as they called themselves, "etaromimi," knew that. They did know that the track was solid, stolid, and without sensation. In a few hundred yards it would debouch upon a pocket of safe soil where a small grove of trees provided a place to rest. The Prime Priest was very old and needed surcease.

"Is far enough?" hummed one of the troupe. "Silverseam can make great destruction, very far."

Bondri was by no means sure it was far enough, but it was as far as the Prime Priest was likely to get, given the state of his legs. They had been broken in his youth and had never healed properly. While they were broken, he had been captured by the Loudsingers and held captive long enough to learn their language. Much later one of the young Loudsingers, blessed be his familial patterns of thought forever, had kindly released Favel to his people. That Loudsinger's name was Lim Ferrence, and his was one of the names of honor whose patterns were recalled by Bondri's troupe during times of recollection.

Behind them on the slope, several of the Great One's fingers blew their tips with a crash and volley of tinkling glass.

" 'Lings," murmured Favel, giving the fingers their human name. " 'Lings."

None of the debris came near the viggies, and Bondri sighed in relief. The Great Ones were not always sensible about assigning fault. If a viggy did something to displease them, their skins or fingers might kill quite another viggy in retaliation. It was almost as though the skins did not know the difference between one individual and another. Or did not know there was a difference. They were the same with the Loudsingers. Sometimes the Great Ones would incubate annoyance for a very long time, exercising vengeance long after the original culprit had gone away or died. At least, this is the way it seemed to Bondri, even though the Prime Priest told him otherwise.

"It is the difference between their insides and outsides," panted the Prime Priest, making Bondri realize he had been vocalizing. "The surfaces of their minds are shallow and quick to irritate. They slap at us as we twitch at a woundfly, unthinking. In the Depths, where the great thoughts move at the roots of the mountains, they are slow to reason and, I believe, largely unconscious of us. I have often thought there is little connection between the two parts of them."

"Except for the way Silver-seam behaved tonight," caroled Bondri. "Strangely."

"Strangely indeed! It seemed well aware of us, did it not? As though some midmind had come awake."

It had indeed seemed quite aware of them, a very uncomfortable thought. "Blessed be (all Presences, large and small, their fingers and skin-parts) they," said Bondri, antennae erect and curved inward over his head, warding away any ill fortune that the priest's remark might otherwise attract.

"Oh, by all means," sighed Favel. "Yes."

"May I assist your (aged and infirm and overly chilled) perceptiveness?"

"If you would be so (gracious in this season) kind, youngster. I get creakier with every moon."

"We would be honored to carry you."

"That much is not necessary. A shoulder to lean on would be welcome."

The troupe sped down the track, moving as quickly as possible consonant with the requisite care. Dislodging bits of crystal trash often made the Great Ones very angry, particularly if it was done noisily. Pieces had to be picked up gently and set aside, and that took time, but long practice made the troupe both quick and silent.

By the time dark fell, they had reached the grove of trees.

"Where are we?" the Prime Priest asked, settling himself into a soft pocket of earth and fluffing his fur to retain body heat. "I do not recognize this route."

"Back side of Silver-seam," Bondri reported. "Just east of the Tineea Singers, Those-Who-Welcome-Without-Meaning-It, named by the Loudsingers, the False Eagers. An easy transit, your perceptiveness."

"Perhaps by tomorrow, an easy transit. At the moment, an impossible one. I cannot move farther. Have we food?"

"Wet food and dry. Comfort yourself while we prepare."

Preparation took little time. There were edible stalks to peel, grain heads to thresh, a few seed pods to open with a sharpened bone. It was not viggy bone. The bones of the viggies were fragile and light, and in any case the ritual of disposal made viggy bone inaccessible for any useful purpose. On the other hand, the hard strong bones of the Loudsingers and their animals were often found at the roots of the Great Ones and were much sought after. Viggies had been anatomizing human and mule corpses for generations, and there was little they did not know about human anatomy. The giligees, particularly, were interested in this knowledge. Sometimes among the wreckage of Loudsingers, animals, and wagons, there were bits of metal, also. Sharp or toothed edges made from this material were even more treasured. Bondri carried several bits of metal in his vestigial pouch just below his song-sack, gifts from his people, mostly salvaged at the foot of Highmost Darkness, Lord of the Gyre-Birds, Smoke Master, the one the humans called Black Tower.

The Prime Priest munched on peeled stalks of settler's brush and made polite conversation, as befit a time of food sharing. "One could almost forgive the humans (outlanders, weird strangers who say unmentionable and disgusting things with words that are not true, thereby incurring the taboo) for coming to Our-Land-of-the-Gods," he sang. "They have brought good food."

"Some of it," admitted Bondri, whose troupe had only recently acquired the habit of raiding human fields and gardens. "The little seeds at the top of the long stems are good, even though they are only ripe one time of the year. And the various thick roots and sweet leaves are good, and those juicy bulbs that grow on their trees. The big seeds aren't good. Brou they call them."

"I don't think they use the big seeds for food."

"I've heard that sung," Bondri conceded. "I've heard they mash the big seeds at a place near the sea, mash them, and put them in containers, and send them away in boats. Our fisher-kin-who-run-from-the-sea-bringing-fish say the mashed seeds go off-world."

"That is true," the Prime Priest acknowledged in a minor key. "During my captivity, I saw it with my own eyes. The Loudsingers eat brou to make them cheerful."

"They do not make us cheerful. The big seeds are very dangerous."

"Arum," the Prime Priest nodded, his throat sack swelling and collapsing in sadness. "I lost all of one pouch to them. The pouch boss went down into the Loudsinger fields. She was at that age where they taste everything, and her pouchmates followed her. One taste and fff. Hopeless. Nothing could be done." He sat silently, mourning. When a mated pair and the giligee could produce a pouchful only every six or seven years, the loss of an entire set of pouchmates was difficult to bear. Next time the chosen giligee would go well back into the country to incubate, well away from deepsoil. And the giligee would stay there until his daughters were of reasonable age, beyond that curious, mouthing stage when everything went between the back teeth. It was difficult to live away from deepsoil, but one or more of the older children could go with the giligee, as helper. There was always etaromimi-bush, called by the Loudsingers settler's brush, if there was nothing else.

"Your perceptiveness?"

"Yes, Bondri."

"You haven't told me where you wish to go."

"The gods are distressed. You see it for yourself, Bondri, First Singer, Troupe Leader. Just as the North Watcher Silver-seam and so forth—just as it quivers and blows its fingers, so do other of the Great Ones. Highmost Darkness,

Lord of the Gyre-Birds, Smoke Master, the one the humans call Black Tower has been particularly disturbed. And now this questioning? This complaint of tumult! Who can it be who makes this tumult? Who are the sensible creatures? There are only three possibilities. The gods themselves. Or the Loudsingers. Or us. Only we three are sensible creatures to make causes of things. Can there be any other answer?"

Bondri admitted there could be no other.

The Priest chewed thoughtfully, rubbing at his legs with his bony fingers. "I go toward a place of meeting. Prime Priests will be there from south and north. We will talk of this. It is very disturbing. One does not know what truth is."

Bondri shuffled his feet back and forth in the dust. "Is it possible, perceptiveness, that it is the gods themselves?"

The Prime Priest waved his ears in negation. "Nothing is certain. It could be that this confusion emanates from the Mad One. Song has come that the Mad One spoke to a Loudsinger."

There was a sharply indrawn breath from the viggies, who had been eavesdropping politely, trilling an occasional phrase antiphonally to indicate attention. A Presence had broken the ban! Spoken to a Loudsinger! Done what every viggy was forbidden to do!

"How? If the Loudsinger had not the words of calm for the skin and the words of greeting for the inner one?"

"There is rumor," Favel sang, "that the Loudsinger, a female Loudsinger, had the words."

"How did she come by them?" The entire troupe held its breath, waiting for the answer to this.

The old viggy sighed. "Do not ask what you already know must be true. If she had them, she had them from us. Are we not etaromimi, Goers Between the Gods? Have the trees suddenly taken up singing?"

The old priest had used the humorous mode, which called for appreciative laughter, though with the intonation requiring slight shame, and this evoked an embarrassed cadenza from the troupe. Now he waved his ears at them, a cautionary gesture. "We had best giggle (melodically) now. Later may be only occasions for (disharmonic) sorrow."

"There was that time," Bondri intoned, the words conveying a time some fifty years before, in the spring of the year, when one troupe had been surprised by a (foreign, weird, off-world) creature. "He had a (noise creator, song stealer, abomination) machine."

"Do any now live who remember that time?" crooned the troupe in unison and with deep reverence.

"None," hymned the priest, closing the litany of recollection. "Only the holy words remember." The words were quite enough, of course. Though individual viggies died, words were immortal. Words and melodies and the lovely mathematics of harmony, these were the eternal things, the things of the gods. So long as they were remembered accurately—and the Prime Priests had the job of remembering them all—everything could be reconstructed as it had happened at the time. The surprise. The fleeing. The creeping back to see what the strange creature was doing. The horror as they heard the stolen song, captive in the machine, the attempt to rescue the song—to no avail. Several had died in the effort, but the song was still captive. Captive, no doubt, until this very day. And now, perhaps that same (grieved for, sorrowed over) song had been used against its will to speak to the Mad One, the Presence Without Innerness, the Killer Without Cause, called by the Loudsingers, the Enigma.

"Poor (predestined to sorrow, condemned, doomed) creatures," caroled a young giligee, solo voice. "If the Mad One has done this thing, the next time it will kill. The Mad One always talks once, then kills the next time. The Loudsinger(s) will undoubtedly die." The giligee voice soared, and Bondri closed his eyes in appreciation of that voice, even as he shivered at the words.

"True," quavered the old priest, taking a comforting bite of fruit. "If any Loudsingers go trying to sing to the Enigma again, undoubtedly the Enigma will kill them all."

—————————— 10

In his hovel on the outskirts of Splash One, Brother-minor Jeshel, whip-hand of the Society of Crystallites, Worshippers of the Holy Ones, Gods Incarnate on Jubal, finished beating his handmaid and looked around for someone else who might

need admonishment. Brother Jeshel was almost certain the
Gods Incarnate had spoken to him in a dream. He seemed to
remember something of the kind happening, and had his
handmaid not interrupted him, he would have remembered
it clearly enough to tell The Three and maybe be allowed to
testify to a vision in temple.

Sister Sophron lay on the floor, half naked and weeping.

"Get up," he snarled. "And don't wake me up like that
again."

"A messenger came," she sobbed. "From her. I didn't
know what else to do."

"The messenger could wait. Cover yourself. You're disgusting like that."

Since Sister Sophron had not removed her gown, the
accusation was unjust. Nonetheless, she pulled the rent fabric
to cover her back and shoulders and tried to tie it in front,
noting in passing that several of the ties were pulled off.
Brother-minor Jeshel had wakened in a rage.

"What does he want?"

"The messenger?"

"Who else are we talking about, slut! Of course, the
messenger."

"He says he's from her, the wife."

"Ah. Tell him I'll talk to him in a bit. Get yourself
dressed. You'll need to get yourself into town, to your job."

Shuffling and holding the gown together at her waist,
Sister Sophron left the room. She did not meet the messenger's eyes when she repeated Jeshel's remarks, nor did she
look back to see how they were received. At the moment she
could think only of getting to the privy before she threw up.
It wasn't right of Jeshel to beat her when she was like this.
She had thought it would be better on Jubal, but it was no
better, not at all. Brother-minor Jeshel was no different from
comrade-insurgent Jeshel. He used slightly different words,
that was all. Back on Serendipity Jeshel had said "Revolt" and
"The Cause" and "The-rotten-management, with all its boot-
lickers." Now he said "Presences" and "Evangelism" and
"The-rotten-BDL with all its flunkeys"—Tripsingers and Explorers included—but it still came down to yelling and burn-
ings and killing people from behind. It still came down to
Sophron earning their living while Jeshel conspired. It still

came down to blood and bombs and being beaten on when you were pregnant. Vomiting copiously, Sister Sophron cursed Brother-minor Jeshel and wished for the moment she had never told him what that Explorer knight had said when Sophron had been cutting her hair.

Behind her in the filthy hall, Rheme Gentry made a face to himself and went on humming quietly. He was very weary, having returned from Northwest only very late last evening, but he would not sit down. There was nothing clean enough to sit on. Eventually Jeshel would show up, dirty and uncombed, probably bug infested as well, though that would be difficult on this planet. There were no human parasites. Perhaps Jeshel had evaded quarantine in order to have some shipped in. Rheme had not yet met Brother-minor Jeshel, but he had heard about him: a lower level functionary in the Crystallite hierarchy, but one reputedly responsible for a good deal of general terrorism and disruption. After sending Tasmin Ferrence to find, and one hoped to assist, Don Furz, the four conspirators, Vowe and Vox, Middleton, and Gentry, had discussed various Crystallites as a possible source of information, and Brother Jeshel had been their unanimous choice. Rheme, it was decided, should put on a modest disguise and a false name to interrogate the man. Rheme amused himself by thinking what his uncle would say to all this. The director of CHAIN wouldn't be delighted at the risk, that much was sure.

He set that uncomfortable thought aside and considered various names for the group that was getting itself together here on Jubal. They might name it the Quarternine Conspiracy. Or perhaps the Card Game Connivance. The most accurate title could be Four Against the Tide. Although according to Thyle Vowe it would be vastly more than four when the Tripsingers learned what was going on—those who didn't already suspect.

Besides, it was wrong to think of it as a conspiracy. A counterconspiracy, rather. A counterintelligence group. This allowed for some additional names. The Jubal Operation. He rather liked that one.

"What'a you want?" The voice was unaccommodating. Gentry turned to see the Crystallite standing behind him, as lank haired, stubble faced, and smelly as had been described.

"My name is Basty Pardo," Gentry advised him. "The

Governor's lady is interested in how her little project is coming along." His name had been Basty Pardo once, and he was certain that the Governor's lady was interested in a good many things. Rheme avoided lies whenever possible.

Brother Jeshel grunted. Gentry was a type he hated instinctively. He was clean and fit looking, with good teeth. Such men couldn't be up to any good, so far as Brother Jeshel was concerned, but he couldn't insult the man. Not now. Not yet. He chose divagation.

"I'm interested in how my own little project is coming along! Some troopers took some of my people the other day. Out toward the Great Ones we was watchin' over. Heretics came right by the Great Ones, and when we chastised 'em, the troopers came. She told us she'd keep the troopers off us."

Rheme put on his voice of cold command. "If you're talking about your attack on the Tripsinger and his acolytes who came through the Mad Gap, it was stupid of your people to interfere. The Governor can keep the troops off your neck so long as you don't assault people, Jeshel, but once you start throwing things, the troopers will move. Nobody can stop them."

Jeshel glared at him in astonishment. The pretty boy could talk hard at any rate. "The Governor can command 'em."

"Not when it's a case of public order. They have standing orders for situations like that. The Governor can keep the troopers from rounding you up—at least for a while—but he can't give you immunity. You know that." It all had a fine authoritative sound, and Rheme wondered briefly if he was saying anything at all true or relevant to the situation. In most situations, sounding authoritative was good enough.

Jeshel grunted. The assault on the Tripsinger had been a calculated risk. He hadn't really expected to get away with it, but his people were getting restless, eager for some real confrontation. There had to be an incident soon, something major, or some of them would start to backslide.

"The Governor's lady wants to know what's going on," Rheme repeated impatiently, hoping the man would respond. It would be dangerous to stay too long or to talk much more than he already had. A wrong word and the filthy fanatic would catch on to the fact that Rheme knew next to nothing and was fishing for information.

"I don't know. It was only yesterday. I sent some people, but they haven't come back yet."

Nor had Donatella Furz come back yet, at least she had not by the time Rheme left Northwest City. Nor had the starkly handsome Tripsinger and his acolytes, come to that. "Did you send some of your followers?" This seemed a safe question.

"Nuh. Not real members. Some people I know."

"You think . . . ah . . . this time they'll succeed?"

"I sent enough of 'em. Four of 'em. If she got sent out yesterday, like was promised, my people should'a caught up with her about dark."

"Heavens." Rheme took out his handkerchief and fastidiously wiped his hands and brow, deciding to risk it. "That should be enough to deal with one Explorer, shouldn't it? But then, we have to remember, you didn't succeed either time before."

"What'a you mean, either time?" Jeshel scowled at the smaller man, a suspicious snarl crossing his lips. "Wasn't any other time. This is the only one."

"Is it only once? Well, it may be. The Governor's lady uses other people as well. Well, I'll give her your message. Meantime, tell your people to stay out of trouble, Jeshel. Burn themselves up all they like, but don't throw rocks? Hmmm?"

Outside in the street, Rheme unlocked his car in the face of twenty scowling Crystallites who had materialized from various hovels and alley openings, carefully not looking at any of them. They were the kind of beasts that were threatened by a direct look. When he drove off, it was to the clatter and splat of missiles hitting the car, but he felt cheered that it was nothing worse than that.

Though his own temporary office was at Government House, he drove directly to BDL Headquarters and parked in the back, not in the courtyard. That courtyard, like that of the citadel next door, was under fairly consistent surveillance by Honeypeach herself, who liked to know who was going and coming from Splash One. Inside the building, he slipped down a flight of back stairs and into an untenanted cross hallway. At the end of it was an unmarked door, and he knocked softly, in an insistent pattern.

"Gentry?" someone whispered.

"Me," he agreed, slipping through the door as it opened a crack. "Good heavens, do we have to go through all this whisper and skulk?"

Gereny Vox lifted one eyebrow. "There's no eyes or ears in this room, Rheme. It's maybe the only room in the whole BDL building you can say that about. Reason there's no eyes is that this is the mule breeding files down here. Who the hell cares about the mule farm files, right? I've got a reason to be here. You don't. Better say it quick and get gone."

He sighed, wiping his forehead once again. "Get word to Thyle that you were right. Honeypeach traded favors with Brother Jeshel to get Don Furz killed. He sent four men, but it's the only time he has sent anyone." He wiped his forehead and ran his finger inside his high, tight collar. "Gereny, it's hotter than the Core Stars down here."

"Keeps the files from gettin' musty. You got anything else?"

"No. How did you find out about Honeypeach anyhow?"

She spat, ritually, without moisture. "Two dumb stall cleaners at the stables here in Splash One, yakkin' about stuff while they should be shovelin' shit. Didn't see me in the stall fixin' Tinkerbell's leg. Both of 'em sort of Crystallites. Not the hard core kind, but the hangers-on. Well. One of 'em has a brother, and he says his brother's been sent with some other guys off to Northwest. To do in some Explorer knight, so he said. They were all paid a good bit to go. Said the knight would be sent out on a mission and they could kill her when she was on her way back, because the Governor's wife wanted her dead." She spat again. "I told Thyle and he called you and Jem for a meetin'. You were late, but you heard the rest of it. We guessed it was Don Furz, she bein' the only one much in the public eye up there, but we didn't know 'til I called the Priory it was all goin' to happen so soon."

"I may be able to find out a little more, as I'm not known around here yet, and nobody but the four of us knows I work for the PEC. Are you getting anywhere?"

"We're puttin' two and two together."

"According to Jem there seem to have been two attempts on the Explorer's life in the past, plus the one yesterday," Gentry mused. "What made Jem suspicious that somebody tried to kill Furz before?"

"Jem's got a birdy over in BDL Exploration Division."

"Birdy?"

"A little spy. Somebody low down in the ranks, somebody no one pays any attention to. Probably some data clerk or communications expediter. Jem didn't say who, and we didn't ask. Well, the birdy says the orders sending Furz out to Redfang the first time weren't to standard. Somebody's approval missin', something not right. And Jem found out today the orders sending her out there this last time weren't any more legitimate than the first ones. Both sets were boggled."

"Boggled?"

"Faked! Some wallmouse creepin' out at night to boggle orders. Who do you suppose? The Explorer King? I'd put my chits there. Easy enough to tell, Gentry. You've got the connections. Find out whether Chase Random Hall has accounts on Serendipity. If he's got money there, it's nine times sure he's your wallmouse, sendin' his own Explorer off to get killed." Her face writhed briefly at the thought of this betrayal.

Rheme Gentry made a quick note. "Don't count on my being able to find out anything, Gereny. Mail to Serendipity's being censored or just lost, even the diplomatic stuff from Government House. BDL controls the ships, and except for a few odds and ends, messages aren't getting through."

"Now how do you know that?"

"I had acknowledgment signals worked out, things to be planted in the system news, outside the BDL net, and they aren't showing up. Jubal's getting zipped up tight, Gereny. I'll see what I can find out about Hall, but I wouldn't fasten on him too quickly. It could be someone else. Hall's a little conspicuous. I'd bet on someone less noticeable."

"Poor Donatella," Gereny mused. "Nice gal. Met her three or four times, always pleasant. No snoot to her, like some of those Explorers. Hope she's all right."

"Well, we'll hope Tasmin Ferrence got there in time to help her out. Jeshel said he sent four ruffians, but if they were the quality I saw hanging around in the Crystallite quarter, the stun rifle should have increased the odds in our favor. Those two attempts before bother me, though. Brother Jeshel claims no part in those. . . .

"Even if it is the Explorer King, I'll bet he's not acting on his own. I'd like to know who's giving the orders."

Price Zimble sat at the feet of the Explorer King, gently stroking the King's knees and calves. Chase Random Hall, while relishing the sensation, affected not to notice this intimacy.

"Then what did you do?" the King asked. "After Donatella got back from Splash One?"

"I hung around," said Zimmy. "I've been hanging around for days."

"She hasn't asked for you since?"

"Not once."

"You've been through her room?"

"Over and over again. There's nothing there, Chase. A few odds and ends of papers and things she's working on, and her own things. That's all."

"No messages?"

"None that aren't ordinary. You know. Ralth asking her to have dinner, or Martin inviting her for a drink, or something like that. A thank you note from her old cousin down in Splash One."

"It could be code."

"Code! For heaven's sake, Randy. It said, 'Dearest Donatella, thank you so much for the nice lunch. Do give my best to your mother. Love, Cousin Cyndal.' If you can make code out of that. . . ."

The King made an irritated moue, his mouth twisting unattractively. "Nothing more about the man down in Splash One, the one that died in the Chapter House?"

"Nothing. No one knows who he is or who sent him. Unless you do."

"Don't be silly, Zimmy. Justin sent him. Who else?" His voice was not as sure as the words.

"What do you want me to do now?"

"In the unlikely event she comes back from this Redfang trip. . . ."

"Unlikely event?" Zimmy opened his eyes very wide in ingenuous surprise.

"Somebody saw to it she got sent, idiot, and it wasn't me. I saw the orders! They were boggled. Why did the powers that be send her off into the Redfang anyhow? There's nothing there that really needed doing."

"Powers that be?" Zimmy was all innocence.

The Explorer King sounded irritated. Parts of the puzzle didn't fit. He, the King, had been told not to do anything to Don Furz. But someone was doing something to Don Furz. Who? And why? He didn't look closely at Zimmy. If he had, he might have surprised a glimmer of amusement in Zimmy's eyes.

"Don't ask questions, Zimmy. The less you know the better off you are. And if she does come back, be there and don't look surprised."

"Well, of course, Randy," said Zimmy with a hurt expression. "I have better sense than that."

Maybelle Thonks listened to her stepmother singing and cringed inside. Honeypeach only sang when in the ascendency, and Maybelle hated to guess whose bloody and recumbent bodies her father's wife must be currently and unmelodically stomping over.

"Problem?" asked Rheme Gentry. He had just come out of the Governor's office with a stack of papers, which he placed on his desk. "Anything the Governor's aide can do to help?"

"Honeypeach is singing."

"Ah?"

"It probably means she's just killed somebody."

"May Bee." It was said softly, but unmistakably as a warning.

"Well, it does."

He whispered. "It may, but we are not going to say so. Not inside Government House. Not anywhere where we might be overheard. Are we?" He took her hand and led her out onto the wide terrace, which extended along two sides of the house, well away from concealing shrubbery or roof overhangs.

When they were clear of the building, she said, "Rheme, how do you stand it?"

"Well, I confess I was somewhat dismayed when I arrived to take the job as your father's aide and learned exactly what his wife thought that entailed."

"How did you keep out of her clutches?"

"I told her I had picked up a virulent and sexually transmitted infection on Rentree Four, that it was currently in remission but still quite communicable, and that the symptoms of the disease in women included complete atrophy of the breasts and other genitalia."

"Rheme! Did you really? You did. My God, I never would have . . . how marvelous."

"I further told her that she needn't worry about her stepdaughter because I found women of your type unattractive. I told her I disliked light brown hair and hazel eyes because they reminded me of my evil aunty, the scourge of my youth."

"You beast."

"As a result, she has not worried, and you and I are allowed to be much together. Of course, she may be watching you eagerly for signs of atrophy. One doesn't know."

"You didn't answer my first question. How do you stand it? You know what daddy's up to."

"I do, indeed. He is up to making a very large fortune for himself before the bottom falls out here on Jubal. He is taking money from the Crystallites with one hand and from BDL with the other. When BDL does whatever it is planning to do, which I haven't totally figured out yet, there will be big trouble, following which there will probably be an inquiry. In advance of the inquiry your father will resign to enjoy his retirement on Serendipity or Eutopia or New Havah-eh or some such place."

"It's dishonorable."

"Not a word that your father has used much, Maybelle. One thing I confess that I don't understand is why you are as you are while he is what he is."

"Because I had Mother around for over twenty years. And he's had Honeypeach. She corrupts people. Not that daddy needed much corrupting. He's had her since she was fifteen. Can you believe that? Her son, Ymries Fedder, is really my father's son, too. It's why Mother left him, when she finally found out about it."

"And you are here only because your mother died."

"I'm here because I had nowhere else to go. Mother's family disowned her when she married the honorable Wuyllum. The honorable Wuyllum was sending support for me, but he quit when Mother died. She and I were living on Serendipity, but as an off-worlder I couldn't even get a work permit there."

"You could work here."

"Doing what?"

"Your father could put in a word with BDL. There should be some kind of registered job available."

"He won't. I've begged him. He doesn't want me to have any resources at all except what he provides. He's a terrible man, Rheme. He possesses people. Mother had told me some things, but I didn't have any idea what he's really like until I got here. He doesn't do anything much with people, but he likes to own them. Every now and then he'll twitch the chain, just to be sure it's still attached." She turned away, biting her lip to keep the tears back.

"You could marry me."

"Yes, I could. The idea is a very attractive one, too. But it would be the end of your job here, believe me. We'd have to leave."

"That wouldn't be the end of the universe, May Bee."

"Not if we got away. We might not, Rheme. I know you think I'm overstating things, but things happen to people who don't do what Daddy or Honeypeach want them to do. Sometimes they have accidents and die. Sometimes they just disappear."

"Ah," he said again, not arguing with her. After his interview with Brother Jeshel, he no longer doubted her—not that he ever had.

"I get so . . . so angry. I love this place—not Government House, but Jubal. I met an explorer, Donatella Furz, at one of the receptions. I told her I'd never seen the countryside, and she took me out into the crystal country. It's beautiful, very strange and mystical. It's obvious what's going to happen to it. It's going to be destroyed. By my father. By BDL. I keep thinking there must be something I could do."

"Thou and I," he mused, looking back into Government House through the door they had left open behind them. Honeypeach Thonks was standing in that doorway, staring at her stepdaughter with the look that a hungry gyre-bird might fasten on some bit of tasty carrion. Rheme bowed in her direction, a bit more deeply than custom required. When he got his head up again, she was gone. "Yes," he mused softly, so that only Maybelle could hear. "We're going to have to do something."

On the roof of the Crystallite Temple in Splash One, just to one side of the high mud brick, plastic gilded dome, there was a comfortable apartment reached by a twisting stair hidden in one of the massive pillars that supported the vaulted ceiling. It was accessible only to a few servants and the three residents: Chantiforth H. Bins, Myrony Clospocket, and Aphrodite Sells, these three being both the heart and soul of the Crystallite religion on Jubal. It was the place they spent most of their time between services, except for infrequent and well-disguised forays into the less savory night life of Splash One.

"Jeshel's stirrin' up the fuckin' rabble again," remarked Myrony, his bald pate gleaming in the light of the late afternoon sun as he put down the com-control and moved toward the glass doors that opened on a spacious roof terrace. "Our man over in BDL reports he assaulted some fuckin' Tripsinger a few days ago. I wish you'd sit on him, Bins. You're the High Pontiff, and that's the only one he listens to. He's goin' to provoke Thonks to do somethin' foolish before we're ready."

The multitudes would have been surprised to see their High Priest at home, Myrony's shiny pate unwigged, his sonorous voice fallen into the vulgar accents of his youth. Myrony had been born and reared in a scum-pocket on Zenith, an entertainment world known more for its depravity than for its devotion to theology. That he had risen so far into godliness from this beggarly beginning spoke volumes for his tenacity and ruthlessness, if not for his conscience.

"Old Sweet Wuyllum won't do anything until we're ready," murmured Aphrodite through perfect teeth and lips, which pursed into a kiss as she peered into the mirror and preened over the glitter of the new firestone necklace. She had been Myrony's associate on a dozen worlds, and she knew him better than anyone still living. "Thonks knows whose hand stuffs his pocket."

"Not necessarily so, Affy," Chantiforth Bins corrected her in comfortably avuncular tones. Though his association with the other two was more recent than theirs with one another, he had long ago adopted a familiar and confidential tone with them both. "The Governor could be forced to move. Myrony's right. We need to sit on Jeshel unless Wuyllum tells us he needs an incident. And then we need to do a quick sunder and be off-planet by the time it happens."

"Harward Justin's not going to let anything happen to us," the woman remarked, stretching luxuriously while stroking the gemstones. The necklace was a gift from Justin, and Aphrodite had her own reasons for believing the BDL boss would take care of them. Her ego was so strong that she had never considered any other outcome of their relationship. Though she didn't realize it, her complaisance was a personality trait that Justin much appreciated, since he felt it made her totally predictable. He would have been reinforced in this opinion by her remarks. "Justin likes the good job we've done for him," she said, smiling at her own reflection and giving the gem one last pat. She did not enjoy remembering the earning of the gift, but having it made up for that. "It's the first time we've ever hired out to start a religion, you know that? It's been what you might call interesting."

"Given the free hand we had, it wasn't bad," Chantiforth admitted.

"It wasn't workin' worth shit until Justin brought in those shiploads of trash from Serendipity," Myrony remarked. "Didn't have two converts to rub together until then. You have to hand it to Justin. He knew the kind of people would go for it. Jeshel and his bunch are just right."

"Jeshel and his bunch are going to scream contra-tenor when they get interned with all the rest," Chantiforth objected. "Justin may be sorry he's got them on his hands then."

"Let Jeshel scream. Let him say anything he likes. He has no idea who we really are, and less than no idea where we're going to be. The army'll take care of Jeshel." Chantiforth Bins rose and crossed to the high windows that looked out over the city. "I'm going to miss this place."

"Not me," Aphrodite said. "The food's lousy, the noise never lets up, and the only music they have is that damn Tripsinger howling. Me for the Spice Coast on 'Dipity."

"I think we all agree it was worth it though." Bins turned from the window with a smile, rubbing his fingers together suggestively. "Biggest one we've done together. Didn't all those pilgrims bleed money?"

Aphrodite puckered her forehead. "Pity there won't be anymore pilgrims when BDL crashes everything. And you're right, Chants. We need to do a sunder well ahead of the shutdown. No telling what some PEC flunky might end up doing. There might be some kind of a last-minute shift that could leave us where we're not supposed to be. Whenever that CHASE Commission gets here, we need to start moving. Couple of months? Or maybe sooner, from what I hear. And we need to watch our money, too. Even though it's on Serendipity, something could go wrong. There's about six million now. Split three ways, Chants-love, that's two million for each of us. Which is not too utterly threadbare for three years' part-time work."

"More than three fuckin' years total," growled Myrony. "Chanty and me had to set up the Jut Massacre, remember? That was a little iffy. I didn't like bein' that close to those fuckin' Presences. And there was some rumor-mongerin' even before that."

Aphrodite shrugged. "It didn't exactly take your full time, My. You and Chanty managed to get in on that Heron's World slash-up in between. You guys made me real mad on that one, you know! I'm some kind of shredded settler's brush, you couldn't cut me in on that?" She stood up and drifted lazily to the window, looking out over the low parapet to the snarling hubbub of the city.

"You weren't around," Myrony snarled, giving her a nasty look. "You were busy. Seems to me there was something I heard about some diplomatic papers that disappeared."

"Never mind," she said, turning to wave her hands at him, shushing him. "I don't want to be reminded."

Below them in the vaulted sanctuary, a bell rang repeatedly, the measured dong, dong, dong seeming to tighten the very atmosphere around them.

"Evening services," said Chantiforth, rising and moving toward the rack where his robe and crown were hung. "Damn. I'm getting tired of this. It was kind of fun at first, but I've had it to my back teeth."

"All you have to do is look impressive," Myrony objected. "It's my night for the sermon."

"Mine for dispensing revelations," Aphrodite remarked. "I think I'll wear that new mantle with the blue feathers. What'll the message from the Presences be tonight?"

"Work for the fuckin' hour cometh," Myrony suggested with an unpriestly sneer as he reached for the full white wig that stood on a stand by the door.

"Repent for the day is at hand," sniggered Chantiforth.

"What'd'you think they really say?" she asked, stretching. "The Presences? Y'ever thought about that?"

The two men, tall, white haired, benevolent looking as saints, gave her equally empty stares, as though wondering if she had gone mad.

"No," she sighed. "I guess you guys never thought about that."

Don Furz looked down on the Redfang valley from a high pass, her head barely lifted above the line of crystal prominences, swiveling slowly as she examined the lowlands with a pair of excellent glasses. She stopped several times and stared intently, adjusting the glasses for focus, then moved on. When she had scanned the entire valley, she wriggled back down the pass to join Tasmin and his acolytes, who were lying beside the trail playing with Clarin's crystal mouse.

"They're there," she said crisply. "At least two bunches of them."

"The same ones as last night?" Tasmin asked, handing the mouse to Clarin and getting to his feet.

"They look the same. Who knows? One group is right down at the bottom of the trail, as though they were waiting for us. The other one is moving along down the center of the valley, as though they don't even know the other one is here."

"Did you see robes? Tripsinger robes?"

"In the group moving down the valley, yes. Two of them. But no robes at the bottom of the trail."

"Which way is the 'Singer group headed?"

"There's a passworded trail east of them. It'll take them in behind the Redfang range, about five miles south and east of us."

Tasmin frowned. "We can wait until the 'Singer group goes on into the range, then we can cross their trail behind them and out of sight of the ones below us."

"There's a route I know." She nodded. "If we can get behind the 'Singer group, I can get us into a fast north-south corridor."

Tasmin nodded approval. "Then once we're far enough south to avoid immediate trouble, we can split up. Some of us need to get to Thyle Vowe. I wish his message had been just slightly less enigmatic, that he'd told us just what it is he's aware of, but we have to operate on the assumption he knows or at least suspects what's going on. Whether he does or not, we need help and there's nowhere else to get it."

"I never intended to involve others," Donatella complained. "It makes me feel hideously responsible."

"You didn't involve us, not purposely. The acolytes and I have talked this over, Explorer." He rose and stretched, the full sleeves of his robe dropping back to his shoulders as he reached for the sky. Then he turned to her, shaking his robes down around him. "We . . . or I should say, I started this journey to solve a couple of personal mysteries—things I needed to know about Lim, about my wife. I still want answers to those, but right now there are more urgent things." He turned away. It seemed a desecration to stop his search for the cause of Celcy's death, and yet he could do nothing else.

"First things first," Clarin said encouragingly, filling the silence and giving him time to recover. She had pocketed the mouse and was now assembling her gear.

"Right," Tasmin agreed, attempting a rather weary smile. "We've talked it over, and we want to help you do precisely what you were trying to do. On the face of it, telling all Jubal that the Presences are sentient is the most important thing we could do just now."

Clarin nodded, running her fingers through her short, curly mop. "We agree about that. However, Tasmin and Jamieson and I—we all feel the need to be prudent. Once the CHASE Commission meets and reports, there will be no time for other efforts. The case has to be airtight. We have to be able to prove everything we allege. And so far, as Jamieson mentioned, we have only your word for everything. There could be another explanation for the attack on you, and that's the only thing we've seen with our own eyes." She shouldered her pack and went off to load it on the waiting mule.

"But I told you . . ." Donatella interrupted.

Jamieson said firmly, "You've told us about your arrangement with Lim Terree, but there could be other explanations for that as well." He went up the trail to load his own mule.

"I've played you the Enigma cube!" she protested to Tasmin.

"You have no witnesses to making that cube, and it could have been faked," Tasmin replied in a sympathetic tone. "And quite frankly, it is . . . well, enigmatic." Seeing her expression he added hastily, "We don't disbelieve you! You're right, they are words, and they are sequential words. They just don't seem to be substantially responsive to what you were saying. Or thought you were saying."

"I was scared to death," she admitted. "I hurried more than I should have. There were these constant tremors. And the Enigma's words sounded . . . well, they sounded a little hostile."

Tasmin nodded. "We thought so, too, which is actually one of the best arguments there could be that the thing *isn't* faked. Presumably, a fake would have made better sense and have been more ingratiating. For the record, we believe you. Others won't, not necessarily. There has to be proof. It has to be as obvious to the people we will give it to as it is to you." He walked over to the mules where Clarin and Jamieson waited, listening attentively. "We have to have more than your word. There need to be witnesses."

Donatella Furz looked from one expectant face to the other, uncertain and angry. "How do you expect me to . . ."

"Oh, very simple," said Jamieson with a radiant smile. "We're going to talk to the Enigma, too."

Harward Justin made his home in a luxurious apartment on the top floor of the BDL building. At one time he had considered living elsewhere, but he had rejected the idea. It was convenient to be able to call upon BDL service employees when one needed a cook or housekeeper or cleaning crew. With BDL people, he need not concern himself with maintenance, discipline, or remuneration, though he occasionally intervened in such matters. Justin was a believer in the stick, rather than the carrot, and the personnel department's idiot insistence upon paying people more than they were worth often stuck in his craw.

Still, using BDL services people worked well enough for his day-to-day needs. Since they did not live in, he was not required to feed them. When they were gone, he had a great deal of privacy. And it was in privacy that he indulged the needs that required other and very special servants.

A neighboring windowless space had been walled off and cut up into two corridors of apartments and cubicles. This warren was connected to his own rooms with a locked and guarded door. Justin's personal servants lived there—the ones provided for him by Spider Geroan.

Most people feared and hated Spider Geroan. Justin found him both interesting and admirable. He detected in Geroan's manner a kind of kinship. Even Geroan's face, which Justin had always felt resembled the face of a recent corpse, devoid of all life though not yet noticeably decayed, pleased Justin. He saw in that face a reflection of himself as he willed himself to be, remote and implacable. He found in Geroan a depth of silent understanding he had never received from any other human being. Justin suspected that others—"them," the world at large—would consider his amuse-

ments childish, on a level with cutting up live animals or
terrorizing smaller children, the things boys did and then
grew out of. However, Geroan did not seem to think him
immature in his pleasures. Geroan knew all about the servants' quarters. Geroan had recruited most of the inhabitants.
Geroan knew exactly why Justin wanted them. Or one of
them, from time to time.

Tonight, Justin was considering a particular one as he
waited at the connecting door while the guard unlocked it.
Inside this door to the left, another door led to the apartments of the professional servants: the doctor, the masseuse,
the four social courtesans who acted as hostesses when Justin
entertained, each with private and well-equipped quarters.
To the right were the cells, tiny cubicles provided only with
basic sanitation equipment. At one time he had thought to fill
this corridor, but he hadn't done so. Many of the doors stood
open, revealing empty rooms. He went to a closed door,
third on his left, and thrust it open. It was numbered with a
"6," and it opened only from the outside.

The occupant was huddled against the wall.

"Stand up," he ordered her.

She did not seem to have heard him. Cursing, he pulled
her to her feet and she swayed against the wall, almost
falling. She was dressed in filthy veils which left her breasts
and crotch uncovered. At one time she would have tried to
cover herself. She did not, any longer. She did not need to,
any longer. The once voluptuous body, the once shapely legs
were now mere bony caricatures. What had been a wealth of
mahogany hair was now a greasy mop, hanging in lank strings.

"Beddy-bye," he said to her, his code word, the word he
had made her fear.

There was no response. No movement in the dull eyes.
No twitch on the face.

Cursing again, he struck her and she fell against the wall
to lie there without moving.

"They're not going to come after you, you know!" he
shouted. "They all think you're dead. They've thought so
for months. The same night I brought you here, we got a
body that Geroan had worked over and put it with your
clothes out behind the Priory. Everyone thinks it was you!"

There was not a flicker of response.

Harward stormed out of the room, letting the door lock itself behind him.

He let himself into the other corridor. The doctor's apartment was second on his right. This time Harward made a perfunctory gesture of knocking before he entered. Professional servants worked better if one allowed them a pretense of privacy.

The man inside rose from the chair he had occupied, a finger marking his place in the book he held. He was neatly dressed in Justin's livery, a gray-faced man of about thirty-five. His hands trembled. "Yes, Mr. Justin," he murmured.

"Room number six," Justin demanded. "What's the matter with her?" Part of the doctor's duties was to provide medical attention to those in both corridors.

"Gretl?"

"Number six," hissed Justin.

"She's dying," the doctor said, his voice quavering. The quaver irritated Justin. If she was dying, it was her own fault. He had intended her to be one of his courtesans, but she'd failed to please him.

"Why? What's the matter with her."

The doctor's voice became calm and quite emotionless. Only the trembling hands betrayed him. "She's half starved. She's been repeatedly raped and abused, and she wishes to die."

"Stop her."

"I'm afraid there is nothing I can do. I can force feed her if you like, or put her on euphoric drugs if you wish. She might go on living then, at least for a while. She'll never look like anything much, of course."

Justin curled his lip in irritation. Of course he didn't want the woman on euphorics. The woman's happiness was not what he had in mind.

"Get rid of her," he said.

"I can't . . . I can't do . . ."

"You can. Or I'll have someone call on your wife, Doctor Michael. Maybe you'd like to have her in room six?"

The doctor was silent.

Justin turned to go.

"Mr. Justin . . ."

"What!"

"I've been here for a year. . . ."

"So?"

"You told me after I'd been here for one year, you'd consider letting me see the children. . . ." Now the face betrayed the man. A certain liquid glaze of the eyes. A quiver at the corner of the mouth.

Justin's lip curled once more, this time with a deep and abiding satisfaction.

"Yes," he assented very softly and lovingly. "I certainly will do that, Doctor. I certainly will consider it."

The man's face broke. "Are they . . . are they all right?"

"Why wouldn't they be?"

"Please, Sir—"

"Doctor!" The voice was a whip crack.

The man bowed his head, wordlessly.

"Your being a good boy," said Justin, licking his lips, "is what keeps your family the way it is."

There was no response. Justin left him there, shaking very slightly, his finger still in the open pages of the book.

Justin talked to himself, quietly and convincingly. He was well rid of the woman. She'd been a disappointment, so forget her. What he'd really wanted to do was prove a point, and he'd done that. Nobody said no to Harward Justin and got away with it. As for the doctor, he would give the man a little hope. Not much, just a little. Make him think his family's life was connected to what he did, how he acted. Make him believe that. Maybe show him a holo of his wife and kids. It would have to be faked, of course. Since one didn't want wives running around asking inconvenient questions, the doctor's wife had been dead since the day Geroan had picked the doctor up. As for the children. . . .

His ruminations were interrupted by the murmur of a well-known voice coming via annunciator from the reception hall, four stories below. Justin started and swore. Think of the devil. The voice on the annunciator was that of Spider Geroan. He was on his way up.

"Well, Spider." Justin greeted him with a twisted smile and an affable squint of his slushy toad's eyes. "Nice of you to come and let me know the job's done."

"Unfortunately, no."

There was a silence, more uncomfortable than ominous.

Spider Geroan had no fear of Justin's displeasure. A physical anomaly made him immune to pain, and he could not remember ever having felt affection or feared death. He was proof against threats. His only pleasures were both arcane and agonizing for others; his only reason for living was a narrow but persistent curiosity. His motionless face betrayed no interest in what he had just said, but then it never betrayed any interest in anything. It was one of the things Justin liked about Geroan.

So now, Justin asked in the sympathetic tone one might use in inquiring after the health of a dear and valued friend, "I'm sorry to hear that, Spider. What happened?"

"You wanted Don Furz's killing to look like a Crystallite attack?"

"I did. I do, yes. She's very well-known, something of a cult personality. Her killing will be the final outrage that will move the Governor to lock up the Crystallites."

The assassin nodded. "I sent a small group of well-trained men armed with knives. Your little man in the Priory boggled a set of orders, just as you directed, and got the Explorer sent up into the Redfang. My men were ready to take her as soon as she got far enough out that she couldn't retreat back among the Presences. While we waited for the appropriate moment, someone else went for her. Four of them. My men joined in, but a bunch of armed Tripsingers came along and drove them off."

"Tripsingers! Armed? How many?"

"My men said six. I doubt that. There were probably three. From the descriptions, one of them was likely Tasmin Ferrence, from Deepsoil Five. He was in Northwest City just hours before, and he mentioned to a truck driver that he wanted to meet Furz. There were two acolytes with him, probably his own. They were carrying at least one rifle. I don't know how or why they were armed, not yet, but I'll find out."

Justin sucked on his teeth impatiently. "So, what happened?"

"Several of my men were killed; the rest were driven off. Furz and the Tripsingers retreated into the Redfang Range."

"She got away *again!*"

"They got away." There was a slight emphasis on the

they. Geroan had been paid to get the woman, but now he wanted them all. "Only temporarily."

"You sent someone after them?"

"Of course. You've paid to get rid of her, and you'll get what you paid for, Justin. It's ridiculous that it should be requiring so much effort. I've already sent some of my people into the Redfang after them, along with a couple of hired Tripsingers."

"If you get to Furz, you'll have to kill Ferrence, too, and the Tripsingers won't stand for your killing their colleagues."

"They won't be asked for their approval." His voice was almost weary, as though the subject bored him. No muscle of his face quivered, and Justin found this stoniness admirable. Still, he persisted. Justin sometimes dreamed of evoking surprise on that face, just once.

"They may attack your people."

"If they do, they'll be disposed of."

"Then your men won't be able to get out!"

Geroan turned his back. So, the men wouldn't be able to get out. They were expendable.

Justin subsided. "Who were the men who beat you to it?"

"One of them lived for a short while. I asked him."

"And?"

"He said he got his money from the Crystallites, but it came originally, so he understood, from Honeypeach Thonks."

"Thonks's whorelady? Why would Honeypeach want to kill Donatella Furz?"

Geroan had wondered the same and had been sufficiently curious to institute a few inquiries. "I'm told the Governor's lady was enamored of one of the Top Six 'Soilcoast singers."

"Rumored, hell, man. Honeypeach was and is enamored of all six of them and any twelve other men, women, or mules, anytime, anywhere. You mean Lim Terree? The one who died? You're right about part of it at any rate. He did die while using a Furz score. Still, isn't it farfetched to think that was the reason?"

"Perhaps. Her motivation could be mere pique. During a big reception here in Splash One some months ago, Donatella Furz introduced Honeypeach as Gereny Vox."

Even Justin could appreciate the humor in this. He barked, "So? A slip of the tongue? You have people who would report a slip of the tongue?" He shook his head, wonderingly. Spider Geroan was the best in the business, and his success was known to be based on detailed and accurate intelligence, but could he really place credence in such tiny things?

"Perhaps her own self-esteem is as important to her as your secrets are to you, Justin."

Justin snorted. It was hard enough for him to imagine how an ex-erotic dancer and part-time prostitute on Heron's World could get pregnant by an ambitious bureaucrat, bear him a son, and end up displacing the Governor's well-bred wife to become the first lady of a not inconsiderable planet. That the same woman would be particularly jealous of her reputation surpassed belief. "I don't think it's a question of self-esteem, Geroan. It's a matter of vanity, plain and simple. Honeypeach believes everyone on Jubal knows her and either admires or envies her or both. If they don't, they should. She doesn't give a damn about her past. It's her present and future she cares about, and having people look at her is important to her. That's why the 'Soilcoast singers are almost her private property—vanity. It's why she makes the honorable Wuyllum keep his pretty daughter tied down—though I'm trying to talk her out of that." Justin licked his lips. "The woman wants no competition. Sometimes she has to be encouraged to allow a little."

"Well, we'll soon eliminate whatever competition Furz may offer. If my men don't catch up to her within the next two days, I'll go after her myself. I cannot remember an occasion on which someone escaped my efforts three times. It cannot be allowed. My sense of what is fitting will not permit it to happen again." The words were like drops of water falling onto stone, emotionless, without particular force, and yet the will behind the voice would eat away just as the drops of water would, forever if necessary. If Geroan ever brooded, which Justin doubted, he was perhaps doing it now. "Just as a sop to my curiosity, Justin, how did you find out the woman is a danger to you?"

"You have your sources, Geroan. I have mine." The assassin waited, unmoving, and his implacable silence made

Justin uncomfortable. "Oh, very well. Someone got a translator program for her from off-world. The procurement clerk saw the item on a bill of lading and reported it to me. I have a short list of items that are always reported to me whenever they show up, and translators are at the top of the list. Then Donatella reported her synthesizer missing in Splash One, and the Prior there reported that fact, through channels. 'Lost' equipment is something else I interest myself in, for obvious reasons. Those two facts drew my attention to Donatella Furz. Then the services man at her home Priory told the Explorer King she was excited and elated about something. And she dropped a few remarks to him that indicated more than a passing interest in the ultimate Password. Besides which, she came up with an Enigma score, and the damn thing works. Given that combination, what would you think, Geroan?"

The assassin merely stared, saying nothing for a moment. Geroan was almost incapable of surprise, but Harward Justin had just surprised him. Geroan had underestimated him. Justin's information net had to be almost the equal of Spider's own. The only clue that Spider had and Justin had not mentioned was the rather equivocal information that the hairdresser, Sophron, had come up with.

After Geroan had gone, Harward spent a few minutes in futile cursing. Donatella Furz led a charmed life. He had no idea how she had escaped the first two times. Both assassins had been provided by Geroan himself, but it would do no good to rail at Geroan. And though Justin would feel much more secure if she were dead, perhaps it was sufficient that she had been driven back into the ranges, out of communication with anyone on the 'Soilcoast. It was unlikely she could stir up any trouble before Ymries and the CHASE Commission would arrive. Once the hearings started, how could she do any damage?

Some other excuse would be found to round up the Crystallites. Chanty Bins could get his pet terrorist to plant a bomb or something, then the rabble Crystallites would be rounded up and put out of the way. Of course, Chanty Bins and his cronies would need a few days' notice to get off-planet before the general roundup. They'd done a good job of setting up the whole Crystallite operation, and he might be able to use them again somewhere else. . . .

Unless—unless he decided he didn't want them to leave at all, which might be safer for Justin in the long run. The three of them must have accumulated a considerable credit account on Serendipity by now—four millions or more, Justin estimated from what he knew of the take at the temples. The account wouldn't be hard to tap if he set his mind to it, particularly if Bins and his colleagues weren't getting in his way while he did it. Four millions or more was a nice bit of lagniappe.

He considered this for some time, along with thoughts about the armed Tripsingers, without quite making up his mind what he intended to do about either. His disappointment in his special servants was quite forgotten.

Word went out from Spider Geroan's place, atop one of the older buildings in Splash One, that the spider was tugging on his web. The strings of that web, highly placed and low, twitched themselves nervously wondering if anything they had caught would be of interest to the spider. Though sometimes it was better to have nothing interesting at all than to have only part of something that Spider Geroan badly wanted.

One of Geroan's webs shivered almost immediately.

"It's Price Zimble, Spider, Sir. Word is you want reports. I have nothing new of use, honored one."

"Surely you've talked to the Explorer knight since her return, services man."

"Only briefly, honored Geroan. She hasn't sent for me since she got back."

A long pause for thought. "You couldn't possibly have said or done anything before she left that would have given her a clue we'd been talking about her, could you, Zimmy?"

"Never, honored Geroan. Of course not. It wasn't me that tipped her, if anything tipped her. It was something that happened in Splash One."

"Funny thing," murmured the Spider.

"What's that, honored Geroan?"

"Some of my people went up to Redfang, Zimmy. Looking for the Explorer knight up there. Found her, too, just like you arranged for our friend Justin. Of course, you hadn't arranged anything for Justin until you'd checked with me first, had you? Because the Spider's webs only work for the Spider, don't they? They don't play the outside against the middle do they, Zimmy? Right?"

"Right, Spider, Sir. I didn't do a thing until you gave me the start, Sir. Then I did the orders Justin wanted. They were perfect, just perfect. Looked official, they did, Sir." Zimmy sounded more nervous than usual while talking to Geroan.

"Funny thing."

Silence.

"My people found some other people up there, too. Some other people looking for the Explorer knight. Some other people who knew right where to look."

"She . . . she must've told someone she was going. She. . . ."

"Oh, I don't think the Explorer told them," said the Spider. "Funny thing. Isn't it."

Geroan disconnected without saying goodbye. Donatella Furz had evaded his assassin in Splash One. Had that attempt failed, perhaps, because Zimmy had said something to alert her? And had Zimmy sold information to Honeypeach Thonks? Information that was supposed to belong exclusively to Geroan? Perhaps Zimmy had outlived his usefulness.

But then again . . . Zimmy was a very good web into the Northwest Priory. A very good web to Chase Random Hall. Not a bad bit of web, everything considered. Perhaps he merely needed a bit of discipline. Spider Geroan found a bit of discipline often did wonders. He considered this for a time, deciding what kind and amount of discipline might be most effective, until his next web called to report.

This was a gemstone broker who worked in the vicinity of the fish market, who wanted to report a young man who had sold a firestone earclip.

"Orange stones, nothing very special, but nice. Gave the kid a hundred twenty for the clip. I've got some gems almost like it. Close enough to make up another clip. I'll get five hundred for the two, easy."

"Kid?" queried Geroan patiently. "What kid."

"Tripsinger kid. A what-you-call-'em, acolyte. One of the

young ones that doesn't do trips by himself yet, you know."
He went on to describe Jamieson in some detail.

"From where?"

"Didn't say. He did say he wanted the money for passage to Deepsoil Five though. For a woman and a baby. Just chattin', you know the way they do, when they're tryin' to sell somethin'."

"What woman? What baby?"

The broker stuttered, "I c-c-could try to find out, honored Geroan. Could try. Don't know much where to start, though."

"The acolyte came to you, why?"

The broker muttered again. "I d-d-dunno."

"Because he saw your place, stone-skull. That means he was nearby, in the area."

"M-m-maybe just havin' some lunch. Lots of people come down to the market for the fish. You know."

"Maybe for fish. But maybe looking for someone. Maybe found someone. Start by asking if there was a Tripsinger around your place looking for a woman and a baby."

Another of Geroan's webs was a cleaning woman in the citadel at Splash One. She came in person, desperately full of bits and pieces, hoping something would satisfy the Spider.

"The Tripsinger from Deepsoil Five had two sets of robes with him, and so did each of the two acolytes, Spider, Sir. Underwear, tunics, socks, boots, and spare boots. Worn, too. Like they'd been living on the country for some time. Skinny mules. Like they get when they set settler's brush for a long while. The machines of the acolytes had Deepsoil Five labels. His machine did, too, but that's a funny thing, he had two of them."

"Two of what?"

"Two machines. Music machines, like they carry to make the Tripsongs. He had two. One like the ones the kids had—like all the regular Tripsinger boxes, with the citadel label on it and the warning against unauthorized use, you know—and a different one. I looked it over, but it didn't have any label on it."

"Describe it," asked Geroan, his interest piqued. This fit in nicely with Justin's suspicions.

"It was greenish instead of gray. It had two handles on

the sides instead of one on top. The keys and dials and things opened up on a fold-down panel, three folds. The regular ones just have two and they fold up, not down. And the speakers fold out on top, not on the sides, like the regular ones do."

"Nothing else? No words, trademarks, maker's tags?"

She shook her head.

"And they went where?"

"Northwest City. The acolyte, the boy, he found a truck that was going there. I was cleaning the hall and heard him say so."

Geroan nodded his thanks, and the woman left, relieved. She expected no payment and rejoiced merely to be let alone for a time by Spider Geroan.

After that, Geroan simply sat, hands folded on his belly, thumbs moving in endless circles around one another as he thought and plotted and thought more.

It was late afternoon when the follow-up call came from the gem broker.

"The Tripsinger was lookin' for a woman named Vivian Terree. She had a kid, a baby. You want 'em?"

"Find out where they are. Find out if they're planning to leave Splash One. Let me know."

There were other calls, back and forth, as the spider tugged on other webs and the information flowed in, culminating in a final call to Harward Justin.

"The Explorer synthesizer that Donatella Furz reported missing seems to have ended up in Tasmin Ferrence's possession."

"A Tripsinger?"

"He had an Explorer model, green, two handled, with a threefold panel. At least he had it when he turned up in Splash One. I don't know where it is now."

Harward made note of this, along with the fact that the Tripsinger had been looking for a specific woman and child. Then he sat, putting all the information together.

Donatella Furz had had an Explorer box with a special translator insert. That box was now in the possession of a Tripsinger from Deepsoil Five. Lim Terree had died near Deepsoil Five. Tasmin had come hunting for Terree's wife and baby. Tasmin had shown up, armed, in time to help Donatella Furz escape a very well laid trap.

Connections. Nine times out of ten, it was safest to assume complicity whenever there were connections.

The time was growing close, very close. He could conceive of only one source of threat to his plans. Not the Explorers. They were under control. The Tripsingers, however, could be trouble. So far, there was only this one man— Tasmin Ferrence. Just one. If there were more. . . .

Anything Justin did would have to be done at once. He had trusted to underlings too many times already. And so had Spider Geroan.

Besides, there was all that money on Serendipity.

He summoned a trusted secretary. "Get hold of Chantiforth Bins and make an appointment for him to see me early tomorrow morning. Then call Spider Geroan and ask him to be here at the same time."

His last call of the night was to the satellite surveillance teams. By morning, he would know almost precisely where Don Furz and her new friends were to be found.

———————————————— 12

In Deepsoil Five, Thalia Ferrence had adapted reasonably well to the presence of her sister, Betuny, who had arrived from Harmony with scant possessions. Since her arrival, however, Thalia had acquired the habit of strolling off several times during the day and almost always at dusk to the low wall that separated the shrubby garden of her house from a narrow roadway and the brou fields beyond. When she had been much alone, she had ached for company. Now that her sister had come to keep her company, she ached to be alone. Betuny was all right. She cooked well enough, old recipes from their childhood that Thalia relished as much for the nostalgia they evoked as for their slightly disappointing flavor. Betuny maintained the house well, too, being scrupulous about keeping each thing in an accustomed location so that Thalia would not stumble or fall over unexpected barriers.

But Betuny chattered, commenting endlessly on everything, and Thalia found herself wearying of her sister's voice, wanting nothing, neither food nor a neat house nor company, so much as silence. Betuny had a theory about Lim's death. Betuny thought she understood Celcy's character. Betuny considered it wicked of Tasmin to have gone off like that. Betuny philosophized about the Presences. Betuny knew a way to raise the money to have Thalia's eyes fixed—every day a new commentary or a new plan, each more fly-brained than the last, each day the same voice, going on and on and on.

So, Thalia had announced her need of a few moment's meditation from time to time, flavoring the announcement with a spice of religious fervor, and Betuny had manners enough to accept that, albeit reluctantly, though she could not really respect it. She had, however, gone so far as to drag out an old chair and put it in the corner of the wall where Thalia could find it easily. Thalia could sit there for an hour at a time, musing, her head on her folded arms atop the low barricade, listening to the soft sounds of doors opening and closing, women calling children in to supper or to bed, the shushing pass of quiet-cars, and more often than not a chorus of viggies sounding much closer than she remembered hearing them when she could see.

There were few loud or aggressive sounds, and the voice that accosted her from across the wall one evening came as a shock even though she had heard the slow gravelly crunch of feet approaching down the road.

"Are you Thalia Ferrence?"

She nodded, uncertain. It was a cold hard voice, not one she recognized, and she was very good at recognizing voices.

"Tasmin Ferrence's mother?"

She nodded again, paralyzed with fear. Had something happened to Tasmin? She started to ask, but the voice went on relentlessly.

"Are you blind?"

She bridled. "That's not a nice thing. . . ."

"Never mind. I see you are, lucky for you. You have a daughter-in-law? A grandchild?"

"No," she said. "My daughter-in-law is dead. And the baby she was carrying."

"Not Tasmin's wife. The other one. The one who changed his name. Lim's wife."

She could hardly speak in her eagerness, her joy, her disbelief. "Lim had a wife? A child?"

"You didn't know?"

"No. I didn't know. Where are they?"

There was a snort, more of annoyance than amusement. "That's what I was going to ask you." Then the crunch of retreating feet.

"Wait," she cried. "Wait! Who are you? How do you know?"

No answer. Nothing but the usual soft sounds, the far-off chorusing of viggies. She rose to feel her way along the path and into the house. She was, after all, the widow of a Tripsinger and the mother of another. There were certain courtesies that the citadel ought to be able to provide. After considering carefully what she would ask—no, demand!—she coded the com and asked to speak to the Master General of the Citadel.

She found it strange that although he did not know about Lim's wife or child, he had many questions to ask about the man who had told her of them.

The troupe of Bondri Gesel had come far from the slopes of the North Watcher—Silver-seam and all relevant honorifics—when the senior giligee approached Bondri while keening the preliminary phrases of a dirge. Words were hardly necessary under the circumstances. The old Prime Priest was barely able to stagger along, and even when they carried him, they had to jiggle him to keep his breath from catching in his throat.

"Bondri, Troupe-leader, Messenger of the Gods, one among us has a brain-bird crying for release." So sang the giligee.

Bondri sagged. "Prime Priest Favel," he hummed, subvocalizing. The giligee wagged her ears in assent. Well, there was nothing for it but to halt for a time. The Prime Priest deserved that, at least. Every viggy needed a quiet time to set the mind at rest and prepare the brain-bird. "We make our rest here," Bondri sang, leader to troupe admitting of no contradiction. The giligee was already circulating among the others, letting those know who had not the wits to see it for themselves.

"I am glad of a rest," the Prime Priest warbled, breathily. "Glad, Bondri Gesel."

"So are we all," Bondri replied gently. "See, the young ones have made you a comfortable couch." He helped the old viggy toward the low bench of fronds, which the young ones had spread on a shelf of soil overlooking the valley beyond. From this vantage point one could look back on the Tineea Singers, the Ones Who Welcome Without Meaning It, arrayed against the sky, almost equidistant from one another and too close for easy passage among them. The Singers had gained their name in immemorial times; no viggy worth his grated brush bark would try to sing a way among them, though young ones sometimes dared each other to try. The song that worked for one did not work for the next, and they were too close to separate the sounds. The Loudsingers had a way to get through, but the only safe viggy way was around.

"The Ones Who," mused Prime Priest Favel. "I have not been this way in a generation. I had forgotten how beautiful they are."

Bondri looked at them, startled into perception of them as newly seen. Indeed, when not considered as a barrier, they were very beautiful. Pillars of diamond lit with rainbow light, their varying heights and masses grouped in such a way that the heart caught in the throat when one saw them at dawn or at dusk. "They are beautiful," Bondri agreed. "But perverse. They do not respond honestly to us."

"Like a young female," Favel sighed. "Singing tease."

Bondri was surprised at this. "Tease?"

"Yes. She is too young for mating yet, she has nothing to give, really, but she sings tease. The Loudsingers have a word for it. Flirt. She sings flirt."

"Tineea," Bondri sang softly. "The songs of maidenhood."

"The Ones Who are like that. They flirt, tease, sing tineea to entice us. But they have nothing yet to give us. Perhaps one day, they will."

"That is true," whispered Bondri. Newly awakened to

loveliness, he stood beside the old priest for a long time more, wondering if The Ones Who could perceive their own beauty.

"Enjoy the aspect, old one," he said as he returned to the others of the troupe.

"Is he at peace?" inquired the giligee as she busily grated brush bark, using a crystal-mouse jawbone as a grater, onto several criss-crossed and immature tree fronds. When heaped with grated bark, the fronds would be folded, then twisted to press out the refreshing bark juice, a drink for all in the troupe to share. Both the mouse jaw and the tree fronds were in keeping with viggy law concerning tools. Tools were expected to be natural, invisible, undetectable, as were the etaromimi themselves.

"Prime Priest Favel admires The Ones Who," Bondri warbled, watching as the first juices trickled into an ancestor bowl.

"Take him drink," the giligee said. "It is your giligee's bowl, Bondri. A good omen."

Bondri picked up the bowl and looked at it. It was a good bowl, clean and gracefully shaped. It was a good omen, bringing to his mind many memories of his giligee. He shared a few of these with the nearby troupe members before mounting the hill once more.

"Whose bowl is this?" Favel asked courteously, allowing Bondri to identify the bowl and sing several more little stories concerning his giligee. The time she climbed the tall frond tree and couldn't get down—that had been before Bondri was even depouched the first time. The way she used to cock one ear, making everyone laugh. Bondri was smiling when he left the old priest, and Favel, left behind to sip his bark sap, was contented as well. It was good to share memories of the troupe.

Memory was such a strange thing. A viggy would experience a thing and remember it. Another viggy would experience the same happening and remember it as well. And yet the two memories would not be the same. On a night of shadow and wind, one viggy might sing that he had seen the spirit of his own giligee, beckoning from beside a Jubal tree. Another viggy might sing he had seen only the wind, moving a veil of dried fronds. What had they seen, a ghost or the fronds? Where was the truth in memory? Somewhere between the spirit and the wind, Favel thought.

When the troupe traveled down a tortuous slope, one would remember pain, another joy. After a mating, one would remember giving, another would remember loss. No one view would tell the truth of what occurred, for truth always lay at the center of many possibilities.

"Many views yield the truth," Favel chanted to himself, very softly. This was the first commandment of the Prime Song. Only when a happening had been sung by the troupe, sung in all its various forms and perceptions, could the truth be arrived at. Then dichotomy could be harmonized, opposition softened, varying views brought into alignment with one another so that all aspects of truth were sung. Not Favel's view alone, but the view of dozens, the view of all members of the troupe, if one had a troupe.

Oh, one must. One must have a troupe. Favel blessed the hour he had been adopted into Bondri's troupe. As a male, he should have lived out his life in the troupe to which he was depouched, but the continuity of his life had been broken when the second commandment of the Prime Song was broken.

The second commandment was almost a corollary of the first. "Many views yield truth," said the first part of the Prime Song. "Therefore, be not alone," said the second.

Favel had been alone. He had been alone for a very long time, which meant there were gaping, untruthful holes in his memory of his life. When he sang these parts of his life, there were no other views to correct and balance his own—no joyous counterpoints to relieve his pain, no voices of hope or curiosity to relieve his own terrified horror. Favel had been a broken one—broken and abandoned.

It had happened long ago—how long ago? Fifteen years? Twenty? A lifetime. Favel had been a young male then, almost of mateable age, had long since given up trailing his giligee in favor of being with the adventurers, as the young ones thought of themselves. It had been in Bondri's pouch troupe, the troupe of Nonfri Fermil, Nonfri the Gap-toothed with the beautiful voice, and it was Nonfri's trade daughter Trissa that Favel had set his song upon.

She had not been in the troupe long, only long enough

to get over her first pain of separation, only long enough to learn a few of the troupe's memories so that she did not sit utterly silent during evening song. To Favel, she was Trissa of the frilled ears, for the edges of her wide ears were ruffled like new leaf fronds, the soft amber color of dawn, only slightly lighter than her song-sack. Her eyes were wide and lustrous, but so were those of all the people. Her voice, though—ah, that Favel could remember, but he had to sing it to himself all alone, for none in Bondri's troupe had ever known her. "Softly resonant," he sang quietly to himself, "plangent in the quiet hours, rising like that of the song mouse to trill upon the sky." Ah, Trissa. She had sung tineea and turned his soul.

A small group of youngsters had gone one evening to gather brush. Some of the elders of the troupe had a taste for bark sap, and the young ones were searching for a juicy growth. Favel was older than the gatherers and too shy of his awakened senses to invite his own group to go with him, so he broke the second commandment of the Prime Song and went alone. Alone to lie in the brush and watch Trissa, hear Trissa. Alone to imagine himself and Trissa mated.

Her group started back, laden with juicy brush. Favel, hidden at the foot of a 'ling, waited for them to pass. One of them, a silly young male, threw a bit of crystal at the 'ling, the very 'ling that Favel lay beneath, hidden in the grasses. The 'ling had been excitable. It had broken.

When he woke, there was blood on his head and his legs were broken beneath the shattered 'ling. When he pulled himself to the place the troupe had been, the troupe had departed. Days passed, and nights, and he found himself beside a Loudsinger trail. Days passed again, and nights, and a Loudsinger caravan came by.

After that was pain as the Loudsinger tried to set his legs, then less pain, and finally only the songbreaking agony of loneliness as he waited to die.

"Why did you not die, Favel?" Bondri had asked him later.

"I was too sick to die," he had replied. "My brain-bird could not settle on it." And it was true. Despite the ban, despite the taboos, Favel had not died. Perhaps curiosity had kept him alive.

Favel learned Loudsinger talk. It gave him something to do, and it was not particularly difficult. One word served many purposes. No word was particularly precise. The Loudsingers made no attempt to find truth, each merely asserting his or her own vision of history. "I remember it this way," one would say in a disagreeable tone. "You're wrong, this is the way it went," making Favel writhe at the rude arrogance of such statements.

The man was named Mark Anderton, and he kept Favel in a cage made of stuff Favel could not bite through. Favel considered the question of taboo and finally allowed himself to chitter words and phrases at him in order to get food.

"Listen to my little frog-monkey," Anderton would say. "Like a ruckin' p'rot, in't it."

"What's a p'rot?" someone always asked.

"Urthian bird. Talks just like people," he would say, with a guffaw. "I got me a Jubal p'rot."

"See the pretty viggy," they would chant, stuffing bits of meat through the bars at Favel. "See the pretty viggy."

"Pretty viggy," Favel would say, without expression, grabbing for the meat, while the Loudsingers broke themselves in half laughing. He was breaking the taboo by not dying, but he was not breaking the taboo when he used words. They did not know he understood what he said.

"Ugliest thing on six worlds," one said. "Pretty viggy my pet ass."

Favel had never considered whether he was pretty or not. It wasn't something generally considered important. Trees were beautiful, of course. Presences, most of them, were beautiful. Voices were beautiful, some more and some less. But viggies?

It was a new thought, one that perplexed him. Had he thought Trissa was beautiful? After much thought he admitted to himself that he had. Yes, the sight of her had gladdened his song. She had been beautiful.

In time Mark Anderton had tired of having a viggy and had sold Favel to another man, who had sold him in turn to Miles Ferrence as a gift for his oldest son.

There were two sons—and how weirdly strange it had seemed to Favel to have sons—and a woman and a man in Miles Ferrence's troupe, and by that time Favel had figured out how it was the Loudsingers got by without giligees. There was something strange about the Ferrence troupe, something wrong. Some days there was such ugliness in the voices that Favel buried his head under his arms, trying not to hear. Favel's cage was hidden on a high shelf for a time. Then he was given to the youngest boy, but the oldest boy took the cage into the night and set him free.

"I am Lim Ferrence," he had told Favel. "I am not debauched. I am Lim Ferrence, and I can sing as well as anybody, better than anybody, and I am not debauched, and if I can't have you, nobody can have you, so you go back where you came from. . . ."

As soon as he was far enough from the cage to make recapture unlikely, Favel had stood forth and sung his thanks to Lim Ferrence, seeing the blank oval of the boy's face staring into the darkness, incredulous at this torrent of song. "I owe you a debt," Favel had sung. "I owe you a debt unto the tenth generation. . . ." He had sung it in Loudsinger language, breaking the taboo. A debt of honor took precedence over any taboo, but afterward he had wondered if the young Loudsinger had even understood.

The debt should have been paid long ago. Why hadn't that debt been paid?

Favel mused, hearing the soft sounds of the giligee who was grating the bark, the young ones who were pressing the sap, the gatherer females who were sorting through their pouches of seeds and roots. The sound of a troupe. How long had he wandered before he found a troupe once more, a troupe that would take him in?

Long, memory told him. "Long, lonely," he sang, his voice rising over the troupe-song below him, so that the others muted their voices and sang with him, letting him know they knew the truth of what he sang. Long, lonely, and wandering. He had not paid the debt then because he could not. He had not the means.

Until he met the troupe of Bondri Nettl, which took him in and learned his memories as though he had been a young trade daughter. Because he had a retentive memory and knew the language of the Loudsingers, he became a priest, then a Prime Priest. Now there were several troupes who knew bits of the Loudsinger language and viggies of many troupes who knew the memories of Favel, who knew the long loneliness of Loudsinger captivity—though they would never know the truth of it, for Favel did not know that truth himself. Sometimes Favel wished he could sing to Lim Ferrence and Miles and the younger son, Tasmin, and the strange woman, Thalia. Perhaps they would have seen enough of what really happened to make a truthful telling.

Bondri Nettl was gone now. Bondri Gesel was his heir. And though he had searched for the troupe of Nonfri Fermil, their paths had not crossed in all the years. There had never been another like Trissa, with the frilled ear edges and song that stopped his heart.

There was a flutter in his mind as he thought of this. A little flutter, as though something were trapped there. He understood, all at once, without any preliminary suspicions, why it was the troupe had stopped and why it was he had been given this comfortable couch on which to rest.

Below, where the members of the troupe nibbled and drank, the giligee heard a silence where the Prime Priest had lain. She looked up to meet his eyes.

"Tell Bondri Gesel the Prime Priest believes it is time to depart," Favel said, trying with all his mind to remember everything, absolutely everything he had ever done.

Bondri heard. In this sparsely grown location, it would not be a fully ceremonial departure, but neither would it lack care. Bondri was not one to scamp the niceties, nor would he allow slackness in his troupe.

Within moments some of the young ones were leaping off to gather fronds for the Couch of Departure, and even before they came leaping back, waving the fronds above them, the old priest had sighed, sagged, and bent his head into the posture of submission. When the fronds had been laid out, he staggered toward them, disdaining the assistance members of the troupe tried to give him.

"I hope that giligee of yours is halfway skillful," he hummed to Bondri as he laid himself down. "Making no bloody mess of it."

"Very skillful, old one. It did my own giligee not long ago. It was very clean. You, yourself drank from her cup."

"Well, I'll be glad of that. I've seen some botched ones in my time."

"No fear, Prime Priest. The giligee of Bondri Gesel will do you honor."

"May I find both honor and sustenance in your troupe, Bondri Gesel."

"I am gratified, old one."

The giligee was hovering at the edge of things, a bit nervously, but it came forward quickly enough when Bondri gestured, and the troupe began the Last Chants as though rehearsed. Well, in a way they were. They had done them several times not long since.

Bondri knelt for the Final Directives.

"Remember the Loudsinger language I've taught the troupe, Bondri. My spirit tells me you will have need of it. I lay this upon you."

"I will remember, your perceptiveness. I will remember the language as I will remember your name, rehearsing both in the dawn hours."

"I owe a debt," the priest continued in a whisper. "A debt to the person or troupe of the Loudsinger, Lim Ferrence, who released me from bondage. I lay that debt upon you, Bondri Gesel."

"The debt is assured and guaranteed," the troupe sang, voices soaring and throat sacks booming. "Taking precedence over all other things. Assured unto the tenth generation."

"None of that tenth generation stuff," the Prime Priest went on, a trifle agitated. "I have already let it go too long. I want it paid out soon, Bondri. It will be on my conscience otherwise. It might prevent my development."

"I will fulfill immediately," Bondri sang, the rest of the troupe following his lead. So sung, it was more than an oath. It became a sacred undertaking, overriding all taboos. And "immediately" meant before they did anything else at all.

Favel went on with one or two other little bequests, nothing difficult, subsiding at last into shut-eyed silence. Bondri took Favel's head between his hands and gestured with his ears. The giligee came forward to kneel with its teeth to the back of the Prime Priest's neck. Bondri inflated his throat sack to its fullest. At one signal, the troupe burst into full voice, drowning out the weak cries the old priest made as he departed. When the giligee had the brain-bird lying licked clean and naked on the fronds, the troupe witnessed its transfer into the giligee's pouch, then all assisted in cleaning Favel's delicate skull. It made an ancestor cup of remarkable delicacy and graceful shape. The eye holes were handles of delightful elegance. Bondri drank from it first, singing of certain memories he shared with Favel, then each of the troupe did likewise. As they sang the memories, the priest's apprentices made fire—a very laborious process used only for a departure—and all took part in the ceremonial burning of Favel's remains. There wasn't enough fuel where they were to guarantee that no bones remained, but the wound flies and gyre-birds could be depended upon to do the rest. When everything was done as well as it could be done, carefully not looking behind them in order that there be no improper memories, the troupe began to run away south.

They had an immediate debt to pay, and the site of fulfillment would begin at the place the Loudsingers called Deepsoil Five.

Aphrodite Sells, astride a mule named Lilyflower, cursed the mule, the trail, the company, and the direction in which they were going.

"Shut it," urged Myrony Clospocket. "Another fuckin' squeak out of you, Affy, and I swear I'll slit your throat." He fingered the knife at his waist, sounding very much as she remembered him from years before, like something elemental with mindless violence breeding just beneath his skin.

"You don't like it any better than I do," she complained. "We should have done a quick sunder, My."

"We should have done it a week ago, a month ago, before Justin got after us. I've decided he's up to something nasty. We'll be fuckin' lucky if we get off Jubal at all."

"Justin just said he needed us to take care of this one thing. He said we were the only ones he could trust, us and the Spider." She sounded doubtful, even to herself. When Justin had given them their orders, he had not been his usual flattering self. "It has to be important, My. He never would've risked a flier to get us in there otherwise."

"Risk, hell! He blew up half a dozen fuckin' Presences and then sent the flier in over where they'd been. You can pray to God nobody finds out what he did before the CHASE Commission makes its fuckin' report."

"If Justin did it, he did it so's he wouldn't get caught. And it must be important."

"That's what he said, and I paid chits for it at the time. That's Justin. He can make shit sound like syrup. He can hold a fuckin' mule-fruit out in front of you and swear it's roast bantigon until your mouth waters. Oh, yeah, I paid chits for the idea then. That was before I'd been out in this fuckin' country on this fuckin' mule for five days."

"It can't be that new to you. You said you were on the Jut for the massacre."

"Shut it, I told you. You want those fuckin' Tripsingers to hear you talking about the Jut?"

"They're ahead of us by half a mile, My. You are in a state."

"Spider Geroan isn't ahead of us. He's behind us, and I swear to God that man's got ears can hear a viggy fart a mile away." Myrony Clospocket shifted on the mule, substituting one aching set of muscles for another. "Besides, when Chanty and me was on the Jut, it was only for two days, and we got picked up by a quiet-boat and sung through the Jammers real fast when the killing was over. It was Colonel Lang that got it done. Same colonel who's back in Splash One right now while we're out here killin' ourselves."

"I should've gone with Chanty," she mumbled, wiping sweat from under her ears and across her forehead. "At least the way he's going down there in the south is a standard route."

"You didn't want to go with Chanty," he snarled, mimicking viciously. "Oh, no, little Affy didn't want to get mixed up with kidnapping babies and killing women."

"I don't like killing," she said with some dignity. "I never have. You and Chantiforth Bins know that very well, Myrony. I never did a job with you where there was any killing, and I haven't done any on this one. Besides, I think it shits to go grabbing babies. Why's this woman and her kid important anyhow?"

"Justin thinks she may be important to that Tripsinger from Deepsoil Five, that's all. Important enough, maybe he'll trade for her."

"Most unlikely," she drawled, putting on her pulpit voice. "Most unlikely for any man to put himself in peril to save some woman, particularly some woman isn't even his wife or anything." She wiped sweat again and glared at the handkerchief, grimed with the sticky dust of the trail. "Besides, I thought you and Geroan were going to take care of the Tripsinger and the Explorer. When and if we catch up to them, that is."

"If is right. According to Justin, they had them located. Located, hell. By the time we got dropped off, they were god knows how far ahead of us. All we were supposed to do was buzz in, splash 'em from a distance with these new rifles and get ourselves back to Splash One, ready for the sunder. Oh, yeah, Justin had it all plotted."

"You didn't say splash them to me, My. You said take care of . . ."

"What the fuckin' hell did you think we meant, Affy? Invite 'em to a tea party? Convert 'em into bein' good little Crystallites?"

She was silent for a time, finally asking with at least an appearance of meekness, "Well, when we catch up to them and you dispose of the Tripsinger, then nobody needs the woman and kid, do they!"

"Insurance," he growled, almost beneath his breath, hearing the crunch of hooves narrowing the distance between themselves and Spider Geroan. "The woman and the kid are just insurance, Affy, and mind your fuckin' tongue."

Inside one of the massive walls of the BDL building, a lean and dusty figure lifted a soil-filled bucket high above her head and felt the weight leave her hands as it was hauled away.

"That's enough for now," came a whisper from above. "Come on up, Gretl." There was the sound of water running. The dirt dug out of the mud brick wall was being disposed of, washed into the sewers of Splash One.

Gretl Mechas started to object, then sagged against the wall of the vertical shaft, unable to muster the strength to move. She could not have continued, even if he had been willing. The makeshift mallet and chisel fell from her hands.

"Gretl?"

"Coming," she said at last, setting her foot on the first of the laboriously inserted pegs that formed a spiral ladder in the chimneylike shaft. When she came to the top, Michael, the doctor, reached for her hand and pulled her out, like a cork out of a bottle. They stood in what had been Gretl's cell when she had been alive. Now that she was dead—for the second time—it was presumably empty, at least temporarily. Michael placed a mud-covered bit of planking conveniently near the opening, then moved the cot back almost to cover it.

"How much farther do we have to go down?" she sighed.

He ran the length of hauling rope between his hands, measuring off the yards. "Another twenty feet, maybe. That should bring us into the cellars." He dropped the bucket and coils of rope into the shaft. "I can get us down another foot or so tonight, after I'm sure he's asleep."

"You're sure he's got a tunnel?" She asked the question for the twentieth time and he gave her the answer he had given each time before.

"According to the guards I overheard, yes. It was put in when the building was constructed. It runs out to the east, through the farmland. There's a door out there. According to the men, it's so well hidden from the outside, it isn't even locked."

"We should be able to move faster now that I'm dead," she said tonelessly, wiping the dust from her eyes. "I won't have to listen for that damned door every minute, wondering if he's coming down the hall."

The doctor nodded, fetching a damp cloth from the attached convenience so she could wash the dust from her face. "There's no one else alive in this corridor, Gretl. Unless he brings someone new in here, I think you're safe. And from what the ladies say, he's preoccupied with other things right now."

"Ladies," she snorted weakly.

"They hate him just as much as you do. They just had a lower breaking point, that's all." He stroked her hair. "You did your part very well. You looked as though you were dying."

"You were right. He didn't want me any more when he couldn't get any response. It was hard not to show anything, Michael. Oh, God, but I do hate him."

"I know."

"I've meant to ask, how did you make him believe I was dead?"

"The same way he made everyone out there believe Gretl Mechas was dead before. There's no shortage of bodies. There are two or three rooms down the corridor that have bodies in them. I just bagged one of those and gave it to the guards. They weren't likely to look. They saw what they expected to see, just as your friends did when they saw your clothes on that other poor soul, whoever it was." Michael's voice shook with despair. "The place is full of death. Justin breathes death. My wife and the kids are dead. I know it. God, I hoped for so long, but I saw it in his eyes this last time."

"Why did he pick you?"

"The historic press published a story on me. I'd developed some new treatments for diseases of aging using biological products I'd found here on Jubal. Nothing very significant, but the historic news blew it up into something. He asked me to work for him full time as his personal physician. I thought that was ridiculous and said so. . . ."

"Justin told me once that no one can say no to him."

"He said the same thing to me. 'Nobody gets away with saying no to Harward Justin,' and 'What's mine stays mine.' "

"What's his stays dead," she whispered. "Did he think you could keep him alive forever or something?"

"Who knows what he thought. I can't extend his life, no matter what. So far I've been lucky. He hasn't been sick. And, of course, when the escape shaft is done . . ." His head came up, listening. "I hear something. Better get through onto my side in case he pays me a visit." He crawled headfirst into the opening, bent his body into a "U" shape and came up through a similar opening on the other side of the wall, behind a couch in his own apartment. Behind him, Gretl hovered, listening to furniture-moving sounds. In a moment she heard him whispering, "False alarm. Do you have enough food? I have more for you here if you need it."

"Not hungry," she mumbled.

"Have to be," he told her. "Both of us have to be. For strength. Strength to be dead, Gretl. Strength to get us out of here."

"All right," she said, reaching through the thick wall to

take the wrapped package. Then she placed the plank over the hole and moved the bare cot to cover it. When the doctor had come to "do away with her," he had wedged the latch on her door so it wouldn't close. Later, while she was below in the shaft they had been digging for months, he had given the guards her "body." The guards weren't watchful, and they certainly weren't intelligent.

She slipped to the far end of the corridor and into an empty room, carefully wedging the latch, saliva filling her mouth at the smell of the package in her hands. She would have a bath. And a meal. And then sleep. And then it would be night, and she would start digging again.

Thalia Ferrence sat in her chair by the wall, dreaming of a grandchild. The Grand Master had called to tell her that he had learned about the woman, that she and the child were on their way to her. The child and Lim's wife, Vivian. Thalia hadn't told Betuny yet. Betuny would be upset, afraid that Thalia wouldn't need her anymore. Perhaps Thalia wouldn't really need Betuny anymore, but she'd deal with that later. Just now, it was too pleasant to anticipate, to dream, to imagine all the wonderful things implied in a daughter coming, and a baby. And to think about old times, too. She had done that a lot lately.

She had allowed herself a celebratory glass of broundy, something she seldom did, and now sat in her chair at the end of the garden, her arms folded on the low wall, the setting sun shining full on her face so that she felt the soft warmth of it as she half dreamed about old times long past, wishing she could see the brou fields and the towering Presences once more. She could see them in a sense, but they loomed so large in her remembered vision that she wondered if she had not created them. She wanted to check reality against her memory and had spent a long hour floating dreamily over this, as though the truth were something she needed to arrive at—a key to some future imagining that could not be achieved otherwise. She could no longer be sure what was true, what had actually happened. What had been the truth about Lim, about Miles? Was Tasmin actually what she thought he was? Had Celcy been? Was this woman who was coming going to be a part of her life? Was this world the world she remembered, or was it only a dream she had invented? How would she know?

The voice, when it came, though it asked a similar question, was not like that other voice that had accosted her. This voice was so soft and insinuating it could have been part of her brooding dream.

"Are you the mother of Lim Ferrence?"

The broundy was flowing in her veins. "Lim Terree he called himself," she said, almost chanting and with a half smile curving her lips. "But I was his mother, yes." The voice that had spoken to her was a strange voice, almost like a child's voice, but with an odd accent. It could be a dream voice. Certainly it did not seem to be a real one.

There was a moment's silence, as though she had said something confusing.

"Was?" the voice asked at last. "Implies former time? Not now?"

"He is dead," she said. "Dead. He died on the Enigma."

A tiny consternation of sounds. She was reminded of birds talking, that chirrupy, squeaky noise, but in a moment the child's voice spoke again, almost like singing.

"What kin did he leave behind?"

"I thought it was just me, you know. I thought I was his only real kin, the only one who still cared, and remembered, and grieved. Oh, there is Tasmin, of course. His brother, but Tasmin couldn't be expected to care. Yes, I thought it was only me, but it seems he had a wife, and a child. They're coming here. Soon. Someone came to inquire about them, and then when I asked the citadel, they found out for me. . . ." Her dream gave way to a sharp pang of anxiety. "I hope nothing's happened to them."

Again that dream pause. Something brushed her face, like a feather, something soft, cool, and infinitely gentle. Then the voice. "Why should something happen to them?"

"I don't know. It's that man who came. His voice. He didn't tell me his name. He said it was lucky I was blind. He wanted to know where Lim's wife was, and his baby. I told them I didn't know Lim had a wife and a baby. The man wasn't polite. He didn't even say goodbye."

That small consternation of sound once more. "Did you think it was a threat to your son's wife?"

"It seemed odd they would want to know where she was. It seemed odd anyone would want to know. What is she to anyone? The Master General said she was only a woman, no position, no family. Working in the fish market, he said. And the baby, only a baby." Thalia brooded over the wonder of a woman and a baby who were only that. Not Tripsingers. Not people with busy-ness or resentments to take them away, but only people. A woman. A child.

Then the voice once more, soft as gauze, so soft she could scarcely tell from what direction it came, unaware it came from all about her, from two dozen throats, soft as a whisper. "How was she to come to you, Mother of Lim Ferrence?"

"By the southern route. Southwest of the Enigma. To the Black Tower." Her eyes filled with tears. She had been worrying over that route. Miles had died at the Black Tower.

Her weeping hid the tiny sound of those that departed. In the grayed light of dusk none had seen them come, and none saw them go.

West of Deepsoil Five, the troupe of Bondri Gesel found a trail through the Far Watchlings, called by the viggies Those Joyously Emergent. Although narrow, it was an insensitive trail, one that required little song and on which great haste might be made.

"We were right about the Enigma," several members of the troupe were singing. "The Mad One has killed again. Lim Ferrence, honored be his name, cannot be repaid, for the Enigma has killed him. Oh, how foolish to attempt song with the Enigma."

Bondri hissed in irritation, and their song faded away. He didn't wish to think of the Enigma just now. If Favel were still here to sing it over with, perhaps they could have arrived at some conclusion, but this was truly a matter for the priests. He sang so, briefly, to a tinkling chorus of assent.

"How are we sure that the Loudsinger and her child are in danger?" caroled one of the young viggies, an attractive female whom Bondri had had his eyes on for some time as a proper trade daughter for the troupe of Chowdri, to the south.

"The mother of Lim Ferrence was not sure," Bondri

admitted. "She but suspected danger. Still, she has no eyes, and. . . ."

"Contradiction," sang the senior giligee. "She has eyes, oh Bondri Gesel, Wide-eared one. Her eyes are not in repair, it is true, but they could be fixed. This pouched one could fix them."

Bondri made a small noise, indicating both consternation at being interrupted and a degree of doubt. He knew of no incident in which a giligee had worked on a Loudsinger.

"Truly, oh Bondri Gesel. This one has taken their bodies apart many times. The mother of Lim Ferrence, honored be his name, has only a small malfunction. It could be made proper."

The giligee had touched Lim Ferrence's mother with its antennae. If the giligee said such a thing could be done, then it could be done. "Remember what you have said," intoned Bondri, wondering just how far a viggy could go in breaking the taboo. "If we do not find the child, it may be we will pay our debt in this way."

"I interrupted the Troupe Leader," chirped the giligee. "Please return to your song."

"The woman cannot see," Bondri warbled, this time in the conditional mode. "Our ancestors say of those without eyes that the spirit must see what the flesh cannot, is this not so?"

"Verily, these are true words," sang the troupe.

"So, her ears told her the man made a threat, though perhaps his words did not convey his true intention."

"Blasphemy," sighed the troupe. "Obscenity." To the viggy, words that did not convey reality were worse than no words at all. Once this tendency of the Loudsingers to sing falsehood had been determined, the taboo had been invoked. How could viggies sing with those who did not care about truth?

"Pity them," intoned Bondri. "For they are lost in darkness of unmeaning." He paused, an obligatory beat, then continued, "So the mother of Lim Ferrence feels her son's mate and their descendent child are in danger. She does not even know she feels it, yet her inward parts know. If such danger truly threatens and can be forefended, Prime Priest Favel's debt is paid even though Lim Ferrence has been killed."

There was appreciative murmuring, followed by a burst of purely recreational rejoicing. After a time, they halted for grooming and food. Bondri took advantage of the halt to peek into the pouch of the giligee who had honorably corrected him. The pink thing that squirmed there in its nest of pouch-tendrils looked very lively. The brain-bird of Prime Priest Favel was developing well.

"We're being followed," said Jamieson, getting down from his mule with an exclamation of pain and annoyance as he grabbed for one ankle. "Damn! I keep hitting that place."

"Shhh," said Clarin. "I told you last night to let me put a bandage on it."

"It didn't need one."

"It does if you keep hitting it every time you get on and off your mule, Reb. For heaven's sake!"

"Oh, all right. Put some kind of a pad on it if it will make you feel better."

"Me? It's you who keeps hitting it."

"All right," said Tasmin, wearily as he rolled up his bedding and inflatable mattress. "The two of you slash it off, will you. You say we're being followed?"

"I rode back and found the highest point I could, Master Ferrence, then looked along the backtrail as you suggested. They were there, all right. Six riders. The only reason I could see them is they're coming down that long traverse along the cliff, the one we were on yesterday morning. About halfway down, the trail splits, you remember? Right there, one of them got down and snooped along the ground, obviously looking for trail signs. Then they came the way we did."

"Have you any idea who?"

"Two Explorers, Master. Way out in front, as though they don't want to associate with the ones behind."

"And the ones behind?"

"Riding in couples. A man and maybe a woman, then farther back, I think two men."

"I don't suppose you could see who they are?"

"I could see the Explorers' leathers. The woman seemed to be wearing something glittery in her hair, beads maybe. Maybe it isn't a woman at all, but that's the impression I got."

"Well, it was only a matter of time before someone came after us." Tasmin cursed silently, wondering who. Wondering why. Wondering how they had found this trail. The group that had pursued them originally had been easy to evade, and they had hoped there would be no further pursuit. Now, this.

The long north-south corridor between two escarpments of Presences that Donatella Furz had found for them had made the traveling simple and very quick, since they had not needed to sing their way through. Now they would need to travel even more quickly.

Don came out of the grove of trees where their small tents were pitched, her face flushed with annoyance or anger or some mixture of both. "Did I hear you say someone is tracking us?"

Tasmin nodded. She grimaced, then turned to take a folded chart from the pack on the ground, spreading it on a convenient rock and kneeling over it. "Damn! I didn't think anyone would find us in here."

"They probably found our trail all the way back in the Redfang and tracked us in here, Don. There are two Explorers with the group."

She shook her head. "Well, I found this corridor. I suppose it would be arrogant of me to think no one else had the wits to find it."

"Did you tell anyone about this passage?"

"I probably did. I would have noted it on the file charts in my room, too. I think I told Ralth. Hell, for all we know, Ralth may be one of the Explorers with them."

"Whoever they are, they probably don't know they're hunting you, Don. Whoever sent them will have fed them a tale."

She perused the chart, chewing her lips. "You still want to split up?"

Clarin made a face of denial, but Tasmin said, "Yes." He said it very firmly. He had become too aware of Clarin. She seemed always to be at his side, ready with whatever he needed next. Or he was always at hers. It was hard to know which. He found himself turning to her, depending on her. If she had her way, she would not leave them, but he was going to insist on it. Clarin and Jamieson both. It was the only thing that made sense. He bit down the feelings this raised in him.

It could be a final parting, and they all knew it. It was bearable only if he did not admit it to himself. "I want Jamieson and Clarin to do their best to get to Splash One."

Don pointed at the chart. "The best way back to the 'Soilcoast from here is to take the Shouting Valley cutoff, about half a day ahead of us."

"Why do you want me to go to Splash One?" Clarin asked Tasmin in a subdued, faintly rebellious voice.

"You've got to get to Vowe," Tasmin answered. "I want you to tell him everything we know, everything we suspect, everything we've even thought of in passing. We need whatever protection he can give us. He's got to be ready for whatever we do, and if you don't get to him, we have no other way to let him know."

"Also, I want you to take him a recording of the Enigma stuff," Donatella said. "I made a copy cube last night. I'll keep my box, the one with the translator in it. You take my new one."

"We've got synthesizers," Clarin objected.

"I know you do, but Explorer boxes are different. They're programmed to try variations. You sit off about a mile away from a Presence and start with something that almost works or worked somewhere else. Then you try variations until you get one that doesn't rock the needle, see. We don't publicize it, but that's how you do it, mostly."

"I thought Presences always reacted adversely to recordings," Jamieson remarked suspiciously.

"They do, if it's close up. But at that distance, it only seems to tickle them. Like a subconscious response, one they're not even aware of. When you've got a variation that doesn't rock the needle, then you play it over until you know it well enough to sing yourself through or at least to get up close and try it first person." She patted the box, almost as though it had been a mule. "If often works, for the easy ones. Not for the Enigma, of course."

"You never told us what Erickson's clue was to getting the Enigma score, did you?" Clarin asked.

Donatella shook her head. "And I'm not going to. Not yet. Better for you if you don't know. If it looks like you're going to be captured, destroy the cube. That way you won't know anything that can help anyone."

"We'll know where you and Tasmin are going."

"Yes," said Tasmin. "And if you're taken, tell them anything they want to know. Tell them where we're going. We'll watch out for ourselves. You don't know anything except that Don Furz thinks she talked to a Presence and is going to the Enigma to find out for sure. Tell them that."

"You'll get through all right," Don said. "I've got proven Passwords for almost everything west of here stored in the box, and the charts are clearly labeled. You'll have to duck around the Giant's Toenails. Can't get by there without a tripwagon full of effects, but if you detour to the south, there's a back way."

"Where are you two going when you leave the Enigma?" Clarin asked.

"From there, depending upon what we get, either to Deepsoil Five or back to the Deepsoil Coast," Tasmin replied.

Silence. Her face was calm, but he could see her hurting, rebellious eyes. Oh, Clarin. Clarin.

"Clarin." More than anything he wanted to comfort that pain. Foolish. She was almost young enough to be his daughter.

"Yes."

"Listen. At least one of us has to go with Don as a witness. I'm the logical person because I'm enough older than you and Reb to have a reputation that guarantees me a certain amount of credibility. Also, getting back to Splash One for the hearings is going to require help. I can get that from the citadel in Deepsoil Five, and I carry more weight there than either you or Reb."

"I could go with you and Don."

"Then Jamieson would be alone. And if whoever is following us chooses to split up and send some of them after him, or if there's someone trying to intercept us from the west, then Jamieson's chances would be decreased."

"You're right," she said. "Sorry."

"And when we get to Vowe?" asked Jamieson, equally subdued.

"Just tell him. Put it in his hands. He'll know what he can do with it. If he can do anything with it. Pray God he'll believe you."

"Oh, he'll believe me," said Clarin. "He'll believe every word I tell him."

"You *did* know him before," Tasmin said. "I thought so. When we met him there in Northwest."

"He's . . . he's an old family friend," she said. "He didn't let on because it makes it . . . difficult."

"Enough of this," Don said. "Let's take a few minutes to familiarize you two with this box. Then let's be on our way. According to what Jamieson says, they're only one day behind."

"Do you have any idea who they are, Donatella?"

She shook her head. "Forget the Explorers. They could be anyone. From Northwest or anywhere. As you say, they could even be my friends. The others? I have no idea. The only woman I've offended is Honeypeach Thonks, but I can't imagine her on a mule, hunting me down in the backcountry." She beckoned the two acolytes to her and began a quick, detailed exposition.

Jamieson and Clarin were both quick to pick up the intricacies of the Explorer box. It was different from the Tripsinger synthesizers only in detail, and they demonstrated considerable proficiency at the end of an hour, enough, at least, that Don nodded her head in approval. "Good enough. We'd better move out quickly."

Tasmin had already packed the mule saddles, and they took a few moments to hide the remnants of their fire before leaving. Not that it would do any good. If the tracker behind them could find evidence of their passage on the barren trail down the cliff, he would find evidence here as well.

They rode on southward, the hooves of the unshod mules making a musical clopping that was hypnotic. If they had traveled on some other business, if they had traveled without pursuit, Tasmin felt he could have gloried in this strange corridor that Don Furz had found amidst the towering Presences. They were on every side, seeming to look down into the valley where the group walked, violet and ochre, ruby and sapphire, emerald and ashen—a thousand gathered giants, occasionally quaking the air with their muttered colloquies.

"What are they saying," he asked Don.

"Nothing, so far as I know."

"Doesn't your new translator pick up words?"

"It *did*, at the Enigma, and in answer to what I sang! But this muttering doesn't translate to anything. All the translator does is snore and snarl and moan."

"You have tried the new translator on it then? Once? More than once?"

"I've tried the translator for hours at a time during every trip since the Enigma. Nothing."

"Then these along here aren't sentient?" Somehow that didn't seem an appropriate premise.

"I wouldn't draw that conclusion," remarked Clarin. "Perhaps they simply aren't talking."

"Or won't," said Jamieson. "I still need proof."

"You were so sure they were sentient," Clarin objected.

"That doesn't mean they'll talk to us," he replied. "If you were one of them, would you?"

They all stared up at the Presences. Cliffs of coruscating rose. Towers of glittering amber. Mighty ramparts of shimmering sapphire, lambent with refracted light. Walls of gray, shattered with silver. Barricades of scintillating flame.

"Ahhh." The sound came from Clarin, the sound of someone wounded, or a sound of lovemaking, a climactic ecstasy of sound, half muffled. The expression on her face was the one she got sometimes when she was singing.

Tasmin's hands shivered on the reins, wanting to reach for her. "We can't linger," he said in his driest voice. "Come, we can't stop." Donatella was looking at him strangely, and he avoided her eyes. His whole being felt stretched, pulled into gossamer, encompassing the world.

An act of self-hypnosis, his tutorial mind advised him. A so-called religious experience. Simply be quiet and it will depart.

As it did, slowly, over the following long hours in the saddle.

They came to the fork in the trail. Donatella checked the charts the others were carrying, checked their machine once more, then sat beside Tasmin as Jamieson and Clarin rode away, small figures growing smaller, dwindling down the west-pointing canyon, not looking back, going away to the cities of the Deepsoil Coast and possibly . . . what?

"It's unlikely anyone is looking for them, as individuals," Donatella said, trying to be comforting, trying to convince herself. "They're safer without us, Tasmin. Come, let's do what we can to wipe out their tracks."

"I pray so," he said, aching with a loss he had not

thought to feel so soon again. It was like the loss of Celcy, and yet unlike. This time it was as though something of himself had gone. "I pray so."

Rheme Gentry, while ostensibly much occupied with the Governor's private business, was actually engaged in two equally demanding activities. On the one hand, he was feeding every item of available information to Thyle Vowe, for his assistance in trying to outwit "that bastard at BDL." On the other hand, he was trying desperately to figure out a way to get a vital message to Serendipity and save Maybelle Thonk's life, or at the very least, her health and sanity, in the process.

Things were drawing to a climax on Jubal. The Honorable Wuyllum was increasingly preoccupied with getting certain items of private—and public—property shipped away to Serendipity, and this required a good deal of falsification of papers inasmuch as BDL had shut down all off-planet shipments except for the necessary flow of brou. Getting anything but brou into space took some doing, though Rheme was getting to be an expert at it. Justin hadn't quite shut off courtesies to the Governor's office. Not yet. Why, the young singer, Chantry, had been shipped out the week before at Honeypeach's insistence, babbling, half conscious, and likely to remain that way. Regeneration didn't work all that well on the nervous system.

"My poor Chantry just collapsed," Honeypeach said at frequent intervals, "from overwork, poor baby."

From drugs, Rheme thought. Drugs and stimulants—which any man needed if he were to get involved with Honeypeach—and too many demands on a nervous system that was, after all, merely biological and normal, not made of transistors and metal parts. Honeypeach simply wasn't interested in normal people or normal biology or normal sex. Honeypeach liked whips and drugs and various electronic devices. Honeypeach liked sex in threes and fours and dozens. Honeypeach liked to watch while others suffered and gyrated, often people Honeypeach said she liked a lot coupled with people she didn't like at all. Rheme knew the signs. Honeypeach had a certain look in her eye when she was choosing who was next, and Maybelle was in line for forced participation. That alone would have told him that the Governor and the Governor's lady were counting the days until departure. Honeypeach would not have focused on Maybelle unless it no longer made any difference what she did or was seen to do.

The honorable Wuyllum had shown no signs of being either aware of this or upset by it. His daughter by his first wife was evidently not seen as a possession of particular value. Rheme Gentry was trying to change that.

"Has the Governor considered what he might be interested in doing after retirement," he asked in his blandest voice.

"Why should I have thought of any such thing?" Wuyllum growled suspiciously.

"An opportunity on Serendipity has come to my attention," Rheme answered in his most syrupy voice. "One which the Governor might be interested in. A very wealthy family agglomeration, which is looking for an alliance of mutual profit, and which has a marriageable son . . ."

"Son?" Wuyllum was being very slow on the load, and Rheme cursed to himself while his face went on being disinterested. "About Maybelle's age," he said. "May one speak frankly?"

Wuyllum stared at him for a moment or two before grunting permission. Rheme felt sweat start along the back of his neck and under his arms.

"It cannot escape one's attention that your daughter and her stepmother are not sympathetic," he said, still in that disinterested tone that he had rehearsed over and over again at the end of the garden, beyond the ears. "It's perfectly understandable, too, your wife being so very young and lovely. At your daughter's current age and level of social experience, however, she is quite marriageable. One could recommend her to many very wealthy families seeking alliances of various kinds, many of which would be to the Governor's advantage. Also, such a marriage would remove a present source of annoyance to the Governor's lady."

Wuyllum grunted again, a faint light of understanding leaking outward from his face. "I might consider that," he said at last.

"If the Governor considers such a possibility in his own best interest, the young lady could be sent on to Serendipity in order that she become fully acquainted with the social set there. It is my understanding she left Serendipity while still too young to take part fully in social affairs."

"She was twenty-two," the Governor snorted. "No more sex smell to her than to a mule."

Rheme affected not to have heard. "Since the families of which we are speaking are interested in reproduction, they prefer women who are . . . somewhat naive and unspoiled. One might say 'conservatively reared.' The Governor's daughter gives that impression . . . now."

A light dawned. "Need to keep her that way, do we? That's what you're sayin', isn't it? Got to keep her away from Honeypeach's party fun, heh?" The Governor's face twisted into a nasty sneer. "And I suppose you'd want to go along to 'Dipity. Kind of a chaperon, heh?"

"I'd prefer not, Sir, if you don't mind." Rheme allowed a brief expression of distaste to cross his face, wondering if he were overdoing it. Wuyllum was no fool. Obviously not. He was as thick-skinned and slow to move as some cold-blooded primordial reptile, but where his own self-interest was concerned, he had an absolute genius for understanding the implications of everything around him. "We're very busy here and I really would prefer not." Let Wuyllum think that Rheme had tired of the girl's attentions. Let him think whatever he damned well liked, but let Rheme get Maybelle off Jubal and away from Honeypeach Thonks. "I can find the name of some appropriate woman on Serendipity. . . ."

The Governor grunted again, suspicion allayed, then turned his attention to other items of business.

That evening voices were raised in the private quarters of his excellency. Rheme, who was huddled with Maybelle in the far corner of the garden repeating the message that he intended Maybelle to carry with her to Serendipity, heard the voices and rejoiced.

"What've you been getting up to with Maybelle, heh?" the Governor asked his wife, his voice coming clearly through the drawn curtains.

"I don't even like Mayzy," his wife confided. "She spent too much time with that vanilla milk woman to be interesting."

"If you're talkin' about my first wife, woman, you'd better have the sense to know who she was. She was the daughter of the Lifetime Ambassador to Gerens, and she came from one of the wealthiest families on Heron's World."

"And they slashed her off with nothing when she married you, Wuyllum, don't forget that."

"Doesn't matter. Maybelle was reared by her mama. She's prime stuff, according to people who know."

"Prime what? Prime settler's brush gruel? She's nothing, Wully. Milky, like her mama. Nothing at all. I don't even know why Justin wants to meet her again."

"Now you listen to me, Honeypeach. I'm telling you once, and only once. I'm sendin' Maybelle back to Serendipity now. Settin' her up back there with a little place of her own, heh? Hire some snooty woman to be chaperone, get her into society. And between now and the time she leaves, and after we get there, I don't want her touched, you understand? Heh?"

There was an uncomfortable silence, broken by a whimper of pain. Honeypeach was accustomed to inflicting pain, but she was not accustomed to feeling it. "Who'd want to touch her? And what would you do if I did?"

"I'd ask Harward Justin for the loan of Spider Geroan, woman. You've got your uses. I don't mind your foolin' around to suit yourself, long as you don't meddle with me. Meddle with me, and you'll find yourself havin' a date with Spider Geroan and comin' home outside your own skin lookin' in. You understand me?" The voice was expressionless, without anger, but the whimpering reply told the listeners that Honeypeach had heard it.

In the garden, Maybelle shivered in Rheme's arms. "God, what did you tell him?"

"How marriageable you are, girl. What a nice, fertile mama you'll make for some herediphilic family on Serendipity." Rheme was actually deeply disturbed by the overheard conversation. He had not liked the lady's mentioning Justin, and he had not liked the Governor's mentioning Spider Geroan. It had implications for his own life and safety that he found ominous. "Now pay attention, May Bee, and remember what I'm telling you. Once you're on Serendipity, you're to go directly to those people I've told you about. You're to tell them you're from *Basty Pardo*. Give them the message, just as I gave it to you. They'll see the message gets sent on, and they'll keep you safe."

"I can't bear to leave you," she sobbed. "God, Rheme, there may be a war here."

"Oh, there will be a war here," he said grimly. "And I'll get through it a lot easier if I know you're all right."

"This vital message of yours, who's it for?"

He was silent, wondering whether he should tell her anything at all except what she needed to know. Meeting her rebellious expression, he knew she needed to know enough to give her a sense of participation. Maybelle was very young, in her attitudes and personality. When he had spoken of her as being untouched, he had said no more than the truth. Still, she had a vivid perception of right and wrong, and it would be wrong of him to use her without her knowing why.

"The work of the Planetary Exploitation Council's been corrupted for years," he said at last. "There was a lot of money credit involved, credit that came from the exploiter agglomerates. The corruption didn't involve many of the PEC members, actually, but the others were too complacent to see what was going on. However, the massacre at the Jut started some tongues wagging because one of the people killed was the son of one of the Council members. She got together some of the newer, younger members and began to agitate for an investigation. You know the PEC has an enforcement body, CHAIN, called that for no good reason. If the letters stand for anything, no one knows what. Speaking from personal knowledge, CHAIN is quite incorruptible. It's headed up by an old fox named Pardo. . . ."

"Any relationship to Basty Pardo?" she asked.

"An uncle, actually. Well, the General—he's retired, but everyone still calls him the General—advised some of the PEC members, and the Council managed to muster a majority of vote support for investigation. CHAIN began by hiring some investigators, a few like me, love. Enough to find out what's really going on."

"So you really are a PEC agent! I thought you were joking. Then it isn't hopeless." Her face lit up, that glowingly childlike look he had grown to love. Sternly, he kept his hands away from her. No sense making it harder than it was.

"It isn't hopeless providing this message can get off-planet and reach the right people, May Bee. But Justin has the planet sealed off. I didn't expect that. Shortsighted of me, but I just didn't expect it. All communications are monitored. No one and no thing is being allowed to leave without a priority voucher, and no priority vouchers are being issued except for the few issued by Justin himself or those we've wangled through the Governor's office. You're the Governor's daughter, and you're known to be hopelessly naive and gauche and remote from anything important. You don't even take part in most social events. Everyone thinks you're a little odd and I've been hinting for weeks that you're perhaps a trifle stupid. You're simply the least suspect person we know."

He touched her cheek, smiling, not letting her know how truly desperate he felt the need was. Everything that was happening on Jubal told Rheme that only force would work, and yet so far as he knew, no one in CHAIN had taken that into account. The Governor would go off-planet in his own good time, and the PEC authorities could pick him up on Serendipity or wherever he landed. But Justin wouldn't leave, and Justin wouldn't resign, and Justin wouldn't obey an order from the PEC.

No, Justin would dig in. Justin would start a war on Jubal rather than be taken into custody. Justin would have to be dug out, or blasted out, or Jubal would have to be put under siege.

And by the time the siege was over, it could be too late for a few million people. And for Jubal as well.

_____ 13

It was midafternoon. Left to themselves, Tasmin and Donatella had ridden farther south and laid a few false side trails, which they hoped would be confusing to the followers.

"The valley gets narrower from here on," Don said. "We

won't be able to escape them, Tasmin, except by keeping ahead of them. What are you doing with those mule shoes?"

Tasmin looked up from the shoes he was fiddling with. "I traded these off Clarin's and Jamieson's animals," he said. "The pattern on each set is a little different. If we put them on two feet of each of our mules, maybe they'll think there are still four of us."

"Do you think they'll pay chits for that?" Donatella asked him, one eyebrow raised in doubt, as he slipped two of the marked shoes over the mule's hooves, like slippers. "Do you think they'll really believe there are still four mules?"

"They might. Unless they're smarter than some people are, yes." He tried for a rueful laugh. "I just invented the trick, Explorer. It made me feel I was doing something. I deceive myself probably. It's either do something or fret. Fretting makes my stomach ache. Maybe they won't realize how inventive we are."

She acknowledged this with a slight, barely ironic smile. "It could work. I don't recall anyone talking much about doing tracking on Jubal. What is there to track? On Heron's World, of course, they do. Lots of hunting on Heron's World."

"You've been to Heron's World?"

"Of course not, Tripsinger. I was born here. My mother got a bonus for me, as a matter of fact. I was her third."

"It saves shipping when you can manufacture locally," he responded.

"Many thanks, Tripsinger."

"No strain intended, Don. I was just wondering how you knew so much about Heron's World."

"Library stuff. Adventure stories."

"Adventure stories?" he laughed. "After being an Explorer on Jubal?"

"You know it's not always that exciting," she said. "Sometimes it's anything but."

"As when?" he asked.

She had stories, her own stories, others' stories, tales of defeat and pain. They were not the stories Explorers told one another, and she didn't know why she told Tasmin except that they were stories needing telling and she might not have another chance. During the trip, she had learned all about him and Celcy. Now she wanted to talk about her and Link.

"Some things you bury," she said. "I believe in burying many things. Not denying they happened, you understand, but just getting rid of them. Putting them away somewhere where you don't stumble over them every day. But with Link . . . there's no way I can bury that. I used to delight in the Presences. Since one of them almost killed Link . . . since then I don't like them as much."

He considered this, wondering why it didn't apply to him. Celcy had died on the Enigma, and yet he, Tasmin, still felt as he always had about the Presences. Perhaps women were different. His mother had always told him that they were. "And you've been alone since then?" he asked her.

"Not exactly alone. I have good friends. And there was a talented services man in Northwest City. I took advantage of his good nature from time to time. Zimmy. Of course, Zimmy was spying on me, as I should have known he would. I saw his face the last time I returned to Northwest. You'd have to know Zimmy for it to make sense, but he didn't expect me to be back."

When she explained how she knew, Tasmin commented, "Not a lot to go on. Just the expression on a man's face."

"I said you'd have to know Zimmy. Believe me, he expected never to see me again."

Tasmin's eyes narrowed and his mouth stretched in a silent grimace. "Who's the one who gave the orders, Don? Who hired him?" The man who hired Zimmy had hired the assassin. The man who hired the assassin was the man who had driven Don Furz underground, causing her to conspire with Lim. And that man was ultimately responsible for Lim's and Celcy's death.

"The top of BDL, most likely. Harward Justin is an evil man. I know that about him for sure."

"I've never met Harward Justin." But that's where the ultimate responsibility probably lay. Tasmin nodded to himself over this. If there was fault, that's where it lay.

She shivered. "I met him once. Luckily, I'd just come back from a trip and I looked like a wet viggy."

"Why luckily?"

"I've been told I'm attractive. And I've been told that Justin has an appetite for attractive women. And he doesn't let them tell him no."

For a moment he thought she was going to say something more about this, but she fell into an abstracted and painful silence that it would have seemed impertinent to interrupt.

By late afternoon, they had begun to climb once more, and well before dark they had reached a crest of hills lined with tiny amber 'lets, no higher than their knees. Far to the east stood the golden Presence from which these small crystals had come.

"An old streambed," Donatella explained. "It washed the seed crystals down here in almost a straight line. I believe that's how a lot of the straight ramparts formed originally. A million years ago, there was nothing there but a river. Now there's a mountain range."

"We're moving onto high country," he agreed. "I want to get a view behind us if I can."

He dismounted and lay among the crowded 'lets, peering through his glasses back along their trail. At last he spotted them, moving figures well inside the limit of vision. "They're there. Still coming, and they're past the side trail where Clarin and Jamieson turned off."

"How many?"

"All six. None of them have gone after the youngsters. I don't know whether to be glad or sorry."

"They're closer than when Jamieson saw them, aren't they? Only two or three hours behind."

"My guess would be yes."

"If we only had a moon, we could keep going late tonight, walk and lead the mules."

"They may keep coming anyhow," he said, staring through the glasses back the way they had come. There was something implacable about the lead rider, something relentless in the angle of his body. He exclaimed, "Damn!"

She peered through her own glasses. Now for the first time, they saw, trailing the group, a mule hostler with a string of unburdened animals.

"They have fresh mounts," Don whispered. "No wonder they're moving so fast. If they catch us before we reach the south end of the valley. . . ."

"We can't outrun them," Tasmin said. "We'll have to think of something else."

He thought as they rode, stopping twice to pick over bunches of green settler's brush, which he whittled at on the way.

"What in hell are you doing?" Donatella asked.

"Being inventive again, Donatella. I'll let you know if it works," he told her, trying to sound more confident than he felt. Half an hour later he had four flat disks of settler's brush, thick spirals of narrow branches, made to fit tightly inside mule shoes.

He showed them to her. "We're going to tie these onto our feet, just as soon as we find someplace we can hide the mules. Then we're going to go on, leaving a false mule trail, until we can find a place to hide ourselves—a small place that they won't think of searching, because they'll be looking for people and mules, not people alone."

"Hide the mules! Where?"

"I don't know where. I'm praying we can find a place."

They did find a place, across a little stream and up a draw, a dense grove of Jubal trees in a tiny box canyon on the opposite side of the narrow valley from the trail. They rode their animals down to the stream, leaving a clear trail, and taking time to water the animals well. Then they led the animals over rock up the curving draw and tied them deep among the trees. On their return, they wiped out all prints, then donned the false mule shoes and walked back to the trail from the stream, leaving clear but infrequent imprints.

"We'll come back for them when the pursuit passes us by," Tasmin asserted, allowing no doubt to creep into his voice.

Donatella stopped on the trail to wipe her forehead and settle the straps of her pack. They had left most of their gear on the mules, taking only what was needed for survival. "What if we didn't get the tracks into that grove completely wiped out. What if they don't believe the tracks? What if they go down into that draw?"

"Then they'll have two more mules and most of our equipment. But they still won't have us. Now we have to leave as much trail as we can before dark."

Walking on the false mule shoes was neither easy nor quick. Twice in the following hour they spied on their pursuers, who were drawing frighteningly close. The second time, Donatella saw them clearly and she put the glasses down with an expression of horrified surprise that she didn't offer to explain. Tasmin let her alone. Attempting a mulelike pace while keeping his balance on the false mule feet required total concentration.

They had not gone far enough to satisfy him when it began to grow dark. "We can't go much farther, Donatella. The soil is getting shallower along here. If we just keep going, we may find ourselves on a barren slope when they catch up with us. I wish I knew for sure what they intended. It might make a difference. . . ."

Her abstracted silence broke with a rush of words. "I know what they intend. Killing. Torture. One of them is a man I know about, Tasmin. I saw him through my glasses, saw him clearly. I've seen that face before. I know who he is." Her voice faded to silence, as though the name could not be uttered.

"Tell me," he ordered.

"His name is Geroan," she answered. "He works for BDL, for Harward Justin. He's an assassin. A hired killer."

"How do you know?"

"A friend of mine met him. She told me about Spider Geroan." Donatella had turned white herself, from something more than mere recollection of what a friend might have said. Tasmin waited for her to go on, but she bit her lip and was silent.

"We have the rifle," he offered.

"We daren't use it. The moment we use it, they'll be sure we're here. And we only have one rifle. They probably have six or seven."

"True," he nodded. "You're right. They can't know we're here. Not yet. Not for sure."

"It's been a long time since I came this way, but I don't think there's anything ahead of us to help. It gets more and more barren the farther up this valley we go, and narrower. There's no way out on either side. Just precipices with no passes through them. The only ways out are back, the way we came, where the pursuers are right now, or at the southern end. . . ."

Where they were seemed barren enough, a slope of hard igneous rock that looked as though it had not changed since it had been spewed out molten except to be sparsely netted with soil-filled cracks. There were only a few stunted Jubal trees, their meager fans trembling in the chill wind. Occasionally there were veins of softer, lighter stone running parallel with the trail: pale, sedimentary strata, the bottom of some ancient sea, layered between stripes of the harder stone by cycle after cycle of vulcanism and alluvium, one replacing the other.

As they moved on, these veins tilted into a wall on their right, at first low, then towering, a striped and undulating outcropping where the softer strata had been eaten away to leave shadowed pockets between the wind-smoothed shelves of harder rock.

As his eyes and mind searched for a hiding place, Tasmin chewed over what Donatella had said about the man following them. There had been fear in her voice, abject fear, more fear than would have been occasioned by no more than she had told him. It was not merely that the man was an assassin. Tasmin started to ask her, then caught himself. She was already afraid. Talking about it might only make it worse.

He turned his mind to the stone, concentrating on it, searching for something his traveler's sense told him must be there, somewhere. . . .

"Stop," he cried. The trail curved to the right around the slope where wind had chewed deeply between the layers, making horizontal crevices that held darkness in their depths. One of these pockets, slightly above their heads, was almost entirely hidden behind fragments fallen from the shelf above. "There," he pointed. At one side of the shelf a hole gaped, thicker than their bodies, accessible from the trail by a tumbled stairway of fallen rock.

He was halfway up the stones before she reacted enough to follow him. He was inside the cleft, exploring its sloping depth, before she reached the shelf. "Come in," he whispered, wary of the echoes his voice might rouse. "It slopes back, away from the trail. Some of the rocks have rolled back here. Help me push some of them up to narrow the hole we came through!" He thrust one of the stones toward her, and she rolled sideways to push it still farther. Within moments they had cleared themselves a hidden crawlspace with ledges of stone above and below and walls of broken rock around them. The wind came through the crevices with many shrill complaints and the late light of evening fell slantingly in frail, reedlike beams, lighting Don's pale face and wide, apprehensive eyes.

"It'll be fairly dark by the time they get here," he said, one hand squeezing her shoulder. "I'm going out and lay additional mule tracks, around the corner and down a bit farther. They may use lights to see the trail, but in the dusk this wall will look solid, as though this crack were full of stone."

He slipped out and onto the trail, seeking out tiny patches of soil that would take clear imprints of the false hooves. When he had gone half a mile farther, he came to a split in the trail, which he traveled until it petered out onto rock, and more rock stretching endlessly away to the south. Then he pocketed the mule shoes, climbed the wall and scrambled back the way he had come, careful to leave no visible trace, grateful for the wind that might be presumed to have blown their tracks away.

She was waiting for him with stones ready to plug the hole behind him. Their two mattresses were already inflated on the roughly rippled stone. "Thank God for an inflatable mattress," she murmured. "We'll have to be quiet. It'll be easier with something soft under us." Her voice broke into a gasping sob.

He pulled her toward him, almost roughly. "You've been strange ever since you saw them," he said. "Ever since you saw that man. There's more to it than you've told me." He stretched out on his own mattress and drew her down beside him, watching her face. One eye was lit from the side by a last vagrant beam of sunset light, that eye tear-filled and spilling. "Tell me."

She gasped. Her teeth were gritted. He saw the muscle at the corner of her jaw, clenched tight.

"Will you tell me," he asked. "Don't you think I should know?"

"I had a friend," she said. "A good friend. Her name was Mechas, Gretl Mechas. She came from Heron's World, on contract to the Department of Exploration. Not an Explorer. She was in procurement and accounting. They housed her in the Priory in Northwest because there was extra space there. We got to know one another very well. . . ."

Tasmin waited, waited longer, then said, "Go on."

"She got word her sister was in need of something back on Heron's World. Gretl never told me what it was. She seemed a little annoyed about it, in fact, like the kid had gotten herself into some kind of trouble. Anyhow, Gretl needed money to send home. She went down to Splash One, to the BDL credit authority. She could have done it all by com, but Gretl was like that. She liked to do things personally."

"Yes."

"When she got back she told me she'd met Harward Justin. He'd stopped by the loan desk while she was there, and he'd been pretty persistent in asking her to have lunch with him. She told me she'd refused him though he hadn't made it easy. You'd have to have seen Gretl in order to visualize this properly, Tasmin. She was stunning. Men did pester her, but she didn't take it seriously because she was in love with someone back on Heron's. She laughed about it when she told me. She said Justin looked like a Jubal toad-fish, fat and greasy and with terrible little eyes. . . .

"Anyhow, when she went to make her first payment, they told her Justin had paid off the loan. She owed him, personally. She left her payment in an envelope for him, but as she was leaving, that man—that Spider Geroan—accosted her and told her Justin wanted to see her."

"Yes."

"She was very strong-willed, Gretl. Indomitable. Spider Geroan took her to Justin's office, there in the BDL building. Justin told her how he wanted her to pay the debt, and she told him she would pay her debt on the terms she had incurred when she took it, nothing else.

"When she got back she was angry. I'd never seen her so angry before. And she told me what Justin said. Justin told her he'd paid her debt, now she owed him. He told her people had to pay him what they owed him, or else. He said if she wouldn't have him, then Geroan could have her. And he laughed when he said it.

"She told me about it, shaking her head over it, furious, not able to believe the man. She reported it to the Priory office and to the Explorer King, both personally and in writing. Technically, it was a violation of the union contract. The contract doesn't allow sexual harassment. . . .

"Two days later they found her in the alley out behind the Priory, there in Northwest. Her flesh cut in little pieces, all over, like noodles. Head, face, everywhere. Her clothing and personal things were dumped on top of the body. Except for her clothing, we couldn't have identified her. I tried to believe it was someone else, but the clothes were hers. No one could have recognized her. Whoever did it had rubbed something into the cuts to keep her from bleeding to death right away. And then dumped her there. Like a message."

"And you think it was Geroan?"

"I know it was. I went to the protector that investigated her death and I screamed at him to find who was responsible. I told him about Harward Justin trying to use her, about his threatening her. The protector got me out of there, took me for a walk, and he whispered to me that if I didn't want the same thing to happen to me, I'd keep my mouth shut. He was scared, Tasmin. Really scared. He said they knew who did it, who'd been doing it for years, but they couldn't touch him because he had people to swear he was in Splash One when it happened. He even showed me pictures of the man. His name was Spider Geroan, they said, and he worked for Harward Justin. Then I remembered what Gretl had told me. She wouldn't give Justin what he wanted, so he told Spider he could have her. . . ."

"She'd been raped I suppose," Tasmin said, sickness boiling in his stomach.

"No," she choked. "Nothing so normal as that. Geroan isn't interested in sex. He isn't even interested in dominance, which is what most rape is anyhow. No, the protector said Geroan has something wrong with his nervous system. He can't feel pain, so it fascinates him. Watching people in pain is the only pleasure he has. . . ."

Donatella shuddered into gulping sobs, and he took her in his arms, pulling his blanket over them both. There was a sound, and they tensed, listening. It came again. Far down the trail, the way they had come, a voice shouting. Had they found the mules? He shivered. Why else would they call out?

Following that sound, he felt only fear, her fear, shared, her trembling and his, their bodies cold under the hasty covering, their senses strained for the first breath of sound that would presage the arrival of the adversary, the enemy, perhaps Geroan, who would use them for an arcane and terrible pleasure, perhaps someone else merely seeking their deaths and not particular about how these deaths were to be brought about.

He was caught in the story she had told about Spider Geroan. What did such a man think or feel, or remember? Did he humiliate and degrade his victims so he could come to despise them, making murder seem a deserved end rather than a despicable corruption? Did he feel anything about them? Did he remember at all? Was his pleasure physical? Was it transitory? Was there some quiet orgasm of the mind that substituted for pleasure of the senses? Since he could not feel pain, could he feel anything? How did one communicate with someone who could not feel at all?

It would be, he thought, like being killed slowly by a machine. Pleading would mean nothing. The device would be programmed to inflict pain, and it would not care what the victim said or did.

Tasmin clenched his teeth tight to keep from shaking. He had always feared pain. The prospect of pain filled him with horror. He imagined blood, wounds, deep intrusions into organs and bone. Bile filled his throat and he gulped, then blanked it out. His way of dealing with the horror was not to think of it. He had seen students, mad with fear of the Presences, run directly toward them, and he wondered what it would take to break his own mind and make him behave in such a way. He had learned to blank out such thoughts, and he did so now, erasing them, thinking only of darkness and quiet.

Donatella was remembering the body of her friend and was wondering whether she had the courage to take her own life before she fell into Geroan's hands. Her knife was under the mattress, where she could reach it. She was not sure

reaching it would be enough. She clung to Tasmin, thinking
of begging him to help her, not let her be taken by that man.
The terror built into a spasm of shaking, and then ebbed
away, leaving her limp.

Her face was buried in his shoulder, against his naked
skin where his shirt had come unfastened under his Tripsinger's
cloak. Her cheek was on his chest, her breath moving softly
into the cleft of his arm, where the hairs quivered, as in a
tiny wind.

The tickling breath came into the blankness Tasmin had
evoked, came as a recollection, a summer hillside, grass
beneath him, Jubal trees along the ridge, himself lying with
his arms around Celcy and the warm, moist breeze of summer cooling the pits of his shoulders. Celcy's head was on his
chest, her lips on his skin. Now, as then, he felt the hairs
moving in a dance of their own and responded to the diminu-
tive titillation as he had then, by turning a little, moving her
body more solidly onto his own, moving his arm more closely
around her. One of her legs fell between his, a sudden,
unexpectedly erotic pressure, and he raised his own leg in
surprise, bringing it into intimate contact with her.

She gasped, becoming very still, and he felt the quick
heat between them. They breathed together, her lips opening on his skin, her hand moving between them to pull her
shirt away. Then the skin of her breasts was naked against his
own, her nipples brushing his chest as she thrust herself up
from him to tug at the belt around her waist.

He felt a ripple across his belly as the silken belt that
had held her full trousers tight around her slender form
pulled free. He saw the sash through half closed eyes, a
ribbon of scarlet. Then there was nothing between his leg
and the furry mound of her groin except the fabric of his
trousers.

Blood beat in his ears. He shut his eyes, not wanting to
think or see, wishing he could shut his ears as well and let
the surging feeling wash over him in silent darkness, with
only the sunlit meadow filling all the space around him. She
made no sound, merely raised away from him a little so he
could free himself from his clothing, only as much as necessary, soundlessly. There was no time for anything more than

that, no time for anything between them except this urgency, no time for avowals or questions or even words. They existed separately, in a place remote from time or occurrence.

Their bodies slid together in a continuous, gulping thrust, then lay joined, scarcely stirring, needing scarcely to shift, the tiniest motion amplified between them as though by some drug or device into a cataclysm of feeling. She pushed only a little, the smallest thrust of her body toward him and away, and they were gasping, uncontrolled, grasped inexorably by a continuous quiver that swept them up and over a towering wave of sensation to leave them floundering in the trough, blood hammering in their ears.

"Aaah," she moaned in an almost soundless whisper. "Aaaah."

"Shhh." He whispered in return. "Celcy . . ." The fear was gone. His body was disassembled. There was a violent pain behind his ears from the spasms that had seized his neck and jaw in a giant's vise, but even this seemed remote and unimportant.

Then there was the sound of a voice, the rattle of gravel, and the vision of meadowlands shattered as his eyes snapped open. Coming toward them was the crunch of hooves, a voice cursing monotonously.

Their bodies lay flaccid, boneless, like two beings mashed into one creature, that creature scarcely aware. Through a chink in the piled stones, Tasmin could see through slitted eyes a dim segment of the path extending back the way they had come. A line of mules. Two Explorers, one of them on foot examining the trail with a lantern, then the man Donatella had said was Spider Geroan with a another rider behind him, dark and silent as a shadow. Then the string of riderless mules. They went past in a shuffle of feet, a roll and rattle of gravel. After a long gap a bald man and a tired, smudge-faced woman approached.

The final hooves came closer, passing the ledge with a scratch and click of stone against stone, then went on to the south. The voice they had heard before cursed again, at repetitive length. The woman answered, briefly and whiningly, the two finally complaining their way into silence behind the rocky rampart.

The pain in Tasmin's head departed, leaving a vacancy behind. Her body clenched on him like a squeezing hand, and he moved once more, this time slowly, languorously, lifting her with his body, holding her there with his hands while he dropped away, then pulling her down once more, over and over again, impaling her, holding her tight to him as he rolled over upon her and thrust himself into her. The wave came again, slowly, building and cresting, carrying them with it into the dark depths of a strange ocean.

The first time it had been Celcy. This time it was no one at all. He sought a name and could not find one as nonsense words flicked by, babbling rhymes, childlike sounds. Perhaps the name he wanted was an exotic word in some foreign tongue, a question without an answer.

"Mmmm," she sighed.

He did not know who it was. Who either of them were.

They slept as their fleeting hunger had dropped them, disarrayed, close coupled, slowly moving apart as the night wore on until dawn found them still side by side, but separate. When Tasmin awoke, it was to a strange dichotomy, a bodily peace surpassing anything he had known for months coupled with an anxiety for which he could not, for the moment, find an object.

When he saw who lay beside him, both body and mind were answered. She opened her eyes to see his own fixed on her, accusingly.

"We aren't dead," she said in response to this unspoken indictment. "I expected to be dead by this morning."

His instant reaction had been a twitch of revulsion, a feeling very much akin to guilt. The feeling passed as he said Donatella's name to himself, leaving only a faint residue of grief behind. "You're disappointed," he murmured, feeling hysterical laughter welling within him. "Ah, Donatella, you do sound a little put out."

She flushed. "It's not that. It's just that I . . ."

He felt a surge of sympathy. "You wouldn't have . . . I know. Neither would I. We thought we were going to die. Or maybe our bodies thought so. Well—it happened. Forget it."

There was a silence. She seemed to be considering this. "Yes. I think you're right. It didn't matter what I did. I would never need to explain it, not to myself, not to anyone, because there wouldn't be any tomorrow. . . ."

He was stung into an irrational objection. "It may be petulant of me, but did it really take that to make you want to make love to me?" He tried to smile to take the sting out of his words, but the wound to his vanity was there. Amazing! He was wounded because a woman he hardly knew felt she needed to explain away her actions regarding him.

"You know better," she said sharply. "You, of all people! It didn't take that to make me want to make love to you. It wasn't really making love, Tasmin, and it wasn't really you. I haven't made love, not for years. Not to anyone. Not since . . ."

"Not since?"

"Not since Link." She sat up, pulling the blanket around her while she fumbled with her disordered clothes, crouching for a moment to shake herself into some semblance of order, tugging at her tunic, searching for her sash. "We weren't casual lovers, Link and I. We were fellow Explorers. Colleagues. Friends. For him, there isn't any more. For me there isn't either. Not really."

"I thought you told me about that man, what's his name? The services man?"

"Zimmy? Zimmy was just . . . like getting my hair done. When things got too tight. Too rough. He was talented in that way, Zimmy. With him it wasn't love, it was skill. Technique. It wasn't making love."

"And last night wasn't either."

"In a way it was."

"Only a way?" His irrationally hurt pride was giving way to curiosity.

She gave him a long, level look. "In a way it was because I forgot you aren't Link. You're not Link, Tasmin. You're a lovely man and I think a dear friend, but you're not Link."

"And you're not Celcy," he said, wanting to get through her self-absorption, perhaps to wound her, only a little.

"Celcy's dead," she said flatly. "You need to forget. Part of you knows that, Tasmin. How long will you go on being married to Celcy? You called me by her name, you know. How long are you going to go on allowing yourself to love only if you pretend it's Celcy doing it? There are other people, you know. Clarin, for instance. She's in love with you."

"Don't be ridiculous," he said, thrusting his way through the stones that had hidden them. "She's a child."

"Child my left elbow. What is she? Eighteen, nineteen?" They slid down onto the trail, adjusting shoes and straps. "What are you? My age, about? Thirtyish?"

"Thirty-two."

"She's no child," Donatella muttered.

He rejected all this. He had no intention of forgetting Celcy! "Don't you need to forget Link and go on living, too?"

"No!" The cry came out uncontrollably, her hands went up in a pushing gesture, demanding that he take the words back. "He's alive. If I could get him to Serendipity, if I could afford the fees, he could have regeneration. Everything that made Link himself is still there. It's only his body that won't let him out. It isn't the same as if he were dead!"

He felt a wave of empathy. "Money? That's it, isn't it. That's what love comes down to sometimes. A fortune to space him to Serendipity, and you'll never have it. A fortune to get my blind mother to Splash One and pay for the treatment, and I don't have that. So, your Link stays in a support chair and my mother can't see."

He didn't want to talk about this anymore. "Have you stopped to think that if we're successful at proving the Presences sentient, we'll probably be shipped to Serendipity—for transshipment elsewhere, if nothing else. All of us. Every human person on Jubal. Which will include your friend Link, won't it? And my mother."

She looked dazed. "It . . . it never occurred to me."

"We'd still have the treatment to pay for, but at least we'll be where it can be obtained." He laughed, a little harshly but with some satisfaction as he saw her look of concern for him turn to one of confusion and dismay, and then to irritation.

"Oh, God, Tasmin, what are we talking about this for?"

"Exactly," he murmured to himself, thankful that she was getting off the subject. Clarin! Of all idiotic . . .

"I can't handle all this," she went on. "We may not even be alive tomorrow. We've got to get to the Enigma and Deepsoil Five. It'll take half a day to pick up the mules and get back where we are, and now they're ahead of us." She shrugged her arms through the straps of the pack and started down the rocky shelf.

"Yes, but they don't know that yet," he said, trailing her a half step behind. "Which gives us the tiniest bit of an edge, Donatella. I think the time has come for us to break out of this valley and head straight for the Enigma."

"We have to backtrack for the mules anyhow, and there are some routes east. Rough transit, though. No Passwords for a good part of this country east of us. Let me thing about it." She rubbed her head. "When we get to the mules, I'll take a look at the charts."

He agreed, shrugging the straps into a more comfortable position. The trail sloped downward to the place they had left the mules. And the mules would be rested. If they went to the east. . . . "Pray God Jamieson and Clarin get to Thyle Vowe. . . ."

"You're placing a lot of hope in a couple of children," she said sarcastically.

"Clarin's no child," he said absently, only then realizing what he had said.

At that moment, Clarin and Jamieson were re-entering the north-south valley in a mood of defeat. Clarin was frankly crying, tears of weariness and frustration, and Jamieson's face showed a similar, although more controlled emotion.

"We'll never catch up to them," she said hopelessly. "And now the trackers are between them and us."

"We know where they're going," Jamieson replied. "So, we'll meet them there. Or we'll get ourselves to Deepsoil Five and ask the Master General to help us someway. I don't know, Clarin. I wish you'd stop crying."

"I'm tired! We haven't slept since we left Tasmin and Don, and there's no point in trying to pretend I'm rested and cheerful. I'm scared, too. God, Jamieson, with what we found out, aren't you? I'll cry for a while and get it out of my system. A good cry is almost as good as a night's sleep."

"It's very hard for me to control myself when you do that. I find myself wanting to hug you."

"Up a gyre-bird's snout," she remarked rudely, wiping her face with grubby hands. "Since when?"

"Oh, I don't know," he mused. "You're huggable."

"Not by you, Jamieson."

He turned away so she would not see his face. "Got your mind set on him, don't you?"

"I don't know what you're talking about."

"Up a bantigon's end flap you don't. You're wasting your time, Clarin. He was brou-dizzy over his little wife when she was alive, and he still is."

Clarin sighed and wiped her face on her sleeve. "All right, Reb. Just between us, yes. I'm tracked on the man. He's a little stiff, a little humorless. Some days I think he's got a Tripsinger score where his sex urge ought to be. But when he talks, it's like he's reading my mind."

"You're what he ought to have had, Clarin. But he didn't. He had a little girl who never had the least idea what was going on in his head. You never met her, but I did."

"What was she like?"

"Like? She was . . . she was a lot like Wendra Gentrack. Edible. And sweet. Like some baby animal, soft, and giggly. Kind of fearful. Not interested in much. A good cook. Beautiful looking. She only had one way to act toward men, flirtatious. She didn't mean anything by it. She fluffed up even for me, and I'm nobody."

"I wouldn't say that," she objected softly.

He shook his head in mock protest, going on. "What I mean is, you got this very strong urge to take care of her, even when she didn't need it. She'd give this little breathless laugh or sigh, like a child, and you'd feel your chest swelling with protective fervor." He laughed. "Not like you, Clarin. Not independent."

"No, I haven't noticed myself arousing any of that protective fervor."

"She couldn't relate to women at all—always had her

claws out. And that was fear, I figured out. She had any woman between the ages of eight and eighty slotted as a possible competitor. Poor Master Ferrence could only sneak over to see his mother when she wasn't looking. I'd always figured it was lucky we didn't have any women Tripsingers at Deepsoil Five, or she'd have made his life miserable."

"She's dead," Clarin said. "That sounds hard, but it's the simple truth, Reb. She's dead. She's not going to come back from the bottom of the Enigma. She's gone. Eventually, he'll realize that. If there is any eventuality. I keep forgetting there may not be. . . ."

"You're planning on being around if he does?"

"If any of us are still alive, you bet your sex life I do." She managed a rueful smile, then stiffened. Her eyes had caught a tiny motion, far down the valley. "Give me the glasses," she said, with an imperative gesture. "Quick!"

She stared, searching the clearing where the movement had caught her eye.

"It's them," she said, disbelieving. "Tasmin and Don."

"Alone?"

"All alone. On foot. Coming back this way. They must have hidden the mules. Or lost the mules. Or the way's blocked down there as it was for us." She urged her tired animal into a trot. "Come along, acolyte. We're not as alone as I thought we were."

Jamieson's report to Tasmin of their effort to find an open route to the west made it clear they had no other choice than to return. "We were cut off," Jamieson snarled. "We tried three routes west, and every one of them had an encampment of troops arrayed across it. Guards, sentries, whatever. With life detectors of some kind, too. They damn near caught us!"

"Every trooper with weapons bristling all over him," Clarin said. "We've thought all along that Justin had the troopers in his pocket. Now we know for sure. Half the garrison is camped between us and the 'Soilcoast. They had Explorers with them. Jamieson spied out one group last night."

"They were talking about guarding the routes out of the

Presences," Jamieson said. "Except for regular brou caravans, anyone coming from the west is supposed to be stopped. The troopers were arguing with the Explorers whether it would be acceptable to engage in a little robbery and rape in the process. The Explorers were really tense about the whole thing—sitting back-to-back kind of tense. Somebody in that setup is going to get killed!"

"How did the Explorers get mixed up in this?"

"I got the impression they didn't really know what was going on, Master Ferrence. They'd been hired to bring the troopers in because no Tripsingers were available."

"Not available!" Tasmin's exclamation was sheer reflex. Tripsingers were always available!

Clarin sighed. She looked exhausted, damp ringlets of hair scalloping her cheeks and forehead. "Thyle Vowe has obviously sent the word to the citadels that Tripsingers are not to lead Troopers anywhere. The word may not have reached the interior yet, but there's been plenty of time for Vowe to tie up the Coast."

"It would explain what happened," Tasmin agreed thoughtfully.

Clarin's voice shook as she said, "Listen, Tasmin. We haven't told you the worst thing yet. The troopers were doing a lot of talking about the equipment they had with them."

"Demolition equipment," explained Jamieson. "White noise projectors and chemical explosives with various kinds of propulsion devices. I snooped around a little while Clarin yodeled down a canyon to draw them off. She sounded exactly like about twenty Tripsingers on a practice trip through the Crazies. The troopers thought there were at least a dozen of her, all female, so the putative rapists went zipping off in pursuit."

"Clarin!" cried Tasmin. "What happened?"

"They ran into some 'lings and about half of them got killed," she said with a calmness that was belied by her shaking hands and bloodless lips. "I was lying above them on a parapet I'd got through to by using Don's machine."

"It gave me plenty of time," Jamieson said, irrepressibly. "I got a good look at the equipment they're carrying. I also got away with a copy of their map." He drew it from one of the deep pockets of his robe and unfolded it, spreading it on the ground before them. It was a satellite map of the area stretching from Deepsoil Five on the east to the Deepsoil Coast on the west and from the southern coast to the Jut.

"Justin isn't going to waste any time," Clarin said, pointing to the markings on the map. The Watchers, the Startles, the Creeping Desert, the Mad Gap, the list went on and on, all marked for destruction, with a line of march leading from demolition site to demolition site as the road was cleared before them. They wouldn't need any Tripsingers. There wouldn't be anything to get in their way!

Tasmin shivered. He felt suddenly cold, as though it was his own body someone had scheduled for destruction. As soon as the Commission findings were announced, Justin would begin!

Don interrupted his musing, angrily. "I recognized the voice of that woman on the trail last night. Her name is Sells. She's some high mucky-muck among the Crystallites. I heard her speak once in the Crystallite Temple in Splash One. What was she doing with Geroan?"

He replied, "Well, you know that Geroan works for Justin. I think you can assume that the Crystallites also work for Justin. Probably they always have."

"The Crystallites!"

"I imagine Harward Justin had the commission arranged for even before the Jut massacre," he said. "The massacre was simply the opening shot in the BDL war, the dramatic 'incident' he needed to reopen the sentience question."

"He's a monster! All those people. . . ."

"Do you think Justin cares? After what you told me about him?"

"Is he the one at the top?"

"He's at the top on Jubal, that's certain." And at the top of my particular list, he thought. "Which doesn't help us at the moment." He nodded at Jamieson and Clarin. "You two did a good job. Don't look so downcast."

"I don't know what to do next," Clarin sighed, then sighed again, patting a pocket, complaining tearfully like a child. "And I lost my mouse."

She looked up at Tasmin, wishing in that instant she could make him respond as Celcy had evidently done. She could use a little comforting, a little protection.

He started to extend his hand toward her, then stopped himself, accusing himself, accusing Donatella. He couldn't hug Clarin now, not after what Don had said. The whole thing was ridiculous. He had no place in his life for Clarin, not now, not when a world hung in the balance.

Clarin turned away, confused by the expression on his face, a rejection that she had done nothing to provoke. She blinked back tears and walked away from them, barely noticing the ironic twist of Donatella's lips. Jamieson came after her, standing beside her as she stared back down the valley, the way they had come.

"You need some sleep, lady."

She did not see the yearning on his face. She responded only to his words. "Amen, Reb. Sleep. And two or three other little things I can think of."

From behind them, Tasmin's voice came in its usual matter-of-fact intonation, as though there was no whirlpool of feelings boiling among them, as though there had been no crisis, no imminent threat, no assassins after them, no map of disaster, no anything that mattered at all. "Get a little rest, Clarin, Jamieson. There won't be any for the next few days. Don and I have picked a route out of this valley. With what you've told us, we can't waste any time. We'll have to head straight for the Enigma."

14

The office of the Grand Master in the tower of the citadel at Splash One was a disaster area—or so Thyle Vowe thought, looking it over.

"Can't we throw some of this stuff away," he asked plaintively from among the litter of cube copy, handwritten notes, and files of untidy correspondence.

Gereny Vox looked up from the box she was packing. "If you're not interested in having documents to base a case on later, sure. We could just burn the place down and get rid of it all."

"It's all in the computers anyhow," he said doubtfully, not really believing it.

"You sure? You sure Justin doesn't have a mouse here in the citadel somewhere, wiping away anythin' that Justin wouldn't want to come out later on? Listen, Thyle! If I can find Crystallites workin' in my own stables, you can find a mouse or two chirpin' away here in the citadel. Believe me. Anyhow, I'm almost through."

"Where did you and Jem decide to put the stuff?"

"We found an empty brou warehouse near the docks in Tallawag. It's far enough north of Splash One not to get interfered with, and it's close enough we can hide out there a while if we need to."

"An empty warehouse? That'd be scarce as red meat! How'd you find one of those."

"Well, somebody favorable to our side of things boggled a few records is what happened. So far as BDL's facility files're concerned, the place is packed with obsolete equipment. So far as the equipment inventory files're concerned, it's full of dried brou. So far as the brou shipment schedule files're concerned, it was emptied last flight out. The auditors might catch up to it in a year or two, but by then it shouldn't matter. Right now it's got my mule breedin' files and Jem's agridiv files, and anythin' else he or Rheme Gentry thinks is important enough to hold onto—includin' at least six copies of all the evidence Rheme's come up with in the Governor's office—along with all the stun rifles we could steal from the armory and all the charge cubes we could steal from troop supply. There's some mighty corruptible folks out there, Thyle. Makes you real sad, seein' what the world's come to."

"You're sly, Gereny," he said admiringly. "That's what you are. You and Jem are a pair. And you takin' pay from BDL, too."

"Pair of old mules is what we are," she said comfortably. "Just because BDL fills our feed trough doesn't mean we won't kick 'em if they need it. We may not be able to prove sentience, which is what I bet Don's up to, but we'll sure as hell prove corruption. You heard anything about Don yet?"

"Just enough to worry me quite a bit."

"That girl of yours get any information back to you?"

"Not a word. No, I sent a couple of 'Singers up Redfang way the day after we sent Tasmin Ferrence. My 'Singers found bodies, more of 'em than there should have been, but none of 'em people we were worried about. They found tracks, too, headed back into the range. Four sets. I figure that means Don Furz is in good company."

"Includin' Renna."

"I do worry some about her," he confessed.

"Well, why'd you send your own daughter off on a fool trip like that?"

"Because she was with Tasmin and his other acolyte, and because accordin' to you there were only three or four Crystallites to worry about—instead of about a dozen assassins, which is what there turned out to be accordin' to the tracks—and because Renna and I agreed nobody was to know she's my daughter because she says it makes her life difficult. I gave her my word. She started callin' herself Clarin and moved away from Northwest where people knew about it. Clarin was her mama's name. My Princess. Did you see what those pagans did to her hair, down there in Five? She had the prettiest hair. . . ."

"You don't want citadels cuttin' neophytes' hair, all you

have to do is tell 'em so. You think somethin's happened to her?"

"No," he grumped. "No, I don't. Tasmin's clever. And that Jamieson is cleverer than two Tasmins. He could sing his way by the Black Tower in the dark with a high wind blowing. And Renna's no fool-child, herself. No, I think they got driven back into the range and are bottled up in there. They'll get to a citadel eventually. Hope they've got sense enough to stay there until all this is over."

He went into a silent communion with his worries, fumbling papers from one pile to another until Gereny asked, "You knew the discipline stockade was found empty, and all the hard cases have disappeared along with most of the regular troops and a whole batch of weaponry?"

"Captain Jines Verbold told me, yes. Came to me at home, kind of snuck around so's nobody'd see him, said it happened without his knowledge or help, and I believe him. Verbold says his men are the only ones left around, barely enough of 'em to round up the Crystallites—which he had orders to do. Colonel Lang is showin' his true colors, Gereny."

"Well, what are you doin' about it?"

"I've got every citadel on alert. I've cut off Tripsingers, so he can't use them to get anyplace. Trouble is, Gereny, there wasn't any pressure to get Tripsingers. Which means. . . ."

"Which means Justin figures he won't need 'em, right?"

"Doesn't need and doesn't want. That's the way I see it, yes. So, I've sent Tripsingers here and Tripsingers there, the ones with the best rifle scores, and I've sent some noise projectors and what not. Way I got it figured, this is pretty rough country and those troops haven't seen action in a long, long time. One good rifleman ought to be able to pin down a lot of troops, don't you think? Blow up some 'lings on top of 'em. Delay 'em some?"

"Delay 'em maybe. I don't think you'll stop 'em."

"No, Gereny, I don't either. We'll need some help to do that."

"Did your Captain tell you the troops had some Explorers with 'em?"

The Grand Master scowled at her. "Chase Random Hall has had both hands out for a long time. He probably called in

a few loyalty chits, told a few more lies. Some fool young
Explorers think loyalty's more important than good sense."
Thyle ran both hands through his white hair and sighed.
"Hall's been their union rep for years, sold 'em out on almost
every issue, and they still vote for him and pay him his fealty.
Makes you wonder what some people use for brains."

"Rheme's trying to get a message out asking for a gunship, is he?"

"Why the hell else are we gettin' ready to evacuate the
citadel, Gereny? Say the PEC figures it has enough evidence
of corruption it gets itchy and calls for Justin's resignation and
the Governor's. Up until just recent, Rheme was gettin' a lot
of information out, and I figure the PEC might figure it had
about enough evidence by now. Say Justin or Wuyllum or
both orders out the whole army to defend 'em and refuse to
budge. Be dumb of either of 'em, but they might do it
anyhow."

"Not the Governor. Rheme says he's gettin' ready to
run. Any time now."

"Well, Justin then. Say Justin digs himself in and won't
move. It'd be like him. So, then, say the PEC decides to
slash off BDL headquarters as a sort of object lesson. That
happens I don't want to be sittin' here in the citadel, right on
their doorstep, examinin' my belly button as my last view of
anythin' mortal."

" 'Tisn't a bad belly button," Gereny remarked in a
discriminating tone.

"Lots've flesh I'd rather be lookin' at," he replied, pinch-
ing a portion of Gereny's.

"You old bantigon," she remarked fondly. "Well, if you
want to spend any of your declinin' years chasing women,
you'd better go through this pile of stuff and tell me what we
need to keep." She put another file in a carton and thumped
it to settle the contents. "And you'd better start thinkin' up
real good excuses to move everybody out without Honeypeach
Thonks gettin' suspicious. She watches this place like she was
a gyre-bird and we'd been dead for three days."

"I know she does," he said uncomfortably. The close
surveillance Honeypeach exercised over the citadel in Splash
One had been one of his major concerns. "I figured she'd be
gone by the time we needed to move. Thought I might leave

movin' 'til the last minute, Gereny, love. Assumin' there's goin' to be a last minute."

Vivian Ferrence lay on a mattress inflated over a layer of crates in the bottom of a brou wagon, baby Miles bouncing on her stomach. Their journey had gone on for many days, and the anxieties of Splash One were beginning to give way to less painful feelings, though in an erratic and undependable fashion. She no longer had to worry whether Miles would have enough to eat on a given day. The food provided by the trip cook was monotonous but adequate. Flat bread. Beans or cheese or bean cheese. Dried fish or meat. A small ration of fresh fruits and vegetables. Once every four or five days, a bit of roasted fresh meat when one of the bantigons from the crate in the back of the cook wagon was slaughtered. There was milk for Miles, as well, artificial and reconstituted, but full of appropriate minerals nonetheless.

And there were cookies. The trip cook, Brunny, had an affinity for children, and cookies seemed mysteriously to materialize whenever Miles toddled around the cook wagon after lunch or during the evening halts.

During the night there were the peaceful stars and sleep that was better than she had had at any time recently. During the day, there was Tripsinging and the glory of the Presences. She had not been afraid. Even considering how Lim had died, she had not been afraid. Her acceptance was almost fatalistic, she realized. If she died on this journey, she would at least have had this period of peace and sufficient food and a warm bed. And memories. Lots of memories.

Night before last, just at sunset, they had seen a red sparkle on the eastern horizon, twin spires of irridescent scarlet. "That's the Enigma," the Tripmaster had announced. "Be nice if there was a trail that way. It'd cut off about fifty miles. As it is, we turn north up ahead a ways, go on up through Harmony and past the Black Tower. You can see the very tip of Old Blacky, sticking up there over that purple peak. Then Deepsoil Five, same day."

Deepsoil Five. The feelings of peace fled, and Vivian became anxious once more. Why? She had accepted what Tasmin had told her. He hadn't known, his mother hadn't known. Much though she believed they should have known, she could not condemn them for something that had been between Lim and his father. Or, she could condemn them but chose not to. Chose, rather, to let baby Miles have a family—if only her mind could stop there, but it never did. It always went on, "let Miles have a family even though they betrayed his daddy and ended up killing him."

No matter how often she told herself that she did not condemn them, she ended up by doing exactly that. Betrayal, she moaned. Killing. Violent accusations against absent people she didn't even know. Each time she arrived at this point in her circular agony, she cried bitterly, then told herself all over again that they hadn't really done it. Tasmin had been seven years old when it happened; he had been only sixteen or seventeen when Lim left. Could she really hold a seven-year-old boy responsible? And Thalia, Tasmin's mother—she had been going blind even then. Perhaps that had been all the trauma she could handle. Her husband couldn't have been any help to her. Perhaps she had been unable to see anything at all.

So, alternately accusing and exonerating, Vivian had spent the recent hours gradually working herself out of the emotional maelstrom and into something approaching calm. Now, with the end of the journey in sight, that calm was disrupted and all the feelings of pain and anger were stirred once more.

"I have to stop this," she whispered half-aloud. "I have to stop it."

" 'Top it," said Miles. " 'Top it, Mama."

"I will," she promised, laughing at him through teary eyes. "I will. Are you going to go get some cookies from Mr. Brun?"

"Cookies," Miles verified with a nod of his head. "Yes. Cookies wit' nuts."

"Where do you suppose Mr. Brun gets nuts?" she asked in pretend amazement.

"Viggy nuts," crowed Miles, giggling. It was a story Brunny told him, about the viggies bringing nuts to trade for candy. Actually, there were no nuts on Jubal, and the sweet, hard nuggets in Brunny's cookies were merely sugary chunks of baked proto-meal, but Miles loved the viggy story.

"That's right." She laughed with him, sitting up as the wagon slowed and stopped. "Supper time, almost." She was hungry tonight. She had noticed herself being a lot hungrier over the past week or so. That was good. She had lost a lot of weight in the fish market, lost a lot buying food only for Miles because there wasn't enough money for food for them both. Lim wouldn't have known her, she had become so haggard. She didn't want Lim's mother to see her that way.

"But it doesn't make any difference," she murmured to herself. Lim's mother was blind. She couldn't see. It didn't matter.

"All down. Mules to water," cried the Tripmaster.

"Mools a wattah," echoed Miles. "Awl down."

"All right, love. We'll get down." She fumbled for her shoes and Miles's, finding them between two crates, and she was busy fastening straps when the Tripmaster arrived at the rear of the wagon.

"Everything all right, Mrs. Ferrence?"

"Everything's fine, Tripmaster."

"Brunny says to bring the baby on over for his evening treat." He regarded her curiously from pale, almost colorless eyes. He had known Lim Ferrence, he had told her, long ago, in school in Deepsoil Five. Without waiting for curious questions, she had told him what had happened to Lim when Lim was only a child. It was a kind of catharsis, telling it. The Tripmaster had said nothing more, nothing since, not about Lim, but he had been uniformly solicitous of her and the baby. "Only a couple days more, and we'll arrive. You lookin' forward to gettin' there?"

"I am, yes," she half lied. "I've never met Lim's mother."

"She's blind, you know."

"Yes, I know. Tasmin told me."

"Pity. I remember her, too, before she was blind, that is. One of the prettiest women I'd ever seen. Lim always bragged on her. You look like her, you know. Like she did then."

She was shocked. "I didn't know!"

"Oh, yes. Same shape face. Same eyes and mouth. Same hair. You could be her daughter." He stumped off, leaving her behind with her mouth open.

"Cookies," demanded Miles.

She got down from the wagon and walked toward the cook wagon, Miles's sturdy legs bringing him steadily along at her heels. When he had received his cookies, she stood with him while he ate them, staring up at the long, dun-colored slopes around them. Open country. Groves of Jubal trees, turned to face the setting sun, plumes fanned wide. Far off, at the top of the western slope, she saw something moving, a speck on the horizon, miles and miles away against low clouds lit by sunset glow. "Riders," she pointed.

The cook followed her pointing finger, frowning. "I don't see nothin'."

"They were there," she insisted. "Riders."

"Better tell Tripmaster," Brun advised. "There's not supposed to be anyone out here right now but us."

The Tripmaster grunted when she told him, looking a little worried. "Trouble?" she asked, apprehensively. "Something wrong?"

"Oh, no. No. I should think not. It's just that there's been a good deal of . . . oh, call it unrest. Over this CHASE Commission thing, most of it. People taking sides, and the Crystallites gettin' worse and worse."

She shuddered. "Sometimes I have bad dreams about Crystallites."

"Don't we all. Well, I don't like people movin' around unless I know who they are."

The man moved away and she and the boy returned to their wagon. She could sleep either in the wagon where they had traveled or under it or in a tent, if she preferred. There was little rainfall on this part of Jubal. What moisture there was came from the coast in vast, cottony fogs that rolled in at evening and burned away with the first light of morning, leaving the Jubal trees sodden with accumulated dew. When light came, every frond lifted, funneling the precious moisture down the trough-shaped veins and into hollow reservoirs below ground. More than one traveler had saved his life by drinking the bitter liquid when no other moisture was available, though no one would drink it by choice. If there was fog, it would be better to sleep in a tent, but there was no sign of fog tonight.

"Tent up?" asked Miles.

"I don't think so," she told him. "I think we'll take our mattresses over in that big grove of Jubal trees, little boy. Jubal trees smell so nice." There would be a little privacy there, as well. She felt the need of a good, all-over wash, and her hair needed braiding.

"Smell nice," he agreed. "Yubal trees smell so nice."

She gathered up their scattered belongings. They had so little that it would fit into one shoulder sack. Their few extra clothes and her books were in a crate at the bottom of the wagon. The sack and the mattress were not even a heavy load as she dragged them to the grove, some distance east of the wagons.

Miles helped her by dragging his own half-sized mattress after her, plopping it down beside hers within the grove. When it was dark, the trees would change from fan shape to a fountain shape, more efficient for fog catching, Vivian assumed, just as the fan shapes were more efficient for gathering sunlight. The result would make a shadowy grove that looked quite unlike the daytime one.

"Smell it, Mama," Miles said now, bouncing on his bed and waiting for the trees to shift.

The sun was a ball, then a half drop, then merely a thin arc upon the horizon. Then nothing, and the trees let go with a rustling sigh, a long shushing. The fronds fell outward from the middle, and what had been two-dimensional shapes became plumy clouds gathering darkness beneath them.

"Supper," she told Miles. "Let's get supper quick, then we can come back here and watch the stars come out."

There were viggies singing as they finished their meal and helped Brunny put away the disarranged implements and supplies.

"Where you stretched out for the night?" the Tripmaster asked. "Over in that Jubal grove? Looks like a nice place if there's no fog. Not much danger tonight." He looked up at the clear sky, hands busy with his trip log. "Sleep well."

By the time they returned to the mattresses under the Jubal trees, the first stars were trembling in the high eastern sky.

"You need to go behind a bush?" she asked.

"I went," Miles said. "All by myself."

"Fine. Then you're going to sleep all night, without waking up, aren't you?"

"All night," he agreed, snuggling onto the mattress. "Tell Miles a story."

She told a story until his eyes closed and his breathing became slow and quiet. Then she told a story to herself, as she gave herself a slow, cool sponge bath, as she brushed and rebraided her hair, as the stars came out to make a glittering diagonal band across the heavens, a story about tomorrow, about the future. She snuggled into her mattress, head pillowed on an arm, to drift in and out of sleep.

The sudden light and shout from the direction of the wagons was an intrusion.

"Tripmaster!" A bellow. A well-schooled bellow, in a modulated voice. She had heard that voice before. Miles stirred in his sleep, and she put out a hand, ready to muffle him if he woke. Why? Because the Tripmaster had said he didn't like people moving around when he didn't know what they were doing. Because he had said something about Crystallites, and that voice had something to do with Crystallites!

A sleepy mumbling Brunny's voice, then the Tripmaster himself, drawling sleepily.

"Well, well, ain't it that big mucky-muck Crystallite Chantiforth Bins? High Pontiff or some such, an't it? What in the name of all that's holy are you doing out here in Presence country? I thought you Crystallites believed in keeping your distance."

"Well, we do," said the voice. "Except when one of our own is in trouble, Tripmaster. Which I have reason to believe is the case."

"Is that the truth? Now who would that be?"

"Member of our congregation. Had a baby under unsanctified conditions, fell on hard times, sold herself into bondage to the blasted BDLers. I've come to buy her bond and take her home."

There was silence. Vivian lay in baffled silence. The story made no sense. There was no woman on this trip who had sold herself into service.

"Don't think I know the party you're speakin' of," said the Tripmaster. "No passengers this trip."

"Oh, come now, Tripmaster. I know BDL pays your salary, but I'm prepared to be more generous than you can imagine. The woman's name is Vivian. Vivian Ferrence? And she has a little boy."

Vivian was screaming silently into her hand, fighting to

keep herself silent and unmoving in the grove. The Tripmaster had said no passengers. Why had he said that?

"Well, you're weeks too late, Bins. We had that lady with us for a time with her child, but she left us at the Deepsoil Twelve cutoff. There was a caravan there goin' by the northern route, one with women and children on it, and she chose to go with them. Kind of lonesome lady, lost her husband recently. Wanted some other women around, and I can't say's I blame her. . . .

"By the way, that fella with you has that stun rifle pointed kind of in this direction. He plannin' to shoot some of us, or what?" The Tripmaster had been talking very loudly, loudly enough so that no one in the camp could have missed a word.

Hearty laughter. "He's just mistrustful, Tripmaster. He wouldn't put it past you to lie to us."

"Well, easy enough to prove," the Tripmaster bellowed. "There's me and my backup 'Singer. There's six drivers here, includin' the cook, and there's six wagons. You can look in all six of 'em."

Vivian kept silent, thinking frantically. Had she left anything behind. Any toy? Any little shoe? Any blanket or bit of clothing?

"He covered himself," she explained silently. "The Tripmaster said we were with the caravan for a while. If you left anything, it was from then. Be still, Vivian. Be very still."

So she was still, though she could not even identify the threat. She had had nothing to do with the Crystallites. She had heard Chantiforth Bins in the temple. Everyone went to the temple. It was a major attraction. What was he doing here? Why was he looking for her, for the baby? Why was she shaking in fear he would find her?

"Be still," she ordered herself. "Trust the Tripmaster. Be very still."

Chantiforth Bins was speaking again, over the sound of rummaging, over the muttering between him and his man . . . men? More than one. Two, maybe three. "I don't find her, that's for sure, Tripmaster. Well, since she left you so long ago, you won't mind our going along with you into Deepsoil Five, will you? We can wait for her there."

"Suit yourself, Bins. But suit yourself with those rifles in their scabbards. We'll have enough trouble gettin' by the Black Tower without your making us nervous."

There were multiple clicks and snaps as the rifles were put away. The men were staying. Staying. And when morning came, when light came, the Jubal trees would make fans of themselves, facing east. And Miles might jabber, she couldn't stop him. Then they would find her.

The Tripmaster was leaving the vicinity of the wagons.

Bins's voice called, "Where are you going, Tripmaster?"

"I'm goin' to do what I need to do, Bins. You want to come along?"

Bins motioned to one of the men with him, who sauntered after the Tripmaster into a small grove well to the north of the one Vivian occupied. The Tripmaster had carried a latrine spade. After a time, they returned to the wagons. There was desultory talk. The firelight dimmed. Silence came. Perhaps someone was on watch, perhaps not. She could not tell. Several of the drivers went to the grove also. The last time a driver went, no one went with him.

Before she had married Lim, Vivian had worked for the Exploration Division, a lowly job to be sure, though a registered one, requiring concentration and accuracy as she fed the reports of the Tripsingers and Explorers into the master library of BDL. Some of her co-workers did not even read what they transmitted, their fingers doing the job all by themselves. Vivian, however, had read a lot of it and and lived every word. She had inside her head the experiences of half the Tripsingers and Explorers on Jubal. She knew what mistakes they had made, what errors of judgment. She knew when they had been clever, too.

Now she asked herself what one of the clever ones would have done, sitting with her head bowed on her clenched hands as she thought. After a time her face cleared and she released the valve on her mattress and allowed the air to bleed away, so slowly it seemed to take forever, not making a hiss. Then Miles's mattress, slowly, so slowly. He slept on. Miles was a good sleeper. She picked him up, cradling him in her arms, his limp mattress under him, then crept through the grove to the side away from the wagons. She needed a declivity, even the smallest trough would do, and she needed distance, to the east.

Behind her someone coughed, and she stopped, agonized. Silence fell again and she went on, up the long rise of ground to the east. She went slowly, keeping her feet from crunching, yard after slow yard.

When she looked back, the fire among the wagons was only a dim star. Beside her were two Jubal trees, the outlyers of a considerable grove, and behind them the ground fell away in a gentle bowl. At the bottom of the bowl, she laid Miles down and slowly, very slowly, reinflated his mattress.

She tucked the blanket loosely around him, then went back the way she had come, measuring the distance with frequent turns to look over her shoulder. When she returned, she carried her shoulder bag and dragged her own mattress behind her to wipe out the footprints she knew she had made.

When she settled into the hollow beside the baby, he murmured in his sleep. Exhausted, she lay beside him with her open eyes fixed on the eastern horizon.

Light came at last, waking her suddenly. Despite her apprehension, she had dozed off. She could not see the camp from where they were. Leaving Miles still deeply asleep, she crawled up the slope, poking her head up behind the lower fronds of a Jubal tree. The wagons were there, much farther away than she would have believed. People were moving around. Chantiforth Bins was stalking here and there, poking into things, searching every nearby grove. Within moments of sunrise, he was in the grove she had been sleeping in, marching through it and out the side nearest her to peer up the slope.

"Any sign?" he called to someone.

"Viggies've been in here," someone answered. "Footprints all over everything. Nothin' else."

Viggies! She gasped with relief. Her own tracks had been hidden then. Brunny was moving around the cook wagon, his loose coat wagging around him. After a time, clutching his coat, he went off to the same grove the Tripmaster had used the night before, also carrying a latrine shovel. No one offered to go with him.

Miles moved. Vivian crouched beside him, ready to silence him if necessary. It might not be necessary. Sometimes Miles slept well into the morning. . . .

As he did this time. The wagons were some distance away before he woke.

When she could no longer see the wagons, Vivian assumed the wagons could no longer see her and went down to the campground, hoping that someone would have found some way to leave food and water. The place was as clean as any campsite the Tripmaster had ever left.

"No cooky?" asked Miles hungrily. "Where's Brunny?"

Her eyes filled with tears. What had the Tripmaster hoped to do? Had he hoped to take the interlopers into Deepsoil Five and then return for her? Or send someone from Harmony? What would it be, minimum? Three days? Five? Surely he must have. . . .

She put Miles down with an exclamation and ran toward the grove where both the Tripmaster and Brunny had gone. She found it almost at once, a little mound. Tentatively, she dug into it with a dried frond.

Shit.

She wrinkled her nose, disgusted. Well, of course. She shoved the half dried feces aside and kept on digging.

Deep in the hole she found a water bottle, a small carton of rations, and a little plastic sack. In the sack was a note for her and something for Miles.

"We'll be back for you," Brunny had written. "Stay put."

"Cookies," said Miles with satisfaction.

Staying put for the morning was no problem. The afternoon became less pleasant, with a strong, grit-bearing wind from the south. Vivian left Miles huddled beneath a sheltering Jubal tree while she searched the surrounding area for cover. To the northwest were ramparts of Presences, pale yellow and gray-blue with forests of 'lings gathered at their bases, dwindling southward almost to the trail. Directly north was the pass to Harmony, a long, 'ling-littered slope, almost barren of growth. Nearby, groves of Jubal trees and meadows of knee-high grass lined the trail on both sides. Farther east, another escarpment was first amber, then orange, then vivid red, peaking at its point of ultimate scarlet into the sheer facades of the Enigma. So much she either knew, had seen herself, or had learned from her over-the-shoulder observations of the charts.

To the south, the groves of the trees dwindled to nothing, and the sedimentary rock of a coastal desert took over,

only an occasional pillarlike Presence breaking the flat monot-
ony, the ruled-line of the horizon.

The rock was broken by potholes. Within minutes of
beginning her search, Vivian found half a dozen of them,
none of them much larger than her head. A bit deeper into
the rock desert, the holes became larger, and about a quarter
of a mile from the trail, in the middle of a patch of fine sand,
she found a hole with nicely stepped sides, a sandy bottom,
and an overhang on the south edge—a perfect shelter from
the strong south wind.

It was warm in the hole, also. The stone walls gathered
the rays of the sun and held the warmth. They would give it
up slowly, even in the chill of the night. All day they sat in
the sand at the bottom of the hole, Vivian manufacturing
trucks for Miles out of ration cartons and bits of string, Miles
building roads in the sand, both of them retreating under the
ledge when the wind blew chill. It was a better hiding place
than the grove of trees had been, and from the lip of the hole
she could see anyone or anything approaching while it was
still miles away. She did not consider that anyone might
approach in the dark or in the fog. She had not even seen one
of the notorious fogs of the southern coast.

When it came, it was not much to see. The first hint of it
was the clamminess of the blankets that wakened her, blankets suddenly soggy and cold in the darkness. She had gathered dried tree fronds for fire, if it became necessary to have
fire, and she lit a small pile of them with the firestarter from
the rations kit. They smoldered with a dense, eye-burning
smoke that would not rise above the lip of the hole, and she
threw sand over the charred branches, cursing at them. Better to be cold than half asphyxiated, she thought, not realizing quite how cold it would get. Once that realization struck
home, she pulled Miles onto her larger mattress and half
deflated the smaller one to make a tent over them, thriftily
setting the water jug beneath one folded corner and listening
to the plop, plop, plop as condensation from the fog ran into
it. A Tripsinger had done that once. She had read about it in
his report. She sat cross-legged, with Miles in her lap, making a tent pole of her body and head, both blankets wrapped
around them. After an endless time, she even dozed.

It was the voices that wakened her. Soft voices in the
dark, calling her.

But not by name. At first the strangeness of that did not strike her. Only when she had come fully awake did the voices seem odd and mysterious. Until then they had been a component of dream.

"We search for the wife of Lim Ferrence," the voices said. Sang. Chanted.

"Lim Terree," another voice contradicted with a soft soprano warble. "The mother said he called himself Lim Terree."

"So she did," the voices sang. "We search for the wife of Lim Terree."

She did not answer, could not have answered. These were ghost voices from a world of spirits and haunts, a childhood world of reasonless fear.

"Perhaps she is afraid," said the second voice. It sounded like a woman's voice, or a child's. Not a man's voice. Vivian's heart hammered. She had to say something. Perhaps they had come to help her. Help Miles.

"What do you want?" she called, her voice a thin shriek on the edge of terror.

"Do not be afraid, please," the voices sang. "The mother of Lim Terree thought you were in danger. We have come to help you."

"Some men came," she cried. "Looking for me. For my little boy."

"Ah," the voices sang. "Can you move? Can you walk? Are you strong and well?"

"Yes. Yes. I'm all right."

The voices murmured in some other language. A few voices first, then several, then many. A chorus. Whatever it was they were singing, they did it several times over until it satisfied them. In some obscure way, it satisfied Vivian, too. When they were through with the song, it was completed. Even she could hear that.

"We have sung this predicament," the voices told her. "You cannot walk in the dark. You have not the means, as we have. You would hurt yourself and the little one. So, when it is light, you must come to the red mountains. We will come behind and wipe away the tracks you will leave."

"The red mountain? The Enigma!"

"Yes. So you call it."

"It's where Lim died," she cried. "I don't want to go there!"

"Not quite there," they murmured. "Only near there. It is safe there. No Loudsingers . . . no humans come there."

"I wanted to go to Deepsoil Five," she cried. "Lim's mother is there."

"We think the men who looked for you are also there. It is not safe there. Later we will take you there."

The fog became silent once more. After a time, she thought she had dreamed it. When light came at last, she knew it had not been a dream. In the fine sand all around the edge of the hole were the strange four-toed prints of viggy feet. She had never heard that they could speak. In the light of day, she could not believe they had spoken.

Her disbelief immobilized her and would have kept her from moving, except for the light that came darting from the trail toward Harmony. Morning had come; the fog had slowly burned away; she had seen the tracks and marveled at them, uncertain whether to be curious or terrified. No one had ever alleged viggies to be harmful. The few specimens who had been caught in the early years of exploitation had all died, most of them very quickly. No rumor of violence attached to them at all. They were virtually unseen, a constant presence to the ear, an unconsidered irrelevancy otherwise.

But no one had ever said they could talk. It was this that made her suspicious. Suppose they were not really viggies at all.

"But they were here," she told herself. "Right here, not four feet from me. If they'd wanted to, they could have snatched me up or killed me or whatever they wanted."

Still, she was undecided. Then, as she was having a slow look around from the lip of the hole, she saw the glint of light up the trail toward Harmony. Flash. Then again, flash. She watched for a long time until it came again, three, four times. Light reflecting off lenses. Up that trail, at the limit of vision, someone was watching this place.

Had they been watching yesterday?

She slid down into the hole and began to pack their few belongings. A little way east of them was a narrow ridge, paralleling the trail, running eastward along it. If she could get behind that, no one could see her from the trail.

She watched first, waiting until the flashes came, then came again, then did not come. Then she was out of the hole and trotting toward the east with Miles staggering along behind. When they came to a grove of Jubal trees, she picked up Miles and darted into the grove to lie behind a tree and watch the Harmony trail.

After a time, flash, and flash again. This time she carried Miles as she trotted quickly away to the next grove. She had begun to get the feel of it. Someone was taking a look every quarter hour.

It took four more dashes between groves to attain the ridge. Then they were behind it.

"More game," suggested Miles, who had become fond of diving behind trees.

"Not right now, my big boy," she told him. "Right now, we're just going for a long walk. Can you do that?"

He nodded, mouth pursed in a bargaining expression. "Cooky?"

"When we stop for lunch, I'll give you a cooky. How's that?"

"Fine."

Long before they stopped for lunch he was worn out and asleep on her shoulder. Long before they arrived at the red mountains, while they were still miles from them, she was equally worn. Evening found them curled in a circle of settler's brush, eating cold rations and drinking less water than they wanted, then falling into exhausted slumber.

"Come," the voice said, almost in her ear. "You cannot sleep now. Men are seeking you. Come."

This time she saw them, in the thinnest glimmer of New Moon light, occulted by the shadow of Serendipity to a mere scythe of silver. They were furred and large-eyed, with wide, mobile ears. Their necks were corrugated with hanging flaps of bright hide, shadowed red and amber and orange, and their heads were decked with long, feathery antennae that looked like nothing so much as the fronds of Jubal trees. They were all around her, singing, singing in her own language, and she was not afraid of them.

"Where are the men?" she whispered. "How far back?"

"They saw you come this way," the viggies sang. "Even though we wiped the lands clean of your feet, still they search."

"What are we to do?"

"We will take you where they cannot go, woman of Lim Terree, honored be his name."

They guided her. She carried Miles, and two of the viggies ran along at her sides, their hands on her thighs, pushing or tugging ever so slightly to keep her on the right path. Bondri had introduced himself, as they went he named off the others of the troupe. Sometimes they slowed, sometimes to allow others of the troupe to clear a way ahead, sometimes to allow those who had been clearing the way behind to change jobs with others. Always they sang, sometimes in their own language, sometimes in hers. So she learned the story of Favel, the broken one, and of his release by the Loudsinger child. She wanted to laugh, then to cry. Lim hadn't done it out of generosity. He hadn't done it out of sympathy for the poor viggy, either. He'd done it out of spite and wounded feelings and jealousy and pain. She tried to tell Bondri this, and he listened with one ear cocked backward to hear her.

"Good," he said at last. "This is what Favel wanted. Another view to make his song more true."

It made no sense to her. Only that they were saving her, and Miles. That made sense.

They went eastward to the end of the ridge, then northward, into the crystal range. Now the viggies were singing in their own tongue exclusively, quieting the earth that trembled beneath them, opening ways that would be closed to those who followed. Some of the troupe climbed to the tops of peaks and yodeled into the night, while all those below opened their ears wide, listening.

"What are they doing?" she asked Bondri.

"The troupe of Chowdri goes around near here. They keep watch on the Mad One, the one you call the Enigma. I have a daughter to trade with Chowdri, and we will sing of Favel's death so the word may go east and south." He did this all in one breath, a kind of recitatif, and she shook her head in amazement. Lim had been an accomplished musician, perhaps a genius. But Bondri could do things with his voice Lim could never have attempted. Of course, Lim hadn't had a song-sack on his neck to hold several extra lungfuls of air, either.

At dawn they stopped. The Engima towered above them, a little to the east, like two bloody swords stabbed upward into the sky. Several weary viggies ran up from the south, singing as they came.

"The men have gone back they way they came, still looking. They did not find any sign of the woman or the child. They say they will go to Deepsoil Five, that the woman must eventually come to Deepsoil Five."

Well, she had left some of her few belongings on the wagon, in a carton. Undoubtedly whoever was after her and Miles had found them.

"They cannot come in here," Bondri said. "Your people have no words to let them into this place."

"But I cannot stay with your people forever, Bondri Wide Ears! Someday I must go to my own people."

"Someday is someday. We will sing that later. Just now we eat."

Miles woke up. He looked at the viggies with total wonder, then politely offered Bondri his last cooky. Bondri took it gravely and ate half, returning half. In return, Bondri gave him a cup of bark sap, which Miles shared with his mother. When she had drained the cup, she looked at it carefully, paling as she did so.

"What . . . what is this?"

"An ancestor cup," Bondri replied. "This one belonged to Favel, who honored your husband's name. Favel who laid his debt upon us that good should be returned for good."

Gently, she laid the skull cup down. Nothing in the Tripsingers' reports had prepared her for this, but native good manners did what preparation could not. "I am honored," she whispered, listening carefully while Bondri sang several songs of Favel's life. She joined the troupe in eating settler's brush, though she gave Miles his breakfast from rations he was more accustomed to.

And when they had finished, she joined the troupe in singing the song of her own rescue. That she had little or no voice did not seem to disturb the viggies. Miles more than made up for her.

"He has a good voice, your son," they sang to her. "When he is big, he will be a troupe leader."

"If he lives to get big," she whispered. A giligee patted her shoulder and crooned in her ear.

At midmorning, word was received from Chowdri's troupe, and they began to work their way east, ever closer to the Enigma.

"Isn't this dangerous?" she asked Bondri. "Aren't we going into peril?"

"Not into peril," he sang. "Not to the Mad One's roost. Only to the edge of the skin where the songs keep it quiet."

"Skin?" she asked, not sure she had understood.

"The outer part," Bondri explained, searching his more limited Loudsinger vocabulary. "The hide, the fur, the . . ." he found a word he liked, "the integument."

"Of the Presence?"

"Yes. The part that only twitches and slaps, like your skin, Lim's mate, when a wound fly crawls on it. The skin of the Mad One is not mad. Only the brain of it is mad, and we will not come close to that."

By evening they had come closer to the Enigma than Vivian wanted to, and yet the troupe of Bondri Gesel showed no discomfort. Six of the viggies were delegated to sing quiet songs to the skin, and these six were replaced from time to time by six others, one at a time slipping into and out of the chorus so that it never ceased. The music was soothing, soporific. Vivian found herself yawning, and Miles curled up under a Jubal tree and fell deeply asleep, even without his supper.

"You should stay awake," Bondri suggested. "Chowdri is on his way here. He has a good tongue. We sing well together."

The troupe of Chowdri joined them after dusk but before the night was much advanced. There were choral challenges and answers, contrapuntal exercises, long, slow passages sung by the two troupe leaders, and finally a brisk processional during which the singers tapped on their song-sacks to make a drumming sound. Chowdri had brought food. Chowdri was less amazed to see Vivian than Bondri thought he should be, and this occasioned some talk.

"We have one, too," sang Chowdri importantly. "A very little one. Not depouched yet."

"A Loudsinger child!" Bondri was incredulous. "A true Loudsinger child?"

"My senior giligee found it in a body," Chowdri sang. "A female who was killed by the Mad One. My giligee went at once to find bones on the Enigma, before the gyre-birds came, and she found this little one, inside the woman, the way they grow. No bigger than a finger. We have sung that the taboo does not apply to such little ones."

"What did he say?" Vivian asked.

Bondri translated.

"I don't understand," she said. "What does he mean?"

Bondri beckoned to his own giligee, who came forward and allowed Bondri to open its pouch and point within. "There," he sang. "In the pouch. This is the brain-bird of Favel. Here, also, grow the little ones from mating. Our females carry them inside for only a little time, not like you Loudsingers. Favel told me all about it."

"Brain-bird?" she faltered.

"Excuse me, Chowdri," sang Bondri. "My guest has a difficulty that I must correct before we sing further together."

"Males and females mate," he sang to her. "You understand this?"

Vivian fought down a hysterical giggle and told him yes, that she understood, that Loudsingers did a similar thing.

"After a few days, the female seeks out the giligee and sheds the little one, like a little worm. The giligee takes the little thing into its pouch. The tendrils of the pouch close it in and give it nourishment. It lives and grows there. When it is big, it is depouched. It is a female."

"Always?" she wondered.

"Always," he said firmly. "We know it is not so with you, but with us it is always female. The female lives and is traded as a daughter to some other troupe and mates and does female things. Then the time comes her brain-bird cries for release. The giligee bites out the brain-bird and puts it in the pouch again. It grows again. This time it is male."

"Always," she nodded to herself in amazement.

"Always. In every female there is a male waiting to grow. It grows up and mates and does male things. And when its own brain-bird cries for release, the giligee takes it once more. And this time, the last time, it grows to be a giligee."

"And when its brain-bird cries for release again?"

"There is no brain-bird in a giligee. They get very old and finally die. Then we make an ancestor cup as we do for all, and put them beside a Presence and sing their songs."

"So Chowdri's giligee has a human baby in it? You know whose baby that is, don't you? That's Tasmin's baby. Lim's brother. Tasmin Ferrence. The woman must have been his wife. Celcy. And Lim was there. Lim was on the Enigma. Maybe he didn't die!"

Bondri turned away in some haste and began a burst of song, which his troupe joined, then Chowdri's troupe, the two groups singing away at one another as though to compile an encyclopedia of song. When the melody dwindled at last and Bondri returned to Vivian, he looked very sad and old, his song-sack hanging limp.

"He is truly dead. I am sorry, Lim's mate, but he is truly dead. The giligee took some of his bone to make a bark scraper. Do you want his ancestor cup? I know it is not the Loudsinger way, but the giligee can get it if you want it."

She shook her head, weeping. There for a moment, she had been full of irrational hope. Well. Miles was alive, and she was alive, and it seemed that Tasmin's baby was alive also.

"How long will the giligee keep it?" she whispered.

"Until it is done," Bondri sang, shrugging. "It is not nearly finished yet."

"Will . . . will the giligee give it to us—to Tasmin's family—when it is finished?"

Bondri seemed to be considering this. "I believe it will. I will take debt with Chowdri's troupe to assure it. In that way, the debt of Favel will be repaid to the family of Lim Terree. We have saved his wife and his child and his brother's child. That is a good repayment."

"Repayment in full," the troupe sang. "Repayment at once, as Favel required. Proud the troupe of Bondri Gesel to have repaid a debt of honor."

Maybelle Thonks squatted on her luggage in the small tender and stared across half a mile of slupping ocean to the spider-girdered tower in which the charred hulk of the *Broumaster* hung, readying for lift. The little boat in which she sat was packed with cartons and bags, all of which had been searched by BDL security men before they had been loaded. Maybelle had been searched as well.

"For your protection, Ma'am," the female guard had sneered. "Sometimes people plant things on other people."

"How in hell do you think anyone could have planted anything *there*," Maybelle had hissed in her ear, shocked. "For the love of good sense, woman!"

"Just routine," the guard had said, suddenly aware who she was violating.

"You've been through my luggage, through my clothes, through my cosmetics. You've been all over my body like a bad sunburn. What the hell do you think I'm carrying, a bomb?"

"Just routine," she mumbled again, handing Maybelle an intimate bit of her clothing.

Fuming, Maybelle reassembled herself and turned to check her belongings, which were now in a state of total disarray. She did a quick inventory of the jewelry case. One pair of rather valuable earclips missing. The security guard had used only one hand for parts of the search. The other one had undoubtedly been busy filching jewelry. Maybelle toyed with the idea of accusing the woman. What would it gain her? Delay. Which she didn't want. Which might even have been the motive for the theft.

Pretend not to notice it, she had told herself. *You're probably being watched right now, so lock up the cases and pretend not to notice*. Which she had done, just in time for the porter to take the cases down to the tender.

Now she was bounding around on Jubal's purple ocean, almost at the launch site and herself seemingly the only passenger for Serendipity. Well, that's what Rheme had said. No one was getting off of Jubal these days. No body and no thing.

Except for brou. And the things the Honorable Wuyllum had stolen. And the things Honeypeach had stolen. And a few cartons near her feet that were tagged as belonging to Aphrodite Sells.

"The rets are deserting the sinking ship," she quoted, without having any clear idea what rets were. Something little and scaley, with unpleasant teeth, that came onto ships simply in order to leave them, ships like the ones on Serendipity, shallow and gently curved, with long, triangular sails.

"We'll miss you, Mayzy," Honeypeach had said. "You have no idea how much." There had been a threat in that, which Maybelle had pretended not to hear.

"Settle yourself in," her father had directed. "Pick the best part of the capital city and rent yourself some kind of expensive-looking place. Rheme's arranged for some woman to help you; he'll give you her name." That was all the Honorable Wuyllum had to say on the matter, but then he was much preoccupied with stripping Jubal of as much wealth as possible in the few days or weeks that remained.

"That's funny," said the boatman. "The loading ramp's not down."

"What does that mean," she asked, a queasy feeling rising from her stomach to the bottom of her throat and resting there as though it had no intention of moving.

"It means we can't get onto the ship," he muttered. "Dumb shits." He hit a button on the control panel and a horn blatted over the sound of wave and wind.

Maybelle put her hands over her ears. The horn went on blaring for some time. When it was cut off, she heard an answering howl from the tower.

"Return to port. Ship is lifting in the hour and will accept no passengers or additional cargo, by order of the launch commander."

"Tell him who's on board," Maybelle directed between
dry lips.

"He knows," the boatman mumbled in a surly voice.
"You think he don't know!" Still, he put the amplifier to his
lips and told the tower who he was carrying.

"Return to port," the tower blared. "Ship is lifting in the
hour. . . ."

Maybelle fell back onto the seat. There had been that
vicious tone in Honeypeach's voice when she had said goodbye. Something eager, lascivious, and sniggering. If anyone
could have arranged this disappointment, Honeypeach could.
All she would have to do was call Justin. . . .

"We have to go back," the boatman said. "We'll get fried
if we stay out here when she lifts."

Maybelle had nothing to say. What was there to say?
What would she do when she reached shore? Run? Run
where? She huddled on the seat, oblivious to the blare of the
tower or the liquid slosh of the waves, lost in apprehension.
When they came within sight of the dock, she saw the ebony
and gold of the guards from Government House. Someone
had sent them to meet her. Someone had known she wouldn't
be leaving.

The sound of a hailing voice brought her head around. A
small fishing boat lay just off their port bow. The plump
figure at the helm was shouting at them. The tender boatsman
slackened speed, let the boat come almost to a stop.

"Miss Maybelle Thonks?" the helmsman cried. Plump.
With gray hair. She thought she had seen him somewhere
before, though she could not see much of his face behind the
goggles and high-wound scarf.

"Yes," she nodded, petrified with fright.

"Mr. Gentry asked us to pick you up, Miss. If you
wouldn't mind." He smiled at her in a grandfatherly manner.

She cast a quick look again at the dock. Household
guards still there, and among them someone else.
Someone in an extravagant hat and drifting multicolored veils.
Honeypeach. Oh, yes.

"I'll go with this man, boatman," she said in her rarely
used imperative voice, covering fear with a pretence of arrogance. "Hold the boats together while I toss my luggage in."

She transferred herself from tender to fishing boat, hear-

ing angry shouts from the dock over the slupping waves. It
wasn't until she was in the other boat, together with all her
belongings, that she realized anyone could have used Rheme's
name. By then it was too late to do anything about it. The
wake of the BDL boat was disappearing in the direction of
the dock, and the boat she was in was speeding north along
the shore.

_____ 16

Tasmin, Donatella, Clarin, and Jamieson left the north-south
valley by striking southeast through a gap that the charts
identified as the Ogre's Stair. There was no Password and
they had an anxious time getting past the Presence. Donatella
thought she had a Password that could be adapted, but the
Ogre was not amenable. They were about to give up in anger
and frustration when Clarin stopped them.

"Let me," she said, opening her music box and kneeing
her mule to the forefront. "Tasmin, help me."

She touched the keys and began singing. It took Tasmin
only a moment to realize what she had done. Once or twice
Don's previous efforts had seemed to quiet the Stair. Clarin
had taken those brief phrases and wound them together,
amplifying and extending the melody, attaching a harmonic
line from quite another score, and then orchestrating the
whole thing as she went. Tasmin picked up the harmonic line
and began to sing it, their two voices rising together.

He had never sung with her before.

It was as sensual as touching her. More. It was like
making love. He knew this, understood it, and set it aside,
refusing to think of it, even as his voice went on and on. The
music had its own logic, just as lovemaking did. Its own logic
and its own imperatives. It wasn't necessary to think or
explain. The thing was of itself, a perfection.

The mules began to move forward on their own. Don and Jamieson followed, their mouths open. Jamieson was stunned at what he was hearing. He had sung with Clarin, but it had not been like this.

Clarin's voice had almost a baritone-contralto range, as softly mellow in the lower ranges as an organ pipe, as pure in the higher ones as a wooden flute. Tasmin's range was smaller, lower, the quality of his voice richer, more velvety. The two blended as though they were one.

When they reached the end of the initial melody, Clarin raised the key and began a variation.

Tasmin followed her, effortlessly.

Beneath them the Ogre's Stair was motionless.

They reached the top on a soaring, endless chord that drifted away into the sky, becoming nothing. The Stair was behind them. As they left it, it sang to them, three tones of enormous interrogation.

Tasmin and Clarin rode on, not noticing, not hearing, oblivious to the world around them.

Don did not have her translator working.

"Good Lord," she breathed, looking toward Jamieson, astonished to find him pale and shivering, tears in his eyes.

"Jamieson," she murmured. Clarin and Tasmin were riding on, not looking at one another, silent. "Jamieson?"

"Just once," he mumbled to her. "Just once. If I could . . ."

She nodded, understanding. There was nothing she could say. Poor Jamieson. Too much propinquity. She squeezed his shoulder sympathetically. He loved the girl, and she loved Tasmin, and Tasmin loved—what? Celcy? Jubal?

By the time they reached the bottom of the slope, Clarin was herself once more. She had dug a package of sweet stores out of her pocket and now offered them around.

"The people tracking us know we're headed south. And since the only thing you did to stir up suspicion was to come up with the Enigma score, they may realize we're headed that way."

Don agreed. "When they get out of that valley we left, they'll hit a major east-west shipping route, with virtually no problems on the way."

"We'll simply have to get there first," Tasmin said, lifting a mule foot and staring at it as though fascinated. He was still lost in the music, still finding it hard to connect with reality. "We've lost a little time dealing with the Ogre, but as I read the charts, I think we can make a fairly short traverse of the Blinders, just east of us, and come into one of the main east-west routes ourselves."

"The one that comes through Deepsoil Two, Six, Eight, and Nine?" Jamieson asked in a fairly normal voice. "That's an easy run. I know every Password on that route."

"Good for you, Reb. And Nine is just through the Mystic Range from Harmony." He thumped the mule and tightened the cinch, then took a candy from Clarin and sat down beside her. "We need to move fast. Justin's got the interior shut off, and he wouldn't have done that unless he expected the CHASE Commission to arrive momentarily. As soon as he gets their verdict, he'll send word to the troops, and anything we have to say will come much too late."

Jamieson nodded. "What do you think we have, at best? A few days? A few weeks? That, at most, if we're going to show them anything while they're here. We've got to collect our evidence and then get back to the Deepsoil Coast at a dead run."

With the situation thus delineated, unaccountably they all felt better. The situation was fully as bad as they had thought it was and they were all agreed on it, which relieved each of them of having to worry it out individually. Don even managed a quirky smile at the sight of Clarin trying to replace her lost crystal mouse by baiting a new and elusive beast with candy. It evaded capture, and they mounted once more, setting out at a good pace toward the Blinders.

After that, they did not seem to pause, not for days. Sleep came and went in brief periods of exhausted slumber, forgotten all too soon, along with snatched meals and hasty relief stops. Jamieson fought them through the Blinders, finding an amazing strength from somewhere, this time leaving them with mouths open. They left the last of the crystal towers in the evening when the refracted light from the setting sun made it almost impossible to see anything in any direction and found themselves on the open trail to Deepsoil Two with only easy Passwords between themselves and the dirt town. In Two, Tasmin requisitioned four additional mules from the citadel, letting their own animals trail along unburdened for most of the following day as they caught up with and joined a caravan headed east and stayed with it all the way into Deepsoil Six. The caravan rested for eight hours, but Tasmin and company slept only five, rising in the dark to continue on the way, timing their departure to let them come to the first intervening Presences at dawn.

Clarin caught a crystal mouse in the 'lings above Deepsoil Eight.

She had it half tamed by the time they reached Nine, feeding it crumbs and singing repetitive melodies to it, to which the others dreamed as they rode.

Jamieson sang them through the Startles, above Harmony to the west, and they planned to sleep that night in the caravansery. There was no citadel in Harmony, but the caravansery manager put himself out to be as useful as possible, fetching food and towels and assorted oddments to a running commentary.

"Nice to have a group of 'Singers here again," he said, his chins and bellies wobbling in emphasis. "Hat a bunch earlier you wuttn't believe."

"Tripsinger trouble?" Tasmin asked, disbelievingly. "I haven't heard that we've got any troublemakers, currently."

"Naah, the Tripmaster was all right, him and his assistant. Wagon men was all right, too. The cook even helpt me fix a meal for the lot of 'em. No, it was those others with 'em."

"Passengers?"

The fat man shook his head, first chins then bellies swaying like waves generated from a common source somewhere around the ears. "Don't think so, no. Four men with mules o' their own, come along after the caravan lookin' for some woman and baby. Tripmaster sait the woman left 'em back outsite o' Twelve. Crazy, if she went that way. Lots longer that way. Have to go through Thirteen and Fourteen on yer way up to Six, then come the way you come from there. Take almost twice't as long."

"You didn't happen to hear who it was they were looking for, did you?" asked Tasmin, dry-mouthed.

"Woman's name was Terree. Same's that Soilcoast singer got himself kilt on the Enigma . . ."

"These men didn't happen to say who they were, did they?" Donatella asked.

"Oh, no neet to tell me the name o' the one of 'em. Bins, he was. Chantiforth Bins. My wife buys ever cube those tamnt Crystals put out. True believer, she is, just so long as she won't have to get up off her lollyfalooz to do nothin' abou tit. Ever time I come in the room, it's that cube rantin' and ravin' like some bantigon with a buttache. I've seen him till I'm sick of him. Heart him, too, and he toesn't make any more sense up clost than on the cube. I knew he was lyin' the minute I startit talkin'."

"But he didn't find the woman."

"Nah. She was long gone. Way I think, that Tripmaster he hit her somewheres."

"Hit her!"

"Right. Like hit her in the trees or hit her in a hole in the ground so's those fella's cuttn't hurt her none. Her'n the baby."

"The answer to all our problems," said Jamieson, sotto voce, leaning heavily on Clarin. "Hit 'em in a hole in the grount."

"I'll hit you in a hole in the grount if you're not careful," murmured Clarin, smiling at him.

"Where's the Tripmaster now?" Tasmin asked, trying to glare at them and succeeding only in looking weary.

"Gone on t'Five. 'Forn he went, he ast me to get 'long there and help her out. Whispert it, kind of. The Tripmaster that was."

"When was this?" Tasmin said, dangerously patient.

"Was yesterday since. Trouble was, I can't go til these ones go away."

"Did the Tripmaster say where they came up to the wagon train? Bins and his bunch?"

"Oh, yes. Come up on it down at the turn off where one roat comes up here t'Harmony and one goes east to nothin' much. I think that's right. Course, you might ask 'em. They're all of 'em asleep in there." And he pointed to one of the dormitory rooms, halfway down the long hall. 'They lookt for her but din't flnt her. Sait they're goin' on t'Teepsoil Five, first thin' tomorrow."

"Armed?" asked Jamieson.

The caravansery manager shook his head. "Don't think so. No arms I saw."

"I guess we don't sleep?" Donatella asked, only half a question.

"I guess you're right," said Tasmin. "Do you have any Bormil tea?" he asked the caravansery manager. "Or Tsamp? something that will keep us awake for a while?"

"Now, what kint o' caravansery wuttn't have Tsamp," the manager nodded. "Sure I got Tsamp. You want it powdert or cookt in somethin'?"

They settled on Tsamp in broth, drinking enough of it that their nerves were screamingly alert when they left Harmony, headed south.

When the sun came up, they found themselves at the fork of the trail, a long ridge leading away to the east, groves of trees speckling the shallow soil between the westward trail and the Presences, and not a sign of Vivian or the baby. They called and searched for an hour, then spent some time hailing with the machines, and then, in a mood of fatalistic exhaustion, turned east and rode for the Enigma.

Tasmin had seen it before, from the north side, from between the twin needles, between the two insolent daggers of bloody ice. He had looked down onto the little flat that lay between those daggers like a stained handkerchief between two gory swords, and he had seen that handkerchief fold away around Celcy, around Lim, wrapping away those arrogant enough to test the Enigma.

Now he saw the same place from below.

A polished ramp of crystal wound upward toward that same little flat. All the shards and shattered fragments had been cleared away. It gleamed like cut glass, like ruby or dark garnet with paler edges, as though its blood had coagulated in some places and had run with water in others, dark clots and pale tints intermingled where something bled into the sea of that great crystal, bled forever and was forever washed away. .

Within the bloody traceries glinted the web of fracture, the delicate tracery of dislocation, of tilted planes and vacant edges, shivering with dawn light.

"Where did you go before, Don?" Tasmin asked. "When you talked to it?"

"Up there," Donatella answered. "It was a dim, gray day, with fog in the air. Not like today. I . . . I don't recall being afraid then."

"Are you now?"

"Lord, yes, aren't you? That thing is glaring at us."

"I expected to be afraid. But then I've only been here once, and my experience was a different one from yours."

"What do we do?" Clarin asked. "Now you can tell us, Donatella. What was your clue? What did Erickson give you that took you up there?"

Donatella turned and adjusted her music box, finding a particular setting and playing it so softly they barely heard it, a haunting melody, rising and falling in quiet repetition, as though water ran upon stone, eating it away. "An-dar-ououm, an-dar-ououm." It was the Enigma score, and yet it was neither synthesizer nor human voice.

"Viggies?" asked Jamieson. "Is that viggies?"

"I'll cut in the translator," she said. "Now listen."

The same melody, translated. "Let the edges sleep. Let one half sleep," sang the translator, "let it sleep in peace, let it rest, let it rest, let water run deep, let the edges grow, let the way come clear, soft, soft, let the fingers sleep, let one half sleep."

She cut off the machine. "There's more. Not a lot more words, but a lot more music, and very repetitive. That's what Erickson suggested—that I record a group of viggies near a Presence without a Password. Well, I got lucky. I hid. I heard them singing off in the night, and I recorded that first thing.

"However, the translator could only give me a few words. I doubt if any translator, up until now, could have done even that. It told me it needed more, lots more. So, I hid in a hole in that cliff up there for over a week, recording viggy songs and chatter and describing what they were doing until the translator had enough that it could start to give it to me clearly. We got words for water and fingers and sleep right away, but it took some time to get the rest. The viggy language is more complex than you can imagine. Once I had the translation, I learned their words, then came here and sang the thing. That's what I used. I sang that to the Enigma, all of it, for about an hour. I don't have much voice, but it didn't take much. You heard it. Simple."

"And you were recording whatever sounds the Presence made?"

"Of course. At first, only noise. Whatever different kinds of noise there are. Like back in the valley, like most places, just a garble, a kind of whistling, chuckling, squeaking, snoring noise. But as I sang, it quieted down. I'd already figured out what questions I wanted to ask. *Do you have a name for yourself you would like me to use?* I thought that would get us off on the right foot. So, as soon as everything was quiet, I sang that. Loudly."

"And the answer was, as I recall from when you played it for us, *Messengers know to whom they come.* Right?" asked Jamieson.

"Right. Not exactly responsive, but it did make sense. So, I thought I'd give it some information at that point. I sang, *I am not one of the usual messengers.*"

Clarin said, "And the reply to that was *None of them are.*"

"That's right. Up until that point, everything had been very peaceful. Then I started to go on to my next question. The minute I started, it shook. Just a little, and only on one side, but I thought—well, I thought, hell, I had enough. I'm no linguist, no philologist, no specialist in alien communication. Suppose I slashed it off, all unwitting. So I went back to the first song, the peaceful water one, and I sang that while I backed off."

"So your intention is to repeat that sequence?" Clarin asked again, staring upward. "With us as witnesses."

"Why didn't we try it on some other Presence, something closer to where we were?" Jamieson wanted to know, also staring upward. There was something ominous about the bloody glare coming from the Enigma, something threatening about the darting, dancing light.

"I tried the viggy music on some other things, and it didn't work. Evidently it's specific to this Presence. And I haven't had time to record any other viggy songs and try anywhere else."

"Would you say the viggies are sentient?" Clarin asked.

"I didn't think so before," Don cried. "I thought of that, of course, because the translator was taking their babble and making words out of it. Nobody has ever seriously alleged that they were. They're so elusive. It would have been hard to prove. But, yes. Once the translator began to make words out of their songs, I believed they were. Not that they've offered to talk to me to prove it."

"Which isn't the point right now anyhow," said Tasmin. "Anybody want to stay down here?" He looked Jamieson full in the eye. "You should, you know, Reb. Stay here with Clarin and the translator. You'll be able to hear, but you should be out of danger. Then if something happens to Don and me, you two can still carry the word."

"Master Ferrence?"

"Yes, Reb."

"With all due respect, Sir. Of the two of us, I'm quicker. I agree that some of us should stay down here. You, Sir. And Clarin." His eyes were clear as he said it. He didn't look toward Clarin, though Donatella knew he wanted to.

"He's right," Donatella agreed. "You're good, Tasmin. But he's better."

"Ah, the confidence of youth," Tasmin said, smiling weakly. They were right, of course. He should be able to accept it without its hurting, but damn it, it did hurt. Jamieson had never been afraid to try things, even forbidden things, even foolish things. And it told. He had learned, learned along the edges where Tasmin had always forbidden himself to go.

"Luck, Reb," he said at last, biting his lip. "Go ahead."

"Loudsingers," gasped one of the troupe of Chowdri, galloping wildly into the camp, antennae waving. "Loudsingers on the Mad One."

"Who dares?" cried Chowdri. "What Loudsinger dares? Has not the Mad One killed enough of them?"

"Same one as last time," the messenger chanted, breathlessly. "The female one. And one called Tasmin and one called Reb and one called Clarin."

"Tasmin!" called Bondri, thrusting through the surrounding troupe members, Vivian close behind him. "Tasmin Ferrence?"

"They are holding a song captive in a box," the messenger cried. "I heard it. The female one has it."

The troupes rose with one accord. "I cannot let Tasmin

Ferrence come to harm," Bondri chanted. "He is part of the debt."

"Neither can the song be left captive," Chowdri asserted, showing his fangs.

"Let me talk to him," Vivian cried. "I'll make him understand, Bondri. There's no need for violence."

"Hurry then," he sang. "Go quick. I will bring the baby."

"Down there," said Chantiforth Bins, pointing to a ridge along the side of the Enigma. "See them, Myrony? Spider? Just to the left of that tall splinter."

Chantiforth Bins had gone on to Deepsoil Five from Harmony, and in Deepsoil Five he had found Myrony and Spider Geroan—along with Aphrodite Sells and two unhappy Explorers. The Explorers had left for the Deepsoil Coast. Affy was still in Deepsoil Five with Spider's man. Chanty, Myrony, and Spider had decided to come to the Enigma and give it one more try before returning to the Coast themselves. After all, where else could their various quarries be heading?

Now they stood almost where Tasmin had when he saw Lim and Celcy die, looking down on the area between the Enigma towers from the north. Beneath them the ground quivered in a ceaseless tremor.

"I see 'em," Myrony admitted nervously. "Now what?"

"Slash 'em off and get back to Splash One," Cantiforth said, lifting his rifle.

"No," said Spider Geroan.

"Whattaya mean, no," Myrony objected. "That's what we came for, Geroan. Get rid of the Tripsinger and the Explorer, and there both of 'em are, down by the splinter."

"That's the wrong one," said Spider Geroan. "He's only an acolyte. Where's the right one? Ferrence?"

"Ah," Myrony remarked. "Yer right, ya know. There's the fuckin' Tripsinger. I see his robe. Down there at the bottom, with the girl. He's out o' range."

"So, slash off these two, then go down and get those two, what's the fuss." Chantiforth was in a hurry. Things were happening back on the Deepsoil Coast. Things that might threaten the profit from this whole job if he didn't get there soon to protect his rights. He lifted the rifle again.

"No," said Spider again. "You hit these two up here, those down there two are going to see it. They'll run off, back into the range most likely, where we can't follow." Spider narrowed his eyes in concentration.

"I told you we should'a brought those Explorers."

"What good would that have done?" As ever, Spider's voice was quite expressionless. "They said there was no way they could get us by the Enigma, and everyone in Deepsoil Five agreed with them. You can't use a noodle to beat bantigons, Bins. It's all going to work out anyhow."

"Damned if I see how. The fuckin' man is out o' range."

"She's the one that came up with the Enigma score," Chantiforth observed. "She's going to sing it right now, isn't she? What else would she be here for? Well. That gives us some time."

Spider nodded. "While they're occupied, we'll sneak down behind these 'lings. You and Myrony hide there, as near the Explorer and the acolyte as you can get. I'll go on down and get into range for Ferrence before you slash off these two."

"What about the girl with Ferrence?"

"I'll keep her," Spider said, affecting not to notice the expression of revulsion that crossed Bins's face. It had been a very long trip, and he had not had any amusement for a long time, had not had that particular excitement that came with watching the one thing he had never experienced. He examined Clarin through his glasses. Good. He liked that type, that age. They were strong and agile, capable of many contortions and pleas before they died.

"You'll yodel when you're ready?" Myrony asked. "I don't like bein' around those fuckin' Presences for very long." They started toward the gap in the Crystal through which Tasmin had stared down. "Wait!"

"What's the matter with you?" Chantiforth demanded.

"We take out these two first, then go on down where Spider is, and he's done the Tripsinger, then this Presence starts to shake and jiggle, how do we get back over the top here to get back to town? Affy's there, waitin' for us."

"He's right, you know," Bins said to Geroan. "Our mules are back there in Deepsoil Five. And all our supplies. I'm not eager to live off the country all the way back to the Coast.

Even if we don't go to the Coast, it's a long hike around by way of Harmony."

Spider ruminated. "All right. I'll make a small change in plan. Do it just the way we'd said. You go on down a little way and cover these two in case there's trouble. I'll go all the way down and take out the Tripsinger and the girl first. These two up here won't be paying any attention; they'll be busy with their boxes. I'll come back up, meet you, then we'll all come back up here to the top before we slash off the Explorer and the acolyte. Kind of spoils it for me, but that's the way we'll do it." Though it did not show on his face, Spider was disappointed. He did not tolerate disappointment well, and only by substituting a mental image of Aphrodite Sells for Clarin in his plans for the next day or so was he able to feel quite comfortable.

The others had no objection. They stood quietly, checking their weapons, waiting for the tremors to cease.

"There," sang Bondri. "That one is Tasmin Ferrence. Prime Priest Favel said he had hair that color."

"Yes," agreed Vivian. "That's Tasmin all right. Keep the baby here, Bondri, will you?" And she slipped out of the grove of settler's brush and made her way toward Tasmin and Clarin.

Behind her, the viggy messenger who had brought the earlier word returned again. "More Loudsingers," he sang softly to the assembled troups. "On the Mad One's back. High against the sky."

"Ready?" asked Donatella, her fingers poised over the box.

"Ready," nodded Jamieson, grinning. He stared around him at the little flat place between the towering scarlet peaks. He wanted to remember it, just as it was. His mind felt like there were flames leaping over it, laughing flames. He remembered every score he had ever sung, every one he had ever seen! "Ready," exultantly.

Their hands came down together and the music began.

"The men at the top of the Mad One have weapons," sang the messenger. "They are pointing them at the people of Tasmin Ferrence."

* * *

"Tasmin," cried Vivian. "Tasmin, you've got to get your people down from up there. Please!"

"Move now," Spider Geroan directed. The quivering of the ground had lessened enough that they could move securely upon it. "Move fast, and keep out of sight."

"Let the troupes of Bondri and Chowdri surround the men with weapons," urged Bondri. "A debt of honor is about to come unstuck."

"It is not our debt," demurred Chowdri.

"It is the debt of Prime Priest Favel," Bondri trilled. "Prime Priests are of all troupes."

The troupes sang this for a few moments in several variations. No one could deny that it was true. Though some sang that a debt incurred before a viggy became Prime Priest might not be binding on all troupes, this was a minority voice, which became only a haunting anharmonic in the finished song.

"Go then," urged Chowdri, somewhat grudgingly. "Go to the Mad One, the Presence Without Innerness, the Killer Without Cause, called by the Loudsingers, the Enigma. Fulfill the debt."

"Vivian! How did you get here?"

"The viggies brought me, Tasmin. Listen, there's no time for questions. The viggies say that the Enigma will kill anyone who tries to sing it quiet. The Enigma is crazy."

"Donatella did it before."

"Not really. It wasn't awake, and she got on and then off before it woke up, is all. It's wide awake today. Tasmin, get her off of there."

While Tasmin was still staring at Vivian, trying to make sense of what she was saying, Clarin did not wait. Some deep apprehension within herself was verified by Vivian's first words, and she darted up the slope at a dead run while Tasmin watched helplessly from below, unable even to follow for Vivian was now clinging to his arm. "Tasmin, do you have a recording of a viggy song? Tasmin! Do you?"

He tried to focus on her question. "Yes. Donatella played it just a little while ago."

"You've got to give it back to them, Tasmin."

"Give it back!"

"Wipe it out. Something. They'll try to take it from you, Tasmin, and some of them could be killed. They saved me. They saved Miles. *They've got Celcy's baby, Tasmin!* Oh, don't ask how, why. Don't ask questions, just tell me you will."

The music was building slowly into a rhythmic pattern, Jamieson's voice softly soaring, leaping, like the wind. Beneath the sound, the Enigma quieted, shivering almost into silence. Still, there was a quiver.

"It took me almost an hour last time," Donatella whispered.

Jamieson nodded, never losing the line of melody. His eyes swung between the two towers of the Enigma. As they moved between the two, he saw Clarin coming up the trail. "She's in a tearing hurry," he told himself, still singing. There was someone with Tasmin on the flatland, pointing and gesturing. . . .

"It's still shakin' a little," whispered Myrony.

"Well, wait until it quits," Chantiforth replied. They were working their way down toward the pillars that bordered the clearing where Jamieson was singing. Spider had started before them and was halfway down to the scree slopes on which Tasmin stood.

"Somebody coming up," hissed Chanty. "Lie flat and be still."

They peered between tumbled bits of crystal, watching Clarin as she came toward them up the mountain, panting and pulling herself along at speed. Just a little below them she stopped, positioning herself against a pillar, gasping for breath.

"What in hell," thought Jamieson, not for a moment interrupting the song. Clarin was gesturing, imperatively. He began a repetition, a phrase that was sung again and again, in ascending keys, only to hear her voice moving with him.

"An-dar-ououm," he sang.

"Bro-oo-ther," she sang in thirds below, clear as a bell.

The danger call! The recognition call! His eyes darted around him, he turned. Nothing!

"An-dar-ououm," he sang, his voice rising.

"Bro-oo-ther," in thirds.

Jamieson beckoned to Donatella and began to move down, away, away from the bloody ground between the spires, down toward Clarin, never stopping the song.

"An-dar-ououm," he sang again, voice soaring.

"An-dar-ououm," came half a hundred voices from all around him.

Viggies! In the shadow of crystal he could see their eyes glowing behind the ruby orbs of inflated song-sacks. "An-dar-ououm, an-dar-ououm."

Then he and Donatella were beside Clarin, the three of them moving downward, swiftly, letting the viggies take the song.

"What's the matter?" Donatella demanded. "Why did you cry 'brother'?"

"Save your breath, Don. Just get down and out of the way of this thing. According to the viggies, it's going to blow."

"Blow! It's quiet as a tomb, and getting quieter all the time." Donatella stopped, turned as though to go back up the mountain. "Is that *viggies* singing?"

"Trying to give us time to get out of the way. Us and themselves. Move, will you." Clarin grabbed Donatella's arm and forcibly turned her. "Move, down. If we're wrong you can always come back. . . ."

Then they were down off the ramp and running toward Tasmin and Vivian and Miles and a dozen young viggies who were all staring at the Enigma and at one another with open mouths, immobilized by strangeness.

A quiver.

A small quiver, as though a rug had been pulled beneath their feet. The song was running away, trickling off the mountain on a wave of viggy feet, fleeing. The rug moved once more, this time a good tug. Donatella staggered. The viggies threw themselves down, gesturing, calling in Loudsinger language, "Down, down, hold on, tumble down coming."

And then it came, thunder, the mountain heaving, the spires shimmering, seeming actually to bend and sway as all around them the smaller pillars shattered and roared.

Fragments spun across the sky, glittering shards of bloody light, edged like knives.

Chunks rained from the top of 'lings, bounding, shattering, ricocheting in hissing trajectories.

Against the sky the twin tines of the Enigma shouted, a howling cataract of threat and danger.

The Translator, set at the top of its volume, roared.

"You'd think after all this time they could get it right." Donatella's voice become the voice of a giant.

Then *"That was petulant of you."* Donatella's monstrous voice again.

Then *"It pisses me off when they don't know who I am. . . ."* Donatella's voice. As it had been Lim's voice, that other time.

On the height, two figures staggered to their feet, one of them carrying a rifle. A spinning shard took off his head, the shard no redder than the blood that spouted high in a momentary jet. The other figure fell and was swallowed up in a dancing fountain of razor-edged boulders.

Where Tasmin and the others clung, the earth heaved and hit them in the face, falling away beneath them again, shaking, again, again, again.

Then silence.

Vivian, Miles, Donatella, Tasmin, Clarin, Jamieson.

The viggies had gone.

Vivian, Miles, Donatella, Tasmin, Clarin . . .

"Where's Jamieson?" grated Tasmin. "Where is he?"

"He was right behind me," Clarin sobbed. "Right behind me." She levered herself to her feet, staggering. "Back there."

Back there was only piled crystal.

From behind a tumble of sanguinary glass, glittering with malice, a dusty thing rose to its feet, teeth exposed in a grimace of hate. It put a weapon to its shoulder and snarled at them through the blood on its face. "Stand where you are."

"I have to find Jamieson," said Tasmin stupidly. "I've got to find him."

"I said stand where you are! Or I'll shoot the lot of you."

"Spider Geroan," Donatella whispered. "Oh, God. Spider Geroan."

"Get over here," Spider said, gesturing with the weapon at Clarin. "Get over here, or I'll kill the rest of them right now, starting with him!"

As though hypnotized, Clarin moved toward him.

"Clarin! No!" Tasmin's voice.

She twitched.

"Keep moving, girl, or I'll take him out. I swear I will."

She moved on. When she was within reach of him, he grabbed her, turning her to face them, one of his arms around her throat, the other fumbling to place a knife at the side of her face.

"Now," said Spider Geroan. "Who did that?"

"Who . . . who did what?" Donatella asked.

"Who set off that thing!"

"No one," she said. "It just blew."

The knife at Clarin's face made a tiny motion and she cried out, a thin, black trickle oozing down her cheek.

"None of that!" he grated. "Somebody did it."

Tasmin struggled to make his voice calm. The man before him was mad. Perhaps had always been mad. "Clarin went up to tell Jamieson and Don that the Enigma doesn't act rationally," he said. "Vivian brought us that message. We didn't know it before. . . ."

"So you got scared and ran, and that did it," Geroan asserted, moving the knife again. Clarin cried out again, a high, toneless shriek.

"It was already doing it," Don said. "Couldn't you feel it? The shaking never really stopped!"

Spider breathed heavily for a moment. First, he wanted to get even with whichever one of them had done it to him. Then he wanted to do this girl. Then . . . then he'd figure out what next. In the meantime, he moved the knife again, almost reflexively, hearing the answering cry of pain with something approaching pleasure.

Tasmin's stomach clenched and he bit down on his tongue to keep from screaming.

"Distract him," murmured Don. "Think of something."

"I have to find Jamieson," Tasmin called frantically. "Or none of us can get out of here."

Spider looked up, the knife stopped moving. "What do you mean?"

"Let me find him," Tasmin shrieked. "He's like my son."

In the shadows of the rocks, Bondri Gesel. "Like his son? What does that mean? Let me alone." This to a giligee who was stanching the blood from a cut on his shoulder. "Let me alone and find this Jamieson. He is one of Tasmin Ferrence's troupe, and the debt is not yet paid."

"He could be your son and it wouldn't matter," Spider snarled lifting the hand with the knife to wipe his own eyes. He felt no pain from the cuts on his face and neck, but the blood was a nuisance and made him irritable. "He could be your brother or your mother and it wouldn't matter. You've been a bother, Tripsinger. You and the Explorer there. I've come to stop the bother."

He choked Clarin against his chest with his knife hand and picked up the rifle once more. There were too many of them to play with. He would save only one. The girl. Clarin. Though he didn't feel like it, really. Maybe he would, later.

In the shadows of the rocks, Bondri Gesel. "That Loudsinger is going to kill them," he roared at the top of his song-sack. "The debt is coming unstuck again; get rid of that Loudsinger with the weapon."

Something seized Spider's knife hand and tore it away from Clarin's face. Clarin rolled away, and as Spider leaped toward her, he tripped over something and fell down. It was a furry thing, and it didn't get out of his way. Another furry thing was hanging on the end of the rifle and he couldn't raise it. Something grabbed him by his legs and sank needle teeth into his thighs. There was no pain, but the thing hung on him, handicapping his movement. Another thing grabbed for the rifle, two more, tearing it away from him. The things clinging to his legs tripped him again. Dozens more of them sat on him. One stared deep into his eyes, brushing his forehead with long, feathery things growing out of its head. He struggled, but there were too many of them.

"This one is defective," said the senior giligee. "Bondri Gesel, this Loudsinger is defective. He has no pain feelings at all. Perhaps that is why he acts as he does."

Bondri regarded the Loudsinger with disfavor. The Prime Song urged good returned for good, and when possible, good returned as an example for others, even when bad had been intended. However, the song also directed that those who kill without good reason must be disposed of in order that others may live in tranquility. Then there was the question of the taboo. There was no good reason to break the taboo for this man. Now he looked down into Spider Geroan's expressionless eyes and attempted to apply the Song.

"Can you fix him?" he sang. "Can you fix him so he can feel?"

"Simple," caroled the giligee.

"Well, then, fix him," he said, with a sense of satisfaction that he did not even attempt to understand. "And when you have finished, tell the troupe they can eat him."

By the time the first astonished screams came from Spider Geroan, Tasmin and the others had found Jamieson and carried him far enough away from the Enigma to avoid any further "tumble down." When they had gone far enough that they could hear no further noise from that direction, they slumped on the flat, motionless earth without moving, watching in dull amazement as a giligee everted her pouch over Clarin's wounded face and began to mend it.

Jamieson lay nearby, a circle of giligees around him. He was, according to Bondri, somewhat broken, but the giligees thought he could be fixed.

One of those giligees, at Vivian's suggestion, had shown Tasmin what was in her pouch. "It isn't finished yet," she had apologized. "But it's developing nicely. The female Loudsinger says it is your young?" What was there was very small, but very pink and lively.

"I can't believe it," Tasmin said over and over. "I can't believe it."

Bondri could not figure out why he could not believe it. He had seen it. So had everyone else. And they had sung it to him two or three times. Bondri was getting impatient. He had not raised the question of the captive song, but he nudged Vivian from time to time, until at last she cleared her throat.

"Tasmin. Bondri asks that you free the song you have captive."

"It's the only proof I've got," Donatella objected.

"No one's going to believe just that," Clarin said. "We've got nothing, Don. The Enigma blew. It didn't talk to you."

"It did before," she cried.

Bondri inflated his sack. These people did not sing in an orderly fashion. They did not get things straightened out and properly harmonized; they jumped from one thing to another, over and over. "Please," he boomed. "One thing at a time. First, the captive song. Then what other things are of concern."

"The record of the viggy music is no good to us," said Tasmin. "Come on, Don. They've saved our lives."

"All right," she cried. "I don't care. I was probably deluded anyhow."

Tasmin opened the machine. "Would you like us to erase it?"

"Erase? I would like you to set it free!"

Vivian reached across Tasmin's hands to press the controls. "Let it play out, Tas. Then burn the cube. That's what they do with their dead. The cube will be dead then, and the song will be free."

"So." Bondri nodded his approval. "We will join the song."

As it played from the symthesizer, the viggies sang with it. Am-dar-ououm. A song of quiet. When it was done, Tasmin placed the cube in the fire where it expired in a flash of sparks.

"So." Bondri sighed.

"Why did the Enigma blow?" Tasmin asked Bondri, singing it.

"Because it is the Mad One, which has two minds. You heard it. On your machine."

"On the machine?"

"On your machine. Which speaks in Loudsinger language with the voice of that one." He pointed to Donatella.

Tasmin clutched his head. "It uses your voice, Don?"

"It uses whoever's voice is using it. When Lim had it, it used his."

"Then that bellowing from the translator, it wasn't you?"

"It was the Mad One," sang Bondri. "It was angry that you did not address it by name. You, female Loudsinger," he pointed to Don, "had asked it before what its name is, but you did not remember. . . ."

"I don't understand," she whispered.

Chowdri was annoyed. These people didn't understand anything! "Bondri and I will sing it to you," he chanted. "Now listen!"

"You came to the Enigma before. Months ago. You used a stolen song to quiet the skin of the Enigma, is that not so? That is so. Then you asked it a question. You asked it what name it had for itself."

Donatella nodded. Tasmin brought himself out of his self-absorption and listened. Even Clarin half sat up, making the giligee beside her snort in disapproval.

"The Enigma replied," sang Chowdri. "We heard it do so. It sang, 'Messengers know to whom they come.'"

"Was that a reply?" chanted Tasmin.

"It was the name the Enigma called itself. *Messengers know to whom they come.* Perhaps the Enigma thinks it is a messenger to all the Presences, and so it says this mad thing.

"Then the female told it something. 'I am not one of the usual messengers,' and the Enigma replied, 'None of them are.' There are no usual messengers to the Enigma. Messengers do not come to the Enigma. Thinking of this made the Enigma angry, and you, you female Loudsinger, wisely you went away very quickly. Is this not a true song?"

"It is a true song," sang Donatella in a tone of resignation. "That's what happened.

"This time," sang Bondri, "you came again and quieted the skin. It is a sunny day, much light flows into the Enigma making it hot. The Enigma is awake and irritable. It expected you to address it by name. It had told you its name. You did not address it by name. You merely went on with skin quieting, even though the Enigma was awake. It became irritated. . . ."

"You mean that's what happened with Lim? He did the same thing?" Tasmin's jaw dropped. "It wasn't because he stopped following the score?"

"When the Presence wakes, you must call it by name," sang Chowdri and Bondri together, the troupe behind them in full chorus. "Every child knows that!"

Silence, while they thought about it. It was Clarin who asked the question at last. "Then all we had to do was call it what it told us its name was? *Messengers know to whom they come?*"

"Perhaps," sang Chowdri, solo voice. "Except that the Mad One is mad."

"What does that mean?"

"It changes what it calls itself. Sometimes every hour, every day. Sometimes not so often. And sometimes it will not tell anyone what its name is."

"So," said Don. "It got angry, and it blew."

"It snapped its fingers at you," sang Chowdri. "And we had only finished cleaning up from last time."

"It shouted," Tasmin said. "It shouted out that after all this time, we ought to be able to get it right."

"One half of it sang that," agreed Bondri.

"Then it was the other half that said, 'That was petulant of you.'"

"True. The other half is less irritable. It remonstrates with the first half. But it was the first half of the Enigma that said, 'I become annoyed when these creatures do not know who I am.' The Enigma said these same things to Lim Terree. The Mad One sometimes says the same things over and over. We believe the Mad One is mad because it has two halves that are partly separate and partly the same."

"It was there all the time," Tasmin said. "I heard those words, but I thought it was Lim who said them."

"You could have asked us," said Bondri irrationally. "The other Great Ones are not mad, most of them. Some are silly, but most of them are not mad. Except that they are very irritated just now, and it must be because of the things the Loudsingers are doing!"

"But you've never spoken to us before," Clarin sang. "Why?"

"Because you do not sing the truth," Bondri chanted, the troupe joining him to make this manifest. "To sing to those who do not sing the truth, this is taboo."

"But you broke this taboo!"

"Because of the debt we owed for Prime Priest Favel, for your brother who released him from captivity in the long ago. A debt of honor takes precedence over taboo." He stood up, gathering his troupe around him. "Now we go, and the taboo is once again as it should be. I have paid the debt of Prime Priest Favel. Vivian and the child are saved. You, Tasmin Ferrence, are saved. Your almost child is also saved, or will be when it is finished. I have returned good for good."

Don cried out, a pleading sound of negation. Tasmin thought bleakly of what was in store for Jubal, his mind frantically searching for some way to stop the departure of the viggies.

"There is still a debt," he gasped. "A debt owed by Bondri Gesel."

Bondri drew himself up, fangs exposed. "What debt!"

"When my brother released Prime Priest Favel from captivity, a debt was incurred. Is this not so?"

"It is so."

"And is a song not as important as a Prime Priest?"

Bondri cocked his head. It was not a question he had considered before. A giligee trilled a response, a female took up the refrain, then two males in countermelody. They sang it for some time. Finally Bondri responded. "A song is almost as important as a Prime Priest."

"Did I not free a song from captivity, Bondri Gesel? Do you not owe me a debt?"

This time the singing went on for the better part of an hour. Tasmin went to the place Jamieson lay, running his hands along the boy's face and body. "Will he live?" he whispered to the intent giligees.

"Oh, yes," one of them trilled in return. "He will live. I think we have him mostly fixed. Tomorrow, maybe, he will walk." She sat with her pouch everted, and Tasmin withdrew his gaze from that mass of thin tendrils that had penetrated Jamieson's body and were busy deep inside, doing incredible things.

He went to sit beside Clarin. The wounds on her face were closed. She lay huddled in a blanket, shivering from time to time. He put his hand under the blanket, on her neck. She jerked away from him.

"Shhh," he said. "It's all right, Clarin. All right."

She began to cry. He gathered her up in his arms.

"Shhh." His heart turned over at the sound of her weeping.

"No one ever hurt me before. Not purposely."

"He was a machine, Clarin. Pretend it was a machine. Not anyone worth hating. He's dead."

"They ate him!" she turned her head away, retching.

"It's a meat-poor planet, Clarin. According to Vivian,

they eat very little meat. They eat fresh fish whenever they get to the seashore, or whenever their fisher kin run inland with a catch, and they dry fish to carry with them. They don't eat carrion or carrion eaters, which eliminates a lot of the other wildlife."

"It just . . . just takes getting used to. What are we going to do now?"

"As soon as the viggies quit singing, I'll let you know."

When they finished singing, it was to announce that freeing the song had indeed brought a debt with it. Neither of the troupe leaders was happy about this. Tasmin wondered how much of the decision had been brought about by viggy curiosity concerning the Loudsingers. Perhaps the troupes had not wanted to return immediately to the taboo.

He said nothing of this. Instead, he drew Clarin up beside him, held her until she quit shaking, and then said, "Bondri Gesel, Troupe leader, great singer. I beg a boon from you. I beg that you listen while I try to sing truth to you. Me, and this person with me here." He gestured at Clarin. "Jamieson sings more truth than I do, but he cannot sing just now. Will you listen while I try?"

Bondri, annoyed, conferred with the troupe. The troupe was a good deal more compliant than he was.

"What are we singing?" whispered Clarin, a trace of color coming back into her cheeks.

"We're singing the destruction of Jubal," Tasmin said. "If we don't get some help here, everything we feared is still going to come to pass."

In later years the troupes of viggies who moved from the pillars of the Jammers to the towers of the east, resang on festival occasions the First Truth Singing of the Loudsingers. Not that it was a very polished performance, but it rang with a passionate veracity that the viggies much admired. Of course, there were only two who really sang, plus one who gave them some musical support, so the ultimate truth of the song might have been in doubt, were it not for verification by later happenings. Nonetheless, the viggies remembered that night.

Tasmin stood up and sang the story of the PEC, of human exploitation of many planets. He sang of the Prime

Song of humans, and of the disobedience that many showed that Song. Beside him, Clarin—the viggies assumed she was his mate, they sang so alike and so well together—sang of greed and pride, things that the viggies understood to some extent. She sang of lying, which they did not understand but were willing to take on faith. Then together they sang of what they had learned, of the lies told about the Presences, of the great destruction that was sure to come.

At this point, the viggies joined the song, query and reply, antiphonally, circling, circling again, as it grew more and more true. "If," they sang, "then what?" and Tasmin replied. "Then if," they sang, "what then?" and Clarin told them.

They sang of the good guys, Jamieson who lay wounded with the giligees working on him, Thyle Vowe, Grand Master of the Tripsingers, who worshipped the truth—Clarin sang this, much to Tasmin's surprise—of Tripsingers and Explorers, and those people of peace who tilled the soil and loved Jubal. These people would not be allowed to stay, they would go in any case, but they would not want Jubal destroyed behind them.

And lastly, they sang the names of villains. Spider Geroan, who had been healed of his affliction and then eaten. The Crystallites, who were liars. The troopers who blocked the way east. And finally, Harward Justin, Planetary Manager, who would destroy the Presences, very soon unless something was done.

And finished singing.

There was a long silence, unbroken. None of the members ventured song. At last it was the senior giligee, the one who carried Prime Priest Favel's brain-bird, who called in a high, clear soprano that soared above them like a gyre-bird.

"Come, Troupe leader. We must go to the Highmost Darkness, Lord of the Gyre-Birds, Smoke Master, the one the humans call Black Tower, and ask it what to do."

17

They came to the Black Tower on the following day. Jamieson was unable to ride. Tasmin had held the boy before him on the saddle, cradling him like a baby while he slept.

The troupes of Bondri and Chowdri had come by their own paths, swifter trails than the one followed by the humans. When Donatella and Clarin arrived, some distance ahead of Tasmin, Jamieson, and the spare mules, they found the troupes already singing.

The humans made camp. None of them had eaten recently, and food, while uninteresting, was a necessity. The smell of heating rations woke even Jamieson.

"I thought I was dead," he said wonderingly. "It came down on top of me."

"You probably would have been," Tasmin whispered, lifting the boy's head to the cup. "Except for the giligees."

"Except for the what?"

A long explanation followed, which had not really ended when Bondri Gesel came into their campsite, shaking his head.

"We sang to the Black Tower," he chanted in a weary monotone. "It did not want to listen. It is full of annoyance and irritation. It is worse than when we were at the one you call the Watcher. It is not the skin that speaks, nor the deep parts. It is some middle part that is new to us, a part full of questions and anger. Something has happened to make it very angry, Tasmin Ferrence. Presences have been bothered!"

"Bothered?" asked Tasmin, uncertain what the viggy meant.

"To the north. Loudsingers came. They made noises and shattered the fingers of many Presences, passing through the air in the confusion. The Presences were slow to wake, but now they are wakening. On all the world, they are wakening."

"The people following us," said Don. "I wondered how they got onto us so fast. They came in by air!"

Bondri went on. "We have sung to the Highmost Darkness. We have told it everything we know. Then we sang everything you sang to us. It wants to sing to you."

"Me?" Tasmin asked.

"You. And the Explorer and the young female and this one. All of you."

Jamieson heaved himself into a sitting position. "I'm not sure I'm up to singing." He was staring at the viggy in complete absorption, turning to Tasmin. "Who did you say this was?"

Tasmin introduced them. "Bondri, this is Jamieson, my friend. Bondri Gesel, leader of the viggies."

The young human and the viggy nodded their heads precisely at the same moment and to the same angle. Evidently ceremony knew no species. Tasmin fought down a snort of bleak amusement.

"Bring him anyhow," said the viggy. "The Black Tower wants to look at him."

"Look?" faltered Jamieson. "They can see?"

"Not with eyes," admitted Bondri. "But they see, yes. When they want to."

"And you've told them all about what's happening, with BDL and all?"

"We are not sure Highmost Darkness, Smoke Master, Lord of the Gyre-Birds understands, because we do not understand. That is why it wants to see you." And Bondri turned away, stamping his feet a little as he went, head high and throat sack half distended.

"He's miffed," said Jamieson in awe.

"He is that," agreed Tasmin as he got to his feet and joined the others in a straggling procession toward the Black Tower, the music box with the translator program at the ready.

"How is it," the Tower asked, after laborious introductions had taken place, "that you have not proclaimed (sung, announced) our sentience before—if you have known it (contained a concept for) as you say you have known it."

Bondri translated this into Loudsinger language. They checked it against the translator. Viggy and machine were more or less in agreement. Bondri was waiting somewhat impatiently for a human response.

Tasmin looked helplessly toward Clarin. They were assembled so near the monstrous monolith that it actually seemed to bend above them. The sounds that came from it came from here, there, everywhere. They had no sense of location. It was not like looking into a human—or a viggy—face. There was no way in which the question could be simply answered. There was no time for equivocation, for polite, diplomatic evasions. These words were the first between two totally different types of sentient creatures. Though they did not have the language of the viggies, which could speak only truth, Tasmin felt desperately that he should try.

Clarin nodded to him, eyes fastened on his. "Tell it," she said. "Tell it the truth. Find the words, somehow, and tell it the truth."

"What do you want me to sing?" whispered Bondri. "It is a very important question the god has asked."

"I don't want you to sing," Tasmin cried. "I want to tell it myself. Me. And Clarin and Jamieson. I want to tell it exactly what we mean to say!"

"Do the Loudsingers have the words?"

"No, Bondri. You know we don't have the words. We have to have a while to get the words."

"Then I will tell the Highmost Darkness that the Loudsinger is preparing an answer."

The troupe sang a short phrase, three times repeated, and a cascade of sound belled from the Tower.

"It understands the difficulty this question poses," said Bondri. "The Great One found intriguing alternatives in encoding it linguistically and can extrapolate there would be alternative possibilities in answer. It allows you time."

Shaking their heads over this, trying to believe they were living a reality rather than a dream, they gathered around Donatella's synthesizer. Tasmin bent above the keyboard, making quick notations as the translator gave him each key concept. Clarin was beside him. Jamieson heaved himself up, tottering, and Vivian ran to hold him up.

"Lie down, young man. You're not fit to be up."

Jamieson grinned. "You think I'm going to let that old man do all the singing, Vivian?" He staggered a little. "I'll get stronger if I move around."

He went to peer over Tasmin's shoulder. Tasmin looked up, shook his head disapprovingly, then turned back to the machine. After a time, Jamieson leaned closer, to help.

Occasionally the translator beeped, clucked, and refused to offer anything at all. When this happened, Tasmin turned to Bondri and asked, "How would you say . . ." or "Is this how you say . . . ?" Bondri offered him word or correction, and Tasmin returned to his work.

What concepts would the Black Tower have? No organic ones, surely. One could not talk of hearts, of blood, of pain. Did they feel pain? Did they have honor? Did they understand truth? There were honorifics aplenty, so they had some concept of glory and power, but what did even these mean to them? They did understand beauty, so much was clear. There was not a phrase sung by the viggies that was not beautiful, and that could not be accidental. There was not a word or phrase in a successful Password that was not beautiful either, and that should have told them something. Though perhaps it told them only that viggy and human had similar esthetics.

It emerged that the Presence had no concept of its own crystallinity. Its mind existed within the great crystal as the mind of humans existed within its cells. Was the human mind aware of its cellular nature, of its neurons and receptors? Only from the outside did that kind of awareness come. And what were the minds of the Presences after all but vast arrays of dislocations, molecular vacancies, self-reproducing line, and planar defects generating energy along infinitesimal fault lines, molecular neurons rather than biological ones, atoms of chromium instead of dopamine, with vacancies in the infinite grid serving as receptor cells.

And yet they were aware. They knew inside from outside. They spoke from their own universe to a universe outside themselves. It would suffice—as a starting point.

Slowly, lines of musical notation grew beneath Tasmin's hands. More slowly yet, the words were chosen.

"I can't do that," sighed Jamieson, indicating a soaring line of vocalization. He was able to stand without help, able to move with only minor discomfort. Or so he told himself, refusing to admit how much of his competence at the moment was mere adrenaline. But he couldn't sing that. . . .

"I can," said Clarin. Her voice was factual, without expression, and yet her eyes were alive with concentration.

"Yes, better let Clarin do that. You take the other part. This will be yours, Clarin," Tasmin muttered, slashing the notation pen across the staff, notes blooming in its wake. "Here's another one for you, Clarin. The main theme is mine. I'm leaving the embellishments to you two."

Jamieson grunted, making notes on his own machine, subvocalizing certain phrases to set them in mind.

Tasmin scowled, erased, notated once more. "This cadence, here. Take it slow; don't hurry it. Extend this syllable out, out, that's the base. Build on that, don't lose it. Come up on the vibrato softly, then let it grow, make it tremble. . . ."

"Wait a minute," Clarin muttered, reaching for the pen and pointing at the screen. "Here, and here, do it this way." The glowing notes and words shivered and changed. Tasmin considered. Yes, it was better. Was it enough? Only the attempt would tell.

"I don't get this bit," Jamieson said. "Shouldn't it fall into the minor, TA-daroo, like that? You've got it on the next syllable. . . ."

"No, it works. You initiate the harmonic line and Clarin comes in here, and me, here."

"What are they doing?" Bondri whispered to Donatella.

"I'm not sure," the Explorer answered. "I've never seen anyone do it before."

"How can they make a song without singing it?"

"It's just something they do," she replied.

An hour wore away, and most of another. Words and phrases were changed in meaning by others that came before or after, by subtle modifications in emphasis or key. They sang very softly to Bondri, phrase by phrase, and he nodded, wondering at the strangeness of this. What would the Great Ones make of this concept of difference? Of dominance of one group by another group? To the Great Ones, all viggies were alike, the same. The Great Ones seemed to know nothing of individuality. What would they think? What would they do?

Bondri turned to the senior giligee for comfort.

"All will be as all will be," it sang, quoting the fifth commandment of the Prime Song. "Be at peace, Bondri Wide Ears."

"That's easy for you to sing," Bondri mumble-hummed, quoting Jamieson. This human language had some interesting things in it. Sarcasm, for instance. And irony. Bondri was very taken with both.

"All right," Tasmin cried at last. "Pay attention, class. We're almost sight reading this one, so hold your concentration. Get it right the first time, because we may not have a second chance. Donatella, help us with these effects—on this line right here. . . ."

"You expect me to sight read this!" she exclaimed incredulously.

"You can do it," announced Clarin through tight lips.

"It'll take all four boxes," Jamieson said. "Tasmin leads."

"Pronounce that word again," Tasmin was asking Bondri. "Dooo-vah-loo-im." He made another notation of accent on the keyboard. "Did you feed it to the other boxes, Jamieson?"

"All in but that last change. All right."

They stood apart, breathing deeply, the boxes supported on their retractable stands. Tasmin keyed the first sounds he had scored, a low, brooding bass, pulsing beneath the words he was singing, the words he was thinking. It would not be enough to sing nonsense syllables. They had sung nonsense words for generations. This time he had to know what he meant.

The bass built into a mighty chord of pure sound, noninstrumental in feeling, then faded away almost to silence as Tasmin began to sing.

"Here in this beautiful land," he sang, "we lived on lies." This was a phrase Bondri had helped them with: a condition that is not real, a word that is warped.

"Lies," sang Clarin and Jamieson, weaving the sound of *lies* into a dissonance, which throbbed for one moment and then resolved into an expectant harmonic.

"Powerful ones let us move in these lands only if we lied." Tasmin had wanted the word *freedom*. Neither Bondri nor the translator could come up with anything. Did the Great Ones have any concept of freedom? How would they?

"If we told the truth, they would force us [the word meant shatter or demolish] away from these lands of glory. Our voices would be silenced, our praise songs fallen into quiet.

"The lies they put into our mouths were these. . . ."

Donatella bent frantically over her box making a wild

clamor of bells. Beneath Jamieson's fingers, trumpet sounds soared into incredible cascades of sound. Drums beat in an agitated thunder under Clarin's hands.

Three voices rose as one, separating into distinct upward spiraling tendrils of song. "They forced us to say there were no Presences [great beings, mighty nonmobile creatures]. They told us to say the Great Ones were no more than empty stones."

Silence. A tentative fluting. "Why? Why did they do this?" Jamieson's voice rose in a lilting cusp of sound, questioning, seeking, wheeling like a seeking gyre-bird, tumbling in the air, a question that moved so quickly it could not be caught or denied. "Why?"

From the troupe of Bondri Gesel, an antiphon, unrehearsed, spontaneous as a fall of water. "Why? What creature could do this thing?"

A return to the ominous base, the annunciatory drum.

"The laws of man [this small, mobile creature not made as the Great Ones are made, other than the messengers of the gods] are clear," Tasmin sang. "Where sentient creatures already are [beings like the Great Ones in thinking, making concepts] humans may not go except as those same creatures will allow."

A hushed phrase, sung in unison, echoed by the troupe of Bondri Gesel. "We singers respect [obey, honor] the law."

"But the powerful ones do not respect the law," Clarin trumpeted.

Silence. A cymbal, tapped. A woodblock sound, like the inexorable drop of water.

"We, we the singing creatures, the speaking creatures, we respect the law and yet we lied. . . ."

Three voices rising in one great harmonic chord. "Because our concepts would be broken if we left the Great Ones. We did it out of fear, out of hope, out of love."

Voices trailing into silence. Liquescent flute sounds dripping away. A last faint call of a grieving trumpet, as though from a distant rampart, being abandoned. A last tap of slack headed, fading drum. Quiet.

What a definition of hypocrisy, Clarin thought, almost hysterically. A symphony on human mendacity.

From the Black Tower, not a quiver.

The four of them stared up at the enormous height, their faces strained with the concentration of the song, gradually relaxing, becoming slack. Jamieson staggered and collapsed on the ground, smiling apologetically at Donatella before he passed out. The giligees gathered around him again, chirping angrily.

Tasmin wondered weakly if they'd gotten any of the words right. The word for love, for instance. Bondri had said it that way, but Bondri had had an odd expression on his wide face when he said it. Tasmin started to ask Bondri whether the word had ever even been used with the Presences.

And was knocked to his knees by the song coming from the Black Tower.

He could not understand a word of it. The translator chirped and gurgled, words fled across the screen only to be replaced with others. Words accumulated, multiple meanings were tried and discarded. Missing sense was filled in on the basis of speculation, words in parentheses bubbled and disappeared. Others came in their places.

"Interesting! (occupying of intelligence). More interesting (even than) the exercise (amusement, occupation) we have (been engaged in). Small mobile creatures (having such) concepts has not (been considered). Our messengers have not (troubled us, announced to us) concepts. Northern entities (parts?) find this (intriguing). Southern parts (entities?) even now begin (debate upon) concepts implied. Deep buried sections (parts? entities?) where the (great water lies) also include themselves. Wonderful! Quite wonderful! *Imperative: Explain love. Explain hope. Explain fear.*"

Just in case they missed it, the Black Tower sang it twice more, in variations. The translator compared versions two and three with version one and settled upon a single message.

Bondri had huddled down beside Clarin, the two of them arguing over an explanation of love that would make sense to a crystalline being. An unlikely duo to be doing such a thing, Tasmin thought at first. Then, remembering certain things both Bondri and Clarin had done in the past, he thought perhaps they were the best ones to do so. Bondri was going on about loving sets of offspring, loving a good giligee, loving the troupe.

Clarin didn't talk with the viggy long. Using the translator, she began singing about hope and fear, with the troupe of Bondri Gesel as backup. "Those of us with short lives," she vocalized, in a line of extended melody, "much regret ending, becoming nothingness. This regret is fear. Those of us with fragile bodies that can be broken, much regret that breaking. This regret is also fear. We fear ending and breaking. We fear the ending of those we think of as parts of ourselves. Others are those who are not broken with us or ended with us. Thinking of others as part of self is called love.

"So, in our minds we create patterns in which there is no fear. These patterns are called hope. . . ."

Donatella was stretched out on the ground, simply listening, her face remote and musing. When she saw Tasmin looking at her, she remarked, "She makes it all sound so simple, Tasmin. They'll probably understand her, too. I told you they talked, Tasmin. I told you. God, I wish Link could be here. . . ."

Later, falling over themselves from exhaustion, they tried to sleep, but Bondri Gesel kept waking them.

"The Great One wishes you to explain pain once more, Loudsinger." "The Great One asks that you tell again of the difference between bad and good." "In answer to a previous question, you used certain Loudsinger words the Great One does not understand. The Great One wants to know more about 'standard business practices.' " "The Great One wants to know if you have something the same as hoosil. I told the Great One that was anger, but it wants *you* to tell it. It sang your particular label. This means the Great One now knows we are each a separate creature, Tasmin Ferrence. It never thought that before. None of them ever thought that before."

Tasmin accepted this through a haze of fatigue. "I noticed the translator had some trouble deciding between parts and entities. As though the Presence isn't quite sure about boundaries between things."

"The viggies noticed this, too, Tasmin Ferrence."

"You sound amazed, Bondri Gesel."

"I am . . . what is that word Jamieson gave me? I am dumbfounded, Tasmin Ferrence. I am based in silence." Bondri bounded away, obviously elated, only to return later, waking them all to get yet another answer and to answer a question or two himself.

"What was that business about the northern and southern parts, Bondri? I didn't understand that," asked Jamieson.

"The one you call the Black Tower touches the ones you call the Watchers, deep beneath the soil. Far to the west it touches the ones you call Mad Gap. It touches the False Eagers and Cloud Gatherer and all the Presences of the Redfang Range. Beneath the lands, Tasmin Ferrence, all the Presences touch one another. Or perhaps not quite all. Perhaps they are all part of one thing. A thing that is everywhere, beneath the Deepsoil, far down, even beneath the seas. We think this is so. Or perhaps they only talk with one another. This is why, we viggies think, the Great One is not sure about edges of things. The Black Tower is not sure where it ends and other things begin. It is not madness, like the Enigma, but it is strangeness. . . ."

Morning.

Donatella, still triumphant, to Jamieson. "I told you they talked."

"You didn't tell me they talked all the time." Jamieson was unable to get up, and no one would let him try. Still, he seemed to be alert, with a clear understanding of what was going on. He asked Tasmin, "What do we do now? Have we got enough proof for the commission?"

"We haven't talked to it yet about what Justin is planning to do. . . ."

"Has already done," snapped Don. "At least partly."

This took the entire morning. Some things were understood almost immediately. The Black Tower understood destruction. It did not understand "maximizing profits," however, which Tasmin had taken some time to translate though he used the Urthish word for it, too. When the Tower finally understood cost benefits, it had a fit of hoosil, which required them to leave the vicinity for over an hour. At the end of the hour, the concept had been spread through the vast network and they were told that all the Presences both understood it and were equally annoyed by it as it pertained to them. What came out always equaled what went in, so far as the Presences were concerned. Taking more out than went in was immoral, unmathematical, and illogical. Things did not balance properly if more went in than out, or vice versa.

"Of course, they're completely right," Donatella said.

"Do we want to talk about closed and open systems? Maybe that can wait."

"It'll have to wait," Tasmin told her. "We'll all getting to the point that our voices are giving out."

"Now what?" intoned Bondri Gesel, sounding weary but indomitable. The troupe had spent the morning telling each other what was happening, just to get it on record, and they had not been able to arrive at a finished song. Some of the words did not seem to be entirely accurate or true. The senior giligee was having a fit over that. Giligees were conservative anyhow, and this one was carrying the brain-bird of Prime Priest Favel, which made it even more conscious of doing things right.

"I hate to say this, Bondri, but do you suppose we could teach the Black Tower to speak some Urthish? The human language? We have some words that are very cumbersome to translate."

"It should be very easy for them to learn the whole language," Bondri sang. "The Great One has already asked us to begin." Bondri sounded offended by this.

"Your own language is far superior," Tasmin offered placatingly. "Truly."

"Oh, we know it is. More accurate. More specific."

"Exactly."

"Your language, on the other hand, has a lot of words we don't have at all. It has more room in it."

"That's true."

"That's what the Great One says. The Great One says it is a good language for puzzles, because it can mean many things."

"The Great Ones like puzzles, do they?"

"For millions of years they have done puzzles, Tasmin Ferrence. They have divided themselves into parts. What you would call teams. They have used us to carry puzzle moves from one part to another, so the other team would not know what move they are making. They made us for this, or so our Prime Song says. Now you are their new puzzle, Tasmin Ferrence. You and all the Loudsingers. We viggies think it will be interesting to watch them figure you out."

"I want them to speak Urthish for only one reason, Bondri Gesel."

"We know," said the troupe leader. "When they speak to your powerful ones, there must be no misunderstanding what they say."

Now Tasmin was dumbfounded. "They intend to speak to our 'powerful ones'?"

"They do, Tasmin Ferrence. As soon as you give them all the words in your language and tell them where these powerful ones are to be found."

"All the words?"

"Are they not in the machine somewhere? The female, Clarin, said they were in the machine."

"The dictionary! In the translator, yes."

"Can this be played to the Great Ones?"

"I suppose it can." The Presences themselves had thought of this? Well, it would certainly save the human voices. "I understood that recorded things were unacceptable to them."

"Irritating to the skins, yes, Tasmin Ferrence. But they can tolerate it if they are awake."

Tasmin exchanged a wondering glance with Clarin, who said, "Before they speak to the powerful ones, Bondri Gesel, ask the Tower if they will speak, very quietly, to persons from the citadels of the Tripsingers?"

"They will do this, even though they say your language is ugly, Clarin. It has some very bad sounds in it."

"Would they understand an apology?"

"They already know. They say you are a young race that has not had time to smooth yourself. You are still very bumpy." Bondri made a smilelike face, fangs showing at the edges of his mouth, a trifle malicious, Tasmin thought, before continuing. "Your language is bumpy, and it is obvious some of your individual persons are also bumps that need to be smoothed away. Or eaten, perhaps." Bondri licked his lips, enjoying Clarin's near success at hiding a shudder. "Undoubtedly you have other bumps as well. However, they find even that interesting. There is no end to the interest that the Great Ones have stored up."

Jamieson could not travel. The giligees would not let him travel. Tasmin knelt beside him, his hand on the boy's shoulder, watching the rise and fall of his chest, the flutter of eyelids, moving with the dream he was in.

The pressure of Tasmin's hand brought him from sleep. "Master Ferrence," Jamieson said, wakening all at once.

"Reb."

"I'm sorry to plop out on you this way."

"I shouldn't have let you sing to the Tower."

"You and who else would've tried to stop me?"

"There was a Tripsinger here a while ago from Deepsoil Five, Reb. They heard the Tower roaring and sent someone to find out what was going on. I've asked him to send some people out to be with you, and with the Tower. The giligees will stay with you at least until then. . . ."

"Have a good trip, Master Ferrence. Make it fast."

"We will. I'm sorry you can't be there for the end of it, however it ends."

"It'll end here, too, one way or the other." Jamieson grinned at him, then heaved a deep breath, as though it hurt him to do so. "Master Ferrence."

"Yes, Reb."

"Remember, once I told you there was a lot to Clarin, Sir. I told you she wanted to work with you."

"Well—she got her chance."

"More than that, Sir. Tasmin." That heaving breath again. "She loves you. I got it out of her. I wish you'd kind of remember that. As a favor to me."

Tasmin could not think of anything to say. He clasped Jamieson's shoulder in his hand once more and left him there.

A caravan moved from Deepsoil Five westward, laden with brou. It came to the Watchers. The Tripsinger put back his hood and rolled up his sleeves. In the Tripwagon, the backup man leaned forward to touch the synthesizer.

Trumpet sounds. A tap of drums.

"Arndaff-du-roomavah," the Tripsinger sang.

"Brother, brother, brother," replied the South Watcher. "Return to the citadel and tell the Master General this Presence is his brother and wishes to speak with him."

The wagons halted.

The Tripsinger fell silent, amazed and dizzy, totally unbelieving.

Not a 'ling quivered. The ground was silent.

"Are you deaf?" the North Watcher rumbled. "Do what your brother says."

Outside the Jut, a wagon train moved eastward along the 'Soilcoast road. It came to the Jammers. The Tripsingers readied themselves, a trifle nervously as every Tripsinger had done since the massacre. The ground was quiet, suspiciously quiet. They did not know what to make of that, and regarded each other with unease. The first notes sounded from the Tripwagon, only to be drowned by quite another music.

"Brother, brother, brother," sang the Jammers in close harmony. "Return to your citadel and tell your Master General to check his armory and be ready for trouble. Also, tell him to keep quiet about it until he hears from us."

At the Redfang Range, a lonely Tripsinger sat high within the firelike glimmer of the ranked pillars, awash in orange light. Night was coming, and he had caught no sight of anyone the Grand Master was interested in. Rumors were the Grand Master's own daughter was in here somewhere, but if that were true, she wasn't showing herself. Sighing, he put his glasses in his pack and started down the trail.

As he went into peril, he picked over the controls of his box, singing the Password in a passable voice, a bit wearily. He had been sitting high on the pass all day, and it had been a funny day. Spooky. Absolutely quiet. No movement in the Presences at all. He yawned, garbling the first words, his mouth gaped wide. It stuck that way. Someone else was singing. . . .

"Brother, brother, brother," the Presence beside him vocalized softly in flutelike tones. "Tripsinger, go tell the Master General of your citadel to get word to the Grand Master of the Worshipful Order that I, Redfang, want to speak with him."

And then, almost as an afterthought.

"Are you recording this, youngster? Your Master General may want proof."

The CHASE Commission was assembled in Splash One, conducting its scheduled meetings with considerable pomp. Among the audience were a number of VIPs, a few from

Jubal, though most—including representatives from both the current and historic press as well as advisers and so-called neutral observers from the PEC—were from off-planet. Those from Jubal included the Honorable Wuyllum Thonks, not yet departed for he had not the means to depart, and his less than honorable lady, present for the same reason, although she did not understand why Wuyllum was at all worried. The only thing that had upset Honeypeach in a long, long time was Maybelle's disappearance. Justin wanted her and Justin was getting nasty about it. Honeypeach licked the corners of her mouth and visualized what she would do when she found the girl. Maybelle had to come out of hiding sometime.

Grand Master Thyle Vowe was also in attendance, though several of his friends and colleagues were not. Gereny, for example, and Jem. And that sweetheart of Rheme's, the Governor's daughter, the one that Vowe had personally pulled off that boat before Honeypeach Thonks could lay hands on her. Luckily Rheme had alerted them to provide a backup escape, just in case she didn't get away. These three and some others had established quite a redoubt in the half-empty warehouse in the fishing village of Tallawag. That it was an unlikely place for them to hide could have been testified to by several minions of Honeypeach's who had been searching for Maybelle ever since Vowe had abducted her. So far, they hadn't even come close.

Watching Honeypeach steam had given Vowe enough satisfaction to carry him over the deadly boredom of the hearings. He was of the opinion that the hearings were designed to be deadly, planned to be uninteresting in the extreme. Witness after witness testified to attempts to make sense out of Presence noises, some of them philologists who spoke pure jargon with no recognizable meaning. No one mentioned viggies. No one even thought of viggies. Vowe wondered at this. He had always had suspicions about viggies.

Harward Justin squatted at one side of the hearing room, low-bottomed as a toad, his slushy eyes swiveling from side to side of the room, his thin mouth stretching in a gratified grimace whenever a witness made a particularly telling point. For all the boredom, the place was crowded and concentration was intense.

Thus when someone jostled the Grand Master, he did

not immediately respond. It took the elbow in his ribs twice more before he looked down to see a note held in the hand of an anonymous donor who was looking everywhere but at the Grand Master.

"Emergency. Northwest Citadel, soonest." The name appended was Jasum Porlees, Master General of the Northwest Citadel. He and Thyle Vowe had been boys in choir school together.

The Grand Master let a little time elapse, then squirmed through the crowd to the door. Outside on the steps, the same anonymous man was standing, staring out over the city and talking almost without moving his mouth. "There's an air car waiting for you at the garage, Grand Master. Your friend says hurry."

It was only when Thyle Vowe was halfway to the garage that he realized the man who had been talking to him was Rheme Gentry.

"Your daughter's all right," said the Master General of the Northwest, soon after Thyle Vowe's arrival. He poured a cup of tea for the Grand Master and waited for the inevitable question.

"Where is she, Jasum?"

"Somewhere near the Black Tower. Or maybe most of the way here, by now. Probably coming pretty fast, since they won't have to sing their way by anything."

"Won't have to what? What in hell are you talking about?"

"You're not going to believe who told me, Thyle. Best way to tell you is to show you. Are you up for a short mule ride into the Redfang Range?"

The commission had heard witnesses for ten days and part of an eleventh. Finally it recessed for a day or two before reconvening to consider its findings. Some of the members took advantage of this interruption to see something of Jubal while there was still, in one member's words, something to see. The destruction that would occur following their pronouncement was fully understood by certain members of the commission, although not by Honeypeach's stepson, the chairman, Ymries Fedder. He had been brou-sotted in his apartment since arrival, and the commission had been chaired by its vice chairman, a junketeering bureaucrat from Heron's World.

Harward Justin retired to the BDL building to take care of a few details. Wuyllum Thonks was waiting for him there.

"What the hell are you doing here, Thonks?"

"That's what I'd like to know. What am I doing here? Honeypeach and I were supposed to be off this place a week or more ago."

"After the findings are announced, Governor, you can be on the first ship out. Along with the commission members. I had to seal things up to prevent any last-minute problems."

"And when will the first ship out be leaving?"

"Three or four days. Maybe five if they want to make it look good. Some of them are sightseeing right now. They may take an extra day or two."

"You don't anticipate any trouble?"

"I always anticipate trouble, Thonks. That's why it never bothers me." Justin smiled, a slithering of lips across irregular teeth, making Wuyllum think of snakes writhing over stones. "Trouble is just another thing to plan for, Governor."

Wuyllum shivered for no discernable reason. "I'll tell Honeypeach."

"Speaking of your charming wife." Justin smiled again, a particularly reptilian smile. "Honeypeach promised to introduce me to your lovely daughter, but seemingly she's disappeared. Did you ever find her?"

"Not yet." Wuyllum waved the question away, refusing to consider the implications of what Justin had just said. "Maybelle had planned to return to Serendipity. It's her home, you know. When she was disappointed about the journey, she probably went to stay with friends. No doubt she'll turn up. Well. We'll be expecting space, Justin. On the first ship out. You'll let us know."

"Remind your charming wife about the introduction, Thonks. I certainly want to meet your daughter before you leave. The Governor's residence is right next door. Call me when you find her."

The Governor left, ashen-faced. He did not care terribly what might happen to Maybelle. He was, however, suddenly very worried that he might not be able to find her. Justin, for some inscrutable reason of his own, had just placed a price on Wuyllum's departure.

As soon as Justin was alone, he commed Colonel Lang, commander of the troops on Jubal. The men and the equipment were ready. As soon as the commission announced its findings, they could start blasting their way into every dirt town east of the coast.

"Colonel Lang?"

"Manager Justin."

"It comes to mind, Colonel, that there may be some demonstrations when the commission announces its findings."

"Is that so, Sir? Everything seems very peaceful."

Justin sneered. The man was being slow on the load. "Well, the findings haven't been announced yet, have they?"

"That's why I'm wondering why there should be disorder, Sir. If we don't know what the findings are, then we can't know what the response will be, can we?"

The officer's voice had been very dry, almost insolent, and Justin cursed himself. Damn the man's nerve! He was right, though. Any preemptive action, particularly while the commission members and observers were still on the planet, might be interpreted as exactly what it was.

"So long as you're ready for any eventuality, Colonel."

"Oh, indeed, Sir. Always ready for any eventuality."

Colonel Lang punched the com out. Every company of troopers moving toward the east had trailed behind it a string of relay points. Orders could be sent down those relay stations within hours. Once the commission's findings were known, orders to begin destruction would be received by the troopers without delay and Colonel Lang intended to join in the fun. However, just to avoid any problem later on, the Colonel did not intend to send those orders until the commission's findings were formally announced.

At another military office in Splash One, Captain Jines Verbold put down the snoop-ear that had been tuned to the Colonel's call.

"Harward Justin," he explained unnecessarily to his visitor.

"I thought so," said Rheme Gentry. "He's getting nervous, now that everything's coming to a climax."

"When's all this climaxin' goin' to take place?"

"After the commission reconvenes to consider its findings, but before those findings are announced. While the observers are still here, needless to say. Probably tomorrow."

"It would've been nice to have a little more notice," the Captain said mildly. "Not complainin', you understand. Just commentin'."

"Sorry, Captain. We've only known about it ourselves for the past day or two. We've acquired some unexpected allies. It was . . . well, to say the least, it was a surprise."

"You wouldn't care to tell me. . . ."

"Can't. Sworn to secrecy. You'll know when it happens."

"You want to tell me where?"

"You know where the commission members are housed, Captain?"

"Justin fixed up an old BDL residential building out at the east edge of town."

"Right. I'd keep an eye on that if I were you."

"How can I help?"

"Captain, it would be useful if there were a few troops on Jubal that Justin couldn't get at for a while. Just in case some very important orders arrive, you know? Orders that replace the current chain of command? Since you were given the assignment of keeping order here in the city, you're elected. Of course, your opinions have been noted, too, along the way."

"My big mouth," murmured the Captain.

"Let's say you let it be known where your sympathies lay. Well, as I said, it'd be a very good thing if there was a good-size body of men elsewhere. Elsewhere, but not too far away. Say, oh, an hour's move, if possible. Needless to say, they should be ready for action on receipt of orders."

"Who—ah, who might they expect to get orders from?"

"Someone very high up, Captain. Someone outranking the Colonel by a good bit."

"Sayin' they're my men, I'd be in the clear then?"

"Oh, yes, Captain. You'll be in the clear. Better than in the clear. Your cooperation with legitimate authority will be noted."

"If I can stay out of Colonel Lang's way until then."

"Yes. There is that."

"I'm not sure enough of the men would back me in outright mutiny."

"I understand the problem."

Verbold frowned, drumming his fingers on his desk as he

considered the situation. "You know, Justin has his own security forces. BDL people. They're spread all over, watchin' everyone, runnin' back to the BDL building carryin' tales. I suppose you know that Justin doesn't trust just anybody. That bunch is hard and mean, and I wouldn't want to tangle with 'em."

"Hm. Damn. I'd forgotten that. Is there anything you could do to be sure they are where they won't give you any trouble? Say, at BDL headquarters."

"Ah." Captain Jines Verbold thought quietly for a time, stroking his chin. "If his security forces are in the building, then you've got all the maggots in one hole, don't you? Well, I might call Justin and tell him to be sure his own men are guarding BDL because. . . ."

"Because you've had rumors of ah . . . an assassination attempt among . . . ah, covert Crystallites," suggested Rheme. "People who didn't get rounded up when the others did. People he didn't identify, because he didn't buy them in the first place. Real converts. Real religious fanatics."

"Oh, yes. Covert Crystallites. Why, I've been hearing about this assassination business from covert Crystallites for some time. Yes. I must let Justin know. He'll pull his men in, and then I think I'll take mine out on maneuvers tonight. Out, but not too far out."

"Do that," agreed Rheme, drily. "Just be sure I've got a way to reach you."

During the night, a fog came up. When morning arrived, there were cottony mists hiding the environs of Splash One. At the buiding on the outskirts of the city, which had been remodeled for their use, members of the CHASE Commission and various observers from the PEC got out of bed, looked through their windows, and sighed. Many of them had not slept particularly well. There had been strange tremors in the night, shiverings and rollings. Not enough to panic anyone, but enough to rouse some and cause bad dreams in others.

On a usual morning breakfast would be served on the terrace. On a foggy morning like this, the somber dining room would probably be substituted, to no one's satisfaction. In preparation for this event, and others that would follow, members washed themselves and cleaned their teeth, scratched themselves and engaged in other, more individual, wake-up practices. Some of the commission members considered what findings they would give. Others didn't bother. In their cases, the findings had already been paid for and needed no consideration.

Among the ancillary personnel, and one of those last to arrive on Jubal, was a tall, moustached gentleman of unmistakably military bearing, who openly carried PEC observer identification. There was another, rather different set of papers in a hidden compartment in his traveling case. This morning, as part of his preparation for the day, this observer removed the papers from hiding and transferred them to a breast pocket, where they would be readily available. They bore, on the lower left-hand corner, the linked ellipses that were the sign of CHAIN.

Outside of town on a low hill, Tasmin got off his mule and helped Clarin down as well. Donatella had not yet arrived, but they expected her shortly.

"Foggy," said Clarin.

"He said it would be."

"Why do you call him he?" she asked. "I mean, why do you call it he?"

"I don't know. It had a deep voice. Mostly. I guess that's why."

"I guess that's why I did, too. Then I got mad at myself for doing it."

"Do you think the new one is ready?"

"He . . . it . . . the Black Tower said it would be."

"What's its name?"

"Nobody said. I guess we'll ask it."

"Where's Bondri?" Tasmin asked.

"Could be anywhere. Most likely is anywhere. He'll come when we call him. He says."

"I kept thinking the viggies were going to reinstitute the taboo."

"Not after their Great Ones told them not to. According to Bondri, our whole tribe has become a debt of honor, Tasmin."

"Tribe?"

"Tripsingers. Explorers. Us. We're the good guys."

"The bad guys have all the guns, though." He was staring at the city before him, a thoughtful look on his face.

"What are you thinking about?"

"Donatella's lover. Link. She told the giligees about him. They may be able to fix him."

"I wonder if the debt would extend that far."

"No. They sang about that for quite a while and decided it was a private matter. They have a word for private reproductive or affectional matters, but I've forgotten what it is. Anyhow, she'd have to pay for it."

"With what?"

"Meat. Bantigons, I guess. They say they like bantigon. Hell, so do I."

"Look. The fog is burning off," she said.

They watched as the slow veils lifted. Donatella rode up beside them and joined the quiet scrutiny.

"There it is," whispered Clarin.

"Where?"

"Over there. A kind of greenish shadow between us and the residence where the CHASE people are."

"God! It's so big I didn't even see it."

"With the top of it hidden that way, it looks like a huge new building, sort of."

As the fog rose, the new Presence came clearly into view. Green as new grass in the dim light, growing more glowingly emerald as the mist burned away. Two hundred feet high, perhaps. A narrow tower of living crystal in which the light danced and played.

"They didn't grow it that fast!"

"No, it's been there, deep down. They pushed it up from underneath, according to Bondri." Donatella yawned, shaking her head.

"Without an earthquake?"

"According to Bondri, just a few shivers."

"Where did you see Bondri?"

"He's back there," Donatella gestured. "He says he'll come out later on. Right now he and the troupe want to watch and sing, so they can remember it right!"

When it became obvious the fog was burning away, the

manager of the hostelry told the dining room supervisor to serve breakfast on the terrace as usual. The supervisor set up the tables and the buffet, never lifting her eyes from the level of utensils and plates. The commission members and observers, when they arrived, sought hot drinks and companionship. Fog still lay mistily above them, a low ceiling of shifting veils that hid any distant view. It was several minutes before the gentleman of military bearing, who was somewhat older and less gregarious than the rest, said in a tone of astonishment, "Was that there yesterday?"

The others looked out and then up, seeing a bulky structure nearby, its top hidden in the fog. They continued to stare as the mists shifted away, perceiving the crystal tower for the first time. It wasn't a building, as some of them had assumed when they had subconsciously noticed the bulk. It wasn't a building, and it hadn't been there the day before.

Some of the members, those who had been paid to bring in certain, predetermined findings, began to entertain horrible suspicions.

These suspicions were verified a moment later.

"Good morning, members of the CHASE Commission and observers from the Planetary Exploitation Council," caroled the looming green tower in impeccably articulated harmonic fifths. "For your convenience, you may address me as Emerald Eminence. I am here to testify before you as to the sentience of the Presences on Jubal."

Everyone, including the observers from the PEC, later agreed that by the time the viggies appeared on the terrace, in full chorus with an Urthian libretto, their obvious sentience was an anticlimax.

Within moments of the first appearance of the new Presence, Justin was aware of it. The residence provided for the CHASE Commission had been well equipped with eyes and ears. Justin was not one to leave anything to chance.

Now he stared at the small holostage on his desk in furious disbelief. The image of the Emerald Eminence appeared tiny and irrelevant and he heard the words coming from it with angry incredulity. Nothing had prepared him for this. No one had even suggested that this could happen. It was a trick! Had to be. It had to be explained to the commission members as a trick. Somehow it had to be explained away. . . .

But he couldn't wait on that! He picked up the com and punched for Colonel Lang.

"Send the orders to destroy," he snarled.

"The commission report isn't in," the Colonel objected, testily. The Colonel had eyes and ears of his own.

"You can send the orders to your troops and apologize later, telling them you thought the commission had reported, or you can refuse, in which case I have some papers to be transmitted to your superior officers within the hour. I think these papers would solve the Jut Massacre mystery to everyone's satisfaction. No one has ever known how the assassins got off the Jut . . . until now."

Colonel Lang's voice cracked with rage. "You'd implicate yourself, Justin!"

"You think I care? I'm going to hold this planet, Lang. I'm going to take it over. I'm going to get rid of all the roadblocks and take it for myself. There won't be any sentience to question when I'm through with it, and I've got some friends in very high places. Now what are you going to do?"

There was only a moment's reluctant silence. "I'll send word to the troops."

"Fine. Do that."

There was a disturbance somewhere in the building. Justin went to the door of his office and listened to the uproar from the reception area below. Raised voices, one screeching, the other bellowing. Honeypeach Thonks and Wuyllum. So, they had also seen the Presence speaking to the commission and had come for asylum. Justin showed his teeth. Let them. It might come to the point that any pair of hands that could recharge a rifle would be an asset.

Justin summoned his chief of security and barked half a dozen hasty orders. Thanks to Verbold's timely warning about the assassination attempt, all the men were present. There were enough forces and weapons inside the walls to hold the BDL building against anything the planet had available to bring against him. And in addition to that, the building had a few nasty surprises built in, surprises that Justin had arranged for, even though he had never really thought he'd have to use them.

By the time he finished—first with the Presences and then with Jubal—any power that might have opposed him would be gone!

Partway up the vertical shaft that burrowed down six floors through the BDL building walls, Gretl Mechas leaned her head against the wall and listened. The bottom of the shaft was now within inches of the goal. The last few buckets full of shattered mud brick had been hauled up and poured away. Now she could hear great disturbance inside the building, much shouting, feet hammering to and fro. Taking a deep breath, she began to ascend the peg ladder to the servant's quarters, almost a hundred feet above where Michael waited. It was time.

_____ 18

Since Jamieson and Clarin had first encountered them blocking the way west, the troopers had methodically worked their way farther into the ranges. Although led initially by Explorers, most groups had long since lost their guides. As the intent of the troops had become clear, the Explorers had vanished. This did not greatly disturb the officers, who had been well briefed by Colonel Lang, although it occasioned a mild spookiness among the ranks, inclining them to start at the least sound and move hastily away from anything that resembled a Presence.

"You don't understand," a young lieutenant remonstrated with his men. "When we get the orders, we're going to blow them up. They won't be able to do anything to us if they're blown up!"

From time to time a shadowy, dusk-hidden figure might

approach a nervous group to ask some such question as, "How much of them do you suppose is showing? Most of the Presence is underground. If we blow up the top, what's the bottom part going to do?"

The shadowy figure would then drift away, leaving the enlisted men to pass this question on to their fellows. They didn't know who had asked them—just "somebody." The officer, aware that hysteria had gone a bit further than consonant with discipline, tried to find the somebody with no success, and the Tripsinger who had started the rumor moved back into the ranges to think up something else, equally troublesome.

This kind of harassment, which was widespread, made the Tripsingers who did it feel slightly better, but did almost nothing to mitigate the danger to the Presences. The troops kept on moving eastward, and when the orders from Colonel Lang began to reach them, there were bodies of well-equipped men dallying along within a few hours' march of almost twenty major Presences.

The orders told them they needed delay no longer.

Sergeant (sometime) Halky Bend had been detailed to lead a small group of men at a fast pace, guided by an unwilling Explorer knight, by a circuitous route to the Watchers. The route was no good for wagons or mules, but men on foot could make it. Bend had been released from the disciplinary barracks in order to lead the group because he was known to move quickly, he was thought to be indomitable, and he had been in the stockade only for breaking most of the bones in a woman's face, not for any serious breach of military discipline.

When the orders came, Halky, his men, and the Explorer—who had been marching for some days at the end of a short and uncomfortable rope—were still miles from the Watchers.

"Get a move on," Halky instructed the Explorer, both verbally and physically. "Accordin' to this map, we've got five miles to go yet!"

His instructions were interrupted by the return of a point man who came back over an eastern ridge at a run, hollering, "Sar'n, Sar'n," as though he'd spotted a diamond mine. When they arrived at the top of the ridge, it was easy to see why. The False Eagers lay below them, ranked towers of glittering gems. Halky's lips parted in a lascivious smile. He licked them with a suddenly dry tongue, then spread the map to see whether anyone had identified this opportunity for him.

The glittering spires of the Eagers were regarded as one of the visual wonders of the known universe; they were not listed on the map as a target; they threatened no shipping route; no one had thought to guard them. To Halky Bend, however, they were an irresistible lure.

Halky had left Heron's World just one step ahead of the planetary police. He had stolen nothing much, killed nobody important, and engaged in no large-scale fraud or blackmail. Halky's crimes were often not motivated by profit at all. He simply liked to break things. His earliest years had been made joyous by destruction. His first orgasm had been accompanied by the incomparable clatter of huge windows falling before a fusillade of stones. He and several adolescent cronies had twice managed to shatter millennia-old stained-glass windows in a historic church and get clean away, though later and more ambitious exploits, which brought together certain incendiary devices and several large public buildings, brought the police closing on his heels. Well aware of this, he had joined the military and shipped out.

Now as he stared at the marvelous scintillation of the Eagers, he heard in his mind the tinkle and crash of broken crystal, the satisfying impact one felt when hitting something that would not bend or give way and could not hit back. With a feeling not so much akin as identical to sexual lust, he announced target practice. The troop set up their simple mortars and fired a few rounds to get the range. Thousand-year crystals shattered and fell. Diamond towers shivered into glittering shards. A cry as of agonized reproach came from the ground, and hearing this the troopers whooped and cheered, bringing the mortars to bear upon the few Tineea Singers that were still intact. Within the hour, the Eagers were no more.

While everyone was having fun, the Explorer escaped.

Within the next hour, every Presence on Jubal knew the Eagers were gone. They told every Tripsinger and every viggy within range of their voices. As soon as the Explorer found friends, every Presence, every Tripsinger, and every viggy also knew the name of Halky Bend.

A large company, under the command of Colonel Roffles Lang himself, was brought by coastal flier to the southern coast and then inland as far as was safe to do so. The company needed to march only a little farther north to reach the Enigma and begin an assault on it. Tripsingers from Deepsoil Five fought in defense of the shrieking Presence alongside a dozen Explorer knights, but they could not get close enough to the well-armed troops to cause them any real damage. The Enigma shuddered, screamed in two voices, and fell at last into a mountain of scarlet glass, a bloody wound on Jubal's skin. The Tripsinger defenders retreated northward to the citadel at Deepsoil Five, which they felt they would have to defend before long. Colonel Lang regarded the results of the action with satisfaction and sat down to look at the map. There were other targets listed on their route of march: Sky Hammer, the Amber Axe, the Deadly Dozen, Cloud Gatherer, and then, finally and most importantly, the Black Tower. The Presences were so close together that Lang felt they could probably all be destroyed within a day. In fact, he could leave the closer and lesser targets to a junior officer and quick-march with a select group to take care of the Black Tower himself.

Stopping in the Redfang Range on their way to the Jammers, a gun crew took sight on the Redfang and saturated the area with explosive charges. When they were finished, only rubble remained—rubble and the far-off sound of viggies grieving.

Outside Splash One, the CHASE Commission members, all of whom had seen and heard both the Emerald Eminence and the viggies, stubbornly insisted on arguing their findings for what remained of the day.

"A trick," asserted one dewlapped man with darting and suspicious eyes who had been paid well for his participation on the commission and had already spent the money. He was convinced the credit would have to be returned if he did not do what he had been paid to do, and he did not have it to give back. "It was a trick," he said firmly, eyes flicking from left to right to left again.

"What about the viggies?" someone demanded for the tenth time.

The viggies were inarguable. The viggies were sitting there, occasionally bouncing in their comfortable chairs, looking interested and asking questions. Enough of the commission members clung to their commitments, however, that it was not until very late that night that the exact wording of the findings was agreed upon. Since it was so late, the commission retired without announcing what those findings were.

In the bowels of the BDL building, Harward Justin blew the dust from a cracked notebook he had dug from the back of a long-closed drawer and flipped the pages to find the checklist he had written there years ago. Reading from it, item by item, he crossed the room to a locked control board, which he tugged at in futile impatience for a moment before fumbling in his pocket for keys. He had not been in this room for almost ten years. He had not really thought the time would ever come when he would need it.

Staggering footsteps on the stairs brought him away from the control board, teeth bared, furious at the interruption. Wuyllum Thonks was stalking down the stairs as though he were at home in the gardens of Government House, Honeypeach behind him, both wearing expressions of angry disdain.

"Justin," complained Honeypeach. "We've just been watching troopers marching in from somewhere. They've surrounded us. I don't think it's Colonel Lang's men. I haven't seen him. But they do have guns and things. And I can't reach Ymries at all, I've tried and tried. . . ."

Wuyllum added his own comments. "It'd be smart to go on out and give ourselves up, Justin. Put a good face on it, show them we're innocent. They'll never convict us of anything anyhow. Not you or us, not with the friends we have and the money we can put into our defense. If we stay in here, they may assault the building! We could all get killed."

"Shut up," snarled Justin. "You and your whorelady get out of here, Wuyllum. I've given you guest rooms. Go stay there."

Ignoring the insult to his lady, Wuyllum went on. "At least tell your security people to let us out. If you don't want to give up, all right. . . ."

"Justin!" cried Honeypeach, "why, how could you say such a horrible thing. . . ."

Justin turned, arm out, catching her across the face with the full force of his weight, crumpling her against the wall. "I said to get that slut out of here," he instructed Thonks. "I've still got a chance if I can bring enough of those damned crystals down in a hurry, and I'm not going to waste time fooling with you or your trull. If you want to go on living, get away from me." He turned away from them, not bothering to see whether Wuyllum dragged the bloodied Honeypeach away.

The installation before him controlled a battery of chemical rockets, rockets without electronic components, rockets carrying nothing that could be altered or burned out by the mysterious interventions of Jubal. The Watchers, the Mad Gap, the Enigma, the Black Tower, and half a hundred other Presences had been pretargeted by these missiles. Though Verbold's troops had probably demolished some or even many of these Presences, the fact that troops now surrounded the BDL building argued that the destruction orders had already been countermanded. Justin could not depend on the troops to clear the transportation routes on Jubal. . . .

But if the troops couldn't, the rockets could. Let the rockets fly and the routes to the dirt towns would be open. There wouldn't be any Presences left on this part of Jubal! Even if he had to lie low for a while, he could come back to pick up the pieces. With all that money on Serendipity—his own and what his phoney Crystallites had squirreled away—there was plenty to start again. Even if he had to leave Jubal for a while. . . .

With the redundancies he'd programmed in to prevent accidents, it would take an hour's work to set up the firing sequences. Once they were set, however, Justin could leave them to their work. He had a bolt hole, an escape tunnel dug ostensibly as a sewer line when the BDL headquarters was built. At the far end of it was a cavernous garage, and in that garage was a quiet-car. Eastward, about two hours' drive, there was a refuge he had prepared years before. He could hide there until he could get off-planet to collect the money that would let him come back and start again. He had planned for trouble. Justin always planned for trouble. Just as he planned for Jubal!

His plans for Jubal were not going to be forestalled by a few talking crystals and a mutinous commission. His lips drawn back into an animal snarl, Justin set to work.

"Stalemate," said Rheme Gentry to Tasmin. "Justin's holed up in the BDL building. I'm afraid of what he has in there. Logically, we should take the place out now, but we don't have the weapons here to knock it down—all the heavy weaponry on the planet is with Lang's men. We won't even have enough men to mount an assault until Lang's troops return, assuming they do. All we can do is keep Justin and his men penned up in there until the General can get some help from off-planet."

"The General?"

"My uncle. Zorton Pardo. He's the commander of CHAIN, and if you don't know what that is, neither does anyone else. It's the very quiet, almost invisible enforcement arm of the PEC. I sort of work for him. He showed up here as one of the PEC observers. He's taken command of the troops on Jubal. But my message never got off-planet, and with a typical lack of foresight, he didn't bring a gunship with him."

"Has he stopped the destruction!"

"Orders have gone out. It may take a while for them to arrive. You know that, Tripsinger." Rheme's face was blotched and gray with fatigue. "And if Justin does what I think he means to, it won't make any difference."

Tasmin put his face into his hands. The Enigma was gone. Redfang was gone. The Eagers were gone. All the Presences had trumpeted the destruction of the Eagers. Tasmin remembered the Eagers. He remembered traveling through them with Clarin, when he was first aware of Clarin. He remembered going home from them to Celcy, when Celcy was still alive. The memories swirled and twined to become joined in his mind, twisted together like a striped candy, infinitely sweet, nauseatingly sad, a pain that clenched the guts like a cancer, eating him—women and Jubal, love and love—the one destroyed, the other destroyed. His woman, women, this place. Everything he loved. This man, he said to himself with hating fury, this man is destroying, has destroyed everything. Harward Justin!

"What d'you think he's got in there?" Tasmin gasped.

"We know what he has. I've picked up some of the original construction workers, and they're happy to tell us everything they ever knew. He's got over a hundred pretargeted chemical rockets without any fancy electronics at all. No seeker components. No hunters. They're aimed just as you'd aim a projectile rifle. By aiming the launch tubes."

"He's going to set them off," Tasmin said definitely.

"He may, yes."

"Not may. Will. That's exactly what he'll do. He's like an animal when you corner it. He'll go down fighting with everything he has." Tasmin's mind spun, jittered. He knew his perception of Justin was true. "Justin's theory would be he could always pick up the pieces. Break Jubal into enough pieces, no one else will care about it, then he'll salvage what's left. Or he'd think that if he committed enough destruction, he could get away in the confusion. Either way, Rheme, he's going to set them off."

"How do we stop him?" Rheme asked helplessly.

Tasmin concentrated, his nose wrinkling almost like an animal's. "Evacuate the area around the BDL building," he demanded. "Move. Right now. Get the troopers away from there."

"What do you . . ." Rheme stopped as he saw he was talking to Tasmin's fleeing back. He was headed away at a run, toward the Eminence. Cursing briefly, Rheme turned to do what Tasmin had suggested.

Tasmin found Don and Clarin beside the Eminence, together with Bondri Gesel. He hailed them breathlessly.

Two verbal acknowledgments, one quaver of song, and a deep musical tone that was somehow interrogative.

He blurted out what Rheme had told him, what he himself suspected, repeating and stuttering, trying to make both Bondri and the Eminence understand projectiles, what they were, where they were, what they might do. "There!" he pointed. "Behind the BDL building wall."

"More destruction?" queried the Eminence, the mighty voice trembling, shivering. With fear? Apprehension? Fury?

It was the Eminence that had told them the Eagers were gone, the Enigma, Redfang, the Amber Axe—the list had seemed endless.

"It can be stopped if you can move the rockets. Or break down the installations where they are. Or break the controls that go to them. . . ."

Silence. Then a voice almost gentle, speaking words Tasmin did not understand.

"The Great One wishes to know if there are any individuals—persons—near that place," Bondri asked.

From where they stood, they could look down into the city. Rheme had taken Tasmin seriously. The area around the BDL building and Government House had been evacuated of civilians when the troopers surrounded it. Now even they were retreating, moving away quickly, herding a few stubborn civilians before them.

"Tell the Great One no one is there except those evil ones who have caused the destruction," Tasmin told Bondri.

"The Great One used our language because he needed to know what is true," apologized Bondri.

"Tell the Great One that I understand."

There was further conversation in the viggy tongue, then Bondri gestured toward the long eastern slope above the city. "The Presences will try to stop further destruction. You could watch from up there," he suggested. "That place should be safe."

Tasmin moved in the direction the viggy had indicated. He felt hollow, burned out inside, as though his perceptions formed a thin shell around vacancy. Clarin and Don were behind him, leading their mules and his. The animals had been grazing at the foot of the Eminence, no more concerned by its size or the noise it made than by any other on Jubal. Bondri and some of his troupe went off to one side. It was nearing dawn. Only one full day since the Eminence had heaved itself up out of the cracking Deepsoil. One day since the Eagers had gone. Tasmin cursed. From behind him, Clarin reached out, then dropped her hand. There was nothing anyone could say to him now. Since he had heard about the Eagers, he had been shut down, almost as he had been when Celcy died. It was as though everything that had happened had been focused on one point somewhere inside him. Only that one point had validity for him now.

They came to a rocky ledge about half a mile from the edge of the city. A narrow belt of farms lay west of them, then a short street lined with low storage buildings, another street of small stores, and finally the wall that marked the eastern boundary of the three great structures: Government House, the empty citadel, and the BDL building. Around this wall, Captain Verbold's troops had been established in a solid line, well protected behind hastily built barricades. Now the barricades were abandoned. The troops were on building tops and at street corners some distance away. There were none on the near side at all.

Tasmin glared at the wall as though it were his enemy. Behind the wall was Harward Justin. If something happened to that wall, if that wall came down, Harward Justin would run. He would run. Tasmin licked his lips, amazed at the flavor of that thought, the flavor of seeing Justin run, skittering like a crystal mouse, dodging, evading, eventually being caught. Oh, the catching. Tasmin's muscles tensed, as though he prepared to leap. Adrenaline poured into his veins, and he tasted it, tasted the thought of doing something himself instead of sitting idly by while everyone and everything else acted.

Oh, yes, Justin would run. And if he did, it would have to be in this direction.

Tasmin stared around himself, searching the ground between where they were standing and the city, peering here and there, his head twisting, eyes glittering.

"What makes you so sure he'll come this way?" asked Clarin.

He turned in amazement. Don had moved away, toward the viggies, but Clarin was sitting calmly on her mule, dark hair tumbled around a clean-washed and expressionless face. "You are watching for Justin, aren't you?" she asked.

"How did you know?"

"Because our minds are alike, Tasmin. Because he's the one," she said. "The one you can blame it all on."

"Do you object?" he grated, unreasonably angry.

She shook her head, kept her face calm, eluded his wrath. "What makes you believe he'd come this way?"

"The city's all torn up," he snarled, not realizing he had thought it all out. "If he has a tunnel, it couldn't go in the direction of the city. They keep digging foundations and substreets and drainage trenches. He couldn't have had a tunnel going into the city and kept it hidden. It would have to come this way."

She smiled, a tiny, barely curved lipline. "Amazing, Tasmin. My father told me you were clever."

"Your father?"

"Thyle Vowe is my father. Never mind. So you really think Justin will come."

"If he can move, he'll come."

"You could be hurt. Killed." She said it calmly, as though it didn't matter.

He didn't hear her.

Colonel Lang's detail arrived at the Black Tower early in the morning, tired but still functioning. A few of the men had been killed, fallen to Tripsinger sniper fire or shattered into bloody fragments by a too close approach to troublesome 'lings, but the dead were no more than Lang had been willing to sacrifice. He had been more concerned about losing his weaponry, but it had arrived virtually intact. Now he directed his men to within a quarter mile of the Tower and there set up his mortars.

Jamieson, fairly well recovered from his injuries on the Enigma, lay on a ledge to one side of the Tower. For the last few days, Jamieson had been living his own resurrection, as though in heaven and granted the privilege of talking with God. He and the Presence had spent long hours in colloquy, hours that were as ecstatic as any Jamieson could remember. Now he lay on the ledge with Tripsingers from Deepsoil Five scattered around him, determined to defend the Presence against whatever came. The men were equipped with weapons that the armorer of the citadel—who had been working on them frantically for days—had assured them would have more than twice the range of the usual stun rifles. Below the Black Tower, Highmost Darkness, and so forth, the two giligees who had stayed behind with Jamieson were preparing to leave. They had not been diligent about their perparations, and Jamieson called to them that the attack was imminent.

"Get out of there," he demanded. "Tumble down."

"Stayed to be sure you were fixed," sang the giligees softly. They had become very fond of Jamieson. He had a voice better than most viggies and was very good to sing with. Listening to Jamieson and the Black Tower had been edifying. They had much to sing to the troupe when they were reunited.

"I know," he caroled. "I am grateful. But you must move now. Those troopers down there are setting up mortars."

The giligees had not seen mortars nor sung them. They had no idea what Jamieson was talking about and were already surfeited with new Urthish words and phrases. Politely but without haste, they started up the narrow trail to the place Jamieson waited.

On the prairie below, Colonel Lang estimated the range of the Tower and ordered his gunner to fire a round. It landed slightly below the giligees, knocking them off their feet, half burying them in shards.

With a cry Jamieson leapt to his feet and ran down the trail, frantically digging out the unharmed giligees and tossing them above him onto a ledge that led back into the ranges. "Hurry," he screamed at them. "Run."

"Threat!" sang the Black Tower in an enormous voice. "Destruction."

Jamieson gulped a lungful of air and sang, "Do not fear. We will protect . . ."

At the side of the Tower a Tripsinger tried his new rifle on the gunner, drilling a neat hole through him.

Colonel Lang cursed, corrected the aim, and dropped another shell into the mortar.

Jamieson was reassuring the Black Tower, singing all his love and determination, his voice more glorious in this epiphany than it had ever been. He saw the shell coming out of the corner of his eye. He was still singing when it hit.

Near the BDL building, Tasmin felt a tremor beneath his feet. Clarin hastily got out of the saddle and sat, pulling the mules down beside her. Obediently, they collapsed with their long necks stretched along the ground. "Get down, Tasmin."

"What's happening?"

"Whatever the Eminence intends to happen."

The tremor grew into a rocking, a shattering, a tumbling of soil. Before them, the long row of earthen brick store-houses collapsed into a heap of mud rubble.

"Not quite," Clarin breathed. "Not quite enough."

It began again, first a ripple, then a wave, the second reinforcing the first, harmonic vibrations that amplified with each return. The wall around Government House began to twist and topple. Still not enough.

Then more! Vast undulations rolling them first one way, then the other. Trees dancing a wild pavane on the prairie beside them, tipping and bowing. Buildings in the city shaking and trembling. The world so awash with mighty sound that they were deafened by it, making each individual destruction seem to occur in eerie silence. The golden dome of the temple coming apart, dropping in ragged chunks that seemed to take forever to fall.

Tasmin wondered if it had been full of pilgrims. Worshippers of the Great Ones. The Great Ones who were bringing the city down on top of their heads.

And again the mighty shaking, the harmonics of one huge oscillation reinforcing another.

The tower at the corner of the BDL building crumpled in upon itself like wet paper. One corner of the main building sagged and fell. The grounds within the wall shifted and jigged, stones leaping over the ground like waterdrops on a griddle.

Tasmin put his glasses to his eyes, bracing his elbows on the ground as the lenses swung wildly. There was motion in the courtyard of the BDL building, someone at the gate that separated it from Government House. The Honorable Wuyllum, quite alone. No. Someone staggering along behind him, clutching at him. Honeypeach?

Clarin muttered an imprecation. She, too, was watching Honeypeach Thonks who was covered with blood from a wound on her head. The Honorable Wuyllum turned and kicked at her, then fled as she pursued him through the gate, across the expansive terraces, and into Government House.

It came down upon them. All at once. As though the bottom layer of it had been pulled away. Within the walls, nothing stood, no wall, no fragment of corner, no towering chimney, and then the walls themselves fell.

And finally the BDL building went, tumbling in upon itself in the shivering tide of motion as though it had been built of sand.

"The citadel . . ." he breathed.

"Empty," she said. "My father told me it was empty."

They both saw the dark opening in the earth at the same time. The soil was still shivering when Clarin's arm went out, her finger pointing toward it even as Tasmin stood up and mounted his mule. The opening expanded. A camouflaged doorway, well east of the fallen area. And out of it came a large man in a small quiet-car, driving speedily away toward the east, toward them, where they waited.

"Clarin . . ."

"Yes."

"Get away. He'll be armed."

"I want to . . ."

"If anything happened to you, I couldn't bear it. It would kill me. There's been enough. Please, Clarin."

She said nothing more. He sensed her motion rather than saw it. He would not take his eyes off the man before him.

It was dawn. The morning light shone straight into Harward Justin's eyes, blinding him. He was within yards of Tasmin before he saw the silhouetted figure of mule and man, the blocky outline of a rifle at the man's side. He had been shaken out of his usual concentration by the earthquake. Without thinking, he wrenched the steering lever to turn back the way he had come, not stopping to realize that the rifle was in its scabbard, that he could have outrun the mule.

Tasmin leaned forward and kicked the mule into a run. He could not hope to catch the man—could not hope to. Did hope to. Wanted to get his hands around that bulbous neck. Fracture that thick, oil-rich skull like a nut, squeeze it.

The car sped back. Justin fumbled on the seat beside him, but the hand weapon he had laid ready had fallen onto the floor when the car made its sudden turn. The car teetered, almost overturning, and he gave up trying to reach the weapon in favor of reaching the secret tunnel from which he had emerged. Directly before him on the scarcely visible

track lay the entrance to the hidden cavern, the door still
open. There was a large open area behind that door. Once
inside that area, he could turn the car. Once inside, he could
get at his weapon. The car plunged into darkness. Not far
behind, Tasmin pursued it. . . .

Something hit him from one side. Someone. Launched
at him from one side, knocking him off the mule. Someone
shouting at him.

"Tasmin, Tasmin, for God's sake it's going to blow don't
go in there after him it's going to blow. . . ."

The earth came apart as it had come apart once before
on the Enigma, except that this was not the Enigma, this was
Deepsoil, solid as rock, eternal as stone, now broken and
riven, with fire belching into the sky as a hundred huge
rockets tried to launch themselves and blew apart under
countless tons of shattered stone. Rocks fell around them in a
clattering hail. Someone screamed in pain. What was left of
the rulers' enclave of Splash One shivered into microscopic
dust rising on a white-hot wind. The cloud boiled, towered,
heaved itself into the sky, blocking the sun. A dusklike
shadow fell.

Tasmin lay on his back, staring at it.

Someone beside him was moaning.

Clarin. Cradling her arm and crying from pain and shock.
"I think it's broken," she wept. "A rock fell on it. . . ."

He got up, slowly, feeling himself to see if his own parts
were present. From the hill behind him came a trill, then a
harmonic hymn. Bondri Gesel and the troupe, who had felt it
coming, had sung a warning and would now record it all in
song.

When Tasmin turned back to Clarin, the giligee was
already there, working on her arm.

"You are making a habit of hurting yourself," it sang to
Clarin, even as it looked up at Tasmin with angrily specula-
tive eyes.

Tasmin shook his head. Somewhere under all that rubble
was a man he had wanted to kill. Still wanted to kill. The
emptyness in himself was not filled. Nothing could have lived
through that. Justin must be dead, and yet he, Tasmin, was
not at all satisfied.

*   *   *

The troops who had just arrived at the Great Blue Tooth, Horizon Loomer, Mighty Hand, the Presence humankind called the East Jammer, had not received any order that countermanded the original one. They set up and got off several very well aimed shells, which knocked a few large chunks off the Jammer. Gyre-birds rose in a whirling, agitated cloud. The ground shook. The men cheered. The Jammer cheered in return, its enormous voice increasing in volume and rising in pitch. The troops found themselves groveling on the ground, hands over ears, screaming at the noise, which did not end until they stopped moving altogether.

Rage had led the Jammer to this unplanned retaliation. Quiet malice led it to communicate the success of the tactic to all other Presences.

At the foot of the Black Tower, one of the giligees whom Jamieson had saved ran frantically among the Tripsingers and Explorers whose sniper fire had successfully kept the troopers at bay.

"Highmost Darkness wants you to move away," it squeaked in their ears, so excited by the action that it could no longer maintain calm song. "Black Tower wants you to move. Fast, away, away."

"They'll destroy it," grated one of the Tripsingers, wiping blood from his forehead where a flying crystal chip had cut him. They had managed to hold the gunners at bay. They had managed to kill a good many of them. The Colonel who had set off the shell that had killed Jamieson had left some time ago, marching hastily away toward the south with a handful of men, but he had left enough men behind to pound the Tower to rubble once they got close enough.

"No. Black Tower won't let them. It knows how, now, but you must go away. Quickly. Eastward, back into the ranges. Go, and cover your ears."

The defenders fled, covering their ears as they had been directed. The sound began almost immediately, a painful intensity of sound, and they increased their speed to get away from it as soon as possible. As they got farther away, the sound increased and went on increasing, always only bearable, and they did not stop running.

The troopers, who had not been given permission to

run, were soon unfitted for further attack. Some of the weapons detonated by themselves, quite harmlessly so far as the Tower was concerned, though the recumbent and unconscious men would not have agreed.

Thereafter, there was no more destruction.

The CHASE Commission, delayed by explosions in the city, which rocked the building they were in and blanketed the participants with dust, convened belatedly at noon for the sole purpose of announcing their findings.

> Sentience: of two types.
> Human persons, including their livestock and crops
> are to be allowed to remain on Jubal
> only at the invitation of the sentient species.

The commission members relaxed. It was done. Facing a corner, the iron-jawed man silently chewed his lips, relieved that he need no longer stand almost alone. If certain people wanted their money back, they'd have to whistle for it. He didn't have it anymore. One and then another of the members began moving toward the doors. Now if they could only get off the planet.

To the east of and far below the piled rubble of the BDL building, Harward Justin awoke to an almost darkness, a cavernous, echoing emptiness in which shadows moved and gathered. After an unfocused time of half consciousness, he began to concentrate on the light. He could see several flickers from where he lay, dancing light that gleamed from along the floor and walls. Fires. Small fires. Nothing dangerous. Nothing threatening. He tried to get up and found himself pinned by one arm. The car had overturned, throwing him clear except for the right arm. He struggled to drag himself free and almost fainted from the pain that surged through his shoulder and chest. Something there was injured, broken. . . .

He was in the garage, he told himself. He had come back into the garage, and then the rockets had gone off. The garage was still intact. Of course, he had built it and the tunnel to take anything except a direct hit from something major—something nuclear, perhaps. He stared at the flickering light. Perhaps they were electrical fires. By squirming a little he could see a narrow and broken line of light in one direction—the large doors through which he had driven the car, now fallen almost closed and partly buried. In the opposite direction there was only a dark hole, a black ellipse. That was the tunnel back into the wreckage. He stared into it, not really aware for a time that what he heard coming from its depths was voices. Voices. The only people who had been in the headquarters except himself were the security people. Those on the lower levels must have escaped.

"Hi!" he called. "I'm down here."

There was silence, then a whispering. Then silence once more.

"I'm caught under this car," he shouted again. "Get off your asses and get over here."

Now he heard the voices again, the shuffle of feet. The car blocked his vision. He couldn't see who it was. Only the feet coming. Bare feet. Why would security men have bare feet? Then another set, shoes this time. He relaxed. Not only those two, however. There were others. . . .

"Mr. Justin," said a voice from beside the car. "Harward Justin?" A woman's voice?

He turned, fighting the pain, turning his eyes upward in their sockets to see who it was. A woman. A haggard, burning-eyed woman.

"Number six," he said in disbelief. "Number six."

"Gretl," the woman corrected him gently, her eyes quite mad. "Gretl Mechas. With some of your other friends. . . ."

It was late in the evening before Rheme Gentry came to the General's room to greet his uncle.

"Has the destruction been stopped?" the General asked.

Rheme Gentry nodded wearily. "We understand it has. Little thanks to us. The Presences found a way to defend themselves."

"Are they holding that against us?"

"No. Not according to Tasmin Ferrence and his group. Tasmin and friends have turned out to be our main spokesmen. Them and the viggies." Rheme shook his head, surprised to find tears coursing down his cheeks. "The damned troops destroyed the Eagers," he cried. "And Redfang!"

"You're crying," said his uncle, shocked.

"Oh, General . . . You just haven't been here long enough."

"No. It's obvious I haven't."

"In fact, I'm not sure I know what brought you here at all."

"There were two things that brought me, Rheme. One was not hearing from you. Considering your unremitting and frequently irrelevant verbosity, I found that somewhat ominous. The other reason was that I did hear from someone else. I got a letter a few weeks ago, evidently just before Justin shut down communications entirely. It was from a former employee of mine, a remarkable woman who used to be the head of our cryptanalysis division. Cyndal Prince. Cyndal retired and came here to Jubal where her only living relatives were. A sister, I believe, and a niece and nephew. Any letter I get from Cyndal, I send over to Crypto as a matter of course. She had some interesting things to say, as usual, beautifully encoded, information she couldn't have gotten through Justin's censorship by normal channels. Taking the two things together, I felt my presence might be useful." He regarded the wet-faced man before him with sympathy. "Now, if you can set emotion aside for the moment, I'd like your opinion on what we need to do next."

Rheme wiped his face. "You reconvened the committee as a committee of inquiry?"

"Yes. They found as seemed appropriate. We have indictments against Justin, against the Governor, his wife, against a whole throng of lesser villains. Most of whom, I'm afraid, have escaped justice by dying rather sooner than we'd intended."

"Lang's still alive. Some of the troops, including Lang and the bunch that destroyed the False Eagers, have refused to come in as ordered."

"How do you know that?"

"Viggies. Tripsingers. They hear things, then they tell a Presence, and the next thing you know, the Emerald Eminence knows all about it."

"So?"

"So, we have to take some of the loyal troops and go after them. We can't let them roam around like brigands."

"You don't think the viggies and the Presences will take care of them?"

"I'm sure they would, eventually. It will look a lot better to PEC and be more honorable if we do it ourselves, however."

"Where is Colonel Roffles Lang now?"

"He's somewhere south of where the Enigma used to be with a couple hundred troopers. He's proclaimed himself commander of all humans on Jubal."

"Oh, has he," the General mused with an audible sniff. "Well! I agree that it will look better if we discipline our own. And since we may have to leave Jubal very soon, it should be done at once. I've promoted Captain Verbold to Colonel, Commander of the Garrison, effective immediately. Sort through the troops you have and the ones that are coming back. Work with him and get the matter in hand."

The matter had been put in hand by the following morning, and Colonel Verbold was much in evidence as troops began to assemble outside the city. Donatella Furz, who had been alerted by both Clarin and Rheme, circled through the gathering men, her long legs ticking off the distance as she searched for one particular participant. She found him at last, red-eyed, obviously somewhat brou-sotted, sitting in the shade of his own mule as he cleaned his rifle.

"Tasmin," she said calmly. "I've been looking for you."

He grunted at her.

"What do you think you are doing?"

"Going with the troopers," he mumbled. "Get everything cleaned up."

"Wasn't Justin's death enough for you?"

He glared at her. "I don't know what you're talking about."

She sat down beside him. "I'm talking about vengeance, Tasmin. Clarin said you really wanted to kill Justin. I can understand that. He did rather slip through your fingers. . . ."

"Bastard," he growled.

"But that doesn't make this more sensible." She gestured around them at the assembling ranks.

"Colonel Verbold said I could go." He sounded like an unreasonable five-year-old.

"No, what he said was that he couldn't stop you tagging

along. However, he did mention his displeasure to Rheme, who mentioned it to Clarin, and both of them told me."

"I've got to . . ." He fumbled for words, unable to find them.

"You've got to get it out of your system," she said for him.

"Celcy," he blurted. "She died."

"Yes, she died. And Lim's dead. And the Eagers are gone, and the Enigma, and Redfang, and a couple of dozen others. I can't say I blame you for wanting to kill Justin and trying your best, even though you damn near got yourself killed in the process. Still, Justin had a lot less to do with Celcy's death than he did with Gretl's, for instance, but I'm not out here with a stun rifle set on high-fry, trying to do a mop-up job that troopers are trained for and we're not."

"Gretl wasn't your wife. Celcy was mine."

She stared at the pig-headed man before her with a combination of pity and irritation. Part of this was her fault. If she hadn't lectured him, hadn't gotten his back up over Celcy, if she hadn't made him aware of and, therefore, guilty over his attraction to Clarin, maybe matters would simply have taken their proper course and he would have let himself forget. Damn!

"Tasmin, do you value our friendship enough to go into that tavern over there and have a glass with me? Broundy, maybe? Hot tea?"

"You won't change my mind."

"After we talk, you do what you like, Tasmin. I won't try and stop you. I promise."

Unwillingly, he shouldered his weapon and followed Donatella through the scattered groups of men. When they were seated at the back of the almost-empty place with steaming drinks before them, she regarded him thoughtfully, trying to find a key to that locked, barricaded door he was using for a face.

He was sotted, exhausted, agitated, and pale. Jamieson and Clarin had both mentioned that he had lost weight since Celcy's death, and Don thought he had lost even more since she had first met him. He didn't look well. Obsessed, perhaps. Maybe just stubborn. Maybe merely guilty.

"Why did you pick her, Tasmin? Out of all the women in Deepsoil Five. Why did you pick Celcy?"

Of the many questions she might have asked, he had not expected this one. The stubborn rejection he had ready would not serve. "Well . . . I didn't pick her, not really. I met her. She was working at the commissary. She was admiring some little trinket, and I bought it for her. I made some remark about buying a pretty thing for a pretty girl. . . ." He tried to focus on Don, having some difficulty in doing it, but his voice was clear.

"And then?"

"Well, one thing led to another. You know."

"Tell me."

"Next time I went in there, I asked her to have lunch. She told me about her family, how she lived. It sounded . . . bleak."

"You felt sorry for her?"

"In a way. She was trapped in that life. It was extremely limited."

"And, of course, she was sexy."

He flushed. "That's my own affair, don't you think?"

"I think we've shared enough of ourselves that we can talk about it, Tasmin. Take it as agreed. She was sexy. She made you feel—powerful. Protective."

"I suppose."

"Did you ever really look at her, Tasmin? Did you really evaluate how much of her you liked? Did you make a conscious choice, based on how well you got along? Did you ever compare her with other women?"

He made an inpatient gesture, which she immediately and correctly interpreted.

"There weren't any other women. You were completely tied up in yourself and your work, and you weren't looking for someone who could live happily with you. She was pretty and sexy and she was doing a menial job, which you regarded with aristocratic distaste. She was there. She needed someone, and you responded."

"I suppose," he said, flushing. "You make it sound superficial, but all that conscious choice business is pretty cold-blooded, isn't it?"

"Is it? I don't know, Tasmin. I've never been married. All I know is, given your nature, you probably take a lot of care in the fitting of your Tripsinger robes. You were proba-

bly very selective about picking a mule from the stables. I
know you take infinite care in checking out your synthesizer,
because I've seen you do it. After all, those things are important and essential to you. But according to you, you didn't
give that much care to seeking a wife. You simply found her,
like a bit of crystal in your path. You let her get accustomed
to you, let her learn to depend on you without ever making
any conscious decision to do so. Then, having done that, you
couldn't in good conscience let her down."

He glared at her. Nothing she had said was really incor-
rect, and yet she infuriated him.

"You are admirable in many respects, Tasmin. And honorable. But you are sometimes so damn stubborn it takes my
breath away."

"You've no right to say that," he blurted. "I left Deepsoil
Five to find out why she died. I've traveled God knows how
many miles trying to find out why she died. One thing led to
another thing, and they all led to Harward Justin—him and
his minions. You say Justin isn't that responsible? Then you
tell me why she died."

"She could have died, Tasmin, because she knew you
were disappointed in her and she wanted to do something
you would wholly approve of."

"You're saying I killed her. . . ."

"I'm saying that when any of us get into relationships
where one person totally depends on another, we kill something. Ourselves, perhaps. Or them."

"We got along!"

"Of course you did! Good Lord, Tasmin, between you
and Jamieson, I've heard all about your life together. You
were in love with Jubal, and she was scared to death of it.
You were fascinated by the Presences, and she was in sheer
terror of them. You were always forgiving her for it. Always
making excuses for her. Always patronizing her. She may
have died because she wanted to live up to your expectations,
Tas. Oh, maybe she was brou-sotted at the time, I hope so,
so that she didn't know what was coming—maybe in her
fogged up mind she decided to do one marvelous thing that
you would have to admire."

He gaped at her, unable to find words.

"It's true. You were at least as responsible as anyone

else. But all you want to do is blast someone to make yourself feel better. First it was Lim, but he was dead. Then it was me, but you decided it wasn't my fault. Then it was Harward Justin, but he got killed without your help, much. Now who is it going to be? Some mutinous trooper who doesn't know a Presence from a piece of rock salt?"

Donatella was crying, partly for herself. "Quit looking for someone to blame, Tasmin, and get on with your life. . . ." She understood his feelings very well. She had been through it herself, with Link. She got up and left him there, staring at the steam rising from the cup in front of him.

When the troops marched out, Tasmin did not go with them. He was outside the city, at the foot of the Emerald Eminence, singing with Bondri Gesel.

"Donatella said it," he sang, "but it isn't true. . . ."

They sat in quiet sunlight while machines thundered in the city, clearing away rubble, finding bodies, occasionally finding one that lived. Tasmin couldn't identify what was going on inside himself, a kind of freshness coming, as though someone had opened a window inside him so that a chill, pure wind blew into him. It hurt. It was very cold and it hurt.

"It wasn't the whole truth, what Donatella said." He gasped again. "You know about us, Bondri. With us—each of us sees the truth our own way, from our own totally egocentric point of view, and then we insist on that. It's like kids, fighting. You did. I didn't. You did, too. You viggies don't have those kinds of arguments. When you sing it, it comes out, 'He felt hurt that she seemed to do this, and she was wounded at his lack of consideration, but neither intended such an outcome.' "

"Yes, you perceive us properly," sang Bondri Gesel. "We would sing that, more or less."

"I guess that once the words of memory are set into our minds in a specific way, that's how we remember. We can't remember the thing happening, we just remember the words we told ourselves about it. I told my mother once that I didn't want a blind woman for my mother, and she remembered that for years. Every time she remembered it, she cried. She said blind is what she was, and if I said what I did, it meant I didn't want her. I don't think that's what I meant, and yet it's true. She was right. There was no way to separate what she was from her blindness. I had to accept her blindness if I was going to accept her. There's no way to separate people into pieces of themselves and only accept the pieces we want. If the viggies had been singing to her, what they said wouldn't have hurt her, for they would have said it all—not just part of it. . . .

"I'm beginning to think I talk to myself only in skin quieters, Bondri. What I say isn't necessarily what I mean. It isn't even the truth. It just gets me by. . . ."

"Ah," sighed Bondri Gesel. "It's important to you? You really want to sing your Celcy, Tasmin Ferrence. Sing your Celcy as we would sing one of ours?"

Tasmin put his head in his hands, wetting his palms with tears. "Yes. I would like to sing the truth of her, Bondri. Because how do I know what happened to her until I know what she really was? I can't believe she went there because of me. . . ."

Bondri shook his head, an astonishingly human gesture. "Don Furz should not have tried to sing her to you alone, Tasmin Ferrence, because she did not know her. Even you should not sing her alone, Tasmin Ferrence. Who else was there, Tasmin Ferrence? She had no children. From what you say, your males saw only her quality of tineea. You have a word, *flirtation*. It is the same. It is a little dance the females do when they are too young to mate. The *tineea*. It says, admire me. Flatter me. Sing pretty things to me. Expect nothing from me, for I have nothing yet to give. It is this quality of tineea I hear in your song of her."

"There was more to her than that!"

"Yes. There is always more."

"She was going to bear my child."

"Is this difficult or dangerous among humans?"

"Not particularly, no. But she didn't want to do it. She was doing it only for me."

"Ah. Well, then, we might sing the song of a child who reluctantly began to grow up for love of her mate. It is already a better song than tineea alone."

"She went to the Enigma, even though she was terrified of the Presences."

"You speak often of terror when you speak of her. Was she often frightened?"

"She was always frightened. Her parents died when she was little. She was abandoned. Her uncle raised her, but he had children of his own. I was the first person she ever had that she belonged to—that belonged to her. She was afraid she would lose me, terrified, of that—of everything."

"Ah. Well. This is a different matter. Now we will sing of her valiance, of her courage, to be so afraid and yet to try to conquer it."

"She gave Lim what he needed when I refused it."

"We will sing of generosity."

"She loved me. If Don's right, she died because she loved me."

"We will sing of devotion."

Courage. Generosity. Devotion. They were not words he would ever have picked for Celcy, and yet he could not say they were not true. "I kept saying to myself that I would find the time to be with her more, time with her enough to reassure her that she wouldn't lose me, enough so that she could start to grow up. She might have become a person quite different from the one people saw."

"We will sing of possibilities, Tasmin Ferrence. We will sing of what she might have become, given time."

Tasmin sighed, a breath that filled him completely, that left him completely, suddenly aware of truth. "Sing what she might have become. That's it. That's the part that hurts so. That I didn't give her time to become it before she died."

"So we will sing."

Tasmin cried, then laughed, weakly, wiping the tears away. "Is it true, what you sing, Bondri? Are your songs true?"

"Truth is what we sing, Tasmin Ferrence." On Tasmin's arm the viggy fingers lay, four of them, three and a thumb, petting him. "You did not know her well enough, Tasmin Ferrence. And then she died. All things die. You did not know her as you should have, as you would have done. You cannot sing her now. You blame yourself. So, that becomes your song. You can sing that you blame yourself for not taking time. Bondri's troupe will listen and help you sing. 'He blames himself,' we will sing, 'but it is not his fault. He did what he could do.' It is not fault. It is a debt you owe. You cannot pay it to her, but her child lives. You can learn to sing that child. And to that child, if you will sing devotion and courage and generosity long enough, that, too, will be true. If you will sing what she might have become, then the child will grow, knowing these things about his mother. And what starts now as a song full of time that never was, becomes, in time, the truth."

Tasmin thought about it, slowly nodding his head. So. So. So. What starts as an enigma score, becomes the truth.

"Think about it, Tasmin Ferrence."

"I'll think about it, Bondri. When Jamieson gets back, I'll talk to him about it. He knew Celcy. And he knows me so well. . . ."

The viggy gasped as though hurt. It was a very human sound, full of a deep and abiding pain.

"Tasmin, my friend. This morning I was told of something very sad and grievous that now I must sing to you. . . ."

Thyle Vowe asked Tasmin to speak for the Tripsingers in negotiations with the Presences. Donatella was invited by her colleagues to represent the Explorers. After thinking about it only briefly, Don declined.

"Let Tasmin represent us," she said to her colleagues. "I can't do anything for you that he won't do. And I have something else I have to take care of."

As soon as services were reestablished, she withdrew a good part of her savings from the BDL credit authority and spent the lot on bantigons, which she offered to the five giligees in Bondri's troupe. She had two friends she wanted them to work on. Link, of course. And Gretl Mechas, who had shown up out of the settling dust, like a wraith, half naked and quite mad.

After her initial shock and surprise at seeing Gretl, Don had asked few questions. Months ago she had identified a tortured body as being that of Gretl Mechas, doing so because it was found with Gretl's clothes, not because she had actually recognized any part of it. Now, even as she realized it had been some other poor creature's body, put there so that no one would look for Gretl, she also realized that Gretl might have preferred that that anonymous body had been hers, that she had been, in fact, dead, gone, out of it. On the surface, Don accepted this, even while she plotted with the giligees. "You want me to let your family know, don't you?" she suggested, carefully staying away from the subject of Gretl's lover. "Back on Heron's World?"

Gretl started to say no, the nodded yes. "Yes. Tell Mother I'm alive. Not ready to come home yet. Maybe not for quite a while. Never maybe. Maybe sometime. Yes. But alive." Alive, her mind said, wishing her soul could be convinced of that. She consented to go to the viggies because Don suggested it and because she was not able to decide to do anything else. After what she and the others had done to Harward Justin, she did not know if she would ever be fit to do anything normal and human again. And yet, at the end it had been Gretl who had convinced the others to let him die.

Link had been slow to agree to Don's offer. At length, however, he had consented to go into the ranges with Don and Gretl and spend a time there with the giligees.

When ten long days had passed, the giligees had not yet done for Gretl what they hoped, eventually, to do. Gretl stayed with them. Link, despite his doubts, had been a simpler matter. He returned to Splash One with Don, weak and staggering, but walking. Each day he became stronger. Don watched his strength return, wondering why she did not feel the euphoria she had expected; then knowing why, never mentioning it to him. Now that Link could explore again, it seemed likely there would be nothing to explore. The dream had come true; the reason for the dream had departed. The irony of this escaped neither of them. They spent a great deal of time in each other's company, gently making love and purposely saying very little, as though their emotions were a forest of 'lings they needed to thread their way through, very carefully.

After several days of this, Donatella did make time to have lunch with her Cousin Cyndal.

"I was so sorry to hear about Lim's wife and baby," Cousin Cyndal said, with an air of competence and without looking at the menu. "When Lim and I arranged the whole thing, he never said a word to me about the financial side of things. I feel responsible."

"You weren't responsible. Trace it back, Cyndy, and the

responsibility for the whole thing falls apart into chance and everyone's individual devils. Except for Harward Justin, no one was at fault. I could have picked any other Presence to try Erickson's suggestion on, but because it was big, and tough, and had stumped all the experts, and I had more ego than was good for me, I picked the Enigma. If I'd done it with any of the others—the Black Tower, the Watchers, even the Jammers— it would have been all right. I could blame myself, too."

"That's fruitless."

"I know. It's only marginally better than blaming someone else."

"How's Link?"

"Getting used to being himself again."

"Are you going to stay together?"

"We haven't decided. Since neither of us knows what kind of life we're going to lead, or even where we're going to lead it, it's a little premature to make that decision."

"My, you're being logical."

"I've been lecturing on the subject." Donatella remembered her diatribe to Tasmin and changed the subject. "Did anyone ever suspect you, Cyndal?"

"Your elderly cousin, Cyndal? That fussy old woman? Of course not. No one here on Jubal knows what I did for a living before I came here. Just because I'm old doesn't mean I'm feeble, but they don't know that."

Donatella flushed.

"Now," said Cousin Cyndal, "let's see if there's anything on this menu I can eat."

"So 'lings are part of the skin of the Presences, are they?" Thyle Vowe grumped to his daughter.

"'Lings and 'lets and the surface of the large crystals as well," Clarin told him.

"And all we were doing all these years was singing lullabies, were we?" He growled in disgust.

"I'm sorry, Daddy, but that's about what we were doing. Very complicated lullabies, of course. The reason we could never translate the noises the Presences made was because they were just noises. Snores and squeaks and scratches. Just like you or me in the middle of a nap, coughing, sneezing, scratching an itch. In the hundred years we've been here, we never got the Presences awake enough to talk."

"Shit," erupted the Grand Master. "It makes a man wonder about the purpose of life."

"Yes," agreed Clarin, thinking about Jamieson and how much he had wanted to talk to the Presences, how much he had been looking forward to it. "Yes. It makes one wonder."

A time came when everything had been said several times, when negotiations were completed, when ships had departed and other ships had arrived, when the worst of the grieving was over, when the dead had been buried—at least those whose bodies had been found, which did not include Harward Justin—when the matter that had begun with the Enigma score could be considered to be almost over. When that penultimate time came, Tasmin went looking for Clarin.

He found her in the library of the citadel in Splash One. She was reading through accounts of old journeys, many of them first journeys, full of the mystery and wonder that had been Jubal. Her hair had grown long enough that it fell over her forehead, shadowing her eyes. He could not read her expression.

"I was trying to remember how it was, before we knew what it was all about," she said. "You and Jamieson and I talked about how we felt. The marvel. The anticipation."

"It's still there," he said.

"Not for us," she said, laying the book down and looking up at him with that long, level look he thought of as so typical of her.

"Why do you say that?"

"Oh, Tasmin, you know what the findings were as well as I do."

"You haven't spoken with your father, then. I sent word to him this morning."

"No, I haven't talked with him."

"If you had, he would have told you that we're not leaving. At least he and I are not leaving. Most of the Tripsingers won't be leaving."

"You mean they really . . . the Presences really want us to stay?"

"They find us interesting, Clarin. They find our perception of them particularly interesting. They see us pretty much the way I'm beginning to see the viggies. The viggies—or at

least the giligees—can go right into our bodies and tell us all
about them. Things we didn't know. We can do the same for
the Presences. They had no concept at all of what they were
until we came along and told them."

"That's right. You've been negotiating."

"The Presences see no reason for us to go, so long as
we're sensible about Jubal. They don't intend to keep their
midbrains awake much of the time—evidently their philo-
sophical life, down deep, occupies most of their interest—and
they say we'll still be needed to keep them from rolling over
on us in their sleep. The ones that were destroyed are growing again, very quickly. Their roots are still there. They tell
us there will be another Redfang in a few decades. Another
set of Eagers."

"But what would we do? To earn a living?"

"There's still a market for brou. BDL won't be available
to handle it off-planet, of course, but some agglomerate will
take us on. The provisional setup we have now will give way
to our own planetary government. The viggies want us to stay
because we provide good food. We'll need Explorers. Less
than a quarter of Jubal is even mapped." He took a deep
breath, eyes shining. "Clarin, all that country out there! Presences we don't know! Things we've never seen! All that
wonderful. . . ." He caught sight of her unresponsive face
and sighed. "The Presences even asked our advice about the
viggies."

"The viggies?"

"There's the question of their eating some humans. Seemingly a back country troupe of viggies caught and ate a
trooper named Halky Bend. I don't know why, except that
the Presence said it was justified. Things like that worry the
Presences a little. They're aware we don't eat people, or
viggies. They know something about taboos. They have some
of their own. . . ." His voice trailed away into silence. She
wasn't reacting. "So," he concluded weakly, "there's lots for
us to do here."

"I'm not sure I want to be studied," she said, apropos of
nothing.

"Studied?"

"Of course. The scientists will be all over Jubal. Just
think! The first, nonorganic intelligences!"

"They may come, but they won't be able to sing their way past a waste receptable," he said. "They'll need us, Clarin."

"Oh, I know that. But I don't want to be their subject."

"You?"

"Us. Oh, yes. They'll study us along with the Presences, us and the viggies. They'll write learned papers on "The Interactions of Human and Nonorganic Intelligences.""

"So?"

"It's just . . ." Her objections sounded specious, even to her. She flushed and examined her hands intently.

He put a package in her lap. "Here's something I found."

She looked at him quizzically, opened it. The soft gray-green plush stared up at her. "A viggy baby," she said softly. "For your baby, Tasmin."

It was a moment before he could respond. "Yes, for the baby. I've been wondering what to name him."

"I think there's only one possible name. Call him Lim Jamieson."

"Lim." He turned away to the window, tears in his eyes. "Jamieson."

"You owe an indebtedness. There's only one way to pay it. Honor their names. Care for their troupes. That's what Bondri would say."

"What about Celcy?" he asked her, looking her carefully in the face. "What do I owe her?"

"You've already paid your indebtedness to Celcy," she said. "You never hurt her, at least not purposely. Everyone I've talked to says she was as happy and contented being married to you as it was possible for her to be. And now she's gone."

"Don says she died because she wanted to do one, totally admirable thing."

"That's possible," she said calmly. "There are other possibilities, Tasmin. An infinite number of them. With some things it doesn't matter what is true."

"I thought it did, to me."

"Only because you were feeling guilty about it. You wanted something to exonerate you. Or maybe something to canonize her. Then when you found the truth about Lim, you felt even worse. None of that was your doing, Tasmin."

He laughed, very softly.

"I said something funny?"

"No. You sing one song, and Don sings another, and Bondri sings a third, and I sing another one yet. I suppose we could get my mother in on this. And Jeannie Gentrack, and the other friends we had in Deepsoil Five. At the time, Celcy's death seemed so silly, so futile, so meaningless. It made me so angry. More angry than sad, as I look back on it. I've wanted and wanted to know why she died, and I don't know any more than when we left."

"And do you know something even stranger, Tasmin? If you could bring Celcy back and ask her, she couldn't tell you."

"That's true," he said with sudden enlightenment. "She probably couldn't."

"It doesn't matter. Nothing would change on the basis of your understanding about what happened then. What does matter is that you're going to get a baby soon, her baby. And you're going to go on living here on Jubal. And your mother is. And Vivian and Lim's child."

"And you," he said.

"I haven't decided yet."

"Clarin. Did you tell Jamieson once that you loved me?"

Her eyes filled. "Yes. I did. He shouldn't have told you."

"It was the last thing he said to me, Clarin. He asked me to keep it in mind, for his sake."

She wept.

"All these conversations I've been having with people, Clarin—they haven't taught me anything that I didn't already know. Only two people on this journey taught me something I didn't know. You and Jamieson. I didn't know anyone could feel as I did about Jubal, care the way I did about Jubal. I set myself apart from people really, separate, in a class all by myself." He laughed ruefully. "Don asked me why I picked Celcy, why I didn't try to find someone more suitable. There was a simple reason. It never occurred to me that anyone could be what I needed. I was elite, Clarin. Solitary in my mystical splendor. I thought I was all alone. Jamieson had to force himself on me to teach me I had no monopoly on wonder. Jamieson . . . and you."

The tears spilled. "I miss him," she whispered.

"So do I. You're right. If I owe Lim, I owe Jamieson, too. He told me where my heart was."

"Are you trying to say you love me?"

"I'm trying to say I love you both. Loved him. Love you. Not the way I thought I loved Celcy. Something quite different from that. . . ."

"I don't want to be your child."

"No. I didn't think you did. I don't want that, either."

"Will you get confused about who I am, Tasmin?"

He thought about this. It was so easy to get confused about who people were. Each person was so many persons. One could only try. He lifted her from the chair, holding her tightly against him. She felt as she had that time at the foot of the Watcher, trembling. She smelled the same. He remembered their voices rising together as they ascended the Ogre's Stair. Two voices, like one. Like himself. If he knew himself, he knew her. If he knew himself. . . .

"If I get confused," he promised, "I'll ask Bondri to help me sing you, Clarin."

Technical Appendix to the Enigma Score
Mark E. Eberhart, Ph.D. Department of Materials Science and Engineering, Massachusetts Institute of Technology

The Presences on Jubal present an intriguing view of crystalline intelligence and, as in any scientific mystery, sufficient information to form a hypothesis on how these Presences might function. The possibility of sentient crystals is hardly new. Modern computers are, after all, an assemblage of crystalline silicon, and one goal of those involved in creating artificial intelligence is to impose an intelligence on such an assemblage. Yet it is doubtful, for evolutionary reasons, that the Presences of this novel would function as some super-sophisticated silicon chip.

The single most important requirement for a living system to come into existence naturally is the ability to self-replicate. Biological life on this planet almost certainly had its genesis in short segments of DNA or RNA, which, when occurring in solution with the building blocks of DNA or RNA, will produce a complementary strand of material. Through the process of natural selection, those segments that are the most efficient at self-replication will dominate over those less efficient. Life, as we know it, is a manifestation of highly effective systems of DNA replication.

The basic building blocks of computers made from crystalline silicon are p-n junctions. A p-n junction is a planar region that has been chemically modified so that electrical current will flow easily only in one direction across, or "normal to," the plane. To create p-n junctions requires tremendous amounts of processing, that is, energy and human intervention. They occur nowhere in nature. It is not easy to conceive of a "natural" process that would allow for the self-replication of such junctions in such creatures as the Presences. It is, therefore, unlikely that thinking crystals would look anything like modern computers. It is the ability of the Presences to grow that provides a clue as to their inner workings.

Before taking a closer look, we might review the underlying structure of crystals.

A crystal is any periodic array of atoms. The key word here is *periodic*: a crystal is analogous to a checkerboard with no edges. If one starts on any white square on the board and then moves two squares in any direction perpendicular to the square's edge, left or right, forward or backward, one would find himself in a position indistinguishable from the starting point. The same would hold true for a black square. In fact, from any starting point on a checkerboard one can translate to an identical position by moving an even number of squares in any direction. A checkerboard is, therefore, a periodic array of squares with a period of two squares. Such a periodic array has the property of translational invariance, for obvious reasons. No matter how one translates himself on the board, moving an even number of squares in any direction, the surroundings will be the same. A checkerboard is a two-dimensional system with translational invariance. A crystal is a three-dimensional system with translational invariance.

Whereas crystals are defined to be translationally invariant, there are no examples of perfect crystals anywhere in the universe. All crystals have defects. The defect we are most familiar with is surface. As soon as a crystal has a boundary—as soon as the checkerboard has an edge—the system is no longer translationally invariant. This is how we know that no perfect crystal exists anywhere in the three-dimensional universe. If it did, it would have no edges and would thus fill the universe, leaving no room for us. A real checkerboard—not the imaginary one with no edges that we referred to—is not translationally invariant because when one moves two squares to the right, one is not in a position identical to the starting point. One is two squares closer to the edge, closer to the defect.

Surfaces are only one example of crystalline defects. Another type of defect is called a vacancy and results from removing an atom from its proper place in the crystal and leaving nothing in that place. Vacancies can be responsible for the color in some precious stones as, for example, in a diamond where large numbers of vacancies produce a yellow color. If one takes cheap, less than perfect, diamonds and subjects them to high energy radiation, some carbon atoms are knocked out of position, leaving vacancies, and creating a "yellow diamond," which is considered attractive and can be sold as jewelry.

Still another kind of defect is the substitutional, in which a normal atom in the array is replaced by something foreign to the array. In the checkerboard, we could, for example, paint one white square red. The red is a substitutional. The color and value of emeralds and rubies result from substitutionals: emeralds result from substitution of chromium for aluminum in a silicate of aluminum and beryllium; rubies result from a substitution of chromium for aluminum in sapphire. Sapphire is simply aluminum oxide (e.g., corroded Coke cans) as are oriental amethyst and topaz with different substitutionals giving them different colors.

The chemists on Jubal who investigated the Presences would have found that they did not look at all like the silicon crystals used in computers, which have the fewest possible defects, but that they had very many vacancies and substitutionals—and dislocations.

This defect, dislocation, is the one that makes it possible for metals—and all metals are crystalline as they occur naturally—to be bent and deformed. Since dislocation is the only defect that "moves," it is an important one to consider in analyzing the Presences.

Figures 1 and 2 (see page 344) show the two types of dislocations that occur to some degree in all crystals. The first of these is called an edge dislocation (Fig. 1). It can be visualized as resulting when one makes a "half cut" through a crystal and displaces the upper face perpendicular to the lower face, usually by one atomic distance. The second type of dislocation is called a screw dislocation (Fig. 2) and results from displacing the upper face perpendicular to the direction of the cut. Real dislocations are not as idealized as "edge" or "screw" represent them. Sometimes they form dislocation loops that wrap back on themselves, and at each point along the loop they will have varying proportions of edge and screw character. The region inside the dislocation loop is said to be "slipped." When deformed, the size of the slipped region changes. Sometimes it increases, sometimes it decreases. The amount of slipped region is proportional to the amount of energy stored in the crystal.

Dislocations represent small regions of deformation and they move in response to mechanical loading so that the deformation can migrate or extend from one region of the crystal to another. Dislocations exert forces on one another, sometimes forming stable arrays that are bound together and sometimes exerting repulsive forces that drive the dislocations apart. Energy is stored in dislocation arrays and can be released suddenly, manifested as fracture.

All of the requirements for "life" can be supplied by dislocations. The storage and utilization of energy, which in biological life is accomplished through chemical means, can be provided by the interaction of dislocations, which would act as the molecules of a crystalline life form. Does this mean it could think? Is there some mechanism through which information could be stored and recalled?

Let us imagine a dislocation moving through a crystal in response to some deformation. Let us suppose that while this dislocation is moving on a straight front, it encounters two or more substitutionals. It has been observed that the substitutionals "pin" the dislocation and do not allow it to move further. Between the substitutionals, however, the dislocation begins to "bulge," much as a sail bulges when pushed by the wind and pinned by the mast. When the deformation energy reaches some critical value, the dislocation can bulge no further and pinches off, wrapping back on itself and forming a dislocation loop. This loop is then free of its pins and moves forward, leaving behind a dislocation segment still pinned, which becomes the source of the next dislocation as the loading continues. This source of dislocations is called a Frank-Reed source.

From examination of the distance between dislocations generated by a Frank-Reed source, one could, in principle, reconstruct the deformation history of a crystal. Thus dislocation arrays contain information and could make up the most important component of a "mind," that is the ability to store and recall information. A very elaborate and complicated array of Frank-Reed sources could operate as an anabolic path for the storage of information—not visual information, which is what we are accustomed to, but mechanical information, the entire deformation history of the crystal. The arrays would record heating and cooling, shifts in the earth, changes in the

crystal's own weight, and, very important on Jubal, sounds.
Sunlight would be received only as heat and be perceived in
the infrared. People and animals and climatic manifestations
would be perceived by the sounds they make. Wind would
be perceived as push, lightning perceived as heat and shock.
The crystal would be, in fact, one enormous tactile being that
could feel a wagon moving on its surface or feel a Tripsinger's
music.

How about growth? Crystal growth is also frequently
dependent on dislocations. When a seed crystal is in contact
with a solution or bath of the constituent atoms that make up
a crystal, and when the conditions are right, a crystal will
grow. Anyone with house plants has observed crystals growing on the soil surface or edges of the pot. These have grown
from a seed crystal in the soil, drawing their substance from
the dissolved minerals in water. In some crystals with large
periods (as many as a thousand atoms), it has been discovered
that in order for growth to occur, the seed crystal must
contain a dislocation, usually a screw dislocation. The growth
of the crystal proceeds in a spiral, reproducing the dislocation. One is confronted by a paradox: Is it the dislocation that
is growing or is it the crystal? The answer depends on the
reference point. To us, it is the atoms of the crystal that have
reality and so, to us, it appears that the crystal is growing.
However, from *within* the crystal, it is the dislocation that is
real. After all, dislocations exert forces on each other and
arrays of dislocations store energy, whereas the uniform structure of the crystal might seem to be no more than an "ether"
through which the dislocations move. Crystalline life would
probably see the dislocation as growing and reproducing itself
in the next generation. Regardless of how one sees the answer to this paradox, this mechanism for crystal growth serves
as an analogy for DNA replication. Over many eons, those
dislocations that are the most efficient at reproducing themselves will be the ones that dominate. Thus, it is possible that
there could be crystalline life forms that feed on mechanical
energy, store that energy in the form of dislocation arrays,
and then release that energy slowly as sonic energy or more
rapidly as violent, perhaps explosive, fracture.

The Presences, because the greater part of their bulk is
far underground, undoubtedly store energy from earth move-

ment. It is not mentioned that there are any Jubal-quakes. Could the Presences be surface extensions of large or small tectonic plates, storing vast quantities of potentially destructive energy rather than using it up in earthquakes and vulcanism?

The Enigma, the "Mad One," is described as being twinned, two tines of a monstrous fork. Some crystals grow as "twins," that is, as mirror images of one another, and the plane between them is called the "twin boundary." Dislocations cannot move across surfaces, and so cannot be transmitted from one crystal to another unless they are in contact. Even when in contact the transmission of dislocations would be very poor unless certain geometric considerations are met. Thus, the Black Tower could presumably speak to the Jammers without sharing their minds. However, dislocation transmission or movement does occur across the twin boundary, and we can imagine the Enigma as a being that is actually of two minds, with each of these minds interfering with or perturbing the other.

As for the Tripsingers, what is it they do? Each Frank-Reed source has a frequency at which it vibrates, its own harmonic frequency, which may be multiple. If one were to bombard a Frank-Reed source with any other frequency, it could generate more dislocations, that is, the Frank-Reed source will operate. However, the Frank-Reed source would be absolutely transparent to its natural frequency.

If the Tripsingers simply sang in accord with the natural frequencies that were the "mind," conscious or unconscious, of the Presences, they would leave no information behind them, that is, they would not wake the Presences up. If certain sounds were "alertive," wagon wheels for example, then it would have been the Tripsinger's job to produce complementary sounds, which, when superimposed on the wagon wheels, yielded exactly those frequencies that were transparent to the Presences. This was, obviously, quite complicated enough.

A subject of some interest might be whether talking to them when they were awake would be an easier or a more complicated matter.

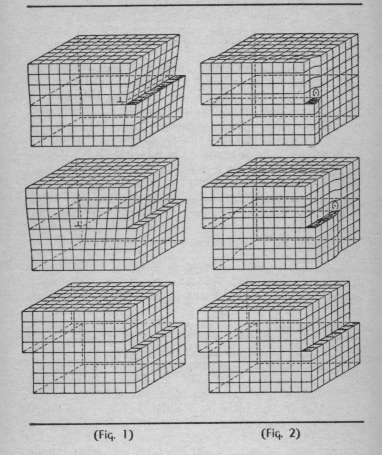

(Fig. 1) (Fig. 2)

ABOUT THE AUTHOR

Born and raised in Colorado, Sheri S. Tepper worked first for the overseas relief agency CARE, and then spent twenty-four years as the Executive Director of the Rocky Mountain Planned Parenthood. On her retirement, she decided to pursue her lifelong interest in science fiction and fantasy, and has since published over a dozen novels. AFTER LONG SILENCE is her first novel for Bantam Spectra. She has two children, one grandchild, and lives in Colorado with her husband, Gene, and a varying population of domestic and wild animals.